The Curious Cases of Sherlock Holmes Volumes 3 and 4

By

Stephen Herczeg

First edition published in 2025

Hardcover ISBN 978-1-80424-582-8

Published by MX Publishing
335 Princess Park Manor, Royal Drive,
London, N11 3GX
www.mxpublishing.co.uk

Cover design by Brian Belanger

To Mum

my biggest fan

To Steve and Sharon

For their ceaseless commitment

to helping others

Contents

Copyright Notices

Illustrations

The Case of the Left Foot ©2024 Stephen Herczeg

The Adventure of the Missing Journal ©2024 Stephen Herczeg

The Man from Moscow ©2024 Stephen Herczeg

The Adventure of the Tesla Coil ©2021 Thaddeus Tuffentsamer

The Strange Case of the Unicursal Hexagram ©2024 Stephen Herczeg

The Disappearance of Dr. Markey ©2024 Stephen Herczeg

The Demise of the Painted Devil
SHAKESPEARE: TEMPEST. Ariel (Act I, Scene II), from William Shakespeares The Tempest, 1611.
Wood engraving after Sir John Gilbert, 1856-60.
Obtained under licence from https://www.freeimages.com/

The Adventure of the Great Wyrley Outrages
Arthur Conan Doyle at his desk at Norwood, ©1894
Credit: The Arthur Conan Doyle Encyclopedia Private Collection.
Obtained under Public Domain licence

The Body in the Box ©2024 Stephen Herczeg

The Possession of Miranda Beasmore ©2024 Stephen Herczeg

A Matter of Tainted Honey ©2024 Stephen Herczeg

Little Boy Lost ©2024 Thaddeus Tuffentsamer

With thanks to:

Thaddeus Tuffentsamer
https://www.amazon.com/stores/Thaddeus-Tuffentsamer/author/B07BQMTHX1

Jeffrey McKeever
http://www.screamingceltstudio.com

Brian Belanger for the wonderful cover designs
Brian did most of the cover designs at mxpublishing.com from 2016 -2023, and does all of the covers over at belangerbooks.com.

Foreword

The world of Sherlock Holmes – as originally laid out by Arthur Conan Doyle – is one in which crimes and mysteries yield, albeit sometimes reluctantly, to logic, to deductive principles, and to common sense. It has strict rules, set character studies, and a certain steadiness. An orderly place, basically.

The world of Sherlock Holmes pastiches, on the other hand…

This latter, shadowed realm of pastiche, homage and re-imagining can be a fraught one, a sort of sandpit where rules are broken with each new tale by each new author. Strict adherents of the canon throw up their hands in horror (or at least mild dismay) when faced with texts which do not stick faithfully to ACD's version of Holmes and Watson, whilst steampunk adherents gleefully insert sleek fighting airships, mechanical computers and other retrofitted technology. There are crossovers with the works of ACD's contemporaries, or ruthless deconstructions of the original stories, and at the same time, writers who are aficionados of horror and the supernatural slide poor Holmes into situations ripe with actual curses, ghosts, demonic presences, and even Lovecraftian monstrosities, oh my oh my.

In this particular collection, Stephen Herczeg employs each and all of the above, though his Holmes and Watson remain fully recognisable and steady, like anchor points. Herczeg seeks above all else to entertain, and although I myself tend more towards a subtle tweak of the original material in my own pastiches, I find it hard to complain about some good old-fashioned entertainment.

Therefore although there are indeed some 'classic' tales here, prepare yourself also for H G Wells's warped science to emerge unexpectedly in a Holmes mystery, for a direct encounter with a subtle cosmic horror from the pages of H P Lovecraft, and perhaps most surprisingly, a distinct nod to Batman! ACD's villain Lysander Stark appears in a major role, as does the strange and arcane Simon Iff from the works of Aleister Crowley. Add in a touch of The Exorcist – or so it seems – and a wicker man, a mention of the real-life George Edalji incident, a serial killer with a gifted mother, and more… well, you get the picture.

Come not with too much canonical prejudice, but simply dip in and enjoy.

John Linwood Grant
Yorkshire, January 2025

The Case of the Left Foot

Christmas was fast approaching when I was finally able to begin tidying up my notes for a case from the previous February that would become known as "The Beryl Coronet". Sadly, for my good friend Sherlock Holmes, it had been several weeks since he'd had an interesting case, and he'd descended through that December into a worrying state of *ennui*, in spite of the approaching holidays. With winter and Christmas now upon us, my concern for him began to manifest itself.

It was then that fortune shone upon us, like the coming of the Biblical Star, when I heard the doorbell ring downstairs that morning. Within moments I could hear Mrs. Hudson, our wonderful landlady, climbing the stairs to our apartments.

Not wishing to seem too eager, I waited until she finished rapping on the door before crossing to receive her.

"Hello, Doctor," she said softly, handing me a small envelope. "Telegram came for him." We both glanced at Holmes's name printed on the outside. "I do hope it brings him out of his room. I know that people get glum at this time of year . . ." she added before retreating downstairs.

Closing the door, I turned and carefully opened the envelope, sliding out the folded sheet. Opening it, the message I read brought a smile to my face. Lestrade needed Holmes's services – something that generally led to some level of intrigue, or at least interest, in my friend's mind.

Reinserting the note into the envelope, I turned to find Holmes entering the sitting room. He spied the message in my hand and said, "What have you there?"

Handing the telegram over, I said, "Hopefully something of a worthwhile distraction for you."

Quickly reading it, he replied, "As you have seen, there isn't much detail, but Lestrade wishes us to join him at Dufour's Place in Soho."

"Strange location to meet," I said.

"Not if there's someone for us to see in the mortuary."

"Of course," I said, remembering the establishment of such in that very place some years back.

"Well, shall we away?" Holmes asked, disappearing from the sitting room to get ready without another word.

***

When I rejoined him mere moments later, Holmes stood unconsciously tapping his foot in repressed impatience. The sniff of a mystery had brought all his senses and expectations to the fore.

We were soon trotting through the streets of Marylebone and eventually into the more decrepit area of Soho. The contrast was striking. In the area near our Baker Street lodgings, the shops were decorated for the season. There was an energy in the air, and a marked cheerfulness as well. This seemed to dissipate as we travelled to the southeast, where there was less opportunity or reason for those around us to celebrate. And yet, if one looked closely, there were still small efforts made to acknowledge the holiday.

The driver turned into the somewhat grim area near Dufour's Place and stopped outside a three-storey Georgian building with a tired, run-down appearance to it.

The structure brought a sense of nervousness to my disposition. Even though I had never attended there, I remembered its history. It had been procured by the St. James Parish well over thirty years before, and a mortuary established to deal with the overflow of victims of the cholera outbreak of the mid-1850's.

I was merely an infant at the time, but part of my medical studies required research and re-examination of such outbreaks, and the lessons learned from their responses. Medical knowledge had advanced from those days, and I sincerely hoped that it was sufficient, but history shows that new variants of diseases are often encountered that force our knowledge and techniques to improve, generally at the cost of many lives in the early days of the process.

Standing before the mortuary, Holmes noticed my expression. "You look confused."

"I'm simply unsure why this building still functions as a mortuary. Surely there are better-resourced facilities."

"Ah, I have heard tell that the high rate of mortality for the area's inhabitants requires such a facility, even to this day. The Parish of St. James maintains the building as a way of helping those families that have suffered a death but have no means to pay the fees required at more salubrious establishments."

"That explains why it's so run down."

"Yes. I think the church's charity can only stretch so far. Renovations are probably well down the list of needs."

A short figure appeared in the doorway, rugged up with a thick coat and hat pulled down to his ears.

"Lestrade," Holmes called, receiving a nod and a wave of a gloved hand for us to join him inside.

Stepping inside the dim corridor, Lestrade's demeanour was dour at best. His responses were shorter than normal, giving me the impression that he was under great pressure over something.

"What do you have for us?" asked Holmes as we were led down the passageway towards a larger and slightly better-lit room at the end. A strong smell of decay and chemicals floated towards us, making my throat constrict for a moment, as it had been a while since my senses had been assaulted in such a way.

It wasn't until we entered the larger room that Lestrade finally answered Holmes's question. "This is a strange one, Mr. Holmes, and worrying." The room was large and rectangular, kept cold by the absence of heating. Several tables lined one wall. Each held objects covered in stained white sheets. I knew by their shape that they were recently deceased bodies, awaiting collection and burial.

My eyes then fell on the subject of Lestrade's despair.

In the middle of the room lay the examination table in question. Instead of the body of some poor unfortunate victim, a solitary shod foot sat in the middle of a clean white sheet. Even from where I stood, I could tell it was a woman's by the size and style of the shoe.

"My Lord," I gasped, stepping closer to peer at the dismembered appendage. It was a left foot, cut off just above the ankle, and wearing a shoe as if its owner had simply misplaced a body part as she strolled towards her place of employment, before being brought here to reside until she came to collect it like an item of lost baggage.

"We haven't examined it, Mr. Holmes," said the policeman. "I knew you'd want to look at it first."

Holmes stood nearby, a speculative expression on his face as he glanced down at the foot, gleaning as much initial information as he could. "Well, Lestrade," he said, "you have my attention. Do you wish to fill me in before I examine this item further?"

"I'll start at the beginning then." Coughing several times to clear his throat, and possibly loosen the built-up taste from the odours in the room, Lestrade reached into his pocket, starting to remove a notepad before shaking his head and simply telling us what he knew. "A little over a week ago, a young lass, Miss Elaine Waterson, employed as the personal assistant to Sir Lyndon Marsden, of Marsden's Fine Apparel for Women – "

"I know that place," I blurted out, receiving a withering look from Holmes. "It's in Mayfair, isn't it?" A harrumphing cough from Holmes stopped me speaking further.

"Inspector," he told Lestrade, "please continue."

"As Doctor Watson said, Sir Lyndon's business is in Mayfair. Very salubrious establishment it is, too, if I may add. I certainly won't be taking Mrs. Lestrade there any time soon. Anyway, Miss Waterson didn't come into work on the Monday of last week, and hasn't shown up since."

"Nothing untoward in that," said Holmes. "Possibly sick, or . . . ." His eyes joined mine in staring at the foot upon the examination table.

"I'll get to that in a moment," said Lestrade. Pulling a piece of paper from his pocket and carefully unfolding it, he placed the page on the white sheet. "This was received on Wednesday of last week."

Holmes and I stepped closer and read the note. It was written in a thin scrawl, and I saw that it was in a woman's hand:

Sir Lyndon Marsden,

We have taken your assistant, Miss Elaine Waterson. She will come to no harm if you comply with our demands.

A personal advertisement will be placed in tomorrow's Times. The addressee will be Mr. Myron Betterman. You are to follow the directions indicated and deliver the sum of one-thousand pounds to the location mentioned.

If you fail to meet these demands, then the results will not be conducive to Miss Waterson's health.

Do not involve the police.

Ignore us at your peril.

I looked back at the dismembered foot and gasped.

"I presume that this Sir Lyndon fellow ignored them?" asked Holmes.

"Actually no. If it weren't for one of Miss Waterson's co-workers, we wouldn't have known about any of this."

Pointing at the foot, Holmes asked, "What led to this then?"

"Ah," said Lestrade, pulling a small piece of newsprint from his pocket and laying it next to the letter. "This is the personal advertisement as mentioned." I had to peer closer, but could make out the slightly smudged print.

Mr. Myron Betterman,

Happy to have made your acquaintance. Leave the item of concern in a satchel before the north face of the statue of the woman in Berkeley Square at mid-day Monday. Come alone. Don't be late.

"Sir Lyndon didn't make it to Berkeley Square then?" I asked.

"He did, but . . . ." Lestrade trailed off for a moment before continuing, "We were informed not long after the first note was received – the lady's co-workers found out, and were concerned. We

– a small contingent of plain-clothed constables and myself – spread out across the Square in anticipation of apprehending the kidnapper."

A wry grin crossed Holmes's face as he turned towards Lestrade. "He didn't show, did he?"

"No," Lestrade answered with downcast eyes. "No, he didn't."

"So it is now Wednesday – two days after this aborted transaction, which seems to have been upset because of the police presence – and more than a week after the lady was taken. You should know, Inspector, that even London's finest look like policemen no matter what their dress – even to the uninformed."

"It would seem that way," Lestrade replied.

"What was Sir Lyndon's response?"

"His rage knew no bounds. My superiors were immediately notified, and that's why I'm now asking for your help. Then there is this," said Lestrade, pulling another piece of paper from his pocket. Unfolding it and placing it next to the other sheets, he added, "This arrived with the foot, early this morning."

"Before I read that, how was the foot presented? Surely not just left on the doorstep."

Lestrade shook his head. "No, no it wasn't. It was neatly wrapped, like a Christmas present, complete with a red ribbon. A gift card on the outside said it was for Sir Lyndon. Naturally, the first staff member to arrive had no clew, took it inside, and placed it on Sir Lyndon's desk."

A grimace crossed Holmes's face. "So the wrapping would be a useless place to search for information. Too many hands would have had the opportunity to touch it."

Nodding to a small table nearby, Lestrade said, "You can still have a look. It has been placed there for your inspection." Pointing to the third sheet he'd laid out, he said, "Read that."

It was neatly wrapped, like a Christmas present, complete with a red ribbon.

Holmes and I bent lower to read the note. I could see that the scrawl was certainly different from the original delicate scratching of a woman. This consisted of a much heavier set of letters, revealing that the author had found it quite a bit more difficult to manipulate the pen than had the person who prepared the first note:

Sir,

You have involved the police. For that, you will pay, as has Miss Waterson.

The sum is now five-thousand pounds.

Deliver this amount to the same location in Berkeley Square by three o'clock this afternoon.

Comply with our demands to the letter, or you will receive several more Christmas presents, each containing another piece.

Come alone.

If any policemen are detected, then you will receive all of your presents at once.

"That is quite the definitive demand," murmured Holmes.

"Yes," said Lestrade.

"I assume Sir Lyndon wasn't happy with this either."

"Not in the slightest. I was called in directly and suffered several minutes of his cursing and red-faced fury before he finally stormed from the room. I had these items brought here as quickly as possible, Dufour's being the closest mortuary to Mayfair, and a sight more discreet for such an affair."

"Can we assume your superiors are not amused either?"

"That's an understatement."

"It's a good thing you brought me into it then."

"Can you find the kidnapper, before it's too late?"

"We don't have much time, and I have some questions that need answering, but I truly believe I can find the kidnapper and the poor unfortunate Miss Waterson."

I saw a slight frown cross Holmes's face as he was casting an eye over the packaging before he turned back towards the disembodied foot. Pulling his glass from an inside pocket, he proceeded to bend closer, examining the wound area closely.

Moving up next to him, I found my gaze drawn to the raw, meaty protrusion sticking from the top of the shoe. After a few moments, Holmes mumbled, "What say you, Watson?"

"The foot size is around six or seven, which for an average woman puts her height at around five-foot-four inches."

"Do we know Miss Waterson's height, Inspector?"

"As the Doctor said: She is five-foot-four inches in height, and of very slight build."

Indicating the amputation site, I continued with my observations. "The cut is clean, but shows a slight roughness, with some tearing. I would suggest it was made with something like a wood saw." Holding my hand out towards Holmes, I said, "Can I borrow your glass for a moment?" Taking the proffered instrument, I focused on the bones themselves. Each had been sawn through roughly, confirming my suspicions. Handing the glass back and pointing at the protruding tibia and fibula, I said, "See here? The cut across the bones is slightly jagged, I would suggest that my observation is correct, and the saw had been dulled before this horrid business. The roughness indicates a bluntness to the blade."

"Excellent. I thought as much myself." Taking back the glass and holding it in front of the Achilles Tendon, Holmes continued. "What do you think of this?"

It took me a moment to understand what he meant, but then I moved to one side. A dark shade ran along the back of the protruding segment of leg, disappearing into the heel of the shoe. "I need to see the foot."

"I agree," said Holmes, "and I would also like to examine the shoe by itself."

Delicately, I unlaced the shoe and prized the foot from within it.

"That was a little more difficult than it should have been, wasn't it?" Holmes asked.

"Yes, it was. I would have expected the foot to have become slightly smaller due to loss of blood."

"Quite, so, "said Holmes, picking up the shoe and studying it. "This is piquing my interest more and more."

Turning my attention to the foot, I rotated it and examined the heel and the Achilles Tendon, following the dark subcutaneous shadow.

"It was removed *post mortem*, wasn't it?"

Surprised by Holmes's quick summation, I nodded in agreement. "Yes. The body lay for quite some time, several hours, I presume, before the removal of the limb." Pointing to the dark shadow on the heel, and the discolouration by the tendon, I added, "Blood pooled here, as indicated by the lividity." Picking up Holmes's discarded glass, I focused on the wound itself. "Yes, I can see a thicker area of coagulation at the site of the cut, which would have been the exit point of the saw if working from front to back of the leg – not something that would occur in a fresh amputation."

"Any idea how long she was dead?" asked Lestrade, his curiosity showing at our discovery.

"I would have to say two or three days, but perhaps more. It depends on whether she was kept cold or not."

"In this weather? I can hardly get warm myself, even by my fire at night."

"Yes. So it could be anywhere up to a week."

"Still, that means it could be our poor unfortunate Miss Waterson."

Nodding, I said, "Yes, sadly."

"Then we've already failed."

"Not so fast, Inspector," interrupted Holmes. "We've only established the fact that the foot was removed from a corpse. Further investigations will be needed to confirm from whom – we have no proof that the foot belonged to the woman in question. It could belong to anyone."

Holmes returned the shoe to the table before pointing to the foot itself. "The owner didn't have regular access to the sort of bathing or grooming facilities one might attribute to an assistant working for a high-end fashion house." Following the direction of his finger, I saw that the foot's toenails were split, and could be called filthy, as well as exhibiting a marked fungal infection. I had been so intent on the wound and blood settlement that I had failed to observe that point.

"And I presume you noticed the slight swelling in the foot?" Holmes continued.

"Yes, I did. I put it down to the lass being a shop steward. Those poor girls are renowned for problems with swelling of the feet."

"Ah, yes, but our Miss Waterson is a personal assistant. We will have to confirm it, but I would expect her to be seated for the majority of the day, with short walking journeys to fetch items for Sir Lyndon."

"Right you are, Mr. Holmes. So if this foot doesn't belong to Miss Waterson, whose is it?"

"If I were to hazard a guess," said Holmes, gazing at the appendage intently for a few moments, "I would say it belonged to one of the streetwalkers who go missing or are found dead at far too regular intervals in our fair city." Turning his attention back to the shoe, he added, "This is where it gets interesting, though."

"Why?"

Carefully picking up the shoe, Holmes examined every side for a moment before continuing. "This shoe doesn't quite fit the foot – it's a bit too small, which is why we had trouble removing it. And it comes from Cobram and Sons of Oxford Street. Their mark is on the underside of the sole."

"That's a very expensive place to purchase shoes," I remarked. "Even for – no offence to Miss Waterson – a personal assistant."

A smile grew on Holmes's face. "Yes, it is quite an expensive item for Miss Waterson to possess. So that leaves us to our next port of call."

"Which is?" asked Lestrade.

"Miss Waterson's house. But first, one last item. Can you find me a sheet of paper?" When Holmes took the foot from me and stepped across to the nearby sink. He dripped some water onto the tips of his gloved fingers, then dabbed them gently onto the underside of the toes and ball of the foot before placing it onto a clean sheet of paper. Once satisfied, he returned the foot to the examination table and held the paper, showing the partial print formed from the dampened ingrained dirt on the base of the amputated appendage.

"And that's for what exactly?" I asked.

"Comparison," he replied.

***

Twenty minutes later, we stepped from Lestrade's carriage in front of a quaint three-storey terraced house in the middle of Chelsea.

"She has the lease of the entire building," Lestrade explained.

"Curious," I exclaimed, gazing at the beautifully presented streetscape before me. "This is an expensive house for a simple secretary."

"Personal assistant," Holmes corrected. "It seems to be the title afforded our Miss Waterson."

"Still."

"Yes, you are quite right," said Holmes, stepping towards the ground-floor entryway. "I find it quite bemusing that the subject of our investigations could afford such a lovely home." He turned toward Lestrade. "And a large home as well. How many servants?"

Lestrade shook his head. "None. All that space, and she occupied it by herself." He extracted a key from his pocket and all three of us filed into the entranceway. Without a word, Holmes headed upstairs, intending to search the lady's bedroom. I decided to linger downstairs and moved from room to room, hoping to gain a sense of the woman that lived there.

The house was sparsely furnished but showed an exquisite taste. I was extremely impressed by Miss Waterson's studious adherence to order. In the kitchen, there was no sign of any used dishes, all having been returned to their places once washed and dried. The parlour was neat and tidy, with no ash spillage from the small fireplace, and no half-burnt coal in the hearth.

Several photographs lined the mantelpiece, each sitting in exquisite silver frames. They showed a rather lovely young woman that I took to be our Miss Waterson, plus a pair of older folk with sour expressions. I speculated that they were possibly her parents. Another lone photograph showed the same pretty woman, but now dressed all in black, with the saddest look on her face. She stood before the doorway of a terraced house, different from the one we had entered. It took me a moment to realise the woman was likely depicted during a mourning phase in her life, possibly for her parents or someone close to her.

After gaining an appreciation for the presentation of the house and its almost museum-display quality, I was disappointed to find a lone ashtray sitting at the far end of the mantel. The stub of a cigar sat within, having burned down after the smoker placed it on the edge until only a small end remained. Sniffing the remains, I recoiled at the bitter stench. It had the hallmarks of an item smoked in the seedy dens frequented by lower-class workers and drunks, rather than something that would be found in such a beautifully appointed home.

Leaving the parlour, I made my way upstairs, joining Holmes and Lestrade in the lady's bedroom. Again, I was met with a well-appointed and neat arrangement. Holmes stood before a free-standing wardrobe, examining the clothing and rack of shoes.

Not wishing to break his train of thought, I stood silently in the doorway and made my own study of the room. Next to the wardrobe was a small dressing table with a mirror. An array of bottles sat before the mirror, with a small jewellery stand to one side, holding a single but striking necklace consisting of a thin chain of gold with a gold heart pendant. The pendant itself held a clear stone in its centre that must have been diamond. The necklace drew my attention almost immediately, as it appeared simple, elegant, and expensive, all at the same time – something that could never have been afforded on a simple assistant's wage. "Had she inherited money, perhaps – enough to explain the necklace and the large house?"

"Not at all," said Lestrade, in answer to my question. "She came from common folk, somewhere here in London. Where she obtained her funds has not yet been established."

Gazing at the contents of the table, I could see that indications that items were missing. Some of the fine facial powder that Miss Waterson used had fallen to the surface, leaving imprints of objects that had been removed. At least two larger items were missing. From my elementary understanding, I speculated that these might be a powder jar and bottle of facial crème. The table was also devoid of a hairbrush, comb, and hand mirror – items I attributed to women of all ages.

I was about to mention this to Holmes when he stepped away from the wardrobe and approached the table. "Items are missing," I said, jumping in to voice my observations.

"Yes. I observed that earlier," he said, leaving me slightly deflated. With his hand pressed to his chin and a finger pointing upwards, he continued. "There are two pairs of shoes missing, and likely some items of clothing, though I can't tell how many."

Joining him near the wardrobe, I spotted the vacant spaces at the bottom of the cupboard.

"She left of her own accord then?" asked Lestrade.

"It would look that way," said Holmes. "But whether that is because she planned a trip, or if she went willingly with her supposed abductor is another matter altogether."

Glancing back at the array of shoes, it was apparent that these sported the same mix of elegance and practicality as that accompanying the amputated foot. Pointing towards a specific pair, I said, "Those look very much the same as the shoe we saw earlier."

Holmes reached for one of the shoes, examining its underside. Nodding, he said, "Yes. Cobram and Sons, inscribed on the base of the sole."

"That's impressive. Two pairs from that establishment."

"Actually," said Holmes, studying the shoe, "we can only be certain that these were hers, but we do now have confirmation that Miss Waterson possessed at least one pair." Turning the shoe around, he held his glass up to the dark writing on the inside of the heel. "Yes, the same size as well."

Carrying the shoe to the table, he pulled out the paper with the foot's imprint on it. Then he removed a small folding knife from his pocket and proceeded to slit the top of the shoe, so that he could then pull it apart and see the inside where the foot normally rested. Then he compared it to the dirty imprint of the detached foot before passing the shoe and the sheet to me.

"Do you see it?"

Lestrade bustled over and leaned in as well. "I do," said the inspector.

All three of us had come to the same conclusion: The feet were completely different, but it wasn't really a surprise, considering the condition of the amputated foot at the morgue. The big toe on the paper imprint was larger than that impressed into the bottom of this shoe, and it appeared to bend towards the right, an indication of the beginning of a deformity from standing too long on rough, slightly uneven ground. The other toes failed to line up evenly as well.

"The shoe at the morgue," explained Holmes, "definitely belonged to Miss Waterson. The patterns within it conform to this matching shoe here – and neither of the Cobram shoes have the same wear as what we see from the amputated foot. It isn't much, but this, combined with the probable evidence that the foot was amputated after death, plus the condition and slight swelling of the detached appendage, allow us to be essentially certain that the foot does not belong to Miss Waterson."

"Then who?" asked Lestrade.

"And why?" I added.

"I think extortion is still our main *modus operandi*. And as to who the foot belongs to, I think I shall make some further enquiries."

"Where?" asked Lestrade.

"I'm unsure as yet, but I believe I already generally know the source of the limb in question. However, there is no haste to determine that at this stage. Our immediate need is to find the whereabouts of Miss Waterson, as there is every chance that she is alive and in good health."

"Marvellous," said Lestrade, his face turning quickly to concern. "But where?"

"Ah, that I do not know," said Holmes as he turned and almost darted from the room in his haste to leave.

Lestrade and I followed him downstairs more slowly, where Holmes was standing at the mantel, examining the cigar stub and photographs. Sniffing the cigar remains, he noted that it was Jamaican in in origin – something rather rare in England, possibly indicating that the owner had brought it himself from the Caribbean. From there, he moved from room to room for some time before ducking into a small nook near the kitchen. The tiny room contained a roll-top desk which clattered when Holmes opened it by the handles. A small array of notes and bills lay upon the green leather of the desk's interior.

Holmes picked up several and quickly read and returned them before holding one before him. "Was there ever any mention of the lady having additional premises in Rotherhithe, Inspector?"

Lestrade shook his head. "No, why?"

"Well, Miss Waterson has several letters and bills, all bearing the same Rotherhithe address. This one," he indicated the page in his hand, "is the latest coal bill." Reading it, he added, "Not very high, which would indicate that the heating isn't used very often."

"Strange," Lestrade noted. "Why would she have bills from another address?"

"Perhaps it's her parents' old house?" I suggested. "There's evidence in the parlour that her parents are deceased. If she has found the money to pay for a residence of this station, she may have been able to afford to keep the other as well."

"Good point, Watson," Holmes said. "It also makes me wonder if Miss Waterson spends some of her time there – perhaps on the weekends when she doesn't need to attend to her employer."

"That might account for the missing items," I said. "And there is the photograph of her in mourning, depicted before another house. That could be this Rotherhithe place."

"Interesting," said Holmes. "I think we should visit it, just to ascertain if our Miss Waterson is there. But first, I feel that we should visit the gentleman that has been maintaining this property for Miss Waterson's use."

"And who would that be?" asked Lestrade.

"Why, isn't that obvious?" asked Holmes, lifting one eyebrow as he turned to glance at Lestrade. "Sir Lyndon, of course."

***

Stepping from Lestrade's carriage for the second time that morning, we found ourselves before an impressive four-story, white-stoned Georgian mansion, taking up residence in the wealthy neighborhood of Belgravia. All around us, the houses were covered with Christmas decorations, but none could compare with Sir Lyndon's home – an enormous wreath upon the door, and smaller ones that matched on every ground floor window. Stretches of garland were draped along the front between the various upstairs windows. It was almost too much, but it certainly outshone the efforts of the neighbors.

"I'm in the wrong business," said Lestrade, glaring at the expansive premises before us. "There seems to be money in selling ladies dresses."

"I think you'll find that the work you do, Inspector," said Holmes, "far exceeds the amount of good created through Sir Lyndon's endeavours."

Lestrade nodded. "But it would be nice to treat the missus from time to time."

"Quite so, and I'm sure you will be able to work your way up to Chief Inspector or even Superintendent in the coming years, which should furnish you with more in the way of honest income to help supplement your lifestyle," said Holmes.

"Well, there's always hope, isn't there."

"It is a wonderful property, gentlemen," I pressed, feeling the nip in the air deep in my bones, "but it's also a bitterly cold day and time is of the essence. Shouldn't we move on?"

"Sorry," said Lestrade, moving up to the front door. The knocking on the door was soon met with a look of slight disdain from an elderly butler.

"Yes, may I help you?" he asked, his eyes peering down his nose towards the three of us.

"Inspector Lestrade of Scotland Yard. My colleagues, Mr. Holmes and Dr. Watson, and I would like to see Sir Lyndon. It is on a matter of urgency, and at his request."

"The master isn't in," began the butler, before a female voice broke out behind him.

"Who is it, Johnson?" the voice asked.

Before the man could turn, a woman that I presumed to be in her late fifties bustled to the front door, almost pushing the aging butler away. "Hello, gentlemen. Come in. It's frightfully horrid out there."

After we'd moved into the entranceway, decorated just as thickly for Christmas, Johnson took our coats and hats while the woman introduced herself. "I'm Lady Beryl Marsden." Indicating a nearby doorway, she added, "Please, let us adjourn to the parlour." Turning to the butler, she directed, "Johnson: Coffee, tea, and biscuits for our guests please." We left a slightly mystified Johnson and assembled in the adjacent room, a welcoming place where a warm fire glowed in the hearth. As we found our seats, I breathed deeply – somewhere in the house, treats were being baked for the holidays, and the odours from the distinctive spices filled the air. "Now," asked the lady, "what can I do for you gentlemen?"

Lestrade spoke up. "I am Inspector Lestrade of Scotland Yard, your Ladyship. Umm, I have been assigned to the delicate matter at your husband's workplace."

"Oh, yes? What matter?"

"Why, the case of a kidnapped employee."

"Oh, dear." Her face showed shock – I wasn't sure if it was from the newly acquired news or the fact her husband had possibly declined to share it with her. "Who? Not that lovely Mr. Benedict?"

"No, ma'am. It's Sir Lyndon's assistant, Miss Waterson."

At the mention of that name, Lady Beryl's face grew dark. "Oh," she said, with such disapproval that I was surprised she didn't rise and usher us from her house as fast as she could.

"You know Miss Waterson?" Holmes asked.

Turning towards him, Lady Beryl's face brightened, either through the application of a careful but well-rehearsed façade, or by way of a genuine interest in our presence. I was unsure.

"You would be Mr. Sherlock Holmes."

"That's correct."

"I'm happy to meet you, Mr. Holmes. I am a long-time friend of Honoria Westphail. I believe you would know her niece, Miss Helen Stoner. Honoria was most delighted by the way you helped her niece – I think it was four or five years ago now – and saved the young lass from a dreadful calamity. She was most effusive and described you in great detail," Then, turning towards me, she added, "And also you Dr. Watson."

Lestrade began to ask another question when Johnson arrived at the doorway. Lady Beryl turned towards him and said, "Ah, good – coffee and tea." Eyeing a small plate of pastries on the side, she thanked Johnson for his thoughtfulness and took the tray from him. Placing it on a nearby side table, she turned and asked us what we would prefer. Lestrade was becoming impatient at the delay, but I knew Holmes would be more than happy to engage Lady Beryl for some hidden details that we were unlikely to gain from Sir Lyndon himself.

Finally, after the coffee and cakes were served, Lestrade was able to ask his question. "Lady Beryl," he started, "we have come to apprise Sir Lyndon of our findings and ask him some more pertinent questions. He had asked that I make a report to him. Can you tell us where he has gone or when he will return? Time is of the essence."

"The last I saw of Lyndon was when he stormed back into the house earlier this morning, not long after the shop should have opened. Within moments, he left once again. He was in a frightful state, such that I didn't wish to even contemplate, let alone become involved. He has been in such a distasteful temper of late. We've hardly spoken a word."

"He hasn't confessed anything to you then?" asked Holmes.

"Confessed?" She gave him a speculative look. "About what? As I said, we've hardly spoken," Lady Beryl answered. "If there's something I should know about, then by all means, please tell me."

It was Lestrade who took the lead. "As we mentioned, there has been a kidnapping: Sir Lyndon's assistant, Miss Waterson."

"Most horrid, but that girl – " Lady Beryl started, but thought better of saying anything further and became quiet.

"Is there something about Miss Waterson that might be helpful?" I asked, assuming an air of innocence.

"Well," she replied, "kidnapping was the least of my worries where that girl is concerned."

"Why is that?" I prodded.

Lady Beryl stared into my face for a moment. Her eyes bore through me as if examining my reasons for the question before she relaxed and let the truth spill forth. By the end of her admission, my heart went out to this poor woman.

Dropping her head, she began to speak, slowly at first, and fighting her inner shame.

"It was around Christmas time last year – Can it have been a whole year? – that I first became aware . . . ." Then she gave a start and raised her eyes to stare at the far wall. "Lyndon and I have been married for many years. Our children are grown and gone off to make their way in the world. I had hoped that the time we now had alone together would re-engender a spark in our marriage, but . . . ." Stopping for a moment, she took a deep breath. I could tell that tears were welling behind her eyes, held in check through sheer force of will. "Last Christmas it was. One day I came home after Lyndon had already arrived, and as Johnson was busy, I put my coat on the rack. I bumped Lyndon's coat and noticed something in one of his pockets. Finding a small box, I almost placed it back without further investigation, but curiosity gained the best of me, and I open it to find the most beautiful gold necklace – a delicate gold chain and a small gold heart pendant with a diamond in the centre. I couldn't believe it. Placing it back where I found it, I assumed that Lyndon had bought it for me, and when Christmas came around, I received a similar-sized box from him."

She took another deep breath and pulled a small kerchief from her sleeve, wiping at corners of her eyes before continuing. "My heart swelled as I unwrapped the little present, but then it sank into my shoes when all I found enclosed was a silk scarf. No sign of the necklace. He had bought it for another. It was then I truly knew that our marriage was nought but a sham."

"Oh, dear," I said.

"But that wasn't the worst of it," she added. "A week or so after Christmas, we had an engagement at the store – to welcome the New Year and congratulate the employees on a job well done for the previous year." Taking another deep breath, she finished off with, "It was then I realised who my 'replacement' was."

"Miss Waterson?" I asked.

Nodding, she continued. "Yes. There she was, as bright as day, dressed in a gown that she had no right to possess. And there around her neck – "

"The necklace," finished Holmes, already knowing the answer.

Turning towards my friend, the tears finally forming and sliding down her face, she nodded and dabbed at her eyes.

"We're so sorry," I stated, my concern for this woman trumping any care for the case at hand. "Have you confronted him?"

A small smile came to her face as she shook her head. "What else is there to do but accept it? I'm a matron, almost in my sixties. I have grown so used to this life. Over the last year, I have simply resolved myself to play the part of a loving, doting wife. I wouldn't wish to throw the spectre of scandal over the lives of my children, and I couldn't live with the shame in polite company."

This was something I had contemplated before. Even though the upper class live lives of affluence and influence, there is – even for them – a simmering underbelly of discontent within their ranks. In this house, it had been made all the more real by the events unfolding over the last week.

I was about to make such a comment when the bell rang. Lady Beryl moved to the connecting doorway to watch as Johnson attended to the newcomer. She must have recognised the visitor, as she sighed before stepping into the entranceway. Instead of waiting for the door to be opened, she turned toward the rear of the house and quickly walked away.

Within moments, a red-faced man appeared. He was portly, balding, and I made him to be in his mid-fifties. He was sweating profusely and breathing heavily from some unknown vigorous activity. As his eyes fell on the inspector, his thin voice bellowed out. "Lestrade, what in blazes are you doing here? Have you found her?" Taking a quick look at Holmes and me, he added, "And who are these two layabouts?"

"Sir Lyndon," Lestrade said, rising slowly to bring a sense of calm to the situation. "This is Sherlock Holmes and his colleague, Doctor John Watson. I've asked them to assist. I didn't think you would mind the added support."

"Holmes? The detective? You must be at your wit's end, Lestrade!" Anger began to bristle behind his thick eyebrows, countered when Holmes spoke up.

"Sir Lyndon, forgive our involvement, but we have already discovered an important fact."

"What?" he almost bellowed.

"We are extremely confident that the foot you received does not belong to Miss Waterson. She may be still alive – something that I believe may not have been the case if you had successfully paid the ransom."

Sir Lyndon's eyes opened wide in anger as he stared indignantly at Holmes. "What are you suggesting, sir?"

"In many of these cases, the kidnappers have no intention of returning their hostage. They merely wait for the funds to be given over, and then they execute the captive to remove any possibility of identification. Scotland Yard's involvement has prevented this occurrence, and probably ensured the continued health of young Miss Waterson."

"Nonsense. This is simply a business deal. This – " Sir Lyndon waved his hand through the air, searching for words. " – this *villain* has absconded with something I want. He has set his terms, and I am happy to meet them. Once I've paid up, he'll hand over Elaine. Simple as that."

"I beg you not to do that, Sir Lyndon," said Lestrade. "This 'villain', as you say, may not hold up his end of the bargain."

Sir Lyndon's face grew dire. "Of course that wasn't Elaine's foot – I never thought for a moment it was. And if you hadn't interfered, Elaine would be back in her rooms by now, and all this would be behind us."

Feeling the need to dissipate the ill feelings in the room and to satisfy my curiosity on one matter, I spoke up. "Sir Lyndon, you seemed very out of breath when you entered. I am a doctor – Is there any way in which I can help?"

His eyes fell on me, almost as if he hadn't taken account of my presence earlier. "I sped home from the bank. I'm afraid I'm a little out of shape. Too much work. Too much food. Why?"

"I had wondered if it was due to smoking. Cigars, perhaps."

I saw Holmes smile at my deftness at recalling the cigar found on the Miss Waterson's mantel. Yet the mystery deepened with Sir Lyndon's answer.

"Smoking? Filthy habit. I have never and would never smoke, and I'm incensed by your suggestion."

Holding my hands up in supplication, I said, "I do apologise. I am a medical man and simply seek to identify the most obvious causes of any malady. I congratulate you on such a stance."

Sir Lyndon's anger diminished slightly. He turned towards Lestrade and asked, "If the foot doesn't belong to Elaine, then who does it belong to?"

Holmes answered for the inspector. "That we don't know yet. But we have investigated Miss Waterson's Chelsea flat, and came here to report, but also to seek out further information."

"Yes?" The man seemed suddenly wary after the mention of the lady's residence.

"The Chelsea flat," continued Holmes. "You arranged that, of course, and you pay her rent and other bills."

Sir Lyndon looked shocked. He blustered his answer. "What? What do you mean? I . . . I don't know what you mean!"

"Come now, sir. It is certainly you who gives Miss Waterson an allowance for clothes, food, and other trivialities. You are a benevolent employer, but surely no one would expect that a mere personal assistant could afford the upkeep on such a residence. There is also the matter of how quickly you took it upon yourself to organise the monies to pay for Miss Waterson's ransom. That is something that any other employer would be very reticent to undertake."

Staring into Holmes's stoic expression for a moment, Sir Lyndon's face relaxed as he became resolved to his unmasking. He took a look towards the open doorway before striding across and shutting the door. Turning back, he answered, "Yes, yes you are right. I'm a damned fool, but have to admit I've fallen for the young lass. Things haven't been well between me and Lady Beryl for many years. I'm old, but still young enough . . . ."

He moved to a large, overstuffed chair and dropped wearily into it. "Elaine and I have formed a . . . a *relationship* over the last year or so. I moved her into the flat to . . . have a place where we can meet. When I found she was missing, and then that damned note arrived, I dropped everything to make sure I could get her back."

His downward gaze had hidden his expression, but as he lifted his face to us, I could see tears forming at the corners of his eyes. "When that God-awful thing arrived, I realised that it could mean the worst, but I still hoped she was alive." Reaching into his jacket he pulled out a thick wad of notes. "I spent all morning arranging for the new ransom. Regardless of what you advise, Inspector, I will happily give it just to have her back safe and sound."

"I hope we won't need to pay it," responded Lestrade.

Staring at the policeman, Sir Lyndon said, "I don't care. I will get her back, no matter what it takes." Abruptly standing, he indicated the doorway. "Now gentlemen, I won't lie, but I have matters to attend to.

By this evening I will have Elaine back, one way or another – with or without your help."

We shuffled out to find Johnson awaiting us with our coats and hats in his arms. As we prepared ourselves for the chill outside, Lestrade made one last appeal. "Sir Lyndon, I implore you to remain at home. Don't give in to these demands. It will not end well."

"Pish-posh!" was Sir Lyndon's only reply. He bustled us from his house, and that angry, red face that was the last sight I beheld there as the door closed quickly.

Holmes wore an expression of irritation before turning from the Marsden house and scanning the street. Then a grin grew on his face as he spied a young street urchin and hurried over toward him. Even from that distance, I realised that the boy must be one of his Irregulars – a fact that became clearer as the day grew long.

***

"He's just going to waste his money and get the girl killed," spat Lestrade, his impatience with Sir Lyndon spilling out from his normally calm but gruff exterior.

"Sir Lyndon will have observers of his own this time," said Holmes with a look in Lestrade's direction. "And they won't look like policemen." Pulling out his watch, he continued, "It's now just past one o'clock. We still have a good two hours before Sir Lyndon pays the ransom. Our next destination should provide some further intelligence as to the overall situation."

Some time later, as our carriage pulled into the more tightly packed and altogether unpleasant area of Rotherhithe, I started to worry that Holmes's optimism might be misplaced. Suspicious eyes followed us as we wound our way through the constricted streets, and I felt their stare stay upon me as we alighted before our destination.

The tiny, terraced house was worlds away from the two elegantly fronted addresses we had previously encountered. This whole section consisted of cramped three-storey buildings filled with various rooms let for lodging. Each of the buildings on this block sported yellowed and peeling paint with faded black trims to the windows. Unlike Sir Lyndon's extensively decorated digs, there was no sign of Christmas here whatsoever.

According to the information gathered at Miss Waterson's Chelsea abode, the apartment we sought was before us, at this address. Its darkened windows and worn and rotting woodwork gave it the appearance of abandonment, but I knew that it was actually a hive of local residents, as were the surrounding structures.

Thinking of the lady's fine Chelsea home, I asked, "Are we sure this is the place?" But I knew it was – this was the house in the photograph.

"This is the address upon the coal pedlar's bill," Holmes replied. Without waiting further, he led us up the stairs and tried to turn the door knob, but it was strangely locked. He tried again, and then knocked loudly. Silence greeted us until he repeated the announcement. Then the quiet was broken by a harsh voice from the basement alcove of the neighbouring house.

"She's gone out!" it cried.

The three of us turned and glanced towards the owner of the voice. There, below street level, sat the solitary figure of a woman, who I made out to be well into her seventies. She sat on a rotting armchair, surrounded by a cloud of smoke from the cigarette hanging from her lips.

"What do you mean, 'She'?" asked Lestrade. "How do you know who we're looking for?"

"Ain't but one lady lives in that building. She bought it somehow and kicked everyone else out – even the ones that had nowhere else to go. Keeps it locked up, except for when she comes by sometimes."

This was news. How could the lady have the resources to acquire this property – even as run-down and filthy as it was?

"Do you know when she will be back?" asked Lestrade.

"Why? What has she done now?"

"What does this lady look like?" asked Holmes. The woman was silent for a moment, weighing her suspicions, before relenting and giving a good description of the missing personal assistant."

"Do you know when she'll be back?" asked Lestrade again. "We simply wish to speak with her – to ensure that she's in good health."

"Looked pretty healthy to me. I'm more worried about why you men want to talk to her." Before anyone could answer, however, the old woman continued, blowing out a huge cloud of smoke. "It's none of my business. Her mother, God rest her soul, would turn in her grave, I tell you."

"And why would that be?" asked Holmes.

"Well, ever since Elaine started coming back, she's been – How d'you say? – not her mother's little girl."

"Elaine," asked Holmes. "Elaine Waterson?"

"That's her. Grew up here. That was her parent's house. They let the rooms until they died. Then she took it on. I kept an eye on it for her, but then a few weeks ago, she turned everybody out. I'm not surprised – she isn't much like her mother."

"A bit flighty?" I asked. "Irresponsible?"

"Umm, more a bit of a charva," she said. "And bringin' back the men? What would her mother think? It's like Kings Cross Station here, some weeks."

"Oh," I answered, suddenly taken aback.

"That new one's a big 'un though."

"New one?" asked Holmes.

"Gorgeous he is," the old woman said, a smile coming to her mouth, showing a severe lack of teeth. "Taller than all of you. Broad across the shoulders. Huge bushy beard, and the strangest thing – a length of hair at the back."

"Long like a queue?" asked Holmes. "Or is it tied up?"

"He leaves it long."

"Have you observed any tattoos?"

"I'm not the sort to stick my nose in, but now you mention it, I did. I bumped into them in the street a while back. The big fellow was holding a sack, but I saw letters tattooed on his knuckles. I could only make out an 'aitch on his left hand, but his right had the word *Sultan* on it."

"Hmm," murmured Holmes.

"What does it mean?" I asked.

"Well, the queue might be a tar, worn by Her Majesty's sailors, and the tattoo might be the name of a ship. Often sailor memorialize their first ship that way. Possibly his was the *HMS Sultan*. She was an ironclad in the channel fleet for many years. I think she's now in the Mediterranean."

Stroking his chin for a moment, Holmes finally said, "These new facts, added to the cigar stub we found, may mean that the man was in the Navy, but no longer. Possibly he's moved into the merchant trade." Staring upward into the clouded sky, Holmes thought for many moments, until Lestrade and I became agitated at his silence. I was aware that three o'clock, and the payment of the next ransom demand, was rapidly approaching.

I noticed the old lady gawking at us with a wry smile on her face as she puffed on another cigarette. Holmes finally broke the silence. "Inspector, you may need to send someone to the nearby docks to see which ships are leaving for the Caribbean today – possibly Jamaica."

"Why the rush?" Lestrade asked.

"Our quarry may be planning to leave England this evening, if the ransom demand is met this time. And the cigar is just the smallest indication that the man we seek has Caribbean ties."

Surprise on his face, Lestrade bustled back towards our carriage and spoke with the driver. Then he climbed aboard and they drove away. Holmes turned back towards the woman below us and said, "Thank you, Madam. As we said, we are here to see Miss Waterson. We shall bid you a good day and wait for her inside."

Indifferent, the woman simply continued to puff on her cigarette, adding, "I would take care around that fellow of hers. Big bloke. Seems to have a touch of anger about him too."

"Thank you," finished Holmes before moving again to the front door. Extracting his picks, he made short work of the old lock, and within moments we found ourselves inside.

The house smelled from a touch of hidden damp, and also the heavy tang of the same type of cigar that we'd found in the Chelsea flat. Holmes left me to bustle off toward the bowels of the house, seemingly with a singular idea front and centre in his mind.

I remained in the parlour, awaiting Lestrade's return. Soon he appeared in the doorway, a slight grin crossing his face as he spied me standing before him. "I assume that the front door was unlocked?" Understanding the intent of his question, I simply shrugged, causing an expulsion of breath and a slight shake of his head. "Mr. Holmes – what the devil is he playing at?"

When my eyes shifted to the passageway that Holmes had taken, the inspector started to move in that direction. I began to follow as he passed by, but a sharp retort from a female voice in the entranceway stopped us both.

"'Ere! What's the meaning of this?"

Lestrade and I spun at the sound of the voice and I spied one of the loveliest faces I had seen in my life. "Miss Waterson?" said Lestrade, to which the young woman nodded, tentatively. She was carrying a sack which, from the bit I could see, contained something wrapped in butcher's paper, and one or two green vegetables.

"Yes, and who would you be?" she said, her reaction to our impertinence strong in her voice.

"Inspector Lestrade of Scotland Yard, and this is Doctor John Watson. He is helping me with my investigations."

"Pleased to meet you, Miss," I said, my eyes dropping to her untouched left foot. "I'm glad that you are in full health."

Miss Waterson's eyes followed my gaze, before darting back towards Lestrade. She looked as if she might turn and bolt. "Why are you here? My Trevor will be very mad when he returns."

Presuming that "Trevor" was the fellow described by the neighbor, my retort was cut off by Holmes's arrival in the parlour. "That's if your Trevor returns at all," he said.

All eyes turned towards him. "What do you mean?" said Miss Waterson. "Why wouldn't he return? And who are you now?"

Stepping further into the room, Holmes took a slight bow and said, "I am Sherlock Holmes, consulting detective. I'm helping Inspector Lestrade in the matter of your supposed kidnapping." Holmes's eyes dropped to the woman's left foot, a wry grin came to his face as he said, "And you are Miss Elaine Waterson. It's good to see you fully intact."

"Why do you gentlemen keep saying that? And why are you so interested in my feet?" She glanced down and then asked, "And why won't Trevor return?"

"First things first, I suppose," said Holmes. "The condition of the bedroom seems to indicate that this Trevor, if that is his name, has removed both his items and himself from this abode."

"What?" Miss Waterson cried, before bursting past the three of us and heading into the rear of the house. Moments later she returned, a look of intense shock on his face. "All of his clothes. Everything. Gone. His bag – gone." Tears welled in the corners of her eyes as she glanced up at us. "Is he gone?"

I moved across, taking the sack from her, setting it upon the floor, and guiding the stricken woman to a nearby seat. As we passed, Holmes pulled out his watch and, checking the time, said, "Not quite, but it probably won't be long." Glancing at Lestrade, he continued. "Inspector, it's now two o'clock. We still have time, but it will be close thing."

"What's going on?" I heard the poor woman whimper.

"Ah," said Holmes, "now that's an interesting tale."

We related all that had happened so far. Miss Waterson's face remained placid during the story of the first ransom note, leaving me with a sense that none of that part was new. It was when Lestrade mentioned the delivery of the amputated foot that the lady's eyes grew wide in shock bordering on terror. "A foot? A real foot?" she exclaimed. "Who's was it?"

"Well, supposedly it was meant to be yours, but obviously," Holmes explained, indicating Miss Waterson's intact appendage, "it isn't."

"That's horrible. Why would Trevor . . . ?" Suddenly she went quiet. Her simple retort told Holmes and Lestrade almost everything they needed to know.

"It may be pertinent, at this juncture, for you to relate everything you know on the matter," suggested Holmes.

Miss Waterson seemed to deflate as the pent-up anxiety bled from her body. "It was Trevor's idea. He's lovely. I met him about three months ago. We had a bit of a fling before he was back on ship. When he came home to port, two weeks ago, he told me all about his idea."

"I can only assume that it was you who wrote the first ransom note," Holmes asked. When she nodded, he continued. "Does Sir Lyndon know about this Trevor?"

A shocked look crossed Miss Waterson's face. "No, of course not. Why would I tell him? He'd cut me off straight away." Her eyes grew wide, and tears began to form at the edges. "It's just that Sir Lyndon is kind, but . . . ." her face twisted into a little grimace. "I'm so much younger than him. I . . . I need to be with someone my age."

"Please tell us the rest," I said.

"Trevor wants to leave the sea life. That's all he's ever really known, but he doesn't want to stay in the city. He has hopes to buy a farm in the Cotswolds. We're going to live in the fresh air. Raise some sheep." She hesitated for a moment. "And some children." Looking from face to face, tears fell down her cheek. "I didn't think Sir Lyndon would miss the money. He's been so good to me, and he's so well off.

"He was so very angry on Monday, but I thought it was because his captain said he needed to do one more trip to see out his contract. So he didn't get the ransom?"

"He did not," Holmes replied. "That was when your Trevor devised his second plan – one that was all his idea." He looked at Lestrade. "The heavier script of the second note, with the intent of the Christmas present and the haste to receive the ransom."

"Must have been," answered Miss Waterson. "He's been so quiet since. Kept disappearing for hours on end. Once we sent the note . . . asking for the money . . . we agreed that I couldn't go back to Sir Lyndon. We've been here ever since, in my parents' old house. I woke up this morning and Trevor was nowhere to be seen. I had to duck out to get something for his tea. I wanted it to be nice when he got back. I bought a bit of beef. I thought he'd be here, but – " Sobs broke out of her, followed by a stream of tears. "He's gone!"

It took some time to calm the poor woman down. Holmes pulled out his pocket watch once again and I knew that time was passing. Somewhere Trevor was waiting to pick up the ransom, which would certainly be paid this time by Sir Lyndon.

It wasn't until a knock on the door that Miss Waterson came back to herself. Looking up, she exclaimed, "Trevor?"

It was Lestrade that opened the door to reveal his driver. After a few moments of whispered conversation, he motioned for Holmes and me to join him, away from the young lady. In hushed tones related his news. "There are two Caribbean cargo ships in port. Both are moored nearby – only five minutes away." He looked at his watch. "Nearly three. This Trevor will be retrieving the money now, and heading that way. We can be there well before he turns up." Nodding towards the young woman, he asked, "What about her?

Although we agreed that from a legal perspective, Lestrade had every right to arrest Miss Waterson for her involvement in the original kidnapping plot, we also agreed to defer doing so until we had dealt with the actual mastermind behind the crime.

As we left the house and drove to the docks, Miss Waterson gave us more information about her errant beau, as she now seemed to have turned against him completely upon realizing that he had no intention of returning to her once he had Sir Lyndon's money. The man's full name was Trevor Farnsley, and her description matched that provided by the old woman next door, and included a confirmation that the tattoos on Farnsley's knuckles indeed read *H.M.S. Sultan*. He had described his previous Navy service aboard that ship to her, and after he was discharged several years earlier, he'd found work plying his trade between England and the Caribbean.

The most useful piece of information that Miss Waterson provided was the name of Farnsley's current ship, the *Batavia*, whose home port was Kingston in Jamaica.

The trip in Lestrade's carriage was swift. We arrived at around a quarter-past-three. Leaving Miss Waterson in the custody of his driver, Lestrade went in search of additional reinforcements. After he returned, we went straight to the *Batavia*'s berth and consulted the Chief Steward. The man had the aged look of one who had spent most of his life at sea. A quick conversation confirmed that Farnsley wasn't yet on board, but was due before the ship weighed anchor at four o'clock.

As we deliberated on our next course of action, two more carriages appeared on the dock, filled with officers. Lestrade quickly instructed the constables aboard to make themselves scarce and wait for his signal. The carriages were driven away and hidden behind some nearby buildings.

A few minutes later, a small, filthy-looking lad appeared around the corner of one of the large warehouses. He glanced once behind himself, then over at Holmes before running for all his worth towards my good friend. A short, but agitated conversation ensued before Holmes motioned towards the opposite corner and followed behind the boy. As Holmes passed me, he whispered, pointing down the roadway leading onto the docks. "The lad was there when the ransom was retrieved. Farnsley is on his way – he's coming in a hansom."

"How did he know where to find you?" Lestrade asked.

"I told the Irregulars to deliver a message to any ships leaving this afternoon for the Caribbean. We were bound to be at one of them."

Following behind Holmes, we ducked down the tight alleyway and waited. Lestrade took up station at the closest point and kept watch around the corner. "Here he comes."

Just as the hansom stopped near the gangway, Lestrade hurried away, with Holmes and me hot on his heels. As we closed in, the hansom moved off, revealing a large cloud of cigar smoke circling the tall well-built figure of a man speaking with the Chief Steward.

Lestrade wasted no time, stopping only a few yards from the pair and speaking loud and clear. "Trevor Farnsley, I am Inspector Lestrade of Scotland Yard. We have reason to believe you are involved in the kidnap of Miss Elaine Waterson, and extortion of Sir Lyndon Marsden."

Turning to face the policeman, Farnsley's expression was a mix of horror and rage. He turned in an attempt to gain the gangway, but the Chief Steward swiftly blocked his way. Pointing at Lestrade, he said, "I think you should talk to the policeman first. We don't want no trouble on board."

Rather than talk, Farnsley threw his rucksack to the ground and balling his fists, strode towards the shorter Lestrade. "I've done nothing. Elaine is in her house in Rotherhithe. No harm has been done to her."

"There is the matter of five-thousand pounds that you have extorted from her employer," Lestrade said, keeping his eyes on the larger man.

Shrugging, Farnsley said, "What money? I haven't taken any money." Throwing his hands to the side, he continued, "Search me if you like. I got nothing but a few pounds."

"Ah, but that isn't quite true, is it?" said Holmes stepping forward, his hand grasping his revolver. "I had you followed from Berkeley Square all the way here." He nodded towards the little fellow peeking around the building corner that we occupied moments before. "My spies tell me that you picked up a small leather satchel at the base of the statue in Berkeley Square before hiring a hansom and heading here, with a brief stop at an address in Limehouse. I'm sure we could find the key if needs be, and at that address, a quick search should reveal the satchel, with its rich contents awaiting your return."

Farnsley's expression turned completely to rage, his eyes darting around for a quick exit. As he made to run, Lestrade pulled a police whistle from his pocket and gave two long blasts. Within seconds, the squad of blue-coated bobbies appeared from around several corners and headed towards us. The cigar fell from Farnsley's mouth as he gaped at the constables.

"You're knicked, Farnsley," said Lestrade. "We'll get all the details from you back at the station, but you aren't going nowhere for a long time."

The tall man bellowed with rage and started again towards Lestrade, but the sight of Holmes's revolver stopped him in his tracks. He swore and cursed under his breath until the paddy wagon arrived to take him to the Yard.

***

"So Farnsley confirmed that he never intended to take Miss Waterson with him?"

"No," said Lestrade, leaning back and taking a sip of tea. We were sitting in Baker Street, and around us were a substantial amount of Christmas decorations – holly and ivy and seasonal candles, all brought in by Mrs. Hudson once she'd been able to make the effort while Holmes was away. I knew that he found them distasteful at best, but it pleased our landlady to celebrate the season, and therefore he would put up with it for a while.

"After we began to question him, it all came out. He met Miss Waterson several months ago, in a tiny pub down in Limehouse. His ship was in port. He was out with some of the other boys. They struck up a conversation and then a relationship. On the next voyage away, Farnsley came up with his plan and convinced the girl to go along with it."

"But not all of it?" asked Holmes.

"No. She agreed to ask for the thousand pounds, but knew nothing more about the rest of it. She had dreams of moving to the country – dreams that Farnsley used to his advantage. She thought that he'd already collected the ransom, and that they would leave London soon. But in the end, he only had eyes for the money."

"The cad," I exclaimed.

"Precisely. Well, he'll be at Her Majesty's pleasure for some time to come."

"I have one last question."

"Yes, Doctor?"

"The foot? Whose was it?"

"Ah," said Holmes. "I can answer that, and the inspector can correct me if I'm wrong." Lestrade nodded his approval. "I've made some enquiries, including at a similar building to the Dufour's Mortuary which is set up in Poplar near the parish church. As with many of the city's mortuaries, they overflow with the dead, from disease and the cold weather. I've had word that disreputable attendants have been selling off bodies to medical schools, and even individual students. Procuring a foot would not be difficult if one has the right connections.

"Given the proximity of Poplar to Farnsley's separate Limehouse residence, I'm sure that he had those. The original owner of the foot was probably a poor streetwalker or local resident, which will be easy enough to confirm. Hence, that's why the body had probably been dead for almost as long as Miss Waterson was missing. In order to add veracity to his trick, Farnsley put it into one of the Miss Waterson's shoes – which Sir Lyndon would recognize, since he saw them every day, and in fact paid for."

"Ghastly," I said. "And what of the lady?"

"I would think that she has been through enough," said Lestrade, surprisingly. "In this matter, she did intend to extort money from her employer – or lover, whichever term you'd like to use. But in my opinion, was that any more tragic than the situation she was already in? Indebted, and enamoured by a man twice her age, with no convenient way out of the arrangement? If she's honest with him, he will simply sack her and throw her out of the Chelsea apartment. I've left her to her own reconnaissance in this matter. Hopefully, it will be a lesson hard learnt."

He took another sip of tea. "And after all – it is Christmas. A little seasonal charity isn't amiss."

"Difficult," I said. "But fair."

"Agreed," said Holmes. "And this will stay with her as a Christmas to remember for many years to come."

"Amen to that," I said, staring into the flames burning in our little grate while the sound of carolers echoed up from the street below.

The Adventure of the Missing Journal

It was late one morning in the spring of 1886 that I returned to 221B Baker Street to find Holmes ensconced in his chair in our parlour, with numerous newspapers strewn about the place.

"Catching up on the news, Holmes?" I quipped.

"Yes, Watson, but sadly, the papers are so devoid of anything interesting as to make it hardly worth the effort."

It was then I noticed copies of the Argus and the Crawley Observer, both from far-flung Sussex lying on the settee next to Holmes's chair. "Brushing up on the farming news then, Holmes," I said nodding towards the two newspapers.

Glancing over at the discarded broadsheets, Holmes replied with a grin, "Ah, yes, when London is in such a state of civility, I like to delve into the activities of our neighbouring counties.

"Anything of note?"

Shaking his head slightly, he said, "Nothing in particular. Though there have been a rash of animal disappearances over the last few months. From reading the accounts, they occur singularly from several farms. I would suggest that the animals have broken free and wandered off, rather than the animated suggestion by the reporter that they have a rustler working in the area." Moving his eyes from the newspapers to rest upon my face, he asked, "Anything interesting in your morning patient?"

Removing my coat and hanging it on the nearby rack, I answered, "No, nothing interesting. An elderly lady injured herself in a fall last week. I simply attended to re-examine the wound for any infection and change the dressing. Almost as dull as your crime report."

"Quite so," said Holmes, picking up the next paper from his pile and poring through it.

As it was past ten thirty, I decided to organise morning tea with Mrs. Hudson. Just as my hand fell upon the doorknob, the front doorbell rang out. Hurrying downstairs, I met Mrs. Hudson as she emerged to answer the door. She eyed me with a puzzled expression and said, “Leaving again so soon, Doctor?” before turning the key and opening the door.

We were greeted by the tall, lanky frame of a young police constable. His face flushed red with shyness, he tipped his head, tapping his helmet with one finger and said, “Good morning Mr. Holmes, Mrs. Holmes, sorry to intrude, but Inspector Lestrade sent me.” Accepting the small, folded note from the constable, I opened it and quickly read.

A smile came to my face.

“Oh, this should at least make Holmes a little happier.”

***

After correcting the young policeman’s two counts of mistaken identity, he blushed even more with embarrassment. I led him upstairs and into our parlour, introducing him to the actual Sherlock Holmes before handing the note across to my good friend.

As I had anticipated, Holmes's interest piqued with the location mentioned in the note. "The British Museum," he said, "What could have happened there that Lestrade needs my services for?"

Constable Dewes, as that was the name he introduced himself with, answered. “There’s been a murder, sir, and a robbery.”

My eyebrows rose at the information. “At the British Museum?”

Nodding, Dewes added, “Yes, sir. There’s a very big kerfuffle going on. The Inspector was determined that I bring you with me. I think his words were, ‘Bring Holmes here or don’t come back at all.’”

Smiling, Holmes said, “It must have Lestrade in a tizzy then.” Rising from his chair, he hurried off into his rooms, throwing a remark over his shoulder as he left. “Right then. Give me a few minutes and we’ll be away.”

***

Dewes' carriage drove up and stopped outside of the wonderful neo-Grecian frontage of the museum. The young constable hadn't expanded on anything during our journey, simply saying that the Inspector had instructed him to not taint the facts of the case. "He said something about Mr. Holmes preferring it that way." I glanced at Holmes to see him nod, a wry grin on his face.

We spotted Lestrade standing near the main entrance doors. A glance inside showed a lack of visitors, something strange for that time of day. It was then I saw another two Constables standing at the base of the steps leading to the main entrance, approaching any potential visitors, and politely directing them away from the building.

"Must be a rum bit of work, if they've closed the museum," I said to Holmes. He nodded in answer, but his eyes were already darting to and fro, seeking any clues they could or detecting anything that might be untoward in the area.

Our young chaperone took us past the two guardians and straight to Lestrade. "What ho, Lestrade?" asked Holmes, "What have you got for me?"

The short, slight frame of Lestrade looked even more withdrawn than usual. He shook his head, "I just don't get this one Holmes, don't get it one bit."

"Something must have happened out here, or else you'd be inside."

Pointing to an area between two of the tall ionic columns to the right of the doorway, Lestrade shrugged and said, "These johnnies they employ to guard this place. I wouldn't give you two quid for the lot. There's one that does the outside, two that do the inside. They are meant to relieve each other every hour or so, but we found one of them there. Dead. Don't know for how long. The two inside did nothing when he didn't show up to be relieved. They thought he'd just fallen asleep somewhere. Seems he does it all the time. It was only when the day guards were coming on duty that they found him." He shook his head. "Damn fools."

"Dead?" I asked, "Where is he now?"

"The Museum manager was here almost immediately. Wanted the body taken away as quickly as possible. I wasn't happy, but he seems to know the captain, same club, or something, so I did as asked. He's gone to the Yard, I thought you'd want to take a look before the coroner starts to examine him."

"Any idea what killed him?"

"I couldn't see anything untoward, just a mark on his face. In my opinion, he was slugged with something heavy. Hit his head as he fell. Poor bugger."

Holmes leaned in towards the area, inspecting a mark on the stonework with his glass. "Hmm. Yes, some hair caught on the stone here. A small amount of blood," He stooped to study the ground, "More blood and hair here. It may not have been the blow that killed him, rather hitting his head on the wall and ground."

"Poor fellow," I added out of sympathy for the man just going about his nightly duties.

After another few moments of examination, Holmes stood and stepped towards the entrance doors. A cursory glance showed them unscathed. "They broke in here?"

"That's the queer thing. No, they didn't. From what I can tell there were at least two of them. One broke in through an upper story window, then let in the feller that did the guard. The doors were closed as the miscreants left. The internal guards didn't even realise they had been unlocked."

"I would have thought that would be part and parcel of their rounds," I added.

"Yes, you would, wouldn't you," said Lestrade, huffing a veiled insult at his private contemporaries, under his breath.

Finishing his inspection of the doors, Holmes stepped into the impressive entrance hallway. Joining him I felt a chill run up my spine, something I had always sensed when glancing into the grandeur of the three-story-high foyer of this magnificent building.

"Where did they enter?" asked Holmes, looking for any sign of damage to the upper story windows.

Lestrade stepped next to Holmes and pointed to the high arched roof, with a line of skylights running around the top level.

In the far corner, a single pane of glass was missing, with only small, jagged pieces left in the frame.

"Impressive," said Holmes, moving into the foyer and hurrying towards the stairwell leading to the first-floor landing at the far end of the room. Lestrade and I struggled to keep up. The game was afoot, and Holmes didn't wish it to get away from him.

We caught him at the top of the stairway, glancing across the stone floor, searching for any piece of information that he could find. His head furtively scanned the area, jerking up towards the missing window pane, then down at the landing a full two stories below.

"You can't be serious, Holmes?" I asked.

"I'm not sure yet, Watson, but the journey from that window could only be achieved by the use of ropes or a ladder, which would beg the question of how those items came to be here in the first place."

"Then how did they climb down then?" asked Lestrade.

"That's why I asked. I think my learned friend is calculating whether they jumped, am I right, Holmes?"

"Possibly, but it would take a formidable athlete." He paused for a moment, before pulling his glass from his pocket, once more, and dropping to his knees. After a few seconds, he said, "Aha," and pointed at what I finally saw was a small patch of dust on the grey stone floor."

"What is that?"

"A footprint. Small and smudged," Holmes said, indicating lines of movement away from the initial impact, "But this is where the person landed." Looking to his left, he shuffled across the stone tiles. "They stepped here, then," he rose, examined the thick stone balustrade, before glancing at the floor below. Rushing down, he ducked towards the small archway from the foyer and dropped to his knees once more. "Yes, here, there," he added, pointing at the small dust imprints on the floor.

Joining him on the ground floor, I glanced up to the top of the stairway. "Are you saying our villain, jumped from that broken window, then leapt over the balustrade and dropped to the floor here? That's three stories in a matter of four or five steps."

"Yes, very lithe this fellow, I think," said Holmes. Following behind Holmes, he pointed out another few dusty prints showed the path our perpetrator took, as he made his way to the front doors. Examining the latches with his glass, Holmes murmured to himself, before standing.

"Anything further?" I asked.

Shrugging, he said, "There are small traces of dust on the latches, and several tiny scratches, but that could be from anybody that has secured these doors over the years. Regardless, it would seem that at least one of our robbers came in through that window, jumped down from the first floor, ran along the ground floor and unlocked these doors." Pointing at another set of smudges leading into the building, he added, "The second villain, waiting outside, followed him in. I can only assume, that one killed the guard." Turning towards Lestrade, he asked, "We have a probable means of entry, but now the question is, what did they steal?"

"Ah, that's where I can help," said a voice from beneath a nearby archway.

All three of us turned towards the source. Lestrade, recognising the figure, spoke up, "Ah, let me introduce my colleagues, Sherlock Holmes and his associate, Doctor John Watson. This is Sir Ezekial Zizza, the director of the British Museum."

Sir Ezekial stepped from the shadows and into the well-lit open foyer. He looked to be in his sixties but stood straight and proud. Following in his wake came a shorter and altogether smaller man, with a slight stoop, and wearing thick glasses. "Ah, the famous detective, good, good, I'd like this messy exercise cleared up quickly. Theft of any of our priceless antiquities is theft not against the museum but England herself."

"Was the missing object highly precious?" asked Holmes.

Sir Ezekial's expression showed confusion for a moment. "Ah, no, not particularly, but it was given to the museum and therefore part of England's heritage."

"What was stolen then?"

Turning to the other man, Sir Ezekial said, “I will let Kyle here answer that.”

The smaller man stepped out of the director’s shadow, his glasses making his eyes look enormous and lending him a frightened appearance.

“Ah, hello, yes, um, it wasn’t just the one. We had several, and they all seem to have disappeared.” Turning, he indicated an archway at the far end of the foyer, “One was housed with the medical anomalies exhibit in the basement. The others were stored with other texts in the reading room below the library.”

When the curator stopped speaking, I waited a moment before blurting out my question, “What were?”

“Oh,” he said, his eyes growing even wider, as a look of stark terror at being questioned bloomed across his face, “Oh, I’m sorry, I presumed you knew.”

“Knew about what?” asked Holmes, his voice gentle and more soothing than mine.

“The journals.”

“Journals? Who’s journals?”

“Ah, that is something that none of us knows for sure," Sir Ezekial piped up. "Last year, a doctor of anthropology, Herbert Magaziner, brought the journals to us. It seems that he procured them, of all places, in Fiji. He had been undertaking some studies of the local tribes, when the captain of a ship that plied its trade in the Pacific, met with him and offered the journals for sale. The good doctor read through them, and to quote him, ‘Instead of burning such drivel, I decided to bring them to the British Museum as a curiosity.’ We are always glad to accept new finds. They presented themselves as a slight oddity within the medical texts, and we thought the public might enjoy seeing them on display. Though we've only ever allowed one on the floor at a time. The rest can be read via the library.”

“What makes these journals so valuable then, that someone would risk life and limb to steal them?” asked Holmes.

“Nothing I presume, but I am not well acquainted with the criminal mind,” said Sir Ezekial.

The little man spoke up, "The language is English, and they talk about forbidden arts within the medical establishment. Vivisection. Of animals, something that has been frowned upon for decades, and virtually banned throughout the profession. Whoever wrote these journals was working outside of the influence and control of any medical institution. Which would be why they were found on an island in the Pacific. The captain told of finding the journals among the ashes of a burned down house and compound, but," the Curator's eyes grew wider, "he told of an operating theatre. Still intact. With one remaining patient on the table. Dead."

"Come now, Kyle, these are stories to tell children, not grown adults like Mr. Holmes and Dr. Watson."

"But they are probably true. The journals speak of such horrors. Of methods to reshape animal tissue to make them walk on two legs. Ways of restructuring the vocal cords to grant speech. Giving them opposable thumbs, and even redirecting their nervous system to increase their intelligence."

"Horrible stuff. Should be sold off as material for penny dreadfuls, not seen as any proper medical treatise." The director drew himself up and puffed out his chest. "Regardless, they have been brought into our collection for display and should be granted the proper security they deserve."

"Who wrote these journals?" I asked, "Surely he could not have been part of the British Medical Association. We have a proud history of staying with the bounds of plausible science, not fantasy."

"I am still unsure of the actual owner. I have read through a good many of the journals, but only one has any indication of a name. It was scratched deep into the leather with a knife or something similar. The style made it look as though the writer was indignant of the name they inscribed."

"What name?" asked Holmes.

"Moreau," said the Curator.

The name seemed familiar to me. Something flared in my mind, a memory from years before during my studies at the University of London.

Stroking his chin with one finger extended, Holmes paused for a moment before asking, “Can we see the display case and book store?”

***

Moving through one of the arches at the far end of the room, the Curator, Kyle, led us down two flights of steps into the relative dark of the basement exhibits. The gas lamps were set to a lower power, probably because the museum was closed to the public.

We entered a small room, filled with glass cabinets, arranged in an aesthetic display. Some were tall with multiple shelves; others were more or less glass boxes resting on wooden tables. Kyle moved away and went to several gas lights, turning the screw to adjust the supply and bring an increase of light to the room.

The display cabinets were filled with a disparate array of relics and artefacts all pertaining to the strangest aspects of the medical profession. Deformed foetuses floated in jars of formaldehyde. Skulls and bones recovered from bodies which would have appeared monstrous in life sat upon several shelves. Strange instruments, looking more like implements of torture, but probably used in ancient operating techniques littered other shelves.

Towards the back of the room, we saw the display case in question. It was of the tabletop style, with the main pane of glass shattered, the shards mixed amongst the items on display.

Holmes approached the cabinet and brought out his glass, stooping to examine the edges of the frame, but careful not to touch anything until he had finished his circuit. “How often are these cases cleaned?”

“Every night,” said Kyle.

“Even in this room?” I asked.

“Oh, yes, the children are most fascinated with the morbid curiosities on display. We often find their little fingerprints and smears all over the cases, even though there are signs everywhere telling them not to touch."

Straightening, Holmes put his glass away before retrieving his thin, kid skinned gloves and a small paper envelope. Delicately, he picked something from one of the spikes of glass in the frame before placing it in the envelope.

"What was that Holmes?"

"It appears to be hair. It may be nothing, but I'd like to examine it under my microscope."

"That's where the journal was displayed," Kyle said, pointing to a small, and now empty, plinth in the rear corner of the case, "We generally turned the page every two weeks, to keep it preserved and ensure each received the same amount of light. Yesterday, it was open to one of the more detailed diagrams. I don't know if that attracted a visitor back."

Bending closer to examine the area, Holmes murmured before reaching in and picking out a piece of glass. Holding it up to the light, he turned it from side to side, before placing it back where he found it.

"Anything?" I asked.

"There was a smudged fingerprint on that splinter as if the thief needed to pick it up and move it away from the book."

"So?"

"Well, it indicates several possibilities. Given there are no other fingerprints on any of the shards of glass, I can surmise that there may have been more than one robber, but we already know that from the evidence of the person that opened the front door for another. Whoever broke the glass appears to have lost some hair, the coarseness of that hair indicates it was body hair. The absence of blood indicates that the arms were possibly thickly covered with hair. Again, these are suppositions rather than factual observations at this stage, I would need more evidence to draw a solid conclusion." Turning away from the display case, Holmes stared into space for a moment, before asking Kyle to show us the reading room.

A short trip down a dark corridor followed until we emerged into a large area sporting bookcases along the walls and a series of desks lined up in rows down the centre. Each desk possessed a small gas lamp which I assumed could be used by a person to provide illumination.

Intrigued at the room, I asked, "Have you ever been here before Holmes?"

"Oh, yes, Watson, many times. The museum boasts quite an impressive collection of archaic texts and volumes. The type of which cannot be found in any normal library or bookshop."

The Curator walked to one of the bookcases and pointed to a small spot on the shelf that was devoid of books. "The other journals sat here. There were nine in all."

"I'm intrigued; was their presence well known?"

"I don't think so. We published their reception in The British Medical Association Journal, many months ago, but apart from that their arrival was not heralded in any other way."

"Do you have any account of people interested in these journals? Has anyone read them of late?"

"No, we don't keep a record of that sort of thing. The volumes cannot be removed from this room." He walked across to a wooden box consisting of several small drawers and opened one. "This is the catalogue. The journals were entered under the name Moreau, and had numbers affixed to their spines." Sorting through the cards in the drawer, he pulled one out and held it up.

"The card, I presume," said Holmes.

Nodding, Kyle replied, "Yes. The only evidence that the journals were ever here."

***

"At least two people broke into the British Museum to steal nine journals. The scratching's of someone called Moreau, who supposedly was a vivisectionist, living on an island in the Pacific, working on ways of making animals more like human beings?"

"That seems to sum up part of the equation, Watson," said Holmes, "The other is the dead guard. We only know that he was supposedly killed by one of the intruders. We don't quite know-how and won't until we see the body." Staring out of the carriage as we traversed the streets to Whitehall, Holmes mused, "From what we saw outside the building, we are seeking two very different individuals.

One who is small, extremely lithe, the other, a large individual, who is very powerfully built."

Before leaving in Lestrade's carriage, we had walked around the outside of the building to the area beneath the broken window. What we found was an almost vertical climb of some fifteen yards. Within moments, Holmes was rewarded with the strangest sight. Several footprints were evident in the damp, slightly boggy grassed area at the base of the building. It was a small garden area, overhung with a thick canopy of trees, and therefore not receiving a lot of direct sunlight. The grassed area was damp, and the intruder had walked through to gain access to the Museum's wall.

Kneeling on the damp grass, Holmes brought out his glass and examined the footprints left behind by the perpetrator. Many murmurs echoed up from him, and when finally, he rose, to examine the wall itself, I asked, "What have you got there, Holmes?"

"Something most intriguing, Watson, most intriguing," he answered, before pointing to several dirty marks that rose up the wall on either side of a drain pipe. "The miscreant has tiny feet, which gives me the impression he may be either a midget or dwarf, but incredibly lithe with it." I took in one of the well-formed footprints on the wall, and almost gasped in the horror of the deformity of our villain. The toepads were tiny, ovoid in appearance, and very close together, forming more of a semi-circle rather than the natural straight line of a normal man's foot.

"Good Lord, the poor blighter, what would have led to that level of disfigurement?"

"I do not know, Watson, but it doesn't seem to trouble the fellow. There are no scratches or burns on the paintwork of the pipe, from any mechanical device or assembly of ropes. For all intents and purposes, the fellow seems to have simply shimmied up the drainpipe barefooted."

"Incredible."

"Quite so."

As the hansom pulled into Whitehall and stopped before Great Scotland Yard, I was snapped back to the present when Lestrade said, "Well, you won't have to wait long to see this unfortunate, I'll take you straight down to the room we use as a temporary morgue."

Lestrade led us into the building, then down two flights of stairs and along a narrow, dimly lit corridor, until we came to a large room, with several tables lining the walls. Sheet covered objects lay on a few of the tables, and in the centre was an examination table holding the body we were interested in.

The room was intensely cold but still held the unmistakable odour of rot. Several blocks of ice sat in containers in the corner of the room, providing an extra level of chill to the atmosphere.

"I apologise for this place, it's not what we would prefer, but the local mortuaries have been overrun of late and those upstairs want the costs dropped, so we set this place up. Any bodies we want to examine are kept here until the coroner comes to collect them."

"Damn chilly," I said, "But better that than have these poor unfortunates rotting away before your eyes."

Glancing at me with a slight look of disapproval, Holmes said, "Well, I suppose we should get on with this so that Watson can return to somewhere more comfortable." Stepping up to the examination table, Holmes drew back the sheet covering the body's face. He grimaced as he stared at the strange bruising on the man's cheek. Turning, he grasped a nearby portable lamp, lit the flame from a wall lamp and returned, leaning closer to study the area. "Obviously, this is where the larger man struck the guard," he said, pointing at the odd mark. It appeared to consist of two semi-circular teardrop-shaped halves that mirrored each other with a gap between them. Gently moving the man onto his side, he inspected the damage to the back of the man's head and nodded. "Hmm. Yes, a large wound where he struck the wall," he said before returning the man onto his back and turning towards me. "What do you make of it, Watson?"

"Astounding," I said, "Whatever it was, it hit him with incredible force. That would account for both the mark and head wound. The bruising would have occurred as he lay dying, but the clarity of that bruise is incredible. If I didn't know any better, I would say he was struck with something similar to a cow's hoof."

"That was my impression," Holmes said, "As if the assailant used the foreleg of a bovine as an actual weapon, or." He trailed off for a moment, a slight grin appearing on his face.

"No, you can't be serious," I said.

"Well, until we can eliminate the conjecture, it shall remain."

I shook my head, knowing what he was going to say next.

"This man may have been killed by a cow."

"Impossible," said Lestrade, "Must have been a club, surely."

Holmes was about to speak again when several harsh shouts echoed down the long, darkened corridor and filtered into the room.

"What in blazes?" asked Lestrade, before bolting from the room. Holmes quickly followed. I took one last look at the dead man's face, before pulling the sheet over his head and pursuing my companions.

Heading towards the noises, I found myself amongst the various holding pens set aside for the more detestable, or unstable criminal elements picked up by the bobbies. At the far end of the line of cells, Holmes and Lestrade stood with two uniformed constables. All four stared into one of the holding cells, the bobbies glancing around frantically, with expressions of horror on their face.

"Well, where did he go then?" I heard Lestrade ask as I joined them. I looked at the object of their attention and almost burst into a fit of laughter. Inside one of the tiny cells was a full-grown sheep. As if on cue, it bleated out in a pitiful voice filled with fear and confusion.

"What the devil is that doing here?" I asked.

"The question is, where did the man who was here before disappear to?" Holmes asked.

As I stared at the sheep, I noticed items of discarded clothing scattered across the floor. From my position, I could see that the shirt and trousers were torn as if hurriedly discarded, or burst apart.

Distressed at the lunacy of the situation, and the possible embarrassment it could cause, Lestrade berated the two constables. "Who was in this cell?"

"Ah," said one Bobbie, "He was a drunk, picked up on Great Russell Street, early this morning. The Constable, that brought him in, said he wasn't making no sense, and couldn't form no words. He was brought down here just in case he had a bad turn. Easier to clean up."

"But he's gone, and he left you this little present."

"Seems so, Sir."

"Good Lord man, we'll be a laughing stock if this gets out," said Lestrade, his demeanour becoming increasingly agitated.

"Inspector, if I may, the fact that this, um, fellow was picked up in Great Russell Street, which is near the entrance to the Museum, strikes me as particularly intriguing."

Confused, Lestrade turned back to face Holmes, "In what way?"

"Well, so far we have someone acting like a cat, someone with the strength of a bull, why not a sheep?"

"Come on Holmes, this is no time for games."

Chuckling, Holmes added, "Oh, I do agree Inspector, I do apologise, I wasn't trying to be funny, just pursuing a line of reasoning, as humorous as it may appear." Stepping up to the bars of the cage, Holmes hunkered down and peered in at the frightened sheep. "This little miss has a ring in her ear. It may be worth a look, plus I'd like to inspect those clothes."

"Constable, key?" asked Lestrade. The Bobbie brought out his set of keys and unlocked the door. Holmes stepped into the cell, slowly approaching the ewe which moved away, pressing herself against the very rear of the little room. Gently, Holmes reached out a hand and patted the sheep on the head, before lightly grasping her ear and examining the little brass band.

"Hmm," he said, "It looks like a registered farm brand, but I'll have to check the records to see where this little one comes from." Pivoting around, he deftly retrieved the items of clothing before making his way back to the door to join us outside. Examining the tattered shirt and trousers, a grin came to his face as he found something in one of the trouser pockets. "Aha," Holmes said, bringing out a small piece of paper.

Unfolding it, we found a hand-drawn map of what looked like streets, with an X marked in red on one corner. I immediately recognised the layout as the area we had just visited. A large rectangle was the Museum, and the X represented the corner of Great Russell Street and Montague Street.

"I believe we have found the lookout's clothes," Holmes said.

"What? The sheep?" asked Lestrade.

"Perhaps not the animal, but rather another member of the bandits, who had been stationed at this point," he pointed to the X, "And subsequently enamoured with his own success, may have celebrated a little heavily. How he then escaped and replaced himself with this ovine equivalent is anyone's guess?"

***

Leaving Lestrade at the Yard, I flagged down a passing hansom and told the driver to take Holmes and me to the Smithfield Markets. Stepping from the cab, the smell hit us with full force. Every manner of animal scent assaulted our nostrils, causing me to search the area in case I had stepped into a pile of manure.

"There's nothing quite like the sensory overload that one experiences at the markets, is there Watson?"

"I'm quite sure I've never suffered such an onslaught before. I can tell you that."

I was still a little confused as to our purpose at the markets, but it seemed we were in luck, the day was dedicated to the sale of sheep, cows, and goats. Holmes strode off towards the sale yard and stopped at a small table where a man took down names and numbers from a line of country folk, dressed in their finest for the day. Not wanting to seem out of place, we joined the queue, and waited patiently, glancing around at the hustle and bustle going on around us.

Finally, we reached the table and found a swarthy man, with the reddened cheeks of a heavy drinker, sitting before us. His watery eyes looked at us in suspicion. “This is for registrations. I think you gentlemen may be in the wrong place,” he said.

“Ah, my good man, I do hope we aren’t. I own a small property on the outskirts of the city of London, and I’m afraid that one of your sellers may have lost a sheep on his drive into the markets.”

The registrar’s face screwed up in confusion, “Oh, yeah, how’d you figure that?”

“Well, one appeared in my top field this very morning. I do not run any sheep, and neither do any of my close neighbours, so it was a surprise.”

“Interesting, did it have an ear tag?”

“Yes, a small, metal tag in its left ear, inscribed with the numbers one, one, six and nine, and the letters D, F and C, written below them.”

The man cocked an eyebrow. “Yep, that sounds like what you’d find.” He reached beneath his table and pulled out a thick, bound volume, plonking it down in a cloud of dust, before opening and searching down several columns of numbers. “One, one, six, nine, you say?”

“Yes.”

“Ah, here we are,” the man said, his finger resting on one of the entries in the book. “DFC?” Holmes nodded. “That would be Drayford Fumey, down in Crawley. That sheep is a long way from home.” The registrar moved his attention back to his current work and read down the list of sellers. After a while, he shook his head. "Nuh, he's not registered so far, may be coming in later today or might not even be here. Can't for the life of me figure out how one of his sheep ended up alone in London? I reckon someone's playing a joke on him."

“Do you have an address for him in Crawley?”

“Nah, just asks at the pub or Police Station. It’s not that big a place, Crawley. Everyone knows everyone else.”

Holmes pulled a guinea from his pocket and slipped it to the man. “Thank you, sir, you have done me a great service.”

The man picked up the guinea, eyeing it greedily for a moment before it disappeared. "To be honest, if I was you, I’d find a good butcher and enjoy a nice lamb roast or two. Can't imagine it'd be worth your while taking a sheep back to Crawley."

Nodding, Holmes said, "Thank you, it is an idea, but I'm not sure I could dine on someone else's misfortune."

"Your loss."

Smiling, Holmes moved away through the throng of people and headed towards the holding pens. I assumed he hoped to catch sight of this Fumey character, or something similar. Instead, he took a direct path to the cow enclosures and took up a conversation with a rural looking chap standing next to the largest bull I had ever seen. Within a few moments, a coin slipped from Holmes' pocket into the man's hand. The farmer turned and pinched the bull on the rear, eliciting a loud low of complaint, and resulting in a wad of hair pulled from its rump which was transferred to another small paper envelope in Holmes's hand.

Confused, I broached the subject with Holmes as we exited. "What was all that with the bull?"

"Ah, I wanted to test a theory about that hair we found, and the easiest way was to have something sourced from the horse's mouth, so to speak."

"You've got a strange definition for horse's mouth," I remarked.

***

Back at our Baker Street abode, Holmes sloughed off his travelling cloak and hat and moved to his experiment table, slipping his microscope out of its corner, and extracting both paper envelopes. Within moments of placing the hairs onto a slide and studying them through the scope, he exclaimed, "Aha, come here Watson, let's see what you think?"

Stepping across to the table, Holmes moved away and indicated the scope. Looking through I could see three hairs through the eyepiece. The two longer, thicker hairs at the top of the slide appeared to be the same, the third was thinner and quite dark.

"The two top hairs are identical, except probably for the colour. One's a slightly darker shade. I would say that they were the ones you bought at the market. The bottom is from a different animal altogether, possibly feline or even human."

"Well done, Watson, well done. Now the reality. The top hair is from the market. The second hair is one of those I pulled from the broken glass cabinet at the museum. The third is mine, I pulled one from my forearm for reference purposes."

"Good Lord, are you saying that someone planted bull hair on the cabinet at the museum? Why would they do that?"

"Ah, that may not quite be the answer. I must cogitate on that a while longer. What I do find intriguing is that the farmer I bought those hairs from was from the Crawley area. I wanted to obtain hairs from the common species of cattle farmed around there."

"Crawley," I said, taking one last glance through the eyepiece, before moving away, "What is it about Crawley?"

"That I do not know yet, but we have a lost sheep with a Crawley ear tag, now we have mysterious animal hairs from a species of cow that originates from the same area."

"What does it all mean?"

"I think we need to take a little trip tomorrow," he said.

"To Crawley?"

"Yes. I believe there may be answers to be found in Sussex."

***

The following morning saw our plan begin to unfold. Mrs. Hudson fixed a wonderful breakfast that would hopefully provide us with the energy to complete our journey. The first stop was to find Lestrade and advise him of Holmes' findings. When we mentioned Crawley, he was both bemused and slightly confused.

"You'll want a local to help then?" he asked.

Nodding, Holmes agreed, "That may be appropriate. I've not been in the area for several years."

Pulling out a card, Lestrade wrote a small note on the back and then stared at it for a moment. "You should seek out Senior Constable Brandon Roberts. He's an old associate of mine. Moved back to Sussex after a few years on the beat here. Should know the local area at least." Glancing up at Holmes, he added, "Are you sure this is the best way forward? Everything's happened here in London, what would draw you to Sussex?"

"I can't put my finger on it, just yet, but as more evidence accrues, it all points to that area, as strange as it may seem," Holmes answered, accepting the card, and pocketing it straight away.

Our trip from Victoria station to Horsham was uneventful. I sat hoping to ask Holmes more about his theories, convinced that we were on a wild goose hunt, but remained quiet, accepting of my colleague's mysterious ways. The carriage we hired took us to Crawley and straight to the local constabulary. As I stood and paid our fee, the mid-autumn sun beat down from on high reminding me that the effects of the morning's breakfast were beginning to wear off in such a way that only a late luncheon would appease the gnawing feeling growing inside my belly.

Inside the police station, we found a bored-looking constable writing in a journal. His excitement at our appearance told me more about the lazy feel of the town than I had seen in her streets.

Showing the card from Lestrade, Holmes introduced us and asked about Senior Constable Roberts, but was told he was on a call to a local farm. "Something about a missing cow," the Constable mumbled, before realising what he'd said.

"A shame really," said Holmes, "We wish to consult with the senior constable about a lone sheep that has appeared in London. Supposedly from a nearby farm."

"A sheep?" the Constable asked, a suspicious frown crossing his face. "Do you know which farm?"

"We only have the identity tag in its ear to go by. It supposedly points to someone called Drayford Fumey."

The Constable's eyes grew wide, accompanied by a grin and a chuckle, "You've found Fumey's sheep? He's been going on about that animal for weeks. Badgered the senior constable for days over the lack of information about it." He smiled widely, "Wait till I tell the senior. Where did you find it?" Pulling a small pad of paper towards him, the Constable picked up a pencil, ready to write down some notes, "And who are you again?"

As Holmes told the Constable the details, he madly scribbled on the little pad, then reread what he'd written, chuckling once more. "British Museum? I didn't think the sheep was that remarkable."

"Oh, I think it might be, but not in any normal way," said Holmes, before changing the subject, "Is there a local pub that can put us up for the night? I'd be especially interested in the one frequented by the local farmers, we might be able to catch this Fumey fellow there."

"Oh, that you will, go straight down the High Street and look for the Ploughman, can't miss it. The outside stinks like a barnyard, 'cause that's where Roscoe, the publican, makes the patrons leave their wellies."

"Sounds wonderful," I added with a heavy dose of sarcasm that was lost on the young policeman.

"Please send Senior Constable Roberts down there when he returns. Regardless of the accommodation, we'll at least settle in for a pint or two while we wait," said Holmes.

"Right you are, then," said the constable, as we headed for the entry door.

***

Luckily, we saw the sign for the Ploughman swinging and creaking in the light breeze, moments before the undeniable smell of the country assaulted our nostrils. The source was lined up near the front door. I counted at least four pairs of boots, smeared underneath with all manner of farmyard detritus. A metal boot scraper sat well away from the door and was caked in the thicker muck, rubbed off by the farmers as they arrived.

The building itself was small and built of stones gathered from the nearby fields, locked together with lime mortar, with a well-worn thatch roof sitting atop. A thin line of smoke rose from the chimney, indicating that a fire burned within, which I thought strange on such a wondrously warm day, but soon realised it was from the kitchen out back.

Inside, a pall of cigarette smoke filled the front bar area, making it difficult to see in the dark room. Windows were few and far between, the main source of light provided by several candles sitting in holders along the outer walls and over the bar.

We found the landlord straight away, he was a large, ruddy-faced man and soon handed over a set of keys to a room at the top of the stairs towards the back of the pub. Holmes asked him to make sure that Senior Constable Roberts was informed of our presence, in case he arrived whilst we were upstairs. A quick question of my own found that a good luncheon was available, and I ordered a hearty meal that would welcome us when we came down.

My heart dropped when we were greeted by a lone double bed. I didn't wish to be delicate, but the thought of sharing with Holmes was not high on my wish list.

"Should we see if there's another room?" I asked.

"Later, Watson, later. We have more important matters to attend to first," Holmes answered.

Shrugging, I quickly relieved myself of cloak and hat and followed Holmes back downstairs. Within moments we were presented with a delightful midday meal, washed down with the local bitter. The relief almost made me forget about our sleeping arrangements.

It was as I drained the last dregs of my pint, that the entrance door opened, and the tall figure of a policeman stepped inside. Waiting a moment for his eyesight to adjust, he scanned the room, saw Holmes and me, and headed straight to our table. Removing his helmet, he looked both of us in the eye before saying, "Mr. Holmes?"

Nodding, Holmes replied, "Senior Constable Roberts, I presume?"

"Yes, Sir, I have it on good authority that my old comrade Lestrade sent you to see me?"

Motioning to the empty seat, Holmes said, "Yes. My colleague, Dr. Watson, and I are helping the Inspector with a rather peculiar matter at the British Museum."

“Smith, back at the station, mentioned that you found a sheep?”

A wry grin broke out on Holmes’s face, “As I said, peculiar.”

“And you think it might be Fumey’s? Good, that fella has been pestering me for two weeks now. Probably mislaid the blasted animal on his last drive up to London.”

A dry, crackle of a voice broke through the pall of smoke and addressed the senior constable. “Oi, Roberts, did I just hear youse have found my Dolly?” A hairless, old face approached from a nearby booth. He looked like he’d lived in the sun for the best part of a century, with well-tanned skin and deep crevices running across his forehead and beneath his eyes.

“Hello, Drayford,” said Roberts, “These gentlemen have journeyed down from London, where they believe that have found your sheep.”

“About bloody time,” Fumey added, “Where is she?”

“Well, actually, she is in a cell in Scotland Yard, so she is perfectly safe,” said Holmes with no hint of irony.

“The Yard? What did she do? I can’t pay no fines.”

“I’m sure that won’t be necessary,” said Holmes, “But once we have finished our investigations, I’m sure she can be returned to you.”

Another voice piped up next to Fumey. I made out the face of another long-time farmer, but with much more hair on his head. “Have you found my bull then?” he asked.

From another direction came another question. “What about Neddy? My horse?”

“It’s gypsies, init?” said another from the back.

Within moments, we were virtually surrounded by several older gentlemen who badgered the poor senior constable with a barrage of questions about missing animals, ranging from horse, bull, and sheep, through to a goat, at least two cats and a dog.

It was Holmes that stood and took their questions, answering with, "Now, now, please gentlemen, we are helping Scotland Yard with this matter. At this stage, we only know about Mr. Fumey's sheep. I'm sure once we track down the miscreant, if there is one, it will all become clear. Until then, I'm afraid no amount of questioning will elicit any further details." With an undercurrent of murmuring, the farmers broke away, returning to their seats.

Remaining on his feet, Holmes glanced down at the policeman. "Mr. Roberts, would you have a detailed map of the immediate area?"

"Yeah, back at the station. But why?"

"I believe there may be a pattern to these disappearances that may be worth investigating."

***

Within minutes the three of us stood around a table in the station's main room. Constable Smith joined us and lay down several maps of the area. Roberts pointed to one depicting the area just south-east of the town, a small stream ran through the area, with several ponds dotting it. To me, it looked like very good farming land.

Placing his finger on one of the small areas, outlined in a darker border, Roberts said, "That's Fumey's place there." Pointing to several others, he continued, "Bodie, the feller with the missing horse, Jones, the bull, Creighton, another sheep, a cat from Herring's, a dog from Dalton's."

"Do you mind if we mark off those farms?" asked Holmes, "Just the borders, I think there is already a pattern forming."

Roberts did as he was asked. Smith piped up and added a couple of other occurrences of missing animals. By the time they had finished, a good deal of the area was outlined in a darker shade. Holmes stood, his hand to his chin with one finger raised. "Do you see it?" he asked.

Extending my hand, I pointed to three farms bordering each other that were unmarked. "These three haven't made any complaints."

"No, I've heard nothing from any of them," said Roberts. Pointing to two neighbouring farms, "these are both sheep farms, but," indicating the farm furthest to the south, "I don't think that feller runs any livestock at all."

"Whose farm is that?" Holmes asked.

"A feller called Prendrick. Edward Prendrick. Been there nigh on ten years. Keeps to himself. Most folk around here probably have never seen him, let alone talked with the man."

"What do you think, Holmes?"

"I am unsure at this stage, Watson, but it may be worth investigating these properties. It isn't clear yet, but the evidence points to a connection between these animals disappearing, and the appearance of a sheep in Scotland Yard, which in turns seems to lead back to the break-in at the museum and the death of the guard. We must remember, the death is the main crime here."

"I'd be happy to accompany you," said Roberts, "Smith can come as well."

"There's probably nothing in it," added Holmes, "But if there is, it may be best if the constabulary is with us."

***

The first two farms proved fruitless. Neither farmer could identify whether any livestock had gone missing. Both ran sheep but had seen foxes of late and put any loss of lambs or ewes down to that cause. Although as we left the second farm, the man's wife stepped out and mentioned that the cat that lived in the barn hadn't been around for a few weeks. The old farmer shrugged and hawked a wad of phlegm into the dirt, suggesting a fox as the cause. The wife added another clue, which I thought strange in itself at the time, admitting that a few items of clothing had gone missing from her clothesline at her last weekly wash.

As the sun set, bringing a slightly chilly night with it, I began to lose faith that Holmes was on the right track. Roberts decided to end our search for the night with a visit to this Edward Prendrick, before returning to Crawley and regrouping in the morning.

It was as the carriage bumped its way along an overgrown track, that I noticed a bright orange light filtering through the trees. I prodded Holmes with my elbow and pointed towards it. "What do you make of that, Holmes?"

Glancing at it for a moment, he said, "Hmm. A fire. Out in the open." He nodded towards another soft glow in the distance. "The house is way over there. So, I doubt if it is our Mr. Prendrick."

Roberts stared at the glow as well, before thumping on the roof and calling out. "Smith, stop here. I think we've found those gypsies." As the carriage pulled up, he added, "I heard one of the farmers complain, and we've had some notice that there's a band of gypsies around somewhere. Lawless blighters. Steal anything that's not nailed down. Could be stealing the animals for food, or some such."

Roberts and Smith led the way, stealthily making their way through the thick underbrush towards a dry-stone wall that let onto the wide-open field beyond. From behind the wall, we could see the light came from a large campfire located on a small hillock, some thirty yards away. Several silhouettes, of varying sizes, sat around the flames and passed in front from time to time.

As we were about to vault over the wall and approach, one figure stood up and moved to one side. I couldn't see him clearly, but as he moved into the firelight, I caught sight of his hair, which was curled in such a way to look almost like the horns of a ram.

A low murmur began from the standing figure, answered by the others around the campfire. The rhythm of their voices wasn't such to suggest singing, more a recitation of some form.

Holmes took the lead, scurrying over the wall, stooping close to the ground to avoid detection, and moving closer up the little rise. The rest of us followed in his wake. As we came closer, the figures became more distinct, as did the invocation from the leader.

"Not to go on all-fours; that is the Law. Are we not men?" said the standing figure, immediately greeted with a mix of garbled voices repeating the line. "Not to suck up drink; that is the Law. Are we not men?" Again, repeated, then followed with, "Not to eat fish or flesh; that is the Law. Are we not men? Not to claw the bark of trees; that is the Law. Are we not men? Not to chase or harm other men; that is the Law. Are we not men?"

The standing figure stopped for a moment, as a general murmur ran through the group, followed by several strange animalistic noises and shushing sounds.

"One of us has broken the laws. One of us has brought us all shame. One of us must pay." Looking to the other side of the flames, the Law Sayer, pointed and spoke. "Brother Hannibal, join me."

My eyes grew wide as a huge figure stood and towered above the flames. I almost gasped in horror at his visage. His eyes were large and round, almost filled with iris and pupil. His nose was wide and flat, with huge nostrils. His chin and jowls sported a light covering of red hair. I couldn't tell in the firelight, but I swear he had horns atop his head. Below that head, sat a massive barrel-like chest, covered in the same course hair. Then I saw his hands. Misshapen, with no visible fingers, just a pair of strange clubs, like the hooves of a cow.

Oh, you poor man.

The man, I use the term as I had no other to ascribe him, approached the Law Sayer. A look of hopelessness seemed to envelop his being, and a murmur ran through the group.

"Brother Hannibal," said the Law Sayer, "You broke the law. There are some that say you killed. Another man no less."

"Accident," the large shape said in a deep bellowing tone. "It was accident."

Another murmur rose from the group.

"What does the law say?"

After a moment's hesitation, the accused replied, "Not to chase or harm other men."

"Again?"

"Not to chase or harm other men." Pausing for a moment, he added, "It was accident."

"We must see the Master. He will know what to do."

The large red-haired figure reacted, pulling away from the fire in horror. "No. Not the Master. There will be a return. I do not want to return."

"I think we have our man," Holmes said in my ear.

Overhearing, Holmes' words, Roberts chose that moment to stand up, the light of the fire spilling across his face. "Hold it right there, boyos. I am Senior Constable Roberts. This man is wanted by the police."

The group reacted as one, rising to their feet they turned to face us and broke out in a series of screeches and squeals, all the time backing away from us to the other side of the fire. Their noises were unlike any group of men I had ever encountered, but it was when I stepped forward and saw them in the full light of the flames that my voice almost joined theirs, such was the horror.

Each man, and I use the term loosely, bore severe disfigurements like their larger companion. One group was no more than three feet in height but displayed no kinship with either midget or dwarf. Their eyes were alighted with fire, centred with oval-shaped pupils. Their noses were but small buttons in the centre of their face, their ears pointed and positioned towards the top of their head. Like their larger counterpart, their hands were malformed into tiny clumps of flesh, with small fingers that extended only out one knuckle and sported long nails that upon examination disappeared somehow into the flesh itself.

Another member of the group was similar in that his height was barely four feet. He sported a long face, dominated by the sloping nose, sitting above a wide mouth with protruding teeth from a severe overbite. His ears were large, and lacking cartilage which caused them to fold over.

Two others had long faces with dull eyes. Their hair a closely curled white, that flowed down from their heads as if they wore judges' wigs.

It was when my eyes finally fell onto the features of the Law Sayer that I felt my very sanity depleting. He stood five feet tall, sporting the similar white curled hair as the last two, and the long ovoid face, but the feature I had mistakenly attributed to hair, were, in fact, two curled horns sitting on either side of his face.

As the visual atrocity assaulted my senses, the audible cataclysm began to make sense. The screeches and squeals began to reform into recognisable sounds. Bleats, barks, mews, and the frantic lowing of a cow. As I realised what I was looking at, I made my realisation known. “They're animals.”

“Incredible, isn’t it?” said Holmes, standing by my side.

"What in the devil is this?" cried Roberts, his face a mask of terror.

A call began to rise from the group. "Master. Master. Master."

Holmes stepped forward, approaching the Law Sayer with hands held before him. "We mean you no harm, but yes, this Master, please take us to him."

A voice rose from the gloom. "There'll be no need for that Lucius, I am already here."

All turned towards the owner of the voice. He stood some ten yards away, highlighted by the orange glow of the fire. He appeared to be a man well into his sixties, with a creased face showing both concern and genteelness, and leaning on a cane for support.

"Gentlemen, I think you should follow me back to the house. Lucius, Hannibal, you should come too."

***

Following behind the limping figure, I looked around at the dour and confused faces of my colleagues, then at Lucius the Law Sayer, and Hannibal, who I started to refer, in my mind, as the bull-man. The clatter of our carriage floated through the still of the night. Smith had taken the opportunity and headed off to collect and bring it to the house's forecourt.

The door was opened by a tall, dark-skinned man, with a long face and large nostrils. It was when he bade us entry, by holding up a hand, that was just a hoof with a small hook tied to it, that I realised this was another of the animal men. A horse no less.

"Thank you, Ned," said our host.

I remembered that name from the pub. One of the farmer's had mentioned, Neddy, his horse. Another piece of evidence that meant our host had indeed absconded with the animals. Why? Part of that was becoming clear, the actual purpose not so much.

Ushering us into a large drawing-room, warmed by a small fire, our host motioned towards a sideboard where sat a flask of brandy and several glasses. "Help yourselves, gentlemen. It is a chilly night."

I made my way across and poured one for each of us, and another for the host. As I took it to him, he used the opportunity to introduce himself. “As you may know from the senior constable here, I am Dr. Edward Prendrick.”

Holmes introduced himself, then me. Roberts simply nodded. It seemed he had met the man before.

“Can I ask why you have come to my farm at such an hour, senior constable?”

“Mr. Holmes and Dr. Watson, here, have come from London to solve several crimes.”

“Oh, yes, and what were they?” asked Prendrick, taking a sip of his brandy before gently sitting in a chair by the fire.

Holmes, spoke up as he moved across the room and picked up a small red bound volume from the table next to the very chair Prendrick occupied. “I think you know perfectly well, what they were, sir.” Holding the book, Holmes opened it and read the first page. “Several volumes of notes from a certain, Dr. Moreau, were stolen from a display case and the reading room in the British Museum. Those volumes recounted the science behind, and experimentation on animal subjects, the purpose of which was to create human-like beings.” Turning towards Hannibal and Lucius, Holmes added, “Much like those that we see before us here.”

“A fantastic accusation, Mr. Holmes,” said Roberts, “Surely, these men were simply born with unfortunate deformities and disabilities. What you suggest is beyond comprehension.”

“I would have hoped until I laid eyes on these men. But what evidence we have gathered points directly to my conclusion. It is my assertion that Dr. Prendrick here, sent three of his creations into the heart of London to retrieve the works of Dr. Moreau. A scientist of a like mind as his own. Two of those we have seen. One of the cat-men, and our Hannibal here. The other, a sheep, is locked away in Scotland Yard. What say you, Dr. Prendrick?"

The older man smiled for a moment. “I find humans to be such a violent and self-centred species, and ever since I returned from abroad, have long shunned their company.”

“Abroad? The Pacific perhaps?”

"Yes. I was shipwrecked upon the island of Moreau. I observed his horrifying experiments and unwittingly played a hand in his demise. Once returned to England, I found, however, that I had lived among Moreau's beast-men for so long that I could not adapt to life with other humans. I shut myself away here for a decade before the loneliness became too much for me to bear. My research in chemistry gave way to further investigations into biology. There is an entire field awaiting investigation, but mine allowed me to develop a reagent that can change and re-configure the brain chemistry of an animal, allowing fuller development and intelligence."

"Incredible," I cried, looking once again at Lucius and Hannibal.

"As it is, yes. My successes have been few, my failures far more."

"But your process is not perfected yet, is it?" asked Holmes.

"No, no it is not. If the subject does not receive sufficient injections of the reagent, they regress back to their animalistic nature and form."

"The sheep?" I asked, "It was locked up overnight."

Nodding, Prendrick said, "Unfortunately for Bessie, yes, she returned to her true form. I can help her, if only she were returned to me."

"Moreau's notes? You hoped to find something in them?"

"Yes. I thought them burnt in the house. I never investigated the House of Pain, as the beast-men called it, the place where Moreau undertook his horrible surgeries. I read in the paper that the notebooks had been donated to the Museum, so I sent three of my friends to retrieve them for me."

"A cat, a bull, and a sheep."

"Yes. My comrades still retain much of their animal skills. They were perfectly adapted for the task."

"But one disobeyed your laws."

"Moreau's laws actually, but which one?"

"To not kill. A guard was killed."

Prendrick cried out in shock and stood up. "What? That was never part of my plan?" He looked towards Lucius, then Hannibal. "Is that what this is about? Hannibal, how could you?"

I read in the paper that the notebooks had been donated to the Museum, so I sent three of my friends to retrieve them for me.

"It was accident, Master. He surprised me. I did not mean to strike him. Then he fell and laid still. I am so sorry."

Shaking his head, remorse lit large upon his face, tears formed at the corner of Prendrick's eyes. "We cannot allow this, Hannibal. You know the laws. You broke them. Now you must pay. All must obey."

“No, Master, no.” The bull-man’s eyes grew wide, his expression one of stark terror. “No, I do not want to return. I am a man. I walk on two legs.”

Prendrick stepped towards the frightened bull-man, placing a hand on his shoulder. “I'm afraid I can't allow that. Any man breaking the law can no longer be a man. You can no longer be a man.”

Hannibal threw his hoofs forward, pushing the old man away from him. “No.” Prendrick stumbled backwards, tripping over the edge of the fireplace, and crashing back against the stone surrounds. His head striking the lintel let out a sharp crack and left a smear of blood on the soot-streaked stone. He fell to the floor with a dull thud and lay still.

The bull-man took one look at his fallen master and let out a loud low of fear. “Master?” Taking one step forward, Hannibal stopped when Lucius spoke up.

“He has broken the law. Again.”

The horse-man, Ned, stepped in behind Lucius and pointed a hoof towards the bull-man. “There must be punishment. He has broken the Law.”

Glancing from the Law Sayer to the manservant with those huge dark eyes, Hannibal’s face flashed an expression of abject horror before he pushed past both and bolted from the room. His hoofed feet leaving loud clopping sounds in their wake before the front door crashed open as he exited.

I ran to the fallen scientist and searched for signs of life. “Damn,” I cried when none were to be found.

“Master?” said Lucius, joined by a worried appeal from the horse-man Ned.

As I turned, I saw Roberts run from the room but noticed Holmes standing stock still and glancing down at me. "Holmes, he's dead. We need to stop that beast."

“No. Roberts may catch up with him, but the source of his humanity is gone. You heard Prendrick say it, in a day or two all these men will be nothing more than beasts of the field.”

“If Master is gone, who will be our Master?”

Staring up at their looks of confused innocence, I shook my head.

"We are alone," Lucius said, before turning and stepping from the room, with Ned close behind. The softer sound of their hooves on the wooded floor, echoed back as they stepped out into the night.

"The poor devils," I said, "To have tasted humanity only to lose it in such a way."

"They will be fine. I presume they will not remember once they regress. All that will be left is for Roberts to return them to their owners."

"What about the bull?"

"Honestly? The bull killed a man. If he were human, he would be hanged. I can only think he will end up at the butcher's within a week."

Staring down at the body, I added, "There is so much to learn here that is now lost. Is it that animals are so close to humans that a simple chemical compound can bridge the gap?"

"I have always found the opposite, so many humans are close to the animals, but crossing that void rarely even requires outside assistance."

The Man from Moscow

The story of Colonel Lysander Stark from The Adventure of the Engineer's Thumb.

Metz, France, 1870

The crack of gunfire echoed through the silent night. Stark's head spun in the direction of the sound. He stopped rowing and listened for several moments before expelling his breath in a sigh of relief. The dark, still night belied the distance from the shooter.

Idiots. There's no point shooting at the enemy. We'll have them starved out in six weeks or less. After tonight, nobody is escaping from Metz.

Pushing the oar through the dark waters of the Moselle, Stark propelled his little boat towards the starboard bank. Several dark silhouettes stood well away from the shoreline. Their windows shuttered; lights extinguished. To the uninitiated, the town of Moulins was all but abandoned.

Stepping ashore, Stark pulled the little boat onto the muddy bank, stowing the paddle and pulling out his map and orders.

By the light of the waning moon, he oriented himself and determined the likely direction of his quarry. The hand-drawn map of the area, copied from the intelligence maps used by the high command, bore an X indicating a house on the outskirts of the little town. A single name, Teulet, was written near the house.

Stark's mind raced with images and memories of his recent briefing from Oberst Kruger.

"Leutnant Stark," the older man's creased faced stared deep into the younger officer's eyes, "Bismark wants Metz. Bismark wants the Army of the Rhine decimated." Stark stood stock still at attention, no movement, no expression. Continuing, Kruger said, "This little man, Teulet, thinks it is funny to enter Metz and smuggle the officers out. We have no idea how. We have no idea where. These French must have a network of tunnels or some such, I don't know, it seems fanciful, but our best intelligence officers agree."

Moving around his desk, Kruger spat at the thought of the intelligence officers, "I don't care what these idiots agree to. I want action." Stopping before Stark, he stared straight into the younger man's eyes, "Your commanding officers speak highly of you. They say you are a man of action. Will you eliminate this threat? This Teulet? Is that something you will do for me?"

"Yes, Oberst, certainly," Stark answered, knowing full well that one would never question a superior officer's request. "This French dog is as good as dead."

"Excellent. You will go alone. If you are captured, you know what to do."

Stark's eyes grew wide, but he nodded in agreement. "I will not be captured," he said, a sign of defiance at the thought, but with the dual meaning that his death would quickly follow any seizure by enemy troops.

"Good," said Kruger, placing a hand on Stark's shoulder. "Do this successfully, and you could end this war months earlier. Fail, and you will not have to worry."

Stark unconsciously nodded at the memory, before snapping himself back to the present and setting off after his goal.

The long trudge up from the shore, through the sodden dirt and grass, left his boots and coat streaked with mud and soaked with water. Stark's sense of duty tossed aside any thoughts of his appearance, his focus was on the mission, and the rewards its success promised.

The crunching of gravel under the thick iron and leather heels of Stark's boots was the only sound accompanying him on the short trek to the outskirts of the darkened town. A light breeze carried the report of another gunshot from the far side of Metz. Stark froze for a moment until the echo of the shot died down. He listened for any other sounds before hurrying onto the row of dark houses.

Sidling up to the third house along, Stark edged up to the shuttered window of the rear room and listened. Silence. It was almost midnight, the last German patrol for the night would be coming through soon.

The entire city of Metz was surrounded. The Army of the Rhine had retreated into the Metz fortress, whilst the German forces had surrounded the area. They intended to starve the army into surrender. To maintain order in the surrounding towns, patrols had been established and sent out on a regular basis. But Teulet and his group had successfully begun an operation under the noses of the German commanders, no doubt with the help of other locals. All intelligence pointed to Teulet's group moving the officers in the hours before dawn.

He must still be here.

Stepping up to the back door, Stark grasped the door handle and thumbed the door latch. Pushing it open, a loud squeal erupted from the rusted hinges and the door base grated across the slate floor. Jumping back in shock, Stark moved away and pressed himself flat against the stone wall.

Within a minute, a shaft of moonlight fell on the nervous face of a man of about forty. He appeared almost comical, standing on the threshold in his long nightshirt and holding a long-barrelled rifle.

"Put the gun down, Monsieur Teulet," said Stark, using imperfect French.

The man's face snapped towards the voice. His eyes grew wide as they spied the gun in Stark's hand. Teulet's hands twitched, the rifle swinging slightly.

"Another move and I'll shoot."

Freezing where he stood, beads of sweat formed on Teulet's forehead. "What do you want? I'm just a poor grocer. I have no money."

"If that were true, I would not be here."

"What do you mean?" Teulet deflated. "Your accent. German?" A curse floated out under his breath.

"Yes, and you know exactly why I'm here. I want to know how you keep smuggling the French officers out of Metz."

Teulet sneered. “Never. I will never tell you. You Germans will never win.” The rifle rose and swung round, but the barrel never had a chance to spit death.

A single shot rang out through the silent night, followed by the clatter of a rifle against stone steps and the thud of Teulet’s body collapsing to the ground. “Fine,” said Stark, taking one look at the fallen man, before stepping into the house.

On a side table near the door sat a candle in a brass holder. A small brass platter held several matches. Striking one against the rough surface of the table, Stark had enough light to see by within moments.

The area was small, consisting of a combined kitchen and sitting area, with a passageway leading to the front of the house. A quick search of the room revealed nothing more than cooking utensils, dishes, and a few items of food.

Bedroom?

Holstering his pistol, Stark made his way down the hallway and into the lone bedroom at the front of the house. A bed lay in one corner, with a small table just inside the door.

Excellent.

Passing the candle over the table, the light revealed several maps of the Metz area and a collection of papers. Leaning in, Stark read a list of names and dates. Those in the past had lines ruled through them. A small grin came to Stark’s face at the information before him, especially the map of the Metz fortress with a circle marked on it. From his knowledge of the area, it was a spot near the fortress wall where the sewers let out into the Moselle river.

A perfect spot for those French dogs to escape.

A small sound broke from the darkness in the corner of the bedroom. Stark spun, his hand dropping to his pistol. He brought the candle up before him, throwing light across the dark area. A small movement was accompanied by another sound. The tiny cry of a baby. Stepping forward, Stark glanced down at the cherubic face gazing up at him. Although he’d probably killed the poor child’s father only moments before, his heart leapt at the sight of the baby.

Memories of his own daughter flooded his mind. Her innocent beauty. The love that filled his world on the day she was born. The happiness he shared with his wife during those first few months. Then the darkness. The dire tragedy of her slide towards sickness and eventually death. The last memory of his wife's despair lingered in his mind.

Reaching out a hand, he pointed a finger towards the child. Its eyes followed the finger and reached up with its own. A smile broke out on Stark's face as their digits touched.

His eyes flicked up to the small name carved into the head of the crib.

Elise.

***

Berlin, Germany, 1885

"Oberstleutnant Stark, come in, sit down," said the large swarthy man, his girth threatening to dislodge the arms of his chair. "I have heard a lot about you Stark."

Surprised at the remark, Stark's eyes darted around the sparsely furnished office before he took the proffered seat. "And what have you heard of me, Oberst Bremmer?"

"All good, all good," the large man chuckled, "Do not worry. You are highly regarded amongst my colleagues. That is why you are here."

"That was to be my next question. Why am I here?" Stark asked, his question dripping with suspicion.

Bremmer slid a small cardboard file across his desk and opened it. Whilst reading the front page, he said, "Oberstleutnant Lysander Stark, also known as Fritz. Middle name I presume?" Stark nodded. "Married, oh, I'm sorry. Widowed." Bremmer glanced across the file at Stark's stern expression. "Four years ago?"

The younger, leaner man nodded. "Yes, Oberst, my darling wife contracted a fever. The doctors said it was typhoid. She never recovered."

"Oh, I am sorry, not a nice way to die."

"No, it was not, I thank you for your thoughts."

Turning back to the file, he said, “Ah, you have a daughter. Something to remember your wife by then?”

“No, Oberst, I’m afraid not. The child was a foundling of the war. We had lost a baby many years before. Elise, for that, is her name, brought my wife many happy years."

Bremmer watched for any hint of joy in Stark’s face. “Not you it seems?”

"No. She is a wilful child. One I must pay constant attention to."

Chuckling, Bremmer said, "Yes, I have children of a similar age. It is the younger generation. They have never known hardships like we did. Perhaps we need another war?"

“Perhaps.”

Pausing for a moment, Bremmer read more of Stark’s file, refamiliarizing himself with the contents. “Ah, yes, you were promoted after your little covert undertaking in Metz.” Smiling, Bremmer nodded at Stark. “Good work that. Cut the length of the war by several months.” The younger officer nodded in appreciation. “Then a little fieldwork, mostly desk work. Diligent. Two promotions from Leutnant to Major to Oberstleutnant since the war. Good, good.” Bremmer closed the file and looked up. “You have been described to me as having a particular way about you. One that may fit well within the organisation that I head up.”

“What organisation is that?”

“Well, you may have heard rumours that Field Marshal Moltke wishes to set up a new arm of the military. He has coined the name Abteilung, sort of a revised version of the old intelligence unit used during the war. Our neighbours to the east have been rattling sabres across the edges of Asia and even down towards Africa. The Field Marshall believes it is time to keep a closer eye on them, and perhaps, begin efforts to undermine their endeavours.”

“How do I fit into this then?”

“Ah, well, the Field Marshall needs good men. Men who have no fear. Men who do not back away from getting their hands dirty when required. After Metz, and some of your other activities, you have been singled out as one who would fit that mould.”

“Intelligence?” Stark stared at the Oberst for a moment. “Do you mean assassinations?”

“Only if necessary. More, information gathering. Exploitation of foreign nationals, that sort of thing.” Seeing Stark deflate slightly, the Oberst smiled and said, “Oh, don’t worry. The particular mission that we have for you should allow a man of your talents to express himself adequately.”

“Alright, now you have my interest. What does this mission involve?”

***

Two days later, Stark found himself sitting in a tiny room, devoid of any light source except for the shafts streaming through the two circular openings in the wall before him. On the other side of the wall hung a very intricate still life painting by renowned German artist Georg Flegal. The small holes hidden amongst flowers and fruit allowed for unobserved viewing of the room beyond.

Leaning forward, Stark placed his nose against the wall and stared through the eyeholes as the door opened and a group of men entered the room. The first was Herr Weissman, a short, rat-like little man, that Stark had met the day before, his job was to run the foreign currency section of the Treasury.

Weissman stood aside, holding the door open as three more men entered. The first was Stark’s target. Bremmer had called him The Man from Moscow as if that were meant to lend him any more presence than his physical countenance demanded. Stark simply saw a tall, well-built man, handsome in a severe way, with close-cropped fair hair. His name was Piotr Mazepin, and he held a similar position to Weissman, but from the Russian perspective. Joining Mazepin were two taller, and broader men, dressed in plain, dark suits. Stark could immediately tell they were Russian military, simply from the way they took up positions behind Mazepin as he sat and stood with their hands folded together in front and their legs splayed slightly apart, both sported bulges on their right hip, hidden by their jackets.

Mazepin took a seat at the long table, with Weissman sitting opposite. Both opened their small satchels and took out thick ledgers, placing them down and opening them, as if this were a prelude move to some form of strategic game.

Reading from his ledger, Mazepin spoke first, "By our accounts your treasury holds a million rubles."

"Give or take a hundred thousand. Our current estimates have the total as nearer one and a half million."

"Do you know what denominations you hold?"

Running his finger down a list of figures, Weissman answered, "Five hundred thousand in notes, nine hundred thousand in coins, with the rest made up from various denominations of kopeks."

"That is a lot of ruble coins, I wasn't aware that Germany held such a large amount in coins." Mazepin flipped through his ledger, mumbling to himself as he added up several figures in his head. Finally, he nodded, "Yes, we have brought enough with us, but it will mean our immediate return to Moskva once the exchange is made."

Stark's mind wandered as the two accountants checked their figures and journals. The details didn't matter to him. His role in this affair was to keep a close eye on Mazepin and ensure that he didn't get in the way of the end game.

It was the end game that was interesting.

Bremmer wasn't fully aware of the motives behind the scheme but had explained it as simply as he could. For their own reasons, possibly to save money, the Russians were changing the base metals that constituted the physical ruble coins from gold to silver. To do that, all existing ruble coins were to be taken out of circulation across Russia and Europe and replaced with the new silver standard.

Germany held a large reserve of ruble coins, to enable easier trade between the two countries. The paper notes were well known for their fragility, many in storage had degraded quickly from mould and damp, making them worthless, so that made the coins more attractive.

German intelligence had come up with a plan to perform a double exchange of the Russian rubles. The boffins in the science division had built a coin press, and an agent assigned to Moscow had infiltrated the Bank of Russia and absconded with a set of the original coin stamps. A million rubles worth of coins had been minted using the press and stamps by substituting a lower-cost mix of nickel and copper to form the metal.

Mazepin's presence here was to enable the exchange of the coins. Stark's presence was to ensure that the man from Moscow was none the wiser that his Nation's coins had been replaced.

To ensure that, Stark had other plans in train.

By the end of the tawdry drawn out meeting, Weissman and Mazepin had agreed on the exact exchange figure and set a time to meet on the following day. Stark discovered that the Russians had brought a large, secure horse-drawn wagon with them, containing dozens of crates of coins. It sat inside the grounds of the Russian Embassy and was under continuous guard by the embassy staff, the exchange would occur at the Berlin Treasury building, under the eyes of German army soldiers.

From Stark's observations, Mazepin did not exhibit any suspicion over the terms of the exchange. Handling millions in currency seemed a natural act to him, which made Stark more comfortable that they would be able to effect the switch with no problems but leaving it all to chance was not in his operating parameters. It was when the meeting began to break up and he overheard Weissman invite Mazepin and his two companions out for dinner, that Stark left to prepare.

***

Sitting at one of the larger tables in the bier Halle, Stark glanced around at his companions, four strikingly beautiful women. To the casual envious observer, much too beautiful to be sitting with someone as gaunt and skinny as Stark. He smiled at the fleeting glances aimed towards his group by the other male denizens of the hall. His pleasure was even more enjoyable when he pictured the looks on their faces if they became aware of the origins of the beauties. Each one was a German military officer, handpicked by Stark for this assignment. Bremmer had given him free rein to run the operation as he saw fit and had asked no questions. Results were all that mattered.

Purposely facing towards the rear of the hall, Stark became alert when, Anna, the blonde woman on his left, leaned across and whispered into his ear. "It looks like they are here." Lina and Freya, sitting across from Stark, raised their champagne and sipped, their eyes scanning the faces of the group, picking their assigned targets. Brigit, sitting on Stark's right, sat still, waiting for the group to pass as they were shown to a table nearby.

For the next hour, Stark's group maintained their observances of Weissman and the Russians. He and his four companions kept their alcohol intake to a minimum, while the other table saw a stream of beer mugs arrive, helped by the deep pockets of Herr Weissman.

It was when the group appeared to be quite inebriated that Stark whispered in Brigit's ear. Smiling, she nodded and rose from the table, turning back towards her group and laughing loudly at an untold joke. All eyes from Weissman's table turned towards the tall striking woman. Stark was pleased to see Mazepin gaze longingly towards Brigit. As the woman surreptitiously turned her sight towards the Russians, she noticed it too.

Turning to face the group, she stood with her hands on hips and a pout on her lips, deliberately making and holding eye contact with Mazepin for several seconds before sashaying across to the other table.

"Hello boys," she said, "It seems a shame that four lovely gentlemen like yourselves are sitting here all on your own." She nodded over her shoulder, and added, "Why don't you join me and my friends?" The men glanced across towards Stark and the other women. Smiles crossed the faces of each Russian.

"I think I would like to take you up on that offer," said Mazepin.

As the others joined him and picked up their stools, Weissman left his alone, and said, "I think it is time I bid you do svidanya. I must return to Frau Weissman, plus I am far too old for engaging in such frivolities. I will see you tomorrow at the Treasury building." Waving he strode past Stark's table, nodding to the military officer before striding from the bier Halle.

At Stark's table, Lina and Freya moved their stools apart, allowing Mazepin's aides to place theirs in the gaps. As they sat, both men introduced themselves to the others at the table. Brigit strolled over with Mazepin on her arm. Pointing to her vacant chair, she said, "I am sitting here, please join me, Piotr."

Smiling, Mazepin dropped his stool in the vacant space between Brigit's and Stark. As the two sat, Stark held out a hand and said, "I am Fritz, glad to make your acquaintance, Piotr. Please join us, my companions are very pleasant, but I yearn for some male company."

"I thank you, Fritz," Mazepin said, his voice holding a noticeable slur.

"A round of drinks should welcome you nicely," said Stark, turning and catching the eye of the comely dirn standing near the bar, whilst holding up eight fingers to indicate the number of beers required. The woman nodded and passed on the order to the barman. Within moments the same dirn plonked eight frothy mugs of beer on the table, receiving a chorus of thanks in return. Raising his, Stark said, "To new friends." The toast was echoed back, with each taking a long pull from their mug.

As the beers flowed, thanks to Stark's insistent ordering, the talk became louder. Brigit and Mazepin were deep in conversation, verging on intimacy, while the other Russians engaged in animated conversation with their companions.

Forgetting himself for a moment, Stark sipped his beer and glanced at each of his companions in turn, admiring the beauty of the women and the way they easily fell into conversation with their male partners as if they were lifelong friends. A nagging thought broke through his musings, a thought about his adopted daughter sitting at home. Ever since the death of his wife, the conversations between himself and Elise had drifted more into iciness, lacking any warmth or familial closeness. It was something he needed to address he told himself, but for now he had other business to attend to.

As the next round of drinks arrived, Stark spoke into Anna's ear. "Distract our friend for a moment." Nodding, she rose and stepped around Stark, putting her head into the middle of Brigit and Mazepin, and speaking quietly to them. Glancing around the table to ensure that all of the men were focused on their assigned beauties, Stark withdrew a small vial with a straw attached. He quietly slid the straw into the froth atop Mazepin's mug, before tilting it vertically. A fine white powder slid from the vial, down the straw and into the clear amber liquid below. Within seconds it dissolved. After stirring it, Stark quickly removed the vial and straw, slipping it away inside his jacket pocket, and pushed Mazepin's beer across the table until it clinked against the Russian's empty mug.

As Anna stood and moved away from the pair, Brigit picked up her mug and held it before Mazepin's face. "A toast. This looks like it is turning into a very good night, but it has only just begun," she said, a sly smile on her face, and a come hither look in her eye. Mazepin's eyes grew wide as he realised what she meant. He picked up his beer and clinked glasses with the blonde. "I think when you finish that beer, we might find somewhere a little more private."

To Stark's delight, Mazepin's beer disappeared within a matter of a moment. Brigit's smile turned to surprise. "Okay then," she said, taking a short pull from her mug before placing it down and standing. "I made a promise, I will have to follow through," she added, smiling that devious grin once more.

Taking Mazepin by the arm, she bid goodnight to the rest of the table. Mazepin spoke in Russian, telling the other two not to wait for him. He would join them at the Embassy in the morning, well before their appointment at the Treasury building. They both chuckled and nodded, bidding him a good night.

Stark watched Brigit and Mazepin leave the bier Halle before leaning in towards Anna and whispering in her ear. "We will give them five minutes, then follow. Everything is set, but by the time we arrive, Brigit should have him where we want him." She nodded and took a short drink.

***

The room reminded Stark of the similar set-up at the Treasury building. The difference being that instead of a painting with holes in it for eyeballs, a dark rectangular box sat on a metal frame. One end was pressed close to the wall, a brass cylinder poking through the hole cut into the canvas of a painting hanging on the other side of the wall.

Another smaller hole was cut into the painting near to the camera's lens. Stark bent and peered through into the room beyond. A smile came to his face as he spied the unconscious form of Piotr Mazepin lying on the large bed that dominated the room beyond.

As Stark watched, Brigit and Anna entered the room, they had removed their heavy dresses and wore simple undergarments. They quickly set about removing Mazepin's clothes. Stark moved to the rear of the camera and lifting the dark fabric hood, ducked beneath it.

His first photograph was a little overexposed but gave him a good idea of how much light was trickling in from the bedroom. Pulling the slate out and quickly replacing it, he adjusted the camera and proceeded to capture several key moments. The photographs that followed were all highly staged, but to the uninitiated, and especially to the unconscious man concerned, they were sure to shock and cause immediate consternation.

After almost half an hour, the two girls pulled the bedclothes back over Mazepin before stepping away. He would awaken in a few hours in a strange room, with a head full of agony and fog, and no clue as to what had occurred.

As the girls left, Stark pulled the camera away from the wall and slid the hole cover back into place. He took one last look through the peephole, reassuring himself that Mazepin was fast asleep, and the girls were gone, before collecting up the plates and depositing them in the lightproof satchel.

He had one a short trip to Intelligence headquarters to drop the photographic plates off for processing before he could return home. His part of the adventure had only just begun.

***

The large, covered wagon ground its way across the cobbled street and entered the gates of the Treasury's rear courtyard. The heavy hooves of the four drays crunched on the gravel and bit into the loose stones for purchase. A fine sheen of sweat glistened on their coats. They each let out a short snort as Nicolai pulled on the reins to draw them to a halt.

Watching from the shade of the rear portico, Stark smiled at the idea that these three Russians had been tasked with carting so much currency across the continent in a horse-drawn wagon. Weissman said they had scoffed at using trains for the simple reason that their control would be lessened, and they'd have to organise wagons from the station to the Treasury buildings, adding time and inconvenience.

Stark noticed that Mazepin's eyes were downcast, his head hanging low beneath his hat. He smiled to himself, lightly slapping the satchel hanging by his side. Its presence itself another form of insurance.

Weissman stepped out through the open doors of the rear entrance and threw his arms wide. "Gentlemen, welcome, I hope your evening was enjoyable." All three Russians glanced at the German and mumbled in return.

Sergei dropped to the ground, his shiny, black boots, scraping the small stones. Turning to Mazepin, he held out a hand to help his superior from the wagon's seat. "Gospodin Mazepin is a little beneath the weather this morning." Mazepin swatted Sergei's hands away in annoyance, before dropping down to the gravel driveway.

Even from his position, Start could see the Russian's eyes were glazed almost to the point where he could succumb quickly to sleep once more.

"Let's get on with this, shall we?" Mazepin snapped, reaching into the rear of the wagon, and pulling out his notebook. Reading his entry, he turned to Weissman, "Eight hundred thousand rubles?" Weissman nodded. Speaking to his men, he said, "That will be thirty crates. Your vault is inside?"

"Yes, I'll have my men help."

Nodding, Mazepin said, "Good. Otherwise, this will take all day."

Weissman hurried up the steps, nodding to Stark as he went by. Within a moment, he was joined by four swarthy men, dressed ready for hard work, simply in shirts, pants, and boots. "In the vault, at the rear," Weissman said to the men, turning to Mazepin he added, "Would you like to inspect the exchange?"

"Certainly," Mazepin answered, following Weissman into the Treasury building. Waiting for a moment, Stark turned and joined them inside. As they made their way to the vault room deep in the building, Mazepin's ears pricked.

He stopped and spun to face the source of the footsteps behind him. “Do I know you?”

"Why yes, yes you do, Mister Mazepin, or should I say, Piotr, as that is the name you introduced yourself with last night," said Stark, "You would know me as Fritz, as that is a name I go by."

Realisation dawned on Mazepin’s face, both of recognition of Stark, and of what happened the previous night. Pointing at Stark’s chest, he said, “You were the man with those lovely ladies.” His hand went to his head as a wave of pain ran through it. “Oh, Lord, it was you that kept buying the beer.”

“I was feeling generous, yes,” said Stark, “I only wanted to welcome you to our fine city and enjoy some other company for an hour or two.”

“Some welcome,” said Mazepin, his hand falling to his heaving stomach. Once he was himself again, he asked, “Why are you here? This seems untoward.”

“Ah, yes,” interjected Weissman, “Let me formally introduce you, this is Oberstleutnant Lysander Stark. A member of our military. We thought it might make things simpler if you had an escort to ease things at the border or at least dissuade any potential villains on the way.”

"I do not understand the need," said Mazepin, "Nicolai and Sergei are both well-trained soldiers, and well-armed. We travelled here from Austria without molestation.”

“And that is good, but my Government’s concern is that we wish to see no harm come to you or your men within our borders.”

“More that you wish to have no possibility of a diplomatic incident.”

“There is that as well. Please as your host let Oberstleutnant Stark accompany you to the border,” Weissman held out his hands to placate the Russian, “The other advantage for you, is that Stark here has access to the Government’s funds. It is a good day’s journey to the border, and you will need accommodation and refreshments overnight. So, consider it an act of goodwill on our part."

His weary face showing signs of concern, Mazepin nodded in agreement. “Fine. You will need your own horse, there is only room for three on the wagon.”

“That shall present no problem, Sir, I will need transport back to Berlin anyway, and I have prepared my own ride.”

Down a flight of stairs, they continued along a dimly lit corridor, to a wide-open area with two large steel doors folded back to reveal the contents of the massive room beyond. Wooden crates were stacked against two of the walls, long rows of shelves, stacked with bound wads of paper bills, lined the third. As they reached the vault, the first attendant arrived holding a heavy chest of coins. Weissman nodded towards the far wall, “Place them over there by the wall.” Pointing at the crates lying near the entrance, he added, “In a moment you can begin to take these out to the wagon. Just don’t get them confused.” Smiling at Mazepin, Weissman added, “Would you like to inspect the contents, Sir?”

Nodding, Mazepin dropped down to one knee, and prized the lid off the nearest crate, revealing a mess of shiny and dull gold coins. Scooping up a handful, he held one to the light, examining the stamped seal on one side and the writing on the other. Weissman’s eyes grew wide as he watched Mazepin handle the counterfeit coins. Stark’s hand moved to his holster. It was a last resort, but he wanted to be prepared for any eventuality.

"We have sorted them into denominations of one, three and five rubles, to make things easier for you. There is also a mix of grades. Some were taken from circulation by our staff; most you will find are relatively new."

Dropping the coins back into the crate and sliding the lid back into place, Mazepin grunted as he rose back to his feet, and drew out his notebook. He quickly counted the crates and wrote down the number. “What is the mix of denominations?”

“Ten of five rubles, eight of three and twelve of ones,” answered Weissman.

“Good, good, the sooner we get this over with, the sooner we can be on our way.” When Mazepin withdrew a kerchief and mopped his brow, Stark took his hand away from his hip. A smile played on his lips as he realised this may go smoother than he first thought.

***

As the four draft horses snorted and strained against the weight of the fully loaded wagon, Stark trotted from the small stables at the rear of the Treasury property on his black stallion. He drew level with Weissman, just as the Russian wagon reached the gates and exited. Stopping briefly, he spoke to the Government official. "They don't seem to have any suspicions, which is excellent for us. If they manage ten miles an hour then we shall reach Fürstenwalde near nightfall. I have sent two agents ahead to inform the constabulary and prepare rooms in one of the local inns there."

"I don't think you will have any real trouble. If you supply them enough with beer once more, then all should be fine."

"Though I think they would be a little warier of drinking too heavily tonight. They will simply be very weary and should fall asleep early enough without my added involvement."

"Then away with you. I will await news on your return." Nodding, Stark kicked his heels into the stallion's rump and sprang away after the wagon.

***

The horses did a sterling job, once they were up to speed they settled into a comfortable rate and arrived at Fürstenwalde just as the sky was reddening with the approach of dusk.

Stark, having stayed well behind the wagon, preferring his own company than attempting to converse with the Russians as they were jostled about by the wagon's ride over the often-rough country roads, picked up speed and drew level with the others. "I recommend we stop here in Fürstenwalde. There is a very reputable inn, which has good beer and food."

Nicolai and Sergei nodded in agreement. Mazepin's eyes flickered open as he returned from slumber. "What? What's that you say?" The other two filled him in. Nodding he spoke to Stark, "Very good, lead on. Is there accommodation for the horses and wagon?"

"Yes. There is a stable nearby. It should be large enough. I will also inform the constabulary to lend us a policeman or two to look over the wagon during the night."

"That won't be necessary, we will protect the wagon, but food would be good," said Mazepin, his eyelids closing once more, "Tell me when we arrive." The other two groaned at Mazepin's insistence that they would be in charge of securing the wagon.

Glancing up at the line of houses in the near distance, Stark said, "Well it won't be long till we are there" Looking at the other two, he smiled, "I'll head off and arrange things. There is only one main street, so you should easily find both the inn and stables. Some cold beer would be most welcome, don't you think." The two Russians nodded. With that, Stark trotted off towards the little town.

By the time the large wagon arrived, Stark stood at the entrance of the stables with a short, stocky man dressed in the dark blue uniform of the Polizei, and another dressed in a simple shirt and dark trousers. The simply dressed man pointed to the vacant area before the stable doors, and Nicolai guided the large wagon to the spot.

As the three Russians dismounted from the wagon, the policeman strolled up and bowed. "I am Polizeihauptmeister Mueller. Your wagon will be safe in my care. I have several polizeimeisters who can watch over it during the night."

"That is all well and good, but we would prefer to see to its security ourselves," said Mazepin, much to the continued distaste of his compatriots.

Mueller clicked his heels together and bowed once more. "As you wish, the offer is there." He bid a good evening to the three Russians and Stark, before adding, "Hans here will see to your horses. I understand that rooms have been prepared in the inn for you as well."

As the policeman left, Nicolai spoke to Mazepin," Are you sure you don't want the constabulary to assist us? It has been a long day and a good night's sleep would be most welcome."

Casting a sideways glance at Stark, "I am appreciative of the offer, but the wagon and its contents belong to Mother Russia and has been entrusted to us, I cannot in good faith delegate such a responsibility to foreigners. We will do our duty to the best of our abilities." Patting Nicolai on the shoulder, "You shall take the first watch, we will secure our rooms and return with food and drink."

Stark simply shrugged and said, "The offer is there in good faith. This will be your last night in Germany, I simply thought you would like to relax before returning to your homeland."

"And I thank you, Herr Stark, but we shall handle things ourselves," returned Mazepin, a tinge of anger, or tiredness, in his words, Stark wasn't quite sure.

***

With the approval of the stable master, the three Russians built a small circle of stones and gathered wood from the field next door. Within an hour they had a roaring fire going to take the chill of the night away. They planned to stay together until later in the night, then one would stay on watch while the others slept. Each taking turns for two to three hours at a time.

Several townsfolk gave them disapproving looks as they strode along the street and entered the Inn. Even Polizeihauptmeister Mueller stopped for a moment to examine their temporary campsite and once again offer his assistance. Mazepin thanked him again but declined help. By that time, they each had tankards of frothy beer and were more than set for the evening.

As night fell, Stark appeared in the firelight with the inn's waitress in tow. They each held trays of food, enough for four people, which they set on the crates that the men had brought out from the wagon to use as seats and tables for their beer. A small grin crossed Stark's face as he glanced at how the crates were being used, but it disappeared when he realised they probably contained the counterfeit coins. He asked the waitress to bring more beers, then sat down and joined the Russians as they enjoyed the local fare of bread, sausage, cheese, and pickles, but couldn't take his eyes away from the crates, visions of the coins heating up and possibly melting if the boxes grew too hot.

After a few more tankards of beer, the Russians relaxed and took on the same level of joviality that Stark encountered the evening before. Mazepin was more reserved, still nursing the effects of the chloral hydrate Stark had slipped him. Mindful of the accountant's more alert demeanour, Stark joined in the conversation, swapping stories of his life in the military, with Sergei and Nicolai who shared a history of serving their country.

Nothing untoward occurred throughout their evening until the conversation relaxed and Nicolai stood up to feed more wood to the fire. After throwing a couple more logs into the belly of the blaze, he bent to drag the crate of coins away from the heat of the flames as they started to lick at the new wood. Stark breathed a sigh of relief and took another draw from his beer.

"One thing has concerned me today," Nicolai said.

"What?" asked Sergei.

Turning to Stark, Nicolai asked, "Herr Stark, how far is it from Berlin to this little town?"

Lifting one quizzical eyebrow, Stark answered, "About fifty miles, why?"

Turning to his countrymen, Nicolai asked, "What speed did we average before we arrived in Berlin?"

The other two glanced at each other for a moment before shrugging. Sergei replied, "I have no idea. What do you think?"

"Our trip from Prague to Berlin was about two hundred and twenty miles, yes?" The other two nodded. "And it took how long?" Both shook their heads, with Sergei shrugging. "Well, I think it took us about twenty-eight hours all up, across four days," continued Nicolai.

"Okay, good, we've been travelling for a few weeks," said Sergi, "I for one am thankful that the Germans held so much currency, we have to return to get more, cutting our trip short."

"Yes, what is your point, Nicolai?" asked Mazepin, a hint of annoyance at the conversation.

"Well, the question I have is, that the journey here was fifty miles, it took us just over four and a half hours to cover that distance." The others nodded, with Mazepin cocking his head at the notion. Nicolai swept an arm out towards the horses in the stables. "I don't think our horses have grown more muscles overnight, plus," he said, holding up a finger whilst standing and pulling the cover off the crate, "The horses should be slower with the heavier load. After all, these coins should weigh more than the coins we had in the wagon before we entered Berlin. Isn't that the whole purpose of our trip, to exchange the older heavier rubles made with gold, with the new rubles made with silver?" Adding, "The coins that the Germans gave us should be heavier than the new ones," as he raised a handful of the coins to the flickering firelight.

"I've known you a long time, Nicolai, and have never seen such an intelligent position come from your mouth, but there is something in what you say," said Mazepin, stepping across and scooping out a handful of coins before striding into the stable. The other two followed after him.

Concerned, Stark rose and peered through the gloom after the three Russians.

From inside the stable, a match flamed, a moment before a small gas lamp was lit, throwing a glow across the area. Stark noted that Mazepin had found a bench built into the side wall. He held a coin up to the light, studying it carefully, and turning it over and examining both sides and the edge.

Stepping closer, Stark heard their conversation, his hand quickly slipped to the leather pouch at his right hip and unclipped the fastener.

In the stable, Nicolai's hand dropped to his pocket, he fished inside and brought out a gold coin. "I've had this one on me since we left Moskva, it's an original ruble, I plan to change it over when we return." Mazepin took the offered coin and felt its weight. He picked up one of the coins from the workbench and compared it to Nicolai's. "These should be the same weight."

Giving them to Sergei, Mazepin asked, "What do you think?"

After a moment of holding both in each hand in turn, and comparing their weights, Sergei answered, "They seem to be different." He placed Nicolai's coin down and retrieved one of the German coins. Comparing the two exchanged coins to each other, he finally said, "These are the same weight." Repeating the process with Nicolai's coin, after a moment, he said, "Both of these German coins are lighter than Nicolai's coin."

Nodding, Mazepin said, "I agree."

My Lord, you are right. These are lighter.

Snatching up the German coins and his own, Nicolai repeated Sergei's assessment. His eyes grew wide, and he said, "My Lord, you are right. These are lighter."

All three turned as one towards Stark, who now stood on the threshold of the stable, silhouetted by the firelight behind him.

Mazepin took a step forward, "What is the meaning of this Stark? Is our assessment correct? Are these coins that your Government has exchanged for Russian currency real, or fake?"

"I can only say that my Government would never knowingly deceive another country's officials. You must be mistaken."

"We must return to Berlin. These coins do not seem to be genuine. We must retrieve our currency, and when you can prove the authenticity of these coins, we will undertake the exchange once more," said Mazepin, a hint of authority creeping into his voice.

Stark's hand moved quickly, the Russians' eyes growing wide as they saw the object in his hand. "I think not," Stark said, pointing the pistol at each man in turn.

"You will not get away with this," said Nicolai, his hand grasping for the pistol sitting in its holster on his right hip and raising it towards Stark.

The loud retort of the gunshot echoed across the large room. The horses whinnied in fear, stamped their feet, and tried to pull themselves free. The men ignored them, staring at the bloom of red spreading across Nicolai's shirt. He gaped at his chest, then at Stark, mouthing an obscenity before falling forward into the dirty straw strewn across the floor.

"No, Nicolai," shouted Sergei, ducking sideways and snatching his pistol out. As he raised the gun towards Stark, another shot shattered the still night. Sergei was flung backwards, sprawling in the straw, and lying still.

Mazepin's terrified face turned from his stricken countryman back towards the German. He raised his hands in surrender, he was not armed. "Will you kill me now?" he said, his mouth trembling in fear.

"No. I need you alive. You will make sure that this currency enters Russia and circulates amongst your countrymen."

"I would never do such a thing. Never."

A broad smile grew across Stark's face, he holstered his gun and drew his satchel from behind his back. Snapping the clasp open, he withdrew the cardboard folder within. Grinning malevolently at Mazepin, he said, "Oh, I think you will. Especially after you see what I have here."

***

"Congratulations, Oberst Stark, as you can imagine by your immediate promotion, my superiors in the intelligence division are highly impressed with your performance on this assignment."

"Thank you, Oberst Bremmer, I am honoured and look forward to serving in my new role."

"Yes, yes, we will get to that in a moment. Now," Bremmer said, leaning forward and placing his chin on his steepled hands, "I have read your report, but want to know everything from the horse's mouth, as they say."

"What details would you like?"

"The accountant, this Mazepin, he was the last survivor, but how did you convince him to cooperate."

"Ah," said Stark, a grin crossing his face, "The man from Moscow. Such a sad fellow, and so timid, for such a tall, handsome man." Nodding towards the folder beneath Bremmer's elbows, Stark continued, "I deduced that I needed to prepare in the eventuality that the Russians found out about the counterfeit coins. To that end, if you inspect the photographs in the folder on your desk, you will see what I had to work with."

Bremmer opened the file, his eyes growing wide as he viewed the first photograph, leafing through the others his mouth dropped open at the debauchery portrayed within. "My word," he said, glancing up at Stark.

"Yes, that was Mazepin's reaction when he viewed them as well. He became extremely compliant with my demands when I mentioned that copies of those are held by German agents in Moscow. He almost fainted when I said that any deviation from my demands would see them sent to his wife, and to his superiors within the Treasury." Smiling, Stark waited for Bremmer to finish and close the file once more. "From that moment on, I received no further complaints or whimpers from him for the entire journey to the border the next morning."

"What happened then?"

"Using the papers of the dead Russians, the two agents I sent ahead to Fürstenwalde took on their identities and travelled with Mazepin. Their orders were to ensure that there was no trouble. Once they were at the Polish border, and had crossed into Russian territory, I left them."

"You didn't stay with Mazepin?"

Shaking his head, Stark said, "No need. We have an agent in the Russian border forces. He confirmed our agents' identities, and as I watched him from my horse, I was pleased to see our agent wave them on without another word."

"The dead Russians?"

"Mueller came out of inn not long after my gunshots. Mazepin pleaded with the man that I had killed them in cold blood. Mueller is a good German and simply agreed that it was self-defence. It was then that Mazepin knew all hope was gone. Mueller simply had the bodies buried in the town cemetery."

"Excellent. You have done a magnificent job. We have also pressed more rubles and sent them to our agents in Moscow, if the time comes we will use them to undermine the populace's trust in their currency by unveiling the fakes."

"Thank you, Oberst. What is my next assignment?"

"Ah, now this will be an interesting one for you. How much do you know about England?"

"Nothing really, why?"

"Well, if you take the assignment, you will be there for quite a while. I suggest you take that young daughter of yours. You have said she is spirited. The English countryside might be good for her."

"How long is quite a while?"

"Well let me put it this way. This little exercise of counterfeiting Russian currency was a simple precursor. We wish you to undermine the English economy, slowly but surely, with counterfeit British coins."

"We? Are you talking about the Intelligence division? The German government?"

"Partly. On behalf of the Government, my division has developed a partnership with a private individual."

"That seems peculiar. Who?"

"Well since you would be working with this individual for a while, it is only fair you should meet. He is here in the building."

Standing and moving to the door, Bremmer looked out and motioned to someone in the next room. Returning to his seat, Bremmer said, "He will be here soon."

Within a few moments, a knock on the door was followed by the entry of an extremely tall man. Stark gazed at the thin figure, with his pale clean-shaven face, in confusion.

"This is he?"

"Yes," said Bremmer, "May I introduced Herr Moriarty."

The tall man smiled and extended a hand towards Stark, "That's James, Professor James Moriarty, at your service." Stark could not overcome the uncanniness of Moriarty's resemblance to him. It was almost like looking into the reflection of an older version of himself, if not slightly thinner and more gaunt in the face. He felt Moriarty's recognition of the same, the older man looking Stark up and down, with a wry grin growing on his face.

"I do believe," Moriarty said, "that I could not be more comfortable working with someone who looks the way you do. I think our future endeavours will be most profitable, to both of us."

The Adventure of the Tesla Coil

Staring out across London from the top floor of the manor, my mind drifted back to a simpler time. A time before the new machines. A time before the rise of the steam engines. A time when my good friends were still alive.

Outside, the heat of the summer's day had given way to a cooler evening, the cloudless night allowing the city to be seen in all its glory. Large airships nestled next to the tall buildings of the central district, the chosen transport of the city's busy business leaders. Their happenings played out in towers far removed from the average people who spent their lives in a constant buzz of survival down at street level.

Gouts of orange flame burst from pipes in the sides of many buildings, releasing the excess gas and heat from the steam engines beneath, and reflecting off myriad plates of brass decorating the edifices, a gaudy show of wealth to those same denizens whose sweat and toil built the towers in the first place.

My eyes fell on the newest addition to the skyline. A looming structure, newly constructed and nearing completion, all but dark as if still lying in its womb awaiting entry to the world. I had read in the papers of the mysterious owner and purpose of the building, but the details hadn't concerned me at the time and the facts were quickly forgotten. I assumed that my young ward would have heard of him and could recite the man's history to the letter.

Watching the self-propelled carriages moving their way through the byways of London, and the smaller dirigibles floating above and weaving their way between the buildings, I couldn't help think, what an age of wonder we lived in. Modern man's harnessing of the power of steam had opened avenues to all, negating the reliance on horses for transport and muscle, and bringing about a new era of self-reliance and prosperity.

Though, as history dictates, any increase in wealth amongst the populace brings with it an increase in criminal activity taking advantage of that fortune.

Glancing across London towards the Houses of Parliament, I imagined I could see the busy offices of New Scotland Yard and especially, Commissioner Lestrade, close contact and confidant of my housemate.

As if on cue, a noise echoed out from the bowels of the great house.

Hurrying inside, I stepped into the master's study, devoid of his attendance, but filled with his presence. Upon his large oak desk sat a device that only he and one other possessed. It had been designed by an acquaintance of mine

but brought to reality by that man's grandson, my ward, Sherlock Holmes.

Grasping the earpiece in one hand, and the speaking tube in the other, I addressed the caller. "Hello, Commissioner, how may I help you?"

"Ah, good evening, Watson. Is Holmes in?" Commissioner Lestrade's voice sounded hollow, an effect of the transformation of the electronic signal speeding down the telegraph lines that Master Sherlock had installed for this very purpose.

"The master is preoccupied and asked not to be disturbed, but I can relay your message to him. I'm sure he would quickly rearrange his priorities."

"Good, good," said Lestrade, "Please have him meet me in the vault of the Bank of England."

"Very good Sir. I shall convey your wishes directly."

Lestrade said a quick goodbye and within seconds I was greeted with the hollow sound of silence as if I was listening to the void of space. Hanging the two small devices back on their hooks, I turned and hurried to the bookcase in the far corner of the room.

On the third shelf, an ancient leather volume of Shakespeare's works was connected to a hidden spring system. Pulling the book forward, a loud click greeted me, followed by the slight creak of the bookcase sliding forward and opening to reveal a narrow staircase leading down into the stygian darkness.

As I stepped forward, hidden sensors recognised my approach, igniting light bulbs on either side to illuminate my way forward. Within a minute of climbing down, the staircase opened into an incredibly large cave, hidden deep inside the hill, and well beneath the manor.

This was my master's true den. Of late, it was where he spent most of his waking, and a lot of his sleeping, hours.

Though the cave's current use was not the sole agency of Master Sherlock, that had been the responsibility of his grandfather, Nikola. An incredibly intelligent and inventive man, whom I had the pleasure of knowing for many years before his sudden death. This had been his laboratory, home to all manner of inventions, the most ingenious still stood in the middle of the cave. A large circular coil sat upon three angled legs. It looked like an oversized children's stool, except for the large bolts of lightning that erupted from time to time and arced across the roof of the cave.

The coil was fed by a steam-powered generator, that huffed and puffed in the far corner of the cave, but it was the coil that provided amplified and transmitted power to all the devices spread across the cave, and the house itself.

Chief amongst those machines was the carriage that Master Sherlock used as his personal transport. A sleek, low-slung, black contraption, that belied the bulky inefficient designs of other carriages running off steam engines. Sitting inside the front section was an electric motor, that ran virtually silent unlike the noisy steam vehicles with their coal-burning power plants. The engine was another of his grandfather's inventions that had only found reality when Master Sherlock applied his ingenuity to it.

The electricity provided by the large coil found its way into the storage batteries onboard the carriage. Lying in wait until needed, where it was fed to all four wheels immediately, unlike its steam compatriots which required a build-up of pressure before unleashing their power.

Looking across to the workbench and laboratory area, I was surprised to find it empty. When I'd earlier brought the Master his supper, he had been hard at work examining items and information obtained at the site of a recent death. I was about to call out when I heard thumping noises and several grunts echoing out from deeper in the cave.

Stepping further into the cavern, I turned and spied Master Sherlock engaged in physical training; punching, and kicking a large thick leather sack, filled with sand, and hung from a metal hook embedded in the ceiling of a cave where it sloped down markedly. The Master wore padded leather gloves and performed a series of strikes, punches, and kicks at the bag. Standing there, I marvelled, as I had at many times in the past, at Master Sherlock's skills in both boxing and an oriental martial art he learnt during his travels in the far east.

I stopped near the entrance of the gymnasium area and stood next to a set of hand weights, pondering what Master Sherlock would need while I waited for him to notice me or stop his training.

"What is it, Watson?" he said, without breaking from his regime.

"Commissioner Lestrade contacted you on the communication machine. He wishes to see you at the Bank of England. He didn't say why."

Finishing his exercising with a flurry of short sharp punches to the bag, followed by a winding kick with the back of his heel, he said, "Well, that would be obvious, wouldn't it? There's been a robbery."

Concern crossed my face, as I imagined all the nefarious villains that roamed London, pondering who could be involved. "You don't think it was Miss Adler, do you?"

Glancing across at me with a slight look of derision on his face, Master Sherlock said, "Why would you say that?"

"You have shown a marked interest towards her activities of late."

"She has turned her attention to stealing jewellery of increasing value. The victims of her crimes can absorb the financial impacts but are prone to seek vengeance through their own means. I'm merely looking to find and apprehend her before she becomes a victim herself."

Nodding, I added, "An honourable stance, Sir. Do you wish me to draw you a bath?"

Frowning, he said, "Now, why would I take a bath, that would waste far too much time." Grabbing a small towel from atop a nearby bench, he wiped the sweat from his brow and face before adding, "I assume there's fresh attire for my nighttime persona to don?"

"Yes, Sir, I always make sure all is ready for your nocturnal pursuits," I answered.

As he walked past me towards the nearby dressing room, he dropped the damp towel across my shoulder, smiled, and said, "Thank you, Watson, I really would be lost without you."

Moments later, the *clomp* of thick leather boots on the rocky floor of the cave, announced Master Sherlock stepping out from the dressing room. He was covered from head to toe in the garb of the deepest black, the uniform of the ninjitsu warriors of the far east, the design brought back from his years spent abroad. He had made several modifications, adding a thin layer of strong steel armour plates beneath, and changing the headwear, to expose his mouth, while covering most of the top half of his head, except for eye holes and his nostrils.

Many months ago, when I had asked about that aspect of the design, Master Sherlock stated that he wished to be heard and that he didn't wish to obscure his senses of smell, taste, or sight.

Moving across to a nearby display rack, he took down a wide leather belt, adorned with various pockets and devices, and quickly fastened it around his waist. Whilst he had dressed, I'd ensured that all items were restocked just in case they were needed.

Stepping up to the dark carriage, he bent and pressed a hidden button. The high-pitched whine of several small motors echoed out, and the door slid up to allow him entry.

"This could be virtually nothing, Watson, or again it may lead onto something of possible interest. I am hoping for the latter, but who knows. Regardless, I have other interests on my mind at the moment, so please prepare a hearty breakfast for the morning."

"Shall I turn down your bed upstairs?"

A grin crossed his face, "Do you actually think I'll use it?"

"No, Sir, but one has hope," I said, "I shall refresh the cot down here then, shall I?"

"Good man, Watson, good man."

With that, the door slid back into place, and a higher-pitched whine emanated from the front of the vehicle. It jolted forward and sped from the cave, only the whine producing any noise, and when gone, the silence descended once more.

I had taken it upon myself to chronicle Master Sherlock's adventures, but sadly, always from afar. My life was in this great house, and in my heart, I knew all too well that my days of adventure were long gone. To ensure any story was properly captured, I relied on Master Sherlock's memories, and the answers he gave to my barrage of questions. At other times, I would seek out any others that had provided assistance, such as Commissioner Lestrade, the most senior policeman in Scotland Yard.

***

Given the scale of the matter at hand, Commissioner Lestrade had involved himself directly in the solution. He had faith in the aptitude of his people but would quickly involve the man he knew simply as Holmes, and whose face he had never seen, if he felt that things may be beyond them.

When the small device on his wrist began to flash, Lestrade knew help was close by. He brought about the quick closure of the investigation and sent his people home for the night. After spending several hours at the scene, Lestrade believed there was nothing more they could glean from the evidence at hand, and he was loathe to have the area despoiled any further.

As Lestrade stood waiting in the great vault of the Bank of England, he examined the damage and devastation that had occurred. At the far end, a solidly built two-foot-thick wall of bricks, mortar, and concrete, now sported a massive, almost perfectly round hole, large enough for several men to quickly enter and make off with much of the contents of the vault itself.

Well, that's how it seemed to have been used.

According to the night guard, tasked with performing routine inspections of the vault every couple of hours, he had found the room in this state on his eight o'clock rounds. Two hours previously the vault had been full. Now only a handful of crates and boxes lay scattered across the room.

"These were no common thugs, this took some planning," came a familiar, low, rasping voice, from behind Lestrade.

"They were well-coordinated and thorough," he replied, not needing to turn to identify the voice's owner.

"Time?"

"Guard found it this way at eight o'clock."

"Previous rounds?"

"Six."

"Fast work." The dark garbed figure stepped past Lestrade and began to inspect the room. Experience told the commissioner to keep quiet while Holmes undertook his examination. He simply watched as the man pored over almost every square inch of the room, pulling out a magnifying glass to focus on some minutiae or detail. Lestrade hoped that he could bring some of Holmes's techniques into the training of his men, but the shadowy figure was very cautious about revealing his methods. Lestrade was unsure if it was to protect Holmes's identity further or simply protect his position of trust with the police.

Sidling up to the hole, Holmes peered through into the darkened tunnel beyond. Reaching for a small black cylinder clipped to his belt, he brought it up and pointed it into the darkness. With a *click*, a small beam of piercing white light cut through the gloom. Holmes played it around the area for a moment before speaking. "This is part of the underground system. A service tunnel perhaps." Shining the light on the ground, he added, "Tracks. They loaded everything onto carts and headed off into the bowels of the system."

"Yes. We followed the tracks. They reach one of the underground train lines, so I assume they loaded their booty onto a carriage and exited that way."

"Doesn't sound like common criminals then?"

"No. They were well prepared."

Playing the light across the edge of the hole, Holmes murmured to himself, before leaning in closer with his glass. "This was drilled out, not made by explosives. If they had a steam-powered cutter, the noise would have been horrendous."

"The guards said they heard nothing."

"Intriguing." Running a finger along the edge of the cut, he added, "This was prepared over several attempts as if the perpetrators had been drilling for days in short bursts. Possibly how they kept the sound down." Turning to face Lestrade, Holmes returned the light to his belt before asking, "What was stolen?"

The commissioner pointed to several empty racks, "These held boxes of gold bullion and sterling. I've had the head of accounts here. The poor man was in tears, even though none of the money was his. He said it was near five hundred thousand pounds worth of gold."

"No wonder the gentleman cried, but it's nothing compared to what the head of security will be feeling when he receives word of this." Dropping to his knees for a moment, Holmes examined the spaces where the bullion crates had been. Shaking his head, he said, "Footprints. Overtrodden by your men. I can't draw anything from them." Standing, he moved across to the wall adjacent to the hole. The entire area was covered with small metal plates all with keyholes. "Safe deposit boxes?"

Nodding, Lestrade said, "Too difficult to break into, it seems. They were completely left alone."

"Not completely," said Holmes pointing to one box in particular and pulling the door up to reveal a vacant space behind.

"What?" coughed Lestrade, his eyes wide at the sight. "Why didn't those fools see that?"

"Because only three have been disturbed," Holmes added, indicating the other two. "Can you find out who these belonged to? There is damage on the bottom of each. They were presumably forced open, but to do so in such a random manner gives me pause to think that these were targeted."

Pulling out the small notepad he kept on him as a legacy of his days on the beat, Lestrade copied down the box numbers. "I'll check with the Bank in the morning."

"Good," said Holmes moving back towards the hole in the rear wall. Retrieving his light from its belt clip, he shone the beam into the darkness, and said, "I'll investigate the tunnel and see if I can't find our lawbreakers' destination. Please send me those names in the morning, I'll keep you informed of my progress."

Lestrade nodded before Holmes disappeared into the obsidian gloom.

***

Early the next morning, I found Master Sherlock standing at his workbench. An array of electric lights, mounted among a rack above the bench, threw a bright aura across the object of his interest. As I drew closer, I noticed he had installed a strong magnifier and was meticulously examining the article.

Placing the breakfast tray down on the nearby side table, I joined Master Sherlock at the workbench. It was looking down at the item on the bench that memories I had long since buried came rushing back into my mind.

"Is that?" I asked.

"It appears to be," said Master Sherlock, "I found it in the tunnels leading away from the rear wall of the main vault. After drilling a hole through the wall, and robbing the vault, the miscreants had taken their haul to one of the side tracks and loaded it onto a waiting train."

"How do you know that?"

"There were cart tracks dug into the ground leading away, plus fresh scratches in the metal of the rails. Rails that should not have seen a train in months as the service tunnel was unused. Sadly, I could not tell where they went after joining the mainline, but then I found this tossed casually aside along the tunnel."

We both stared down at the green woollen balaclava. On its own, it would be nothing more than a winter garment to be worn to protect against the bitter cold. But the style of garment and the colour meant so much to the history of the Holmes family and sent me back to a time over twenty years previously, to an event to which I sadly had firsthand experience.

I had been in the service of Sir Mycroft Holmes for many years, enjoying his company and building a strong friendship to complement my position. That time had seen his romance and eventual marriage to Mathilde Tesla, with her father Nikola soon after joining us in the Holmes family manor to pursue his research.

Sir Thomas showed no animosity to the old man. I truly believe he thought him novel and eccentric. I certainly found his inventions fascinating, up until the moment they killed him.

Admittedly, Lady Mathilde's sorrow was short-lived when it was discovered she was with babe. The cavern beneath the manor was locked up, and Nikola's inventions and discoveries were forgotten until a young Sherlock found them years later.

During the early years of Sherlock's life, the manor brimmed with love and humour. The young boy was bright, intelligent, and inquisitive. Something that Sir Thomas attributed to Mathilde's side of the family. The Holmes's were diligent and hardworking, but none had ever shown the level of inventiveness or a thirst for science that young Sherlock indulged in.

It was however that fateful day of young Sherlock's tenth birthday that everything changed for him.

The family was to attend a matinee performance of Alice in Wonderland at the Prince's Theatre in Piccadilly. In a private conversation with young master Sherlock, I found that he didn't want to go, but was doing it to make his parents happy. He stated he would rather attend the exhibition of variations of Watt's and Stephenson's steam engines that were being held at the Crystal Palace. I agreed and promised to ask permission to take him to the exhibit later in the week, which brought a wide smile to his face.

Sir Thomas expressly asked us to leave an hour earlier than the performance starting time, as he had to attend to some business at the Clydesdale Bank in nearby Plough Court. Sherlock and I waited in the carriage, while Sir Thomas and Lady Mathilde went inside. As master Sherlock and I talked about many things, he pointed to a dark carriage that approached and stopped directly outside of the bank.

I almost failed to even notice it until the young master pointed to the driver who wore a dark green balaclava over his face. When the four other men sprang from the cab, each wearing a similar face covering and carrying an unholstered pistol, I shouted in fear.

Glancing around for any sign of a policeman, I failed to notice the young master climb down from the buckboard and race across to the bank building.

Without a second thought, I jumped down, for I was lither in those days, and sprinted after him. I caught the boy just as the first shots rang out within. Holding him in my arms, I dragged him away from the entrance, moments before the doors sprang open and the first of the hooded men burst out and bolted towards the waiting carriage.

The other three followed each man carrying cloth sacks filled most probably with money. As the last man exited, I noticed two horrid details, he held in one hand, both a sack of money, and a long strand of pearls, and his shirt was sprayed with crimson though he did not look injured. He turned once and saw the two of us, our eyes wide in terror.

He brought his right hand up and aimed the pistol towards us. A thin line of smoke rose from the barrel, punctuating his immediate past deed. A cruel smile issued from the mouth hole of the balaclava, as the man thumbed the hammer closed on the pistol and said, “See you later kid,” before he turned and joined his companions in crime.

Moments later the first whistles echoed across the area and men in dark blue uniforms appeared before racing towards the Bank. Still shaking in fear, young Sherlock stared up into my eyes and asked, “Mummy? Father?”

Taking him by the hand, for he had regressed to the little boy he was, we walked up the stairs and through the dark doors. I immediately regretted my actions and wish I could retrace those steps to this day. The image of Sir Thomas and Lady Mathilde lying on the floor, in a spreading pool of their blood, haunts me to this day.

In less than ten minutes, not only had I lost a pair of good friends, but the boy that would be entrusted into my care lost his parents and found his life forever changed.

Finally, after my memory finished, I gasped, “The Robin Hood gang?”

“Only if they’ve found the fountain of youth. They’d all be well into their sixties by now,” said Master Sherlock, “Except of course the member I tracked down. He found his fate at the end of a rope.”

That had been one of the first moments in Master Sherlock's life of fighting crime. Using his freshly honed skills to track down his parents' killer and bring him to justice. Something that the newly appointed Commissioner Lestrade was quite thankful for.

"Could it be someone using their old modus operandi?" I asked.

"Perhaps," he mumbled, turning, and grasping a small pair of tweezers before concentrating on the balaclava. Within seconds he withdrew a long slender filament of metal and placed it next to three others, and a single grain of what appeared to be black dirt.

"What have you got there, Master Sherlock?"

"At this stage I'm unsure," he said, "The black granule appears to be pure carbon, possibly coal. The other four pieces are threads of metal. These may have been picked up by the balaclava's owner either at their hideout or along the way. I'm hoping they will lead to a pathway back to the gang's location." Staring at the young master's face I didn't think he believed what he was saying at all.

"Did you get any sleep last night, Sir?"

"An hour or so," he shrugged, "I have much to do. I'll sleep later."

"You do remember what tonight is don't you?"

A confused look crossed his face, "No?"

"A charity event at the Iceberg lounge in Soho."

Master Sherlock's face screwed up in disgust. "I assume it's hosted by that horrible little man."

"Yes, Charles Augustus Milverton. Contrary to popular belief, he is supposedly a fine upstanding citizen."

"Not in my experience," scoffed Sherlock.

"Regardless, Sir, in your role as an equally fine upstanding citizen and one of London's leading businessmen, it would be well within your interest to attend, if only to be seen."

"Do you know who any of the other invitees are?"

"I did delve into the gossip pages of the paper to undertake my investigations. Nobody knows who is sponsoring the event, but it does appear that many of your contemporaries will be there plus members of academia from London University. My take on it has been that the benefactor wishes to facilitate investment in the University itself, by introducing some of the staff to these businessmen."

A grin appeared on the young master's face, "You may be onto something there, Watson, well done." Thinking for a moment, he then added, "Yes, I will attend. Make sure to have my suit ready, you just never know what will happen where Milverton is involved." I took that to mean more than just a gentleman's formal attire and went about my duties.

***

A *whooshing* sound, followed by a pall of steam loosed from the turbine at the front of the town car, announced our arrival before the Iceberg lounge. A red carpet, flanked by two long lines of braided gold rope, ran from the entrance of the building to the gutter where each steam carriage drew up and deposited its occupants.

As I exited and moved around to let Master Sherlock alight, I noticed a large group of less elegantly dressed people pressed together on the opposite sides of each rope chain. They were either there to catch a glimpse of any person of note or in the hopes of some titbit of currency being flung their way. Their encroachment onto the carpet was impeded by the bulk of two hefty, but well-dressed men. These were obviously two of Milverton's guards, simply standing there, with arms crossed and their backs to the crowds, forming a small but formidable guard of honour for the arriving guests.

Master Sherlock presented just as impressive a figure as his tall, athletic form stepped from the carriage. Murmured questions and gasps of recognition, with whispers of the name *Holmes*, issued from the crowd. Sherlock Holmes was, by virtue of his inheritance, the owner of one of the largest enterprises in London, but rarely entered into the public domain. The business affairs were managed by a long-time family friend and close confidant of Master Sherlock's father, leaving my ward time for himself and his own pursuits.

Stepping back into the car, I watched Master Sherlock ascend the stairs to the front entrance. I had urged him to bring a guest, but he had fobbed me off with his usual mutterings of wishing to remain unencumbered in case he needed to leave at a moment's notice. Having heard his protestations before, I reconciled myself with thoughts that he hoped to encounter Miss Adler, for I knew well that he harboured feelings for the woman, even though she dallied on quite the opposite side of the law as Master Sherlock walked.

At the top of the stairs, Master Sherlock was approached by a heavy-set man, who although short in stature and rotund in appearance, was dressed in an exquisitely tailored tuxedo, with a full white-tie accompaniment, finished off with a satin top hat. He wore a monocle over his right eye, which leant him a permanent sneer on one side of his face, but I noticed he had a long-stemmed cigarette holder clamped between his teeth to disguise the fact.

Charles Augustus Milverton, the owner of the Iceberg lounge, and host for the evening thrust one hand out to Master Sherlock who shook it amiably. I could only imagine the reaction of Milverton, were he to find out about Master Sherlock's other life. For it was via his nighttime activities, that a younger Holmes, just starting his crime-fighting career, had uncovered Milverton's secrets. The evidence gathered and presented to Commissioner Lestrade had relocated Milverton to Wandsworth Prison for a good two years and broken the back of a burgeoning crime syndicate. Supposedly, Milverton had used the last few years to re-establish himself and he now stayed on the right side of the legal system.

A loud, harsh honking from behind, broke me from my musings. Another carriage wished to set down its passengers. Engaging the gearing system and with one last look towards Master Sherlock, I lurched away with a belch of steam and coal smoke and headed for the allotted parking area nearby.

***

Irene Adler's eyes turned away from the elderly gentleman she'd engaged in conversation and settled on the figure at the entrance to the Iceberg Lounge. A smile crossed her lips as she studied the tall, handsome man, a direct contrast to the squat, rotund figure of Milverton at his side.

Sherlock.

Watching with amusement as Sherlock Holmes's piercing gaze scanned across every face within his vicinity and knowing too well that he would be scrutinizing and cataloguing details of each attendee in turn, Irene waited for him to pick her out of the crowd.

It wouldn't be too difficult, she believed, for Irene Adler had eschewed the frumpy look of her female counterparts, with their layers of fabric, and embraced the

fashions of the day, consisting of body-hugging leather and satin. To her, the skin-tight outfit was both a statement and complimentary to her line of work. To the many men in the room, it was a beacon, again proving useful to Irene's occupation, and made for a much easier source of introductions.

A rare smile broke out on Holmes's face as his eyes locked with Irene's. Turning to Milverton he bade the club owner farewell and crossed the floor, the guests parting in his wake, and was soon before Irene.

Standing to his full height, he bowed slightly, taking Irene's hand, and kissing it lightly. "Miss Adler, it has been some time."

Nodding, Irene replied with a grin, "In a public setting, yes it has." The memory of their previous encounter on the ramparts of the Tower of London, where Holmes had interfered in her attempts to secure the Hope diamond for a continental buyer with both physical force and intelligent reason, concluding in a mutual agreement to desist. Her client's outrage and communication to all and sundry within his circle had dented her reputation, but an anonymous deposit into her bank account the next day, matching the client's fee, had been most welcome.

"You are looking most resplendent this evening," Holmes added.

"And you do make a dashing figure," pausing slightly to punctuate her statement, "When appropriately dressed."

Before Holmes could respond with a suitable quip, the figure beside Irene cleared his throat, dragging their attention to him. Irene's eyes grew wide when she remembered the fellow she had been conversing with. "Oh, I'm dreadfully sorry. Professor Coram, this is Mr. Sherlock Holmes."

Holding his hand out, the gaunt man turned his dark piercing eyes up towards Holmes, and said, "I have heard much of you, Mr. Holmes. The bad news about your parents all those years ago."

Holmes was taken aback, mentions of his parents were few and far between given the time that had passed. "I thank you, Sir." Shaking the man's hand, he added, "Professor? Do I take it that you are resident at London University, or have you travelled from Oxford?"

"Pah, Oxford," the man sputtered, "London, for well over forty years at last count. I am the Dean of the Engineering Faculty." Waving a hand around the room, indicating the expanses of gaslights, clockwork engines, and steam lines running the length of the room, he dropped his head before adding, "All these gizmos and gadgets that have come from Watt's engines can be traced back to our work at the University." He sighed, "But, in our innocence, we allowed the designs to freely flow into the industrial complex. Damn stupid that." Looking up into Holmes's eyes once more, his gaze appeared sad, the intensity lost, "And that brings us here, with cap in hand to request monies from the likes of you." Holding up a hand to stop Holmes's immediate response. "I like it less than you would think, but we are at the mercy of industry and have lost many a good academic to employment within these new businesses. Even great minds need to feed their bodies."

"And as one who owes his existence to academia, I can concur with your thoughts."

Coram cocked his head slightly, "I don't follow."

"My grandfather. You may know him or have even worked with him. He was an esteemed academic at London University before he was mysteriously castigated for some affront and banished from the place."

"Who was he? I don't remember." Coram trailed off as a memory came to the fore.

"Tesla. Nikola Tesla. Grandfather on my mother's side."

His eyes opening wide, Coram stuttered, "My word. I never made that connection before. You are the grandson of Nikola Tesla?"

Before Holmes could answer, Coram glanced around, before bidding them adieu and making a hasty retreat.

"What was that all about?" asked Irene, "I hope you haven't scared off a potential client."

"Client? Or mark?"

Irene thought for a moment, "Considering that conversation, neither."

"He may be of no interest to you, but to me, he is a potential lead."

"Why?"

"As part of my private interests, I have been helping Scotland Yard."

"As always."

"Yes. You may have heard of two recent shooting deaths."

Irene's eyes grew wide. "My word, those Oxford professors?"

Nodding, Holmes added, "Yes, but both were originally from London University. The other aspect is that I was called to a break-in at the Bank of England. You wouldn't know anything about that would you?" Holmes studied Irene's expression for a moment.

Maintaining an innocence that belied her profession, Irene answered, "No details, just rumours."

"Rumours?"

"Yes," she said, taking a short sip from her champagne, "There's a new player in town. No idea who it is, but he wants to make an impression, shall we say, on the criminal world. What has Professor Coram to do with this? He's not even a businessman, just a simple academic."

"You were interested in him?"

"Yes, in a professional sense. A client is interested in something he possesses."

"Then we may have similar interests. Coram owned a security deposit box that disappeared in the robbery. His and two others."

"The two Oxford professors?"

Nodding, Holmes smiled, "Yes, well done. They belonged to Doctor Grimesby Roylott and Doctor Leslie Armstrong, both of the engineering faculty."

"You think they are linked?"

"Given they were the only boxes stolen, it seems likely." Looking around the room, Holmes said, "Now where has Coram gone? I feel the need to speak with him once more."

Stepping forward, level with Holmes, Irene nodded past him. “Seems to have found someone else to talk to.”

Coram was visible through a pair of open doors in the far wall. He stood just outside on a small patio, talking animatedly with another man.

“Do you know his companion?” asked Holmes.

“No,” said Irene, staring at the short, rotund man, “Another academic, by the looks of him.”

As they both studied the two men, the sharp retort of gunfire shattered the scene. The tall figure of Professor Coram fell forward, knocking over his companion, and crashing to the paving stones, a fine spray of crimson splattering the stonework. Screams, shouts, and cries erupted from around the room. In their panic, people ran away from the open doorway, pushing and shoving others out of their way, regardless of their identity.

Dropping to the floor at the sound of the gunshot, Irene slowly composed herself and stood up. Glancing around, she found herself alone. Sherlock Holmes had disappeared, the only evidence he was ever there was his jacket, shirt, and tie lying discarded nearby. Her eyes moved to the open doorway, and the corpse lying on the ground outside.

***

At the moment the sound of the gunshot reached Holmes’s ears, he took in as much of the details of the assassination as possible. In his mind, time slowed down as his eyes flicked across the scene. Measuring the angle of Professor Coram’s head as it snapped back from the impact and projecting the path of the bullet as it flew towards its victim.

Within seconds, his jacket, shirt, and tie were falling to the floor as Holmes sprinted towards the open doorway. Stopping for a moment, he glanced in the perceived direction of the shot.

Across the road sat a three-story building. Holmes spied movement in the darkness on the rooftop. Pulling his mask from a hidden pocket in his dark-coloured outfit, he quickly pulled it on, covering his identity, before sprinting across the street. Angling his trajectory to match the path of his target, he quickly closed in on the corner of the building.

As he ran, Holmes pulled one of his many devices from his belt and aimed it towards the roofline. A sharp *snap* was followed by a small piton dart streaking out, trailing a thin, but immensely strong, line of metal strengthened rope. A second later, the dart buried itself deep into the brickwork of the upper story, followed by the line rewinding, pulling Holmes up the building as he ran. A casual observer would have witnessed the incredible sight of a dark-clad man sprinting up the side of a building with giant strides.

Holmes leapt the last stride, vaulting onto the roof and landing with his feet against the sloping slate tiled roof. He let go of the device, letting it clatter against the wall, its purpose fulfilled.

The man in Holmes's sights had reached the corner of the building and was tossing a rope, fastened to a chimney stack, over the edge.

"Stop."

He turned at the sound of Holmes's gravelly voice, a wide grin crossing his face. "Ah, the great detective," he said, slowly raising his hands to reveal he still held the rifle used to cut short Professor Coram's life only moments before.

From the lean, athletic figure, and broad handlebar moustache, Holmes was quick to realise who he was dealing with. "Colonel Sebastian Moran, if I'm not mistaken. World-renowned hunter, a former member of Her Majesty's Army, and as of late, an assassin for hire."

Chuckling, Moran answered, "You have me at a disservice, Sir. You know my name, but I cannot tell yours."

"We'll leave it at that for the moment," said Holmes, "I cannot contemplate any connection between you and Professor Coram, so can only deduce that you are on contract." The clanging of bells echoed up to them, followed by the squeal of brakes as several steam carriages, containing London's finest, slid to a stop in the streets below. "If you tell me who your client is, I'm sure I can arrange it with the Yard to alleviate your sentence somewhat."

Moran took a glance at the gathering beneath them before turning back to Holmes. The smirking grin grew on his face as he stepped up onto the low brick parapet. "My sentence," Moran chuckled, "If the Yard captures me, I'll be swinging in the breeze within a matter of hours. Besides, I may not know your identity, Sir, but are you not the world's greatest detective. He says you are anyway."

"Who is he?" asked Holmes, a hint of frustration leaking into his tone.

Moran laughed out loud. "I think he may be wrong. If you haven't deduced it already. Or at least determined where to find him."

"How could I do that?"

"You were at the Bank of England, were you not?" Moran took Holmes's silence as an affirmative. "Well then, you have everything you need to reckon where to find him."

Filled with confusion, Holmes failed to notice Moran glance up once, then down, before shifting backward. Holmes darted forward, just as the assassin stepped back and dropped out of sight.

"No!" Holmes shouted, reaching the now vacant spot.

The loud drone of several large engines burst from above. Holmes glanced to the heavens to see a large, black airship hovering high above the roof and slowly ascending away. A long, black, rope ladder trailed out from the belly of the behemoth. Within a few seconds, the smiling figure of Colonel Sebastian Moran, clinging to the rope ladder, rose above the roofline of the building, passing within a few yards of Holmes.

"Sometimes it is convenient to have friends in high places, Detective." Waving his free hand at Holmes, he added, "Until we meet again, which I do hope won't be too soon."

With a roar of propellers, the airship lurched, pointing upwards and rising quickly away. Within moments, it had disappeared from view, leaving only the softening whirring sound of its engines in its wake.

As Holmes watched the dark object slowly fade from view, his mind kept replaying the last moments of his conversation with Moran.

I should already know his location.

"But how?" he spat into the night.

With a roar of propellers, the airship lurched, pointing upwards and rising quickly away.

***

The drive back to the manor was rather silent, with Master Sherlock brooding in the rear of the car for the entire journey. I attempted to prompt him for more information about the evening, especially the appearance of the gigantic, black airship, that stole away with the prime suspect. With his continued silence, even under my barrage of questions, I finally gave up and drove the rest of the way in quiet myself.

Before I had even finished the shutdown sequence for the car, dropping the steam pressure slowly to avoid stress on the engine, and bringing the boiler temperature back down to compensate, Master Sherlock had exited and disappeared from the garage. It was times like this that I wished we could develop another of the electric motors that Master Sherlock had fitted to his night carriage so that we could avoid the tedious routines required to start and stop our town car.

After setting Master Sherlock's jacket, shirt, and tie, in the laundry room for later cleaning, thankfully rescued by Miss Adler, I prepared a light snack and some coffee. I had seen these moods before and knew that my ward would set his mind to a deduction for hours without ceasing. I felt he would need nourishment, as I didn't believe he'd had time to partake at the soiree.

As I placed the tray on a small table near Master Sherlock's workbench, I found him hunched over his powerful magnifying glass, staring at the green hood, and the tiny fragments he had discovered.

"I have brought you a light supper, Sir, and some coffee. I thought some nourishment might stimulate your thought processes." I received a simple grunt in return. "Is there anything that I can help with, Sir?"

"What?" said Holmes, finally recognising that I was standing there. He peered up from the glass, first at me, then at the food, then back to me. "Sorry, Watson, that Moran fellow has me confused. He knew about the Bank. He knew that I had been there. That leads me to believe that it was all orchestrated in advance, just to force my attendance. If so, then this," he indicated the hood, "Is the vital clue. But how? There is some sort of riddle here, but I can't put my finger on it."

I noticed something written on the chalkboard nearby and gazed past the young master to see that five sets of letters had been written on it; Sn, Sb, Zn, Mg, and C. I determined that they were connected to the four filaments and black grain that he had discovered on the hood. Even from my rudimentary knowledge of the sciences, I recognised them as chemical symbols. Tin, Zinc, Magnesium, and Carbon. I had no idea of the fifth.

Turning away from the board, my eyes lifted to the large copy of Mendeleev's table of elements affixed to a board on the wall nearby. I found the symbol Sb and realised it was antimony, a nugget of information that may never prove useful again but would stay with me. Each chemical symbol had a number written below it, above them, Master Sherlock had added his number, giving the set of symbols a regular progression and order.

"Master Sherlock, do the numbers have any meaning? I mean in the context of your riddle?"

Sherlock's gaze joined mine. I chanced to glance back at him and saw his eyes widen. He jumped from his seat, and picking up some chalk, redrafted the series of symbols with the smaller numbers sitting above, and the larger numbers below, before stepping away to examine the chalkboard. Pointing at the sets of numbers, Sherlock said, "This series that I have added is a new system currently being determined by a young scientist called Mosely. They are being called the atomic number. The other series are the atomic weights."

"I still don't know what the significance is."

"Moran said, I would already know where to find him."

"Do you know what he meant?"

"No, but..." Stepping up to the board again, the chalk sang, the five atomic numbers, fifty, fifty-one, six, thirty, and twelve; separated and written near the top. Moving away again, Sherlock stared at the numbers for several moments, before speaking. "It's the where. Where to find him." Finally, a broad grin broke out on Sherlock's face. "Do you know the latitude and longitude of London?"

Shaking my head, I answered, "No."

Moving to a large bookcase nestled against the rock wall, Sherlock returned with a leather-bound volume and placed it on a table. Opening it to a map of London, he pointed at the lines running across and down the page. "Zero longitudes. The Greenwich meridian. Latitude fifty-one." Glancing at the numbers, he calculated in his mind, then pointed at a spot on the banks of the Thames near Wapping. Fifty-one degrees, fifty minutes, and thirty seconds north, zero degrees, six minutes and twelve seconds west."

"Isn't that the location of that monstrous new building?"

A broad smile crossed Sherlock's face. "Yes, yes, it is. The Reichenbach tower. Well done Watson, I believe that's where I'll find this mysterious villain."

***

The almost silent night carriage whirred through the streets of London, slipping past surprised onlookers, whose stark, wide-eyed looks suggested their memories of the craft would stay with them for years to come.

Sherlock Holmes slowed down as he reached the building site of the Reichenbach Tower, parking the carriage in the darkness of a side alley out of reach of the waning moonlight, and exited. Standing in the near-black shadows, he blended almost seamlessly with the gloom, only his mouth and chin visible.

Staring up at the building, he formulated a plan.

The Reichenbach Tower was a marvel amongst the newly assembled marvels of the modern age of London. Harnessing the power of steam had leant the last vestiges of the Industrial Revolution a renewed vigour, producing machines of immense complexity, and buildings taller than ever before. No longer was St. Paul's Cathedral the loftiest structure of the city, that honour now stood with this newest of skyscrapers.

It stood fifteen stories high, constructed of dark, black brick, and rimmed with brass and steel plating. The very top consisted of a circular, disc-shaped penthouse, comprised of curved windows running around the entire floor, purportedly giving the lone occupant a full view of the city below. The strangest part of the top floor was the way the penthouse's wall extended well beyond the supporting structure below it. It leant the building the appearance of an enormous candle holder as if the penthouse was waiting for any wax dripping from a towering flame above. It was the huge black airship hovering a hundred yards from the circular room that convinced Holmes the villain was here.

He wants me here. To kill me? No. Moran could have killed me easily. There's something else.

Scanning the shear side of the building, Holmes concluded that climbing the outside was a fool's errand. He'd need to scale the lower floors, then enter and ascend via the internal stairways.

Noticing a small balcony running around a part of the second floor, he brought out his scaling device and pointed it towards the building. With a sharp *snap*, the piton fired out, trailing a fine black line. Holding the device, Holmes vaulted quickly up the side of the building and onto the balcony.

To his surprise a pair of glass and metal doors stood wide open, begging for him to enter. Unhooking and replacing the piton device on his belt, he stepped cautiously in through the doors.

The entire floor was empty, ready for whatever business would eventually be undertaken there. The wall adjacent to the balcony was dominated by a pair of open-cage style elevators, and an entranceway into the stairwell. A single electric light glowed above the stairway; the only light on the entire floor.

Electricity? Not gas. This becomes more intriguing.

Holmes approached, scanning from side to side for any obvious, or indeed hidden, traps. Convinced that his host had no intention of harming him, he entered the staircase and began to climb.

At each exit doorway, Holmes stopped and scanned the floor beyond. For several floors, the area was dark and empty, sending him upwards. He continued to climb until the staircase stopped, presenting him with a closed door and no further route up.

Slowly pulling the door open, he found a darkened room beyond. Stepping inside, the door slammed shut as soon as he let it go, the inside had no handle, and pushing against it only assured him that he was locked inside the room.

Suddenly, several lights illuminated, casting a bright glow around the room.

Holmes's eyes were immediately drawn to the loud clicking of a clock above a door at the other end of the room. The clock was set to two minutes to midnight. In his mind, the time was significant and represented a countdown of some sort. The pipe sitting below the clock proved it. The sound of gas escaping came to Holmes's ears. Sniffing, his eyes grew wide.

Almonds? Cyanide.

Launching towards the door, he soon realised it was stuck fast, and any amount of strength would not dislodge it before the countdown ran out.

Looking down, he saw a small table sitting by the door. It held a single long knife.

Is that it? Death by my hand? Or by poison?

Scanning the room, he noticed other objects. A settee lay along one wall. A single-throw cushion at one end. Against the other wall sat another small table. It held a chessboard with several chess pieces arranged along one side. Above the chessboard was written the words: *None shall take another.*

Holmes stepped over to the chessboard. There were seven queens arranged along one side, with a vacant square in the middle.

One's missing?

Studying the board for a moment, his head snapped around to the settee, and then the knife. Snatching the knife up, he moved quickly to the settee and slashed at the cushion, pulled the stuffing out, and found a small, but hard object inside. Another Queen.

Racing back to the board, he placed the chess piece down and studied the board.

None shall take another. Queens can take other pieces in any direction, except...

Moving the first piece forward two squares, he realised the concept. Each queen needed to sit on a square where they could not take another queen. Glancing at the clock, which was closing in on one minute to midnight, Holmes turned back to the board. Moving several pieces, he scanned the board once more. The fifth and seventh queens were in line.

Damn.

Resetting the pieces, he tried again, redistributing the pieces in an almost circular pattern around the board. A feeling of accomplishment filled him until he saw two on the same diagonal.

Frustration grew in his mind, a glance at the clock only caused more, twenty seconds left. Taking ten seconds to study the board and bring his breathing under control, Holmes reset the pieces, bringing the fourth queen towards the centre of the board, and shifting the sixth further away. Five seconds left; a hissing sound penetrated the silence. The cyanide was building. A quick movement of the first and seventh, then the eighth piece, and Holmes was sure it was done. Two seconds.

No.

Dragging the third piece to the seventh row, just as a clock chimed midnight.

I did it. Why is it chiming?

As the third stroke sounded, another loud click emanated from the door as it sprang open revealing another room beyond. Relief swept across Holmes as he stepped up to the doorway and entered the room. A loud hiss followed him as the gas streamed from the pipe, forcing him to slam the door shut, cutting off any escape back into the chess room.

Staring around the darkened room, Holmes found a feeling of disorientation filling his mind. Light flooded one side of the room as electric globes flared along the adjacent wall, drawing his attention. A door sat in the middle of the wall, the only other visible exit from the room. Noticing writing on the door, Holmes moved across to read it.

There were seven three-digit numbers written in three rows and columns. With three questions marks in the bottom, right corner.

813	274	596
672		384
549	836	???

As he read them, a cacophony of *squeals* and *groans* erupted from behind. Turning towards the sound, his eyes grew wide as he spied a room-wide steel grid-shaped frame grinding its way across the floor towards him. Each vertex of the grid sported a long metal spike, pointed directly at the opposite wall. Holmes judged he had two minutes until the spikes were on him.

Reading the door again, he noticed the set of numbered buttons situated a foot below the puzzle. A frantic minute passed in which Holmes calculated sums and differences, then performed several permutations and computations. Nothing made sense.

The squealing began to play on Holmes's mind, filling him with annoyance, something alien to his mindset. His preferred method of contemplation was calm, in a quiet location, with ample time to dwell on the problem at hand.

Cursing himself, he closed his eyes for a moment, took a deep breath, and stared at the numbers again. A pattern formed. The top row and left column contained every digit, once. Quickly, he pressed the one, two, and seven, corresponding to the missing numbers in both the bottom row and the right column.

A loud *clack* broke through the squealing noise, and the door snapped open. Holmes pushed through into the next room, just as the metal spikes ground into the brickwork on the other side of the wall.

Closing the door, Holmes readied himself for the next trial. As the lock clicked into place, lights flared all around the room, revealing it empty save for an ornate brass caged elevator in the middle of the room. Scanning the floor for any obvious traps, Holmes moved to the elevator and examined it. Nothing seemed untoward, and the elevator presented the only visible exit from the room.

Stepping into the cage, Holmes braced himself for the next phase of this adventure. Immediately, the door swung shut and the grinding of gears echoed out from the walls as the cage ascended through the floor into the room above.

Within a minute, the cage door opened onto the floor of the large circular penthouse. The line of windows looking out across the London skyline was mostly dark given the time and the height of the tower. At one point the windows gave way to a pair of doors, thrown open to the night. A small platform led out, suspended above the drop below. Through the doors, Holmes could see the shape of the large airship, waiting to be called into service. He understood it was common practice to leave airships tethered when not in use but seeing this one floating free left him with a feeling it was being kept ready for immediate use or escape.

He discerned movement off to the right and suddenly several lights flared around the room, throwing brightness across a tall, gaunt figure as he stood up from his desk and moved forward. "Ah, Mr. Holmes, welcome. I'm so glad you could join me."

Still feeling slightly annoyed, Holmes interjected, "A welcome doesn't seem to have been your intent. Not after those two death trap rooms."

"Oh, pish, a man of your intelligence and wit would never have fallen foul of those simple riddles. I merely use them as a form of insurance to stop would-be thieves making their way to this chamber. I never for a moment believed you would succumb." With a flick of a hand towards Holmes, "I think you can dispense with the mask. I discerned your identity a while ago, and you confirmed my deductions yourself when you appeared at the Iceberg lounge and conversed with that Adler woman. "You really should be more careful of your associations. Modern technology is a wonderful thing. I had listening tubes installed all around that room before I organised that little shindig last night."

"Who are you?" Holmes cut the man off. The face, gaunt and skeletal, with a simple whisp of thinning grey hair, was in no way familiar. "And how did you come by the technology to generate electricity?"

"Ah, yes, I apologise. I am Professor James Moriarty."

"Professor?"

"Yes, London University. Mathematics. Though I left there over twenty years ago. Haven't taught or undertaken research since."

"Were you there when Professor Coram attended?" Moriarty nodded. "Roylott and Steinmetz?"

"Well of course, and before you ask, your grandfather also. I knew Nikola Tesla quite well. In fact, I helped in the development of that coil device of his. He charged me with determining a lot of the mathematical equations surrounding the transference of electricity through the air. Though we never completed the project. It was

Tesla's designs that helped me build my own version of the electricity generator, and of course these wonders," he waved a hand at the lights embedded in the ceiling.

Holmes spun, scanning the room. Apart from the light bulbs, the ceiling held a vast network of cables, running in concentric circles, with several thick knots of cable crossing from the edge to the centre and dropping into the midst of a complex series of box-like machines.

"Ah, good," said Moriarty, "You've guessed. Quicker than I thought."

"This entire room is a larger version of Nikola's coil." It was a statement rather than a question.

"Yes, it is."

Studying the array of dark boxes, Holmes added, "It doesn't work." Turning back towards Moriarty, he noticed a grin cross the old man's face.

"Not yet, no. That is why you are here."

Before Holmes could react, two burly men stepped from the darkened gloom at the other end of the room and grasped each of his arms, pinning him between them, he struggled, but rather than enter a physical battle calmed himself. There were more important facts to glean. "Me?"

Pulling a key attached to a gold chain from his vest pocket, Moriarty stepped towards the machine console, inserted the key, and turned it. Immediately, lights sprang awake across the face of each box-like device. "Why yes. You have a working model of this coil. You brought it back to life after your grandfather was killed." Waving his hands around the room, he raised his voice and said, "This. This has been my dream since those days at the University. I, Nikola, and those three buffoons put this design together two decades ago. We saw the coming of the steam age but knew that there was untapped potential in electricity. The inventions that your grandfather designed and built. Engines that could harness the power of the electron. And this, this coil, designed to transmit that energy through the air."

Moriarty stepped up toe to toe with Holmes and stared straight into his eyes. "I have spent the last twenty years building an empire."

"A criminal empire, including the green hood gang. You were responsible for killing my parents."

Faltering at the accusation, Moriarty stepped back. "Not directly, I assure you. Yes, I financed them and took my cut. I used their signature to gain your attention, but what does that matter. The purpose of my enterprises was to accrue money, to build this. Your grandfather dreamed of building a coil of this size, to transmit electricity freely to all of London."

"But you have other plans."

"Well, of course, dear boy. I'm a businessman. Once society realises the potential of electricity, they will toss these steam machines aside." Bringing his hand up level with Holmes's eyes, he closed it into a fist. "Once they have a taste, they will become addicted to it. They will need more, and there will only be one source."

"You?"

"Me."

"But it doesn't work."

"Yet." Pointing a finger at Holmes's chest, "That is why you are here, Mr. Holmes. You fixed your grandfather's prototype. You run this," he waved a hand at Holmes's costume, "This second life on the electricity generated and dispersed through your grandfather's coil. You have already embraced the technology, but you hide it in that cave of yours."

Holmes's eyes grew wide. "How do you know so much about me?"

A nonchalant wave of a hand. "Oh, come on Sir, once I realised who you were, it was a simple matter to send spies into the bowels of your manor house once you left, like on the previous two nights. They returned with explicit details, which matched the knowledge I already had of your grandfather's toils, and your extension of his ideas and dreams. Tonight, you will do that for me."

"Why? Why would I do anything for you?"

"Oh, you won't be doing it for me. You'll be doing it for yourself, and of course the citizens of London."

"That's very magnanimous of you, but I thought the aim was to enslave the populace to your production and delivery of electricity."

Moriarty let out a small chuckle, "Oh, you misunderstood me it seems. When I meant you would be doing for the citizens, I didn't mean providing a means to gain electricity, I meant to stop this enormous bomb from wiping out the entire east end of London."

"What?"

"Did they never tell you how your grandfather actually died?" Moriarty waited, studying Holmes's confused expression. "It was when he tested his coil. The power grew so rapidly it sent an out-of-control pulse through that underground cavern beneath your house, killing him instantly. Whatever you did had solved that problem." Moving back to the console, Moriarty flicked several more switches. Lights flashed up and down several of the rows. "The same will happen with this version. Unless," stepping back, he grinned into Holmes's face, "You repeat what you did and you save all those people, plus you will help engender a new age. The age of electricity."

"I refuse."

"Then you will die along with thousands," Moriarty shrugged, "I will simply invade your manor house and retrieve your design. I'm sure my engineers will have no problems emulating it." Without another word, Moriarty turned away and walked slowly towards the airship platform.

Holmes watched the old man move away. The man that had caused his parents' death. The man that hired an assassin to kill seemingly innocent university professors. The man who would kill thousands to coerce someone into helping him against their will.

"Moriarty," Holmes yelled.

The Professor stopped, slowly turning back towards the detective. "You wish to help willingly."

"No, I just want to know. Why have you had your old friends killed?"

"Oh, simply revenge. They mocked me and caused my dismissal. I thought they could be useful, I presumed they had Tesla's missing designs, but no. Plus, they are the only other people that know about this coil. Eliminating them was simply logical." Looking past Holmes towards the console, Moriarty smiled and pointed, "You might want to turn your attention to that. It won't be long now. And you can't turn it off, this is the only key." Showing the activation key, before putting it back in his pocket, the old man turned and stepped out onto the platform. Reaching into a pocket, he brought a small gun and fired a flare towards the black airship. As the orange flash burst across the sky, the loud whir of engines echoed back.

Can't let him leave. Must bring him to justice.

Holmes pushed left, raising his right foot, and lashed out, kicking down with the flat of his boot into the knee of the man on his right. *Crack.* The man howled with pain as his knee shattered and let go of Holmes's arm, falling to the floor.

Spinning, Holmes blocked a punch from the left-hand man, then drove his right fist into his throat. The man gagged, clutching at his neck with both hands. A kick followed, striking him in the chest and sending him sprawling. The drone of engines filled the area, as the airship arrived to collect Moriarty.

Holmes looked towards the exit doors, Moriarty was stepping towards the gondola of the airship, within a moment he would be away and out of reach. Sprinting towards the open doorway, Holmes pulled a device from his belt and held it out before him.

As he reached the platform, the engines roared, turning the craft around and moving it slowly away from the building. Moriarty stood in the gondola's doorway and shouted, "You don't have much time Mr. Holmes." His smiling face turned first to surprise, then fear, as Holmes raced towards the end of the platform, pointed the device towards the ship, and pulled the trigger.

The piton raced across the gap, piercing the skin of the airship just above the head of the stunned Moriarty. Leaping into the air, Holmes retracted the line and landed deftly next to the professor.

"I didn't see this eventuality," said a shocked Moriarty.

Snatching at the gold chain, Holmes tore the key from Moriarty's pocket. "Firstly, I need this. Secondly, you must face justice." Throwing an arm around Moriarty's waist, Holmes lifted the lighter man and jumped from the airship's gondola. The device fired once more, sending its piton towards the Reichenbach building as both men plummeted towards the streets of London.

Lodging in the metal skin of the coil, the device retracted dragging Holmes and Moriarty quickly through the open space and dumping them onto the wooden platform. The key and chain were knocked from Holmes's hand and skittered into the darker room beyond.

Both men picked themselves up, Moriarty turning to stare at the great airship as it gently veered away. Suddenly, the massive stern engines roared into life, blasting all with a high-powered vortex of wind. Moriarty was driven towards the edge of the platform, his arms windmilling as he lost balance and fell. Holmes dived forward, grabbing Moriarty's hand as he disappeared from view.

"I've got you," said Holmes, straining to bring the older man back to the safety of the platform.

"To take me to justice? I think not," said Moriarty, a smile creeping onto his lips. "Dying at the end of a rope was never part of the plan." With a cackling laugh, the glove Holmes held emptied, and Moriarty's form quickly disappeared from view as it plummeted towards the streets far below.

"Damn," said Holmes, losing sight of the old man within seconds.

***

"But the authorities found no corpse?"

Nodding, Master Sherlock said, "No. When I'd finished stabilising the coil, I made my way back down and could find no sign of him either."

"Very strange."

"Indeed."

"But what of the coil and the building?"

"I have undertaken to purchase the building as part of my company. A team of engineers will examine the coil, using the design of my oscillation dampener that stopped the explosive pulse, as a basis. I truly believe I can complete Moriarty's work, or should I say, my grandfather's work, and create a source of energy that can be shared with millions."

"Nikola would be proud of that."

A smile grew on Master Sherlock's face, "Yes, Watson, I believe he would. And I will rename the tower."

"To what?"

"My grandfather's notes and designs had a single name assigned to his proposed transmission tower, and I think it would be fitting to use the same name."

"And that is?"

"Wardenclyffe."

The Strange Case of the Unicursal Hexagram

"It... it wasn't there yesterday," said a distraught Lady Marjorie, as Holmes leaned in to examine the strange design on the basement door. "I became fed up. We have a dinner party at the French Embassy tonight. Sheldon locked himself in there four days ago, and I hadn't heard a peep out of him since."

"Does he do that often?" I asked.

"Oh, yes, silly man. Normally he will at least accept trays of food and answer when I call, but this time nothing for the last three days. Wilson, our butler, said that the food goes untouched. Such a waste."

"And this symbol. You stated that it appeared this morning," asked Holmes.

"Oh, yes, as I said, I'd become fed up. Normally, I'm happy for Sheldon to go off on these little hermit holidays of his, but we needed to prepare for this evening. I asked Wilson to bring the keys and unlock the door. To both our astonishment, as soon as the key entered the lock, that horrid symbol appeared."

"What does he do down there?" I asked.

"Oh," Lady Marjorie's shoulders deflated, in an expression of resignation, "He's found religion."

Glancing back at the symbol, I couldn't place what religion it belonged to. The design was a hexagram of sorts, in the shape of two overlapping and interconnected triangles, not unlike a Star of David, but with the top and bottom points extending well beyond the rest. In the middle was a flower, or a sort of five-leafed clover.

"Have you ever seen anything like this before, Holmes?"

"I can't actually place it, at this stage," he said, "If it is religious, I would say it belongs to one of these strange new esoteric cults."

I nodded in agreement. I'd read of many new religions springing up. It seemed that any person with half a mind could hang a shingle and call himself a priest or prophet of his own religious order. "Something like those Swedenborgians or that Eliphas Levi fellow?"

It... it wasn't there yesterday.

"Exactly," said Holmes, turning the key still set in the keyhole. It wouldn't budge. Pulling it from the lock, he examined it closely, then leaned in and studied the lock itself. Nodding, he turned back to Lady Marjorie, "Have you had your man check for other keys, just in case this is the wrong one?"

A voice piped up from nearby, "Yes, sir, I did." It was then I noticed the butler standing at a polite distance and just out of sight.

"It's a Beddows lock, put in there by Sir Sheldon himself. He kept one key for himself and gave the other to me, for just such an occasion."

"Intriguing, then, that it doesn't work now."

"Yes, sir, it was annoying. I did offer to bring in a locksmith or even break the lock, but Lady Marjorie preferred a less destructive approach—and was also worried about the master's extended absence. That's why she requested help from Scotland Yard."

It had been an unlikely caller to 221B Baker Street that prompted this entire episode. Holmes and I had been ensconced in the morning papers, enjoying our mid-morning repast, when we heard the bell downstairs. Within moments, Mrs. Hudson had shown the tall, but stout, figure of Inspector Bradstreet into our parlour.

Dropping his paper on a side table, Holmes had risen and met the policeman with some enthusiasm, possibly hoping for another intriguing quest. "Ah, Bradstreet, to what do I owe this pleasure? I do hope something hasn't befallen young Hatherley again?"

"No, Mr. Holmes, nothing like that," Inspector Bradstreet replied, though his demeanour showed a touch of embarrassment at approaching Holmes for assistance. "I've been assigned to a queer case in Kensington, at the residence of Sir Sheldon Tallinger."

"Tallinger?" replied Holmes, shaking his head, "I can't place him."

"Nor I," I piped in. Searching my mind, I failed to find any notable information about the man in my memories from reading the society pages.

"No, quiet family, keep to themselves. Retired from military service, went into some sort of manufacturing business. Retired from that now, as well. It seems to be his normality that's the key."

"Why do you think that?" Holmes asked.

"You'll see when we get to his house."

Within half an hour, we found ourselves standing in the Tallinger house, looking at the strange design on a stubbornly locked door.

"I had one of my best men here," said Bradstreet. "Tried everything, even pulled the faceplate off, but the locking mechanism is stuck fast. I suggested to Lady Marjorie that we may need to break through the door, but she insisted we do everything we can to avoid that. I know that it's probably a simple mechanical problem, but given that symbol, plus the fact that the lock is not that old and seems completely undamaged, I thought you may have some insight."

"Hmm, I will admit that I'm not as intrigued as I thought," said Holmes, his patience a little strained as such a seemingly simple problem. Shrugging, he drew out his lock-picks and set to work. After several moments, and several murmurs and harrumphs, Holmes packed them away and stood staring at the lock.

"Anything, Holmes?" I asked.

"I reverse my previous comment. This is intriguing. None of my picks went even close to opening this one." He looked at the key once more and shook his head slightly. "Yes, from the arrangement of the tumblers within, this is indeed the key to that lock." Inserting it again, he jiggled it several times, before withdrawing it once more. Shaking his head, he said, "This is extraordinary. The key fits. The lock is in good condition. There is no mechanical reason for it not to work." Grasping the doorknob, he turned it and pulled. The door didn't move even slightly. Letting go, he said, "The only way to get through this door is to remove the lock altogether, but I'm not even sure that will work. We may have to break the door apart."

"Even if you tear the wall down, you will never enter that room." The voice that spoke had a deep, resonant tone, one that suggested compliance without any tinge of force.

All three of us spun to face the speaker. I would have placed him in his mid-thirties. With a plain, smooth face, and shock of dark hair, but it was those eyes that held me. There was an intensity in his virtually unblinking stare that drew my gaze to his and held me there until I forced my sight away.

It was Bradstreet who broke the spell. "Who are you, sir? How did you arrive here?"

"And more to the point, what did you mean by saying we will never enter this room?" asked Holmes, his tone less forceful than Bradstreet's.

"To answer the Inspector's questions first. I am Simon Iff. I was invited here by Sir Sheldon."

"When?" interjected Bradstreet, "And where is Sir Sheldon?"

“It was only this morning. And if the message was clear, Sir Sheldon resides within that room.”

“What?” sputtered the Inspector, “How could he have messaged you? If he’s in this room, he hasn’t left for days.”

Iff replied, with a calm, but assertive voice, “That is true. His spirit visited me and asked me to assist. We are associates.”

“His spirit?” cried Bradstreet, “What twaddle. Are you some sort of spiritualist? Come here to prey on Lady Marjorie and Sir Sheldon, or something?”

Holding his hands before him palms up, Iff shook his head and said, “I assure you, Inspector, I am neither a spiritualist nor a charlatan. I do, however, know what that symbol is. It is a unicursal hexagram. We use this particular version as a potent locking mechanism, but only in extreme circumstances. Even with all your intelligence and experience, I doubt you would even be able to break its spell.”

“Spell?” Bradstreet’s voice had risen in pitch to the point where he might lose all control if left unchecked. Thankfully Holmes stepped in at that moment.

“Inspector,” he said, snapping Bradstreet’s attention to himself, “You know me as a man of logic and science. I would have no truck with any self-proclaimed spiritualist or magician, but on the odd occasion I am happy to let someone of that ilk have their time in the sun, if it proves useful.”

“What are you suggesting?”

“Let Mr. Iff here break this so-called spell and allow us entry into the room beyond. If he fails, then we send him on his way; if he succeeds, then we have gained. He has asked for no money.” Turning to Iff, he asked, “I assume you would not ask for recompense?” When Iff shook his head, he added, “Then what is there to lose?”

“Fine.”

Smiling, Iff stepped up to the door, examining almost every inch in the same way that Holmes had only moments before. After a minute or two, he dropped one hand into his pocket and brought out a small metal rod, with a crystal attached to one end. Placing the device in the centre of the flower, he closed his eyes and bent his head forward. A deep murmur arose from Iff, as he spoke in a strange language for several minutes, occasionally moving the device to the six points of the hexagram, then back to the centre.

It was on the third rotation of the metal wand around the hexagram, that a sharp, metallic *click* echoed out from the door. Grasping the doorknob, he turned it and pulled the door open. A breath of stale, foetid air blew up from the dark basement below.

"Candles," Bradstreet yelled at the surprised butler, who rushed off and quickly returned with two fully lit candelabras. Snatching one for himself, Bradstreet hurried to the head of the staircase and began the descent.

I offered to take the second, leaving Wilson on the ground floor, rather than force him to follow us into the bowels of the house.

Trailing after Holmes, I stepped carefully down the steep staircase, and into the chamber below. Bradstreet found the nearest gas lamp and lit it, throwing light across the room.

"GoodLord," I gasped, at the sight of a man lying in the middle of the dusty floor.

"Watson, would you be so good as to test for life signs? Be careful not to disturb anything that may help my investigation, though," asked Holmes.

Handing him the candelabra, I dropped to my knee next to the body. Placing two fingers on his neck, I waited. Nothing. Leaning over I listened intently at his mouth. Again nothing. Foolishly I hadn't brought my bag, leaving it for several home visits I needed to undertake in the afternoon, so turned to Holmes and asked to use his glass. Holding it against the man's mouth, it remained clear for some time.

Shaking my head in sorrow, I gave the glass back to Holmes, before placing my hand on the man's forehead. It was still warmer than the room temperature. Finally, I stood, my head hanging slightly.

"I believe we are too late. This man has no pulse or breath, but he is still warm. I can only conclude that he died almost within the last hour or so."

"Damn," said Bradstreet, "That damn stupid door. We could have saved him. How will I break the news to Lady Marjorie?"

Holmes continued to gaze at the man, without a change in expression. As if staring at a curiosity rather than the corpse of a man who had breathed his last so recently. "Have you nothing to add, Holmes?"

"Not yet, Watson, not yet. You say that he was alive while we were still toying with that infernal door?"

"Possibly, he may have perished just before we arrived. Why?"

"Well, I think he's been lying here for quite some time, possibly ever since he entered the basement and locked that door."

"Why?"

"There are several candles scattered around that have burnt out, and there's a light covering of dust on his person."

I looked back and realised he was right. He had lain completely still for some time to accumulate such a covering. "If he'd been there for so long, why did he only just die?"

"Of that I am unsure." Pointing to the floor beneath the body, Holmes added, "And this design inscribed on the floor. It seems similar to the unicursal hexagram on the door. What do you make of it, Iff?" We both turned to look for the stranger but found no one else in the room.

"I could have sworn he followed us down here."

"I also," said Holmes, "How peculiar."

"I apologise, I was too concerned with the body to take any notice of that man," added Bradstreet.

Glancing around the room, I finally took in the full details around me. Behind us was a large bookcase filled with thick leather-bound texts, and an array of strange objects, some similar to the metal wand that Iff had used. Before the bookcase was a desk, covered with open texts and loose sheets. Moving closer I recognised a diagram of the unicursal hexagram. "Here, Holmes, these may help."

Stepping up next to me, Holmes scanned the open documents and said, "They may, except for the strange language they are written in. I would need to seek out one skilled in that script." Looking closer at the texts I realised what Holmes was on about. Beneath the various diagrams were blocks of text written in a strange form of lettering, which may have been another alphabet, or even some strange form of code.

***

While Bradstreet oversaw the arrival of the coroner's wagon, and the removal of the body of the poor unfortunate Sir Sheldon Tallinger, Holmes and I undertook interviews with the house-staff. As far as we could see, there was only Wilson and Charles, Sir Sheldon's valet, on duty in the house. The latter provided a spark of interest in Holmes's mind.

"Do you find it a little peculiar that there are only two house staff? And no cook? Especially in a house of this size, with an ageing matriarch such as Lady Marjorie."

"I feel that retirement has not found Sir Sheldon in the best of times, so to speak."

We found Charles downstairs in the laundry, shining SirSheldon's shoes, and pressing his shirt and suit. From my observations, Charles looked like a man who'd spent quite a deal of time, the previous evening, imbibing at one of the local pubs. His eyes were downcast and half-closed, his movements slow and stilted, as if to avoid any head shaking.

"If I were you, I'd find some time to yourself and have a good lie down. You could also try placing a wet cloth with a little vinegar sprinkled on it, across your forehead," I said."Should relieve a little of that pain you're feeling."

The valet slowly looked up from his duties, his eyes crossing both of us in a confused manner. "You're not police, are you? What have I done now?"

"Nothing, as far as we know, but what do you think you've done?" asked Holmes.

Dropping his head, the valet stared down at the clothes laid out before him and said, "I don't know what I'm even doing now." He pulled a stray piece of lint from the lapel of Sir Sheldon's morning coat, and added, "I'm preparing a dead man's suit for his funeral, but I feel like I'm preparing my dismissal from this house." Shrugging and turning towards us, his eyes slightly damp, as well as bloodshot, he added, "I'm sure I saw him last night. It could be the drink, but he was outside the house, large as life. And then this morning Mr. Wilson says he's dead." Thumping the bench with his fist, he exclaimed, "What's to become of me now?"

Trying to calm the poor man, I said, "I'm sure that Lady Marjorie will ensure you are taken care of, at least in the short term. You were Sir Sheldon's valet, is that right? That leaves you in good stead for another position with a suitable gentleman."

"I'm also his driver. I also help out Mr. Wilson, as footman, and between the two of us, we take on the cooking duties. It's the only way we get fed."

"Ah, a man of many talents then," said Holmes, "Did Sir Sheldon step out on many occasions? Perhaps to his club, or some other societies?"

Thinking for a moment, Charles wiped his moist eyes on his sleeve, before answering. "He didn't frequent any clubs. Lady Marjorie put a stop to that a few years ago. I heard they couldn't afford the memberships. Of late, Sir Sheldon's only excursions were to the temple."

"Temple?"

Staring at the blank wall opposite for a moment, "The Herminatic Order of the Yellow Dawn, or something like that. Had me drop him off in a rundown building off the Clapham high street, Nelson's Road, or something. He'd be there for hours, a couple of times a week."

"Do you know what he did there?" I asked.

"No. I wouldn't stay around. He told me to be back at a certain time, so I'd go down the pub or come back here, there's always things to be done here. He never discussed anything. I suppose you could ask Lady Marjorie, but pretty sure she wouldn't know either."

I could see Holmes thinking for several moments and could only imagine the cogitations going on inside that brain before he asked another question. "You mentioned that you saw him last night, but surely you knew he was locked in his basement room."

Glancing up into Holmes's passive countenance, Charles paused for a moment, collecting his thoughts, before answering. "I... I know it was probably the drink, but I swear I saw Sir Sheldon outside in the yard. It was late and a dense fog had rolled in. I'll admit I'm lucky I managed to find my way back inside the house. I'd had a few at the Ladbroke, down in Notting Hill, and made my way down the back alley. Pitch black it was, but Mr. Wilson always leaves a light on in the kitchen, just in case. It was when I opened the rear gate that I saw him. He was moving around the yard. At first, I thought he was a burglar or something. I shouted at him, but he just ignored me." Taking a deep breath, he paused once more. "And he was glowing. That's the only way I knew it was Sir Sheldon. He turned around, and looked straight through me, but I could see his face as plain as day. He seemed lost. Looking at him filled me with sadness. Like I'd lost all hope. Then he just disappeared. Took a while for my eyes to adjust back to the darkness, but all I could hear was my heart thumping in my chest. I made my way inside as fast as I could, went to bed and hid under the blankets. By this morning I'd recovered, but I'll never forget that look on his face. And now I'll never see his face again."

When Charles hung his head once more, staring at the suit before him, Holmes and I mumbled our thanks and left him to his sorrow.

"What do you make of that, Holmes?"

"Intriguing Watson, intriguing. There's nothing to say that our victim wasn't playing a prank. You have estimated the time of death, so it would seem that Sir Sheldon was alive at the time Charles arrived home. That's if he even saw anything other than a vision formed of his alcohol intake." Glancing down the tight corridor, Holmes added, "I wish to return to Sir Sheldon's basement room. There's more to see in there, I think."

"I need to leave, as I have several errands to attend to and patients to visit this afternoon."

"Very good."

***

It wasn't until morning on the following day that I laid eyes on Holmes once more. His slow movements and red-rimmed eyes, with dark shadows beneath them, told me he'd had a very late, and sleepless night.

"Are you well, Holmes? You look as if you've patrolled the streets all night after some felon or other. I've warned you about these late nocturnal endeavours."

Sitting and waving away my protestations, Holmes fixed himself a cup of coffee, downing and refreshing it quickly before he finally found the focus to reply. "I spent all yesterday afternoon and evening at the Tallinger house, before taking to the streets in search of answers."

"Did you find any?"

"Yes and no. The questions that keep arising are the most troubling aspect."

"Fill me in then. What happened?"

"After you left, I waited with Bradstreet as the coroner arrived, made his assessment, then removed Sir Sheldon's body to the morgue. There was nothing more either of us could add, though the coroner did come to a similar conclusion as yourself."

"And that was?"

"The poor man died within hours of our arrival. A thermometer confirmed that his body temperature was still quite high, in light of the cool nature of the room. He applied similar techniques as you, listening with a stethoscope for any heartbeat or breath. There was no indication of life. The internal examination will be performed later today, so hopefully, a cause of death will be found."

"Damn shame we weren't quicker then."

"Perhaps." He drew another sip of coffee. "When all had left, I spent the next few hours poring over Sir Sheldon's papers and books."

"From my cursory inspection, he was dabbling in the black arts or some such."

Holmes chuckled. "Not quite. I tried not to take too Christian a view of the works in his possession, but rather a more disconnected look. The books and papers were not of some satanic nature, but of an obscure religious doctrine which is being discussed by some, apparently, under the suggested title of Thelema. Some texts that you saw were in a strange language, others were in English, German and French."

"Thelema? What nonsense is that?"

"It appears to be one of the more esoteric of the new wave of religions that have arisen over the last few decades. Thelema is not yet a full 'philosophy', but an undercurrent which draws on several ancient ideas, from the Egyptian, Greek, and Eastern yoga, and the more modern Qabalah. The ideals behind the movement are not that far removed from Christianity, Judaism or even Islamism. It's the practice that has changed."

"In what way?"

"The open texts on Sir Sheldon's desk point to several rituals whereby the practitioner can seek a higher plane of consciousness through meditation, incantations and the use of herbs, or medicines."

"Drugs?"

"Oh, yes. That may be the key that the coroner will need to seek out. There were many pots of burnt herbs scattered around and containers of powders and liquids on several shelves that would need examining. Probably only stimulants, but possibly poisonous in nature, which could account for Sir Sheldon's demise. I have sent a note to Bradstreet to have them examined."

"Have you drawn a solution?"

"Not as yet, but I feel that Sir Sheldon undertook a course of stimulants, then dropped into a meditative state in search of this higher plane of consciousness. During that experiment, his body gave up and he died, possibly after a few days of oblivion."

"Horrible."

"Yes, but even more disturbing, I'm not completely convinced that he is actually dead."

"What?" I blurted out, horrified at the suggestion.

"It was while I sat reading through those strange texts," Holmes began. "The room grew colder, even though Wilson had stoked a fire for my convenience. Looking up, my sight was drawn to a cloud of fog that had formed in one corner of the room. Perplexed, I studied the mist as it collected and coalesced into an almost human form. The figure floated gently across the space, coming to rest in the centre of that strange symbol. It did not become distinct enough for me to ascribe any identity to it but stayed for several moments before simply vanishing."

"A ghost? You're describing a ghost? Impossible."

Waving my protestation away, Holmes continued. "Highly improbable, I would say, but until we have proof that such cannot exist, I would not call it impossible. As we know there are many strange occurrences in this world, many we have investigated ourselves. Most are a result of simple natural causes, but some have evaded explanation."

"But, you're saying that this spectre—Ghost? Vision?—is Sir Sheldon's spirit?"

"Not exactly in those words, but such is implied in my readings of the Thelema texts completed so far. The adherents of the religion practised a form of meditation that enabled their spirit to escape their physical form and wander the world." Holding his hands palms up before him, he added, "Now, I cannot imbue any credence in that philosophy without further data, so I feel I need to investigate until I can dismiss or prove its existence. In all probability, it was simply a parlour trick involving light and the thick clouds of dust in that room."

"Highly irregular," I said. "But why do you believe that Sir Sheldon is still alive?"

"Ah, that also lies in the texts. There is an explanation that the meditation process, coupled with herbs and other substances, will lower the respiratory system to that of complete hibernation. The effect is that the person will appear, in all regular circumstances, to be dead."

"Preposterous, I examined him myself. So did the coroner."

"Yes, but think back, for how long did you search for a pulse?"

"About thirty seconds. No need after that."

"And breath?"

"The same."

"Did you know that a hibernating bear will breathe once every minute? The heart follows the same pattern, beating only once the animal breaths. If we assume that Sir Sheldon had fallen into a hibernating state, then it is possible that his respiratory system is following the same pattern."

"But…I…that…"

"No need to be incensed, Watson, it is a reasonable suggestion and no smear on your professionalism. It would also account for Sir Sheldon's body temperature at the time." Downing the remainder of his coffee, he stood. "I have sent an urgent telegram to Scotland Yard, but have heard nothing. It is my imperative to seek out the coroner and stop Sir Sheldon's autopsy." Checking his watch, he added, "I just hope we are not too late."

***

At the Yard, we learned from Inspector Bradstreet that Sir Sheldon had been taken to the Royal Brompton Hospital in Chelsea—and that a warning not to begin the autopsy had indeed been despatched, as Holmes had requested. Bradstreet was a little concerned with our presence, and our questions, and chose to accompany us.

Sadly, the coroner was not present when we arrived, forcing us into an interminable wait seated nearby. Bradstreet attempted to hurry up the proceedings by plying the interns and nursing staff with questions, but none seemed to possess any knowledge of the workings within the morgue.

To pass the time, Holmes filled Bradstreet in on all that he had discovered. By the end, the Inspector's face was aghast in horror.

"What you are suggesting is preposterous," he said.

"Echoes of my words," I added.

"As I told Watson, I will not discount anything until I have proof. Much of what I read suggests that Sir Sheldon placed himself into a drug-induced hibernation. All other aspects should have logical solutions which can be established at a later date. For now, the unfortunate victim is our primary concern."

Just as Holmes finished, movement at the end of the corridor caught our attention. Thankfully, it was the same coroner from the previous day, followed by two burly interns who carried a stretcher between them. The bulging of the sheet over the stretcher indicated another unfortunate soul was on his way to the morgue.

As the coroner drew close to us, he stopped and said, "Inspector Bradstreet? Mr. Holmes?DoctorWatson? To what do I owe this pleasure?"

Holmes butted in before Bradstreet could begin. "Sir Sheldon? I have reason to believe he has not passed but is in a deep hibernating state." Pausing for a moment, he added, "I simply hope I'm not too late and that you haven't undertaken an autopsy as yet."

Strangely, the coroner's face broke into a wide grin. "Remarkable that you are here. I stayed late last night to catch up on my workload. Staring down at Sir Sheldon's reposing form, I held my knife above his chest ready to press it into his flesh, when his mouth opened, and he took one long deep breath. To be honest, I was flummoxed. Snatching up my stethoscope, I stood and listened for almost a minute before a single heartbeat echoed from his chest. I've never seen anything like it in my life."

Relief flooded all three of us.

"Where is he now?" asked Holmes.

"We've moved him to a private ward. A doctor has been assigned, with nurses keeping an eye on him around the clock."

"Any change in his condition?" I asked.

"Not as far as I know, but for now it is out of my hands. I was going to drop by later. He's in ward 2C."

After the coroner left, we followed Inspector Bradstreet to the ward. He found the attending doctor and plied him with questions while we stayed back and waited. Finally, Bradstreet joined us.

"I think every person in this hospital finds it remarkable that Sir Sheldon is still alive," he said. I noticed a wry smile on Holmes's lips.

"What are their plans for him?" he asked.

"Well, he is stable, if unresponsive. They feel that he has slipped into a stupor, from which he may or may not emerge. Until they can observe him for several more days, then they are not concerned." Shrugging, Bradstreet added, "My next course of action is to return to Kensington and inform Lady Marjorie." Glancing back at the bedridden man, he added, "Though, I am unsure if having her husband in this vegetative state for some time will be better or worse than having him simply die. I have known of others like this. They simply hang on to life for years, causing nothing but misery to their families with the unknowing."

"Yes, a sad state of affairs," said Holmes. "Though, I feel that we may be able to bring this to a conclusion in a much swifter manner. I need to return to Kensington myself. The answers lie in those arcane scripts of Sir Sheldon's."

"We can ride together, but I must make a short trip to Mayfair on the way. In fact, you may as well come with me."

"Why? Another case?" I asked, hoping that there may be more for Holmes to be occupied with.

"Yes. The sad passing of Sir Hubert Mumford, though from the report I received earlier today, there does not seem to be any foul play. The poor man simply had a heart attack overnight. I have heard he was old and rather portly."

***

"Who was he?" I asked Bradstreet, as we stood in Sir Hubert Mumford's study and watched the coroner's attendants remove the rather overweight figure from the room. Even though they were both well-built lads, they strained to lift the dead man's bulk onto the stretcher and carry it from the room.

"An industrialist. Owned and until recently ran Mumford's Gearing, an engineering business that had a large concern in the rail industry."

Holmes held up a hand to the attendants and asked, "Might I have a quick look at something?" They both groaned as they stopped, bending to place the corpse-laden stretcher once more on the ground.

"What in the devil are you doing?" asked Bradstreet.

"Won't take a moment," Holmes said, moving across to the stretcher and dropping to one knee. He drew the sheet down to reveal the final expression on Sir Hubert's face.

"Good Lord," I exclaimed. As the coroner had covered the body before we arrived, we hadn't been privileged to see the unfortunate man. The stark look of horror on his face was as disturbing as it was incredible.

"He looks like he was scared to death," said Bradstreet.

"That would account for the sudden heart attack, even with his obvious level of fitness."

"Why did you feel the need to look at his face, Holmes?" I asked.

Pointing to the far wall, Holmes said, "That certificate of business registration."

Stepping across I read the framed document, proudly displayed on Sir Hubert's wall. I gasped as I saw the name of the company. "*Tallinger and Mumford engineering*," I read out loud.

"Yes. I think with a little digging, we might find that Sir Hubert's business enterprise was once a partnership. Possibly one that changed recently to benefit him more than his previous associate."

"Sir Sheldon," said Bradstreet, "That's a little too much of a coincidence."

"Quite so," said Holmes, "I think now might be the appropriate time to speak with Lady Marjorie."

***

"He's alive? But, Doctor Watson," Lady Marjorie exclaimed, pointing towards me, "And the coroner. They both said my poor Sheldon was gone."

"Yes, it was only after a more detailed examination that life signs were found. He is being cared for at the hospital and I will keep you informed if there is any change in his condition," said Bradstreet.

Staring at the cups of tea, in light of the stunning news, I stood and suggested that Lady Marjorie may require something a little stronger. "Brandy?"

Glancing up towards me, a slight wetness in her eyes at the hope her husband would be well again, she nodded. Looking around I noticed Wilson was not in sight, probably off undertaking another of the myriad tasks he would need to fulfil given the lack of staff. Moving to a nearby sideboard, I was delighted to find a small set of glasses and bottles hidden away from sight.

Pouring a stiff drink for our hostess, I brought it back and was surprised to see it vanish in one gulp. "Thank you, Doctor, my heart is still fluttering," she said before holding up a hand, "But I think that should do me for now."

"I'm sad to say, though, Lady Marjorie, that our visit here is not all good news," began Bradstreet, "We have just come from the house of Sir Hubert Mumford."

"That cad," came a spiteful reply, seemingly out of character from the lady of the house.

"You know him then?" asked Holmes.

"Yes, I know him." She held the glass out towards me, "I think I will have another; my mood has altogether changed."

I rushed away to pour another glass, while Bradstreet continued. "Unfortunately, Sir Hubert is dead. Possibly a heart attack," he added.

"Good riddance to bad rubbish," said Lady Marjorie, accepting the glass from me and downing the brandy in another swift drink. Pausing for a moment, she placed the glass down and looked at each of our stunned faces in turn. "Oh, don't think of me as so callous. Sir Hubert is no saint. It is because of him that we find ourselves in this parlous situation. All that my husband built up over so many years was spirited away by that man, leaving us near destitute in our dotage."

Glancing around the room, she added, "This house will be next. It is all we have left."

"Can you tell us what occurred," asked Holmes.

"Yes, I have let the cat out of the bag, so I must finish. My husband and Hubert built up Tallinger and Mumford Engineering over many years as partners. My Sheldon was older and reached a point where he believed he had earned the right to retire." She hung her head before the next statement, shaking it sadly before adding, "But Hubert was always the legal man. He drafted a contract with Sheldon to procure our half of the business. Thinking all was in order, Sheldon, my trusting Sheldon, signed everything without reading it. It wasn't until our accountant called to examine the books, that we even realised what had happened. That scoundrel had deposited only one-tenth the value of the company into our account. A mere pittance, but so easily disguised by dropping a zero from a figure."

Pulling a small kerchief from her sleeve, she dabbed at the corners of her eyes. The memory was obviously still very raw and painful. "We spent five years with lawyers and judges trying to overturn the contract. But, Hubert," her face screwed up as she said the name, "had employed better lawyers. The contract was unbreakable. The payment stood, but it only covered the costs of the legal representation. We were almost destitute. A life of toil washed away with too much trust and the stroke of a pen."

"My word," I said.

"I know it hit my Sheldon quite hard, not that he would say anything, mind, but I could see it in his eyes and in his stance, especially on days that found him more despondent than normal. He did talk of fixing things at times, but I knew my Sheldon, and I thought that meant only that he would find the money somehow."

Leaving Lady Marjorie, we spoke briefly in the entry foyer before Bradstreet bade us goodbye and left. I thought about joining him but instead followed Holmes to the basement room.

As he stepped up to the bookcase, overflowing with tomes, many showing their age, with aged and cracked leather bindings, I glanced around the room once again. With the body of Sir Sheldon now removed, I could clearly make out the design painted on the floor. It was similar to the unicursal hexagram we had seen on the door upstairs, but instead of a five-leafed clover in the centre, it sported a cross where each side was the same length.

"It's a simple design change. The Thelema religion seems to thrive on the hexagram itself, with the central motif instilling the usage. The cross seems to be of Greek origin, but I think that is just a coincidence. It could be a plus sign for all I can determine."

"Have you discovered what this Thelema doctrine believes to be the symbol's purpose?"

"Oh, yes, it is used as a doorway into the astral plane."

"The what?"

"The astral plane. The world between worlds, where the spirits live out existence once they have been shod of their earthly bodies."

"Surely you don't believe that."

A fey grin crossed Holmes's face as he stood staring at me. I began to feel uncomfortable as my mind raced that perhaps Holmes was buying into all this crackpot spiritualist guff. Finally, he spoke. "No, of course not Watson. Don't be foolish. There is nothing I have seen, nothing in these books and diagrams, that provides me with enough evidence to believe that a man's spirit can leave his body and walk amongst us."

"Good, good," I said, very relieved, "You almost had me there."

A strangely familiar voice echoed out of the far side of the room. "You might need to rethink that position when I'm done."

We both turned as one to see the same mysterious man from the previous day. "Ah, Mr. Iff," said Holmes, "I do hope you've come to return those items you seem to have borrowed."

"Very good, Mr. Holmes," Iff said, sliding a worn, leather-bound volume from a satchel slung around his shoulder. The book was plain except for the Roman numerals, XXXVI, embossed on the front cover. "You may not know the name, but this is *The Star Sapphire*, volume thirty-six of the intended sacred Thelema texts. Or it will be when Crowley and others have finished."

"I can only assume it is the volume that contains the spell used to resuscitate our poor unfortunate Sir Sheldon."

"Supposedly. Intriguingly enough, I've never seen it used. Sir Sheldon is the first member of our order to actually attempt astral projection. I discussed it with the head of our order, and he was most infuriated, especially when I pointed out that Sir Sheldon had *borrowed* several volumes of the sacred texts." Reaching into his satchel, once more, Iff brought out a metal rod with a small cross affixed to the top. "This is Sir Sheldon's personal magick rood. We all have one; you probably saw mine yesterday when I broke the spell on the door outside."

"I assume your order believes that those can channel your power, or some such."

A slight grin broke on Iff's face. "Yes, you could say something like that. Though I would have to assume that non-followers, like yourselves, would place as much faith in that idea as an antelope would place in a lion."

Holmes nodded, a sly grin on his face. "A curious analogy, but with merit. Why did you choose to return at this precise moment?"

"Ah, now that is interesting. Up until these last two days, I had very little to do with Sir Sheldon. I'm relatively new to our order, and I'm not exactly well set within polite society, but our head priest has taken me under his wing, so to speak, and has tasked me with developing certain deductive skills. One of the associated tasks is to undertake information gathering about other members. Sir Sheldon was one such member."

"Oh, yes," said Holmes, "And to what ends was this information-gathering exercise directed?"

"Nothing illegal, or even immoral by your standards, just precautions. Ours is a very new religion, and therefore comes under greater scrutiny, especially from more established theological organisations."

"Such as the Protestant and Catholic churches?"

"Precisely, so we need to ensure all our members are protected from any salacious inquiries."

"And what did you find out about Sir Sheldon?"

"Ah, yes, our poor Sir Sheldon. I'm only young, so do not have the experience to understand the pain of losing everything that you have worked for during virtually your entire life, but I can imagine an immense sense of despair and animosity has lingered inside Sir Sheldon over the last few years as events have played out."

"I agree. I've seen that sense of hopelessness play out in the most dramatic of ways many times. What more do you know?"

"I know that a certain Sir Hubert Mumford has passed away unexpectedly."

"Good Lord," I said, "How would you know that?"

"I have my ways, Dr. Watson."

"But you had nothing to do with it, I assume?" asked Holmes, his grin had vanished, replaced with a stern countenance.

"And I assure you, that I did not. The poor man was in ill health, his heart simply waiting for any chance to give up. It may or may not have been due to a spectral visitation from the subject of our discussions."

"Sir Sheldon?"

"Yes. I think his resentment towards Sir Hubert overcame him, and he resorted to means that few should even conceive of, let alone enact. The order has tasked me with bringing him to trial before them."

"How do you envisage doing that?" I asked.

"With your help, and that of Inspector Bradstreet's," Iff said, matter-of-factly.

***

"This is all very distressing," said Lady Marjorie upon hearing Iff's request, "I mean, I don't even know who you are, Mr. Iff."

"And that is fair, Lady Marjorie, I can only ask you to trust me, as a member of your husband's religious order. I truly believe that I can reverse the process that your husband has used, thereby bringing him out of his self-induced stupor."

The woman studied the younger man's face for quite some time until Holmes intervened.

"If I may, Lady Marjorie, at some point, I'm sure that Sir Sheldon would need to be brought home from the hospital, if not for financial as well as health reasons. He is in no danger, and his convalescence would be more assured in his own home."

Nodding, she said, "I can see that point. Especially from the financial. Though I'm a little livid at Sheldon for his foolishness."

"I would be more than happy to lend my services to ensure that your husband is made comfortable and well-cared for here," I added.

Heaving a large sigh, Lady Marjorie added, "Fine, then. I shall have Wilson prepare the spare room. I only have one request though; I wish to be present at this *ceremony*."

***

The next few hours were a flurry of activity.

While Iff went into the basement to prepare, Holmes and I journeyed to Scotland Yard to discuss matters with Inspector Bradstreet.

"Spirit? Ghost? Have you gone mad, Holmes?" Like myself, Bradstreet was incredulous when presented with Iff's story.

Holmes, in his inimitably calm way, preceded to soothe Bradstreet's initial anger. "Understandably, Inspector, this is all very peculiar, and I can appreciate your concern. Regardless of what this Iff character says, the delivery of some curative through the casting of this so-called spell may be what is required to restore Sir Sheldon to full health." Pausing for a moment to let Bradstreet decipher his intent, Holmes added, "Besides, we have questions for Sir Sheldon. The strangely coincidental death of his long-time business partner, for one."

"But the coroner himself has signed that off as a mere heart attack."

"And I wouldn't question his findings, but I'm intrigued by any outside forces that may have triggered that heart attack." Holmes took a deep breath, and I could tell that something was troubling him. "I must admit that I have investigated this Simon Iff and he is an enigma. His history is minimal, and the links to this supposed religious sect are vague at best. I don't understand his interest or even his motives in this matter."

"Yes, the Yard has been keeping a close eye on the Hermetic Order of the Golden Dawn for several months, especially an up-and-coming fellow called Crowley, who seems to be making his mark in their circles. Apart from improprieties due to the hedonistic nature of their gatherings, there's nothing we can actually pin on them from a legal perspective." A stern look crossed Bradstreet's face. "Do you think this Iff fellow can restore Sir Sheldon?"

"We can only try. From my reading of the texts, regardless of the religious significance, Sir Sheldon imbibed a strange concoction of toxins that rendered him into a state of deep hibernation, one that modern medicine treats simply as a prolonged stupor. There may be some restorative benefits to the reverse *spell* that is worth trying."

"Fine with me. I'll accompany you to the hospital and we'll arrange transportation. I'm sure they'd be happy to free up the bed."

Two hours later, an ambulance transported Sir Sheldon to the Kensington house, with the two orderlies settling him into his new room. Even with Bradstreet in attendance, we were wary of attracting too much attention to the goings-on and decided to move Sir Sheldon once the ambulance had departed, at which point I assisted Charles in moving his master once more into the basement.

As we descended, I spied Lady Marjorie sitting in a comfortable chair off to one side. I felt a tinge of anxiety over her presence, nothing to do with the subject matter, just the nature of what may happen to her husband.

Engaged in setting several pots of pungent herbs on each of the hexagram's points, Iff noticed our arrival and motioned for us to place Sir Sheldon on the floor, his head and feet positioned to run along the longest axis of the design. Iff placed the magick rood, which he had retrieved during his last visit to this room, on Sir Sheldon's chest, and moved away.

Charles left the basement, taking the borrowed hospital stretcher with him. I quietly moved across to join Holmes and Bradstreet, our eyes all focused on Iff, intent on watching the *ceremony* play out.

The adept of Thelema struck a match and lit each of the small bundles in quick succession, filling the small space with the cloying but sweet scent of the burning herbs. He moved and stood near Sir Sheldon's head, before extending his arms and speaking in some strange, unknown tongue.

"*Fahf adept mgep epgokafahf shuggog*."

I held back a slight chuckle. The guttural tone of this strange language was almost comical in the way Iff uttered it. Holmes turned and gave me a slightly angered glance, before turning his eyes back towards Iff as he continued.

"*Throdog ehye. Hafh fahf shuggoth back l' h' orr'enah ahna. H' uh'e h' gotha nogephaii. H' ymg' ah nyth'drn. H' ahor uh'eor ahnyth ph'nglui h' bthnk*."

Pausing for a moment, Iff threw his head back, his eyes closed, beseeching whatever pantheon of Gods his religion venerated.

"*Nogephaii h' hai!Nogephaii h' hai!*" This last incitement shouted much louder than the rest.

I still swear that the lights dimmed somewhat as if a dark pall or cloud enveloped the room. Then a brightly glowing orb of blue light shone out from the far corner of the room. I know I gasped, and I could hear others inhale in astonishment.

The glowing sphere grew until it was the size of a football. It moved across the room, floating halfway between floor and ceiling, and headed towards the prostrate form of Sir Sheldon.

As it hung in the air above the body, Iff proclaimed another stream of unintelligible words. "*Vulgtmnah ulnah ahf' ymg' ah hai. Nogephaii h' l' c'*."

Slowly, the orb descended towards the body. Casting a dull blue glow across Sir Sheldon's pallid skin, before touching his chest and sending waves of blue light into his body. Dropping further, it seemed to enter his body, and within a moment, the globe disappeared completely, leaving only the strange blue glow on Sir Sheldon's skin.

"*Ymg'ah ehye ephaii,*" said Iff, his voice softer. He moved around and knelt near Sir Sheldon's chest, lightly tapping him on the cheek. "Sir Sheldon. Wake up. You are back in your body."

As shocking as the blue orb had been, what I witnessed next shocked me even more. The eyes of the man, who only yesterday I had pronounced dead, fluttered, and opened.

Their gaze flicked around the room, before finally settling on the face of the man above him.

"Iff?" Sir Sheldon croaked. "What in blazes are you doing here?"

"Welcome back, SirSheldon, now please take your time to gain your senses once more."

"Take my...?" said the older man, as realisation dawned on his face, "Oh, Lord, I did the Star Sapphire spell didn't I?" When Iff nodded, Sir Sheldon dropped his head and muttered, "Damn fool. What was I thinking?" Holding out an arm, he told Iff to help him to his feet. Standing unsteadily, he scanned across the faces in the room. "Who the devil are these fellows?"

Iff quickly introduced us, but Sir Sheldon only had eyes for his poor, unfortunate wife. Taking one step forward, he held out a hand towards Lady Marjorie. "Oh, Maggie, I'm so sorry, I've been such a fool. I believed I could change things, or at least find out how to get our money back." It was then his head snapped back towards the three of us, realisation dawned on his face. "Holmes? The Detective? Bradstreet? Scotland Yard?" His mouth dropped open. "Is he dead? I think he spied me. The last I saw of him, was his hands clutching at his chest. Then I was lost to the void once more." Grasping at Iff's shirt lapel, Sir Sheldon's eyes bulged as he asked once more, "Is he?" As Iff nodded slowly, Sir Sheldon gasped, "What have I done? Even he didn't deserve that." Suddenly, he let out a groan, his hands leaving Iff and grabbing at his chest, as his face screwedup in excruciating pain.

The old knight dropped to his knees with a sickening *crack* before toppling forward. I ran to my medical bag, which I'd made sure to bring this time, not wanting a repeat episode. Dashing back to the fallen man, I urged Holmes or Bradstreet to roll him onto his back. Listening for a much longer period, my head dropped when there was no evidence of a heartbeat.

"Damn," I mumbled under my breath, before reaching into my bag for a syringe. I'd read of small doses of nitro-glycerine being used for the treatment of heart attacks and kept a dose for just such an emergency. Even after the needle emptied into him, Sir Sheldon's body refused to comply. It was a miserable period of time during which I tried all manner of treatments to bring the man back to the land of the living, but this time my diagnosis was correct.

Finally, I turned towards his widow, shook my head slowly and said, "I'm so sorry, Lady Marjorie. There's nothing I can do for him this time."

Instead of an outburst of tears or wailing, she simply stood, looked down at the reposing form of her husband and said, "Damn idiot," before climbing the stairs and yelling back over her shoulder, "Wilson, it's dinner time."

To be honest, I was flummoxed. "Good Lord."

"I think she may have tired of Sir Sheldon's pursuit of Sir Hubert and had already grown comfortable with the fact he was dead or in a prolonged stupor before we brought him back to life, that is," said Holmes.

"Where's Iff?" asked Bradstreet.

Looking around the room, I was surprised to see that the young devotee of Thelema had disappeared. Holmes moved across to the large bookcase and indicated the now-vacant shelf.

"It's not just Iff that's disappeared," he said, "All the Thelema texts have joined him."

"He stole them?" asked Bradstreet.

"Well, according to Iff, Sir Sheldon had already procured them from the Temple, so technically Iff has simply reclaimed them."

Blowing out a lungful of breath in a long sigh, Bradstreet glanced around the area and said, "I have no idea what I'm going to write up about this little escapade. I can't even see an actual crime. Not one that my superiors would believe, anyway. That said, I can't believe what I saw here tonight. Blue lights. Spirits supposedly reinhabiting their bodies. Magic spells. None of it makes sense."

"Only if you look for the impossible," said Holmes. "At its simplest, we have a man who accidentally induced a stupor upon himself. One of his fellow compatriots knew the concoction of herbs that would bring him out of that stupor. The only problem was that the health of the subject was not great and he possibly suffered a heart attack because of it all and died."

"The lights?"

"I'm sure I could find evidence of some simple parlour tricks if you'd like me to investigate. They may have been set up by Iff when he was alone down here."

"Hmm. No matter; do so for your own interest's sake. What about Sir Sheldon's statement of causing Sir Hubert's heart attack?"

Shrugging, Holmes said, "In that, we have no physical evidence. There are no witnesses. Sir Sheldon believed he could leave his body to haunt Sir Hubert. Wishful thinking on his behalf, but pure coincidence is the more likely culprit."

"And Iff?"

"A charlatan, perhaps? But no reward was sought or given. The texts? Perhaps you could pursue him over those, but I feel that they probably do belong to the Golden Dawn. So, again, there does not seem to be any evidence of a crime. I doubt that Lady Marjorie would be willing to press any charges over the matter."

Bradstreet harrumphed, before saying, "I am embarrassed. I feel like a complete dolt. I brought you into this and simply wasted your time. I will think hard before doing such again."

"Don't worry yourself, Inspector. Though we haven't uncovered a crime, I have learnt so much about this strange esoteric religion and ideology that it has been worth my while. I may never use the knowledge, but am still richer for the experience."

"Good, then," said Bradstreet, though I did not feel that he was altogether satisfied. "I will give my condolences to Lady Marjorie before organising for the coroner to call again. "Good day, sirs, and I hope we meet on more favourable terms next time."

As we bid adieu to Bradstreet and listened to his footsteps climbing the stairs, I turned to Holmes and asked, "Do you believe anything you've just said?"

"Now, Watson, that's very cynical of you."

"I mean the blue lights. The whole spiritism thing. The magic spells. True or completely fake?"

"Now, you know me, Watson. I never discount anything until I have facts and evidence. I'm not even sure I will find evidence of chicanery, but I'm not even sure I want to. Perhaps leaving it at that will leave me hungry for more knowledge in future."

"The locked door?"

"That, I think, was a trick using magnets or some such. I'd need Iff's magick rood, to trigger off any hidden mechanisms within that door."

"And this Simon Iff character?"

"Ah, an intriguing man. Shows up at the most opportune times. Seems to possess information that he shouldn't. He's only young, but I think that he has an interesting future ahead. I certainly will be keeping an eye out for anything relating to him from this point on."

With that, we left. My last view of the basement was the unicursal hexagram with its even-sided cross drawn in the middle. A nagging feeling still clung to the outer reaches of my mind, that there was something lying just a little outside the knowledge of ordinary man in all this esoteric doctrine. Like Holmes, I wondered if we would ever again encounter Simon Iff, Thelema, or other members of the Hermetic Order of the Golden Dawn.

The Disappearance of Dr. Markey

It was in late July of 1887 that I found myself extremely occupied with quite a number of patients. Sherlock Holmes, however, found himself in quite the opposite situation. A dearth of interesting cases has plunged him into a drawn-out period of boredom, in which I caught sight of him, on many occasions, unclasping the catch of his neat Moroccan leather case containing the implements with which he partook of his horrid little habit.

Dismissing thoughts of Holmes and his addiction, I journeyed to the abode of Lady Marjorie Ingrum, a patient of mine. I had received a telegram earlier that morning that, even through the medium of the stilted printed word upon the sheet, instilled a feeling of desperation, a certain sense of urgency within me.

I was greeted by Townsend, Lady Marjorie's butler, and was quickly presented to the Lady in her sitting room. Even though she was almost twenty years my senior, her ragged appearance and drawn face made me think she was well into her seventies.

"Lady Marjorie," I exclaimed, moving across and dropping to one knee while taking her hands in mine. "Your telegram sounded frightfully urgent. What is the matter? Have you taken ill?"

A trail of tears scarred the heavy makeup she wore, lending a more sorrowful look to her appearance. A sad shake of her head. "No, Doctor, it isn't me that I've asked you here for." A glance upwards drew my stare in that direction. "It's my son."

As I helped Lady Marjorie ascend the stairs, she told me, "I haven't known what to do with him for many months now. Howard could keep the boy in train, but I've never been strong enough." I had never had the privilege of meeting Sir Howard Ingrum, as he passed well before Lady Marjorie became my patient, but his stern painted expression looked down from an assortment of vantage points around the house. "Wallace was always a willful child, and now in adulthood, is even more so. I know he's a layabout, and Lord knows I've asked him time and again, but coupled with a lazy coterie of so-called friends, he prefers an almost Bohemian existence to seeking out any form of practical application of his skills and talents."

Nothing that Lady Marjorie said came as any surprise to me. I met Wallace Ingrum on a few occasions, mostly as he passed by in the corridors of the house. He always presented an air of indifference or, as it seemed, intoxication, and I think we'd barely exchanged more than a few sentences. Each time he was as Lady Marjorie depicted: Regularly dishevelled, with dull eyes sporting dark shadows beneath them, and a pallid complexion as one who never ventured into the daylight.

It was even less of a surprise when I was led into the young man's bedroom to find him lying fully clothed on top of his bedclothes. The powerful smell of vomit assaulted my nostrils as soon as I entered. I reeled back slightly, before recovering and moving closer to the bed. The source of the rank odour had spilt down the other side of the bed and covered the floor.

Lady Marjorie coughed at the smell and pulled a kerchief from her sleeve. "That wasn't there when I last checked on him." Turning to her butler, she said, "Townsend, have Mary see to that, please." The butler bowed slightly and hurried off.

"How long has he been like this?" I asked, moving to the bedside, and retrieving a stethoscope from my bag.

As I placed the cup on Wallace's chest, Lady Marjorie said, "He came in late last night. A lot of banging and thumping. I could hear him all the way down the hall, and simply presumed he'd returned after an evening with those friends. It was Townsend that found him like this. I asked him to give Wallace a mid-morning call to try and get him to at least rise before midday, but this morning he was unresponsive. I was only relieved that he was simply sleeping and not . . . ."

Her voice trailed off as she suppressed a sob. Turning to catch her expression, I grew concerned for her almost as much as my patient. "Is there something more?"

Nodding, she added, "Yes. I think it's the cocaine."

“He’s a user then?” I asked, turning back, and reaching for the man’s wrists. There were a substantial number of puncture wounds on the underside of his left forearm, a sure sign that he shared a similar habit with my compatriot at home. Scanning the area, I noticed a small glass syringe lying in the shadow of the bed. From its position, I surmised it had dropped to the floor then rolled out of sight.

I checked the man’s chest and noticed a severely accelerated heartbeat, to the point that I was surprised I couldn’t hear the thumping without the aid of my instrument. I placed my hand on his forehead. He was burning up. “Can you ask Townsend to fetch some cold water and some flannel cloths? We need to get Wallace’s temperature down as far as possible.” When Lady Marjorie left, I set about stripping the young man down to his undergarments. The room had a single window, so I drew the curtains, lifted the windowpane, and threw open the shutters. A slight breeze blew into the room. My hope was it could wash across the man’s body and cool him. The only other course of action was to introduce water into his system, but with him unconscious, I could do nothing on that front until he awoke.

Thankfully, Townsend returned in a few minutes, with a young housemaid that I assumed was Mary. Averting her eyes from Wallace’s half-naked form, she set about cleaning up the other side of the bed.

Retrieving the towels from Townsend and the bucket of water that he set down, I dampened and placed them on Wallace’s forehead and chest. By the time Lady Marjorie joined us, it was a simple wait until Wallace regained consciousness. If he showed no signs of recovery in the next hour, I would send word to the nearest hospital and have the unfortunate man moved.

As Mary left with the dirty water, Lady Marjorie asked her to bring tea. I believe it was more to help pass the time than to alleviate any thirst. Townsend brought a pair of straight-backed chairs and a small side table and finished setting them up when Mary returned with a tray laden with a teapot, cups, and a small plate of biscuits.

After Mary and Townsend retreated to the bowels of the house, I watched Lady Marjorie for a moment and noticed her eyes barely leave her unconscious son. Taking it upon myself, I played mother and poured out the tea, establishing the need for sugar and milk as I did so.

"He will be all right, won't he?" Lady Marjorie asked.

"I'm sure he will be." Holding the plate of biscuits out to distract her attention for a moment, Lady Marjorie unconsciously picked one from the plate and bit into it.

After several minutes of silence, broken only by the sound of munching and the clink of china, Lady Marjorie seemed to calm down, possibly in anticipation of her son's recovery. "I have to confess, Doctor, that you weren't the first physician I approached to help."

Intrigued, I replied, "Really? I didn't realise you were seeing anyone else."

"Oh, I don't. It's just that I received a pamphlet from another local doctor who specialises in helping those who overindulge in the drugs."

I thought immediately of Holmes and became even more curious. "What would this physician's name be?"

"Dr. Dermid Markey. He has a practice just south of the River in Brixton."

"But he couldn't help you?"

"No. None of my telegrams were replied to. I stated just as much urgency and almost sent Townsend in person to seek out Dr. Markey's help, but then thought of you."

"I can only assume that Dr. Markey was simply detained elsewhere. It would seem peculiar that he didn't deem it appropriate to at least answer your telegrams."

"I was a little disappointed. From the word amongst my friends, he is very diligent, and quite against this whole epidemic of drug usage, especially amongst the younger generation. I had hoped he wouldn't just save my Wallace and help him recover, but could aid him in overcoming this compulsion to take these nefarious substances."

Thinking of my own version of Wallace sitting at home in Baker Street, I had to agree, and could only hope to find this physician and have him visit Holmes in the near future. I plied Lady Marjorie with more questions, with a view of learning more about this Dr. Markey, and to keep her mind occupied on other thoughts while we waited to see if her son recovered.

***

"Yes, I have heard of this Dr. Dermid Markey," said Holmes, seemingly in decent spirits following a splendid luncheon prepared by Mrs. Hudson. There were no obvious effects from any addictive substances in his system, which pleased me no end.

I had returned to Baker Street after staying with Lady Marjorie until young Wallace showed signs of recovery. Starting with a small series of groans, and a flickering of his eyes, I diagnosed that he was beginning to return to consciousness. Removal of the damp cloths brought out a series of goosebumps when the calming breeze from the windows wafted across his bare skin. His heightened temperature had indeed receded, boding well for him. Deciding there was little more I could do in any practical way, I covered him with his bedclothes and bid good day to Lady Marjorie.

"I think the worst has passed. He will need to sleep the rest of the effects off, but there is little more I can do for now. I'm happy to drop by in the early evening if you like to see how he progresses," I said.

"That would be most thoughtful," said Lady Marjorie, very effusive in her tone now that her son was on the way to full recovery. "You are a Godsend, Dr. Watson. A Godsend."

"I am a simple physician. Assisting the poorly is my duty." With that, I returned in the hope of a late luncheon before more attendances in the afternoon.

"But I neither see any need to meet with the fellow, nor how that could even be possible," said Holmes, a wry grin on his face hiding some snippet of information to which I wasn't privy.

"I simply feel that you may find some benefit from his views on the use of certain substances," I said, nodding towards the contents of Holmes's case on show in the corner. As I noticed his eyes drift in that direction, then back, the last part of his statement made itself known to my mind once more. Confused, I asked, "What did you mean by possible?"

"Ah, well," he said, moving across to a pile of newspapers and rifling through them, before turning back with the issue he sought. Placing the paper down, he opened to a page with a small article titled, "Local Doctor Missing".

I read and was dismayed to find that Dr. Dermid Markey had gone missing over a week before. The article stated that the last sight of him was just before attending a callout. A single witness described the hansom he hailed, but the driver was wrapped up for cold weather, a fact I felt strange given the wonderful weather of the past month. Not a word had been heard of him since.

"That explains why Lady Marjorie had no word from him then," I mumbled under my breath.

"Who?" asked Holmes.

"A patient of mine. I have just returned from helping her son overcome a cocaine overdose."

"Careless," said Holmes, matter-of-factly.

"Quite." Pointing at the article, I asked, "You didn't see fit to investigate this?"

"Not beyond a cursory examination of the facts. I have had no contact with anyone interested in instigating a formal investigation, so there has been no need."

Desperately trying to hide my annoyance at Holmes, I mumbled, "It wouldn't have anything to do with his stance on narcotics and stimulants?"

"Not at all. I will admit I don't like the man's intentions. He wishes to outlaw or bring in a higher level of Government regulation on the availability of perfectly legal drugs." Taking a deep breath to control his rising emotional state, Holmes exhaled slowly then added, "I know you wish for me to stop my usage, but it is all perfectly legal, and I only partake to maintain a level of stimulation in my mind. Besides, the product of the coca plant has proved a boon amongst your professional comrades, virtually replacing the use of ether as an anaesthetic and increasing the safety of many medical procedures."

Not wishing to look him in the eyes, I glanced down at the newsprint once more. A snatch of information buried in the middle of the short article caught my attention. "Did you pick up on this fact?"

"What would that be?"

"Dr. Markey ran for parliament in the last general election."

"Yes, I believe he ran as an independent on a strict platform of drug reform. I think the article mentions the winning Member."

Reading further, I replied, "Yes, Sir Benton McBrough, one of Gladstone's liberals, a backbencher. I haven't heard much about him."

"One can't keep abreast of all of these Parliamentarians. Why are you so interested in Dr. Markey?"

Finally glancing up into Holmes's face, I said, "He's a fellow physician, so there's a natural bond there. From what Lady Marjorie told me, he is a bit of a crusader – a do-gooder, I suppose you'd call him. That drags me closer to him as well. The fact that he is missing disturbs me, and draws me to wish to find him, or at least find out what happened to him."

"Very noble, Watson," Holmes answered, examining my expression for a time, and forming some opinion in that complex mind of his. Standing, he clapped his hands together and said, "In that case, I will seek out the whereabouts of this Dr. Markey. Consider it a favour to you, my old friend."

With that he disappeared into his rooms, leaving me slightly astonished at his change of heart.

***

Never one to dawdle when the scent of a case was in the air, Holmes returned within minutes, ready to depart. Where I had no idea, until he expounded that we were to start at the beginning: The rooms of Dr. Dermid Markey.

Holmes was quite effusive during our hansom journey across the Thames and into the south of London. To my ears, it was partly a relief to see a break in his sombre and distant mood, but also partly a concern that his disposition was due to something other than just the likelihood of an interesting mystery to solve.

As we turned down Kennington Road, Holmes quipped, "We don't come as a pair into this part of the city very often."

"Am I to assume that you travel here by yourself then?"

"Oh, yes," he said, a sly grin on his lips, "There is a definite undercurrent of the ways and wherefores of the criminal underbelly writhing its way through the destitute backstreets of this area. I have spent many a night wandering and slinking my way around in search of information. I'm much happier to be entering the place in the fullness of the day, though. It can be a very rough area at night." He pondered for a moment, then added in a downcast voice, "Which sadly could account as a simple solution to our little mystery."

The cab turned into a small side street and pulled up before a modest two-story yellow brick terrace. A small wooden sign hung next to the front door, the names Dr. Markey and Dr. Carlton were inscribed upon it.

"He has a partner," I said.

"It would seem," replied Holmes. "This should be a good place to start then."

The front door led straight into the surgery's waiting room. It was filled with patients, together with the sound of coughing and the gentle murmurs of discomfort. The only light came from the front window and a sole gaslight affixed above the receptionist's desk.

Holmes strode across the short distance and stood before the young woman dressed in a simple nurse's uniform. I realised the practice was small enough to warrant the duties of nurse and receptionist to be undertaken by a single person. A simple nameplate sat on the desk, informing patients that the young girl's name was Nurse Jenny Calahan.

Within a moment, the lass looked up with a slight expression of surprise, possibly at our manner of dress or stature, and said, "We don't get such fine gentlemen around here too often. How can we help you?"

"Thank you, Nurse Calahan," replied Holmes. "We'd like to speak with Dr. Carlton if that's possible?"

"Is it a medical matter?"

"No. My name is Sherlock Holmes, consulting detective, I have undertaken to investigate the matter of Dr. Markey's disappearance."

"Oh, in that case, I'll see if I can catch him for you."

Just as she finished her statement, voices echoed from a nearby doorway. "Now, Mrs. Withers, please take one each day, and stay off your feet as much as possible. The swelling should go down if you do."

"Oh, I'll try, Doctor," came the reply, "but my 'Arold's a useless fool around the 'ouse, so nuffin' will get done if'n I's just lazing around."

"Fine, but please do try."

As the old woman appeared in the doorway, followed by a young, handsome man in a doctor's coat and carrying a small card with him, an elderly man stood and shuffled across to take the old woman's arm. As they waddled towards the exit, Harold said, "Now, Diedre why's you go an' say that to the doctor?"

"Oh, don't worry 'Arold, 'e knows you well, so it comes as no surprise to 'im."

"Still," finished Harold.

I watched as they exited, then turned back towards the doctor, who eyed Holmes and myself suspiciously.

"And you gentlemen are?"

Jenny piped up, "Oh, this is Mr. Sherlock Holmes, Doctor. He's come to ask about Dr. Markey."

Carlton popped the medical card down on the desk near Jenny and reached for the top one on a small pile nearby. Reading the card he said to us, "Well, I'm sorry, but my waiting room is full. Jenny here can book you in, but it may be some time."

Smiling, Holmes bowed slightly and said, "No problems there, Doctor. I can see you are busy. It is a matter of some urgency, as it's about your partner, but I'm happy to fit in with your schedule."

Regarding Holmes for several seconds, Carlton finally turned away and called out the name of the next patient. "Mr. Gareth Jones?" The call was answered by a scruffily dressed man standing. His actions were immediately met with a short coughing fit, garnering disgusted looks from others nearby. Once composed, he trundled off into the rear rooms, followed by Carlton, who gave Holmes one last look before joining him.

Seeing that there were now two seats free, Holmes stepped across and sat down. I quickly joined him, a little frustrated that we were going to have to wait, but interested in seeing how this particular medical practice operated. My observations were a little short-lived, however.

Almost as soon as he sat, Holmes garnered the interest of the old man seated to his left. He looked well into his seventies, but could have been young as sixty. His face was lined with deep wrinkles, and his weathered and sun-burnt skin looked similar to the cracked leather of an ageing couch.

"Did me ears hear right?" asked the man. "You're Sherlock Holmes?"

Looking him up and down, Holmes gave the man a quick examination, before answering. "Yes. Yes, I am."

"The detective?" Holmes nodded. "Don't you work with the Yard to bring down criminals?"

Smiling, Holmes added, "Yes, I do work with members of Scotland Yard from time to time."

"So what are ye here for? Not here for Carlton are ye? I hope not. He's been me doctor for a while now. Good man. Never had a problem with him."

"No, nothing like that. I'm here to ask Dr. Carlton a few questions."

"About any of us?" asked the man, his expression changing to a look of shock. I noticed at that point, many heads turning our way.

"Well, really I can't say. That sort of thing is private to the case at hand, and nobody can be ruled out until the evidence says they are innocent. Take you for instance. Your accent reeks of Newcastle, but you've been in London for a number of years, or you came from London initially and spent time in Newcastle." Holmes pointed to the man's hands. "You worked the mines. Your hands still have a deep-seated hint of coal dust deep in their pores. That, plus the yellow stains on your fingers, tell me you are a heavy smoker. Both could be the possible cause of why you are here."

The man looked flabbergasted, a common sight following one of Holmes's dissections. He coughed loudly for a few moments, bringing out a kerchief to capture the effluent.

It was then I noticed another man on the other side of the room who had been staring at Holmes quite intently stand up and head for the door.

"Mr. Smythe? You're next." said Jenny, standing and moving around her desk. "Do you not want to see the doctor now?"

"Oi'll come back later," he said, turning slightly, but keeping his eyes on Holmes. "It's a little too busy roight now." As the door banged shut, the other patients turned from staring at Smythe to staring at Holmes.

Shaking her head, Jenny turned and disappeared down the short corridor.

After she had gone, a lady sitting near to me piped up and asked Holmes, "Did you just say that nobody was innocent?"

Holding his hands up, Holmes said, "No, no, I assure you. I merely suggested that until all the evidence is gathered, one cannot rule out the guilt of any person involved. I am only establishing the facts of the case in which I'm involved, but the same concept applies."

That one statement had a galvanising effect on the conscience of the gathered group. Almost as one they stood and headed for the door. Within a couple of minutes, Holmes and I found ourselves alone in the waiting room.

I turned to Holmes and asked, "Did you plan that?"

A wry grin crossed Holmes's face, "How could I have known that the power of a guilty mind could outweigh all logic and reason?"

Before I could answer, Jenny stepped back into the waiting room. A look of shock came to her face as she spied all the empty seats. "What happened?"

"I think they had more pressing engagements," said Holmes.

***

"Well, you have my attention now," said Dr. Carlton, looking very aggrieved that his entire waiting room was now empty, "I have no idea how I'm going to recover the lost earnings that just walked out of here. We barely manage to make ends meet at the best of times."

"I can sympathise with you Dr. Carlton," I said. "I have a number of patients myself that can barely afford to cover the costs of any medications I prescribe before they pay for my services as well. I almost wish that the Government would step in and bolster the medical industry as a whole – to somehow make it affordable for all."

Cutting me off, Holmes added, "Yes, Watson, but you also have patients that could buy you many times over. They afford you a level of fee that, I presume, Dr. Carlton could only dream of." Turning his attention to Carlton, he added, "Again, I can only apologise so many times, but our true quest here today is to ask about your missing colleague, Dr. Dermid Markey."

Carlton sat back, an expression of resignation on his face, which told me he'd been through this all before. "I've told the police everything I know, which is nothing. The last I saw of Dermid, he was heading out on a call, and he never came home. Devastating to his wife, and very damaging to the practice."

"You don't seem too affected emotionally?"

"Well, I've only known him professionally."

"For two or three years, I'd say?"

Carlton looked astonished. "How did you know that?"

"You look about twenty-four years old, give or take a year. Standard medical training should take four years. Unless you are a prodigy, you would have started in your eighteenth year. You have the look of someone from a public-school background. The clothes under your coat are neat and tailored, but starting to wear, meaning you like to appear well-dressed, but are struggling to manage of late. Could be a consequence of this practice's turnover."

The doctor merely gaped at Holmes. I took that to mean his assessment was spot on.

"You mentioned that the practice has been struggling." Carlton nodded in response. "Do you think that Dr. Markey would have taken on a loan to supplement the practice's finances?"

Carlton shook his head. "No. What I have found of Dermid was his pride and insistence on taking every burden upon his own shoulders. I would never believe he would borrow money under any circumstances. Sometimes I consider that a foolish stance, but one I had to admire. Why do you ask?"

Shrugging, Holmes answered, "Just gathering indications of any untoward attention from the more nefarious members of society. What about competitors, enemies, or any disgruntled patients?"

Again, the younger doctor slowly shook his head. "If you were to meet the man, you'd almost call him a saint. His patients all returned to him, time and again, even with another physician not far from here. I didn't know much of his private life, but he never gave me any cause to think he was hated." Stopping, he considered for a moment before continuing. "There was one incident during that d--n foolish foray into politics."

"Yes?"

"A stone was thrown through the surgery window. No note. No follow up of any kind. We didn't think much of it at the time – just youths being reckless."

"Why think of it now?"

"Because it occurred about a week before the vote. We'd never had any other incidents, but, just now, that one stuck out."

"Were there any other incidents during the campaign?"

"Just the idiotic stance taken by Dermid's opponent." He stood and moved to a small window that looked out upon the street. "McBrough stood for several hours on that street corner and handed out free samples of cocaine to any passers-by. I must admit that I watched him between patients. Couldn't believe his actions. An aged politician treating a dangerous drug as if it were sweeties."

"Intriguing. I've always taken the acts of politicians with a grain of salt. They tend to look after themselves first, then their constituents."

"Quite."

"One last question I would ask is about this final call that Dr. Markey went upon. Was it one of his addiction cases?"

A slight nod of the head was followed by a sigh and, "Yes. Damn fool. He would drop everything to go help another of these hopeless cases. They always turn out bad. The patient was either dead or so far gone that he would never recover. If it was a positive outcome, then any fee we recovered was chewed up by the costs of medicines and implements. Dermid would never ask for extra to cover them."

Carlton shook his head. "I warned him it would all go wrong one day."

"How many overdoses did Dr. Markey attend – per year say?"

"Too many. One a week, sometimes two or three. Especially in this area, and down towards Brixton. The loss of time and money on such a quixotic pursuit drove me to distraction."

"And with him gone, you're feeling trapped here? Am I reading that right?" Once again that astonished look crossed his face. "I – I – " He hung his head and shook it slightly, "I can't lie. Yes, I've been making enquiries. Looking for a place in a practice north of the river. Somewhere more salubrious." Looking up, his face took on a haggard, tired expression. "If I stay here much longer, I'll end up like my patients in the waiting room. Old before my time. One foot in the grave, the rest of my life spent just counting down the days."

***

As we stepped into the waiting room, I was a little pleased to see a few more patients had settled in for their wait. Holmes moved across to the nurse and asked, "Would you have the address to which Dr. Markey was last requested?"

Jenny said, "Oh, yes, I do." She flipped pages in a small diary and ran a finger down a column of addresses and notes. "Here. 23 Angel Road in Brixton."

"Hmm. Not a nice part of town," Holmes muttered.

"And the strangest part is, it isn't the first time we've had a call there either."

"No?"

Flipping back a few pages, Jenny pointed to another entry with the same address. I noticed the date on the page was two weeks earlier. "Dr. Markey was on another call, so Dr. Carlton went instead." Her face turned slightly dour, "He wasn't a happy chappy when he returned. He was muttering about a waste of time and something about addicts. I found out later that there was no one home, almost as if it had been a prank. I did mention that to Dr. Markey, but he dismissed it as a misunderstanding."

"Did you tell the police about this?"

"Oh, yes," she said, shrugging, "Not sure they cared or looked into it. Always too busy, the police."

"Quite so. Did you consult them when the stone was thrown through the surgery window?"

"Oh, yes. A young constable came around. Took one look, took some notes. Mumbled something about wild youths in the street, then we never heard from him again. Typical really."

Nodding, Holmes stood still for a moment, thinking on this latest information before asking, "Do you know if Mrs. Markey is in?"

"You might be in luck. She's been in a right state. I think she's looking to go off to her sister's in Windsor for a few days. I have the address if you miss her."

Nodding, Holmes said, "Thank you. I believe that the Markeys live next door, is that right?"

"Yes."

"We'll check there, but return if we need that address."

"That will be fine."

Holmes walked away, while I maintained eye contact with the lovely nurse for a moment before joining him.

***

"Oh Lord, have you found him?" said the distraught looking woman who opened the neighbouring door.

"No, I'm sorry we haven't," said Holmes, "I assume then that you are Mrs. Markey?"

A confused look grew on the woman's face. "Why yes. Who are you?"

"I am Sherlock Holmes, and this is my colleague, Dr. John Watson."

"Sherlock Holmes?" said Mrs. Markey, "The detective?"

"The one and the same. Your husband's disappearance was brought to my attention, and I would like to offer my services in finding him."

"I don't have any money to pay you," the woman said, accompanied by a pained expression of embarrassment.

"And like your husband, at times I do not charge. I believe that he has been offering quite a public service, and I wish to do the same."

Mrs. Markey poked her head out further, her eyes darting frantically to and fro as she scanned the street before stepping back and allowing us entrance. "Please, come in then."

We were ushered into a small sitting room near the front of the house and took the seats offered to us. It was a sparsely furnished and appointed room, a single gaslight providing a trifling amount of illumination. Looking around, I noticed a single framed photograph on the nearby mantel. From the looks of Mrs. Markey in the portrait compared to the woman sitting opposite me, the photo was several years old. It was presumptive, but I took the other two people in the picture to be Dr. Markey and probably their teenage son.

"Now we do apologise for the intrusion," said Holmes, "but I felt the need to speak with you prior to continuing my investigation."

"Thank you for even considering it, Mr. Holmes. The last week has been horrendous. I've never felt more alone. My family are all in Windsor. I'm tempted to visit, but the cost . . . ." She trailed off at that point. I made a mental note that money was high on Mrs. Markey's mind, almost akin to the loss of her husband.

"Firstly, and I'm a little loathe to ask, but is there any reason that Dr. Markey may have willingly gone missing?"

"What do you mean?"

"Again, I'm sorry to ask, but perhaps a lover?"

Affronted, Mrs. Markey sat upright, in a posture of defiance. "Certainly not. Dermid and I are firmly committed to each other." Thrusting out her left hand, I noticed a beautifully crafted engagement ring, with a less ornate but striking gold Claddagh ring. It took me a moment to realise that Markey must be of Irish heritage. "We both wear the same wedding ring, as a way of showing our connection to each other. Dermid rarely takes his off, even when seeing patients." Taking a deep breath, she forced herself to relax before adding, "Besides, he simply wouldn't have the time."

"Ah, that was my next line of questioning. The public service he has taken on, to assist those that have succumbed to addiction and overdose – I assume by your statement that this occupies much of his time."

"Yes. It's a double-edged sword. I can only admire his stance and his actions, but in the same breath, I find it takes him away for so many hours each week. Time he can ill-afford."

"Why is that?"

"It has affected the practice. His paying patients are made to wait while he goes off to help the next unfortunate. As it is, we're only scraping through with the surgery and the house to support."

"Therefore, I can assume that your husband took on no loans to assist with finances?"

"No. He is far too proud to rely on others. He'd rather sell off our furniture before asking for charity."

"I see. Good. I just wanted to ensure that there could be no involvement of nefarious elements looking for recompense."

"Does your son still live at home," I butted in, "or is he making his way in the world? Does he contribute or assist his father?"

With that statement, Mrs. Markey's face became a veil of sorrow. Immediately, I realised my misreading of the photograph. The boy was obviously gone from this world, hence why she had never felt so alone.

Through the onset of tears, Mrs. Markey answered, "No. Jason left us three years ago. Fell in with the wrong crowd. Took to drink and opium. He became Dermid's first overdose patient, and Dermid's first failure. It's what drives him so. He never wants another family to face the devastation that we have."

We were left in silence for a few moments while Mrs. Markey recovered herself, drawing a kerchief from her sleeve to mop the small flow of tears. Finally she looked across at the family photograph, took a deep breath, and slowly exhaled. "It's why Dermid chose to try his hand at politics." Turning she glanced first at me, then at Holmes, "He wanted to take a stand against the proliferation of drugs in the community. He has tried to spread the word through his patients and his work with addicts, but believed that he would finder a greater voice from the floor of Parliament. Sadly, that wasn't to be."

"Yes, he lost to Sir Benton McBrough, I believe," said Holmes, "a long-time Liberal. A very hard task for any man, especially one new to the cut-and-thrust of politics."

"That is true, but he did quite well, almost unseating Sir Benton in the last election. Dermid still aspires to Parliament, and holds out hope that there may be a repeat of the last two year's instability."

"He would be one of the few, other than those unseated by Gladstone's defeat. I don't generally dwell on matters of politics, but I do remember some details of the campaign. Sir Benton spent quite a large amount of effort in undermining your husband's platform."

I piped up as I recalled Dr. Carlton's comment. "Didn't Sir Benton make a bit of a fool of himself by promoting the use of cocaine, and indeed giving some away for free? I thought it very strange at the time."

A surprising smile came to Mrs. Markey's face. "Yes, the man became a little obsessed – or should I say fearful – of Dermid's commitment. I never really took much interest, but some of my friends brought that little incident to my attention. Dermid and I both found it amusing, if not a little disturbing."

"Politicians," said Holmes, a thoughtful look on his face. "Most will do anything to gain or retain power."

***

After bidding adieu to Mrs. Markey, Holmes vowed to keep in touch with any information he uncovered, and we made our way to the high street. Luckily we found a passing hansom and asked to be taken to the Brixton address. The cabbie was very hesitant at first, but a promise of a higher fee soon had us on our way.

The cab pulled up in front of a series of run-down terrace houses and, from the lack of movement within any of them, abandoned.

"Are you sure this is the right address?" I asked Holmes.

He nodded, showing me the piece of paper. "As far as we know."

"Can we at least ask the cabbie to wait? I can't believe we'll be long."

"Oh, come now, Watson – where's your sense of adventure?" Holmes vaulted from the cab and strode across to the reason for our presence.

I stepped out and paid the driver, stopping myself from asking him to stay before he drove away. Looking around, I noticed that the area was a reflection of our destination. The houses weren't quite derelict, but close to it. The street was strewn with rubbish, and there was a distinct lack of carts or wagons. The only bright spot in the street was the modest-looking church opposite. A small sign read "St. John the Evangelist". The doors were shut, and the grounds quiet and vacant – not surprising for the time of the week.

Stepping up to the house in question, I found Holmes standing a few feet from the front door and examining the steps. As I watched, he pulled out his glass and leaned down, peering closely at the area.

"What have you found?" I asked.

"Something strange indeed." He stood up, replaced the glass, and pointed at the area of his concern. "Can you see?"

I examined the spot for a moment before it started to become clear. "My word," I said, dropping down for a closer look. The dust and grime on the step and stoop were quite thick, and as there was no mat on which to wipe one's feet, one could clearly see where the dirt had been disturbed – but only from a single pair of boots that I could see. "What does it mean?"

"I can only presume that, of late, only one person has visited this door." Pointing to the few steps leading up, he added, "And that person only approached the premises and never left. Luckily for us, there hasn't been any rain for the last week or so."

"But if the person entered, then he or she must still be inside."

"Unless he or she left by a rear exit, which may be how the regular visitors gain access as well."

"Should we knock then?"

"We can, but I doubt if there is anyone inside."

The hollow sound of the knocker rang through the house, but there was no noise from within. I shrugged. "Well, I assumed you would be correct, but one must try these things."

Smiling, Holmes reached into his coat and brought out his lock picks. I glanced around to ensure we were undisturbed while he made quick work of the lock and swung the door open. I made to move inside, but Holmes placed a hand on my chest.

"Sorry, but I just want to view the scene before we enter." Intrigued, I followed Holmes's gaze and noticed that the floor within was filthy with dust and grime, much like the steps outside. However, three sets of footprints could be clearly seen in the dust. One set led to the door, with two sets leading away. "I assume you can see the sets of boot prints." I nodded and watched as Holmes stooped down once more, examining each set of prints in turn. Pointing to those leading in from outside, he said, "This pair has the look of boots worn by a city-based man, but this pair," he pointed to the other, "has a wider tread – something akin to a worker's boot."

"Strange."

"Quite," he said, entering the passageway and stepping lightly along the wall, preserving the trail of footprints as much as possible. I followed, shutting the door behind me, and keeping to his trail as closely as possible.

The line of footprints led down the long hallway and turned abruptly into a room at the end. Holmes stopped for a moment, studying the area before disappearing through the doorway.

My first view of the room brought a feeling of surprise. It was a combined kitchen and dining area, with two small windows overlooking a very overgrown rear yard. The state of the area confirmed my view that the house had been unused for some time. In the kitchen area, the small benches lay empty, devoid of cutlery, crockery, or items used for food preparation. The furniture in the dining area consisted of a small wooden table with four chairs, one of which lay upturned in the far corner. A thick layer of dust cloaked every item in the room, the floor especially.

Holmes squatted nearby, his eyeglass hovering above several impressions in the dust.

"More boot prints?"

"Yes. Two more sets in addition to those we have already seen. The scraping of heel marks and footprints through this dirt suggests that there was a scuffle of some kind." He pointed towards two parallel lines running from near the centre of the room towards the double doors that led out to the garden. "A quick summation would lead me to presume that the person entering this room was attacked, knocked unconscious – or worse – and then dragged towards the garden."

"Should we go out and check? He may still be there."

"In time. There are still many clews to uncover in this room." Then, peering closer to the floor, he cried, "Ah, yes!" Looking down, I saw him point to several dark spots on the dirty floor. "This may be blood, but I cannot tell fully in this light."

Noticing a gaslight nearby, I pulled out a small box of matches and endeavoured to light the flame, before giving up in exasperation. "There's no gas," I said, a little confused and surprised.

"That would corroborate with my assertion that this house has been unused for quite some time – at least for normal habitation, that is."

It was then I noticed a candle in a holder on the other side of the room. Deftly skirting around the periphery, I quickly lit it, shining a dull, yellow light across the scene.

"Thank you. Well done," said Holmes, snatching the candle from me and bringing it closer to the area of his attention.

Now that there was a little more light, I took the opportunity to glance around the room and noticed a glint of something metallic in the corner opposite. Pointing I asked, "What's that?" Holmes looked up as I skirted the centre of the room and retrieved the object. It was conical in shape, with circular openings at both ends. The brass had dulled slightly from age and use, but still retained enough shine to catch the light. "Intriguing," I said, "If I had to guess, I'd say this is the end of a stethoscope."

I passed the object into Holmes open palm. He quickly examined it under the glass and nodded in agreement. "I believe you're correct – different to the type you use, but common enough among your colleagues."

"Does that mean that Markey was here?"

"The idea gains credence," Holmes said.

While Holmes continued to investigate the room, my eyes kept wandering to the area outside of the rear doors. It was a singular mess and tangle of weeds and plants, though a pathway of broken cobblestones and tamped down grasses could be seen running through the brush towards the rear of the property. I almost jolted in shock when I felt rather than saw Holmes's presence at my shoulder.

"The owners of this property obviously don't entertain anyone in the rear yard," he quipped.

"I'm more worried about what they hide in there."

"Well then, let's find out, shall we?"

***

The first thing I saw as the door swung open was the definite line of muddied footprints leading up the garden path to the rear step. They had smudged slightly as boots walked back across them towards the rear gate once more.

"The mud only comes one way," I said.

"Yes. The owner obviously realised that his boots were filthy and cleaned them off there." Holmes pointed to a smear of dark, mud on the edge of the top step. Carefully stepping across to the dark patch, he bent down and tentatively poked his finger into the pile. I grimaced, my darkest imagination picturing where the mud came from and what it contained.

As Holmes rubbed the mud between two fingers, then raised it to his nose and sniffed. I said, "Be careful. That could be – "

"Excrement?" he asked before taking another sniff. "In fact, it is. Sheep or – " Sniffing the mud again. " – pig. There's definitely a hint of omnivore in it. Not strong enough for a carnivore. Possibly from a pig, and intriguingly still relatively fresh."

Holding back a sudden urge to gag, I said, "Where would someone find a pigsty around here?"

Wiping his fingers on his kerchief, Holmes said, "I doubt it was actually around here." He stepped to the side of the path and studied the footprints and crushed plants. After a few moments, he said, "Yes, there are actually three sets of prints. The mud-laden boots, plus two others. All came up the path in single file, then two of them moved side-by-side going back out. By the depth of the impressions in the grass, they were carrying something on their way out."

"Or someone?"

"Yes, it's starting to look likely that it was someone."

I followed Holmes as he slowly made his way down the garden path, stopping every once in a while to examine the footprints and crushed greenery. I noticed the privy set against the rear fence. It was unusable due to the build-up of weeds and grass around the door, almost hiding it from view.

The thicker weeds on both sides of the path appeared to have been completely undisturbed for weeks, if not months. Holmes confirmed this by ignoring them completely and making his way through the rear gate and into the service laneway behind. The road was a turgid mess of mud, I hoped it was mud. I knew well that the laneway was probably used mostly by the nightsoil men undertaking their nocturnal duties.

We both studied the wet trails of wagon wheels and horses' hooves, Holmes shaking his head at the state of the area. Any indications of a trap or cart behind our position had long been erased. It was then that Holmes's eyes fell on the rear door of the privy. As he carefully picked his way across to it, I gasped, "Surely you don't need to look in there?"

"Ah, but think on it. The night soil men would know by now that this house is unused, and to save themselves time and effort, would regularly skip this privy. But if you were to discard or hide something, what better place?"

As he slid the door up, I expected no less than a bucket of foul contents, but was greeted with a triumphant "A-ha!" Holmes pulled from the tiny room a brown, leather case. Even from where I stood, I could make out what it was.

Opening and peering inside, Holmes nodded and said, "A medical bag, as I'm sure you already determined. Unless there's a rush on disposing of medical professionals, I'm sure we can establish that this indeed belonged to Dr. Markey."

"The poor man. Where do you think he was taken?"

Peering down the laneway, Holmes gave a tiny shrug before adding, "To that, I have no idea as yet. I believe we need to involve the constabulary, as this case has deepened very quickly."

I was a little surprised that Holmes would look to bring in the police before having established all the facts of the case. It wasn't until we exited back into the street that it became clear.

As Holmes worked his magic and relocked the front door, I scanned the roadway for any witnesses or passers-by that might cause a ruckus, and noticed a young urchin hiding in the churchyard across the street. His attention was focused solely on us, which I thought strange, as I hadn't seen anyone on our way in, and from the looks of the boy, he knew we had entered and had been waiting all this time.

It was as Holmes turned and stepped down to the street level that the boy came out of his hiding spot and raced across towards us. I unconsciously stepped before Holmes as the boy approached.

"Mr. 'Olmes! Mr. 'Olmes!" he cried, alerting my colleague to his presence.

As Holmes stepped to one side, a smile came to his face. I realised immediately that he knew the boy.

"Jenkins, you look thoroughly flummoxed. What's the matter?"

"I'm sorry Mr. 'Olmes. One of our lads lives this way and sent word to Wiggins that you were here. He sent me in a hurry."

"Why? What can the matter be?"

"It's this 'ouse, sir. Do you know whose it is?"

"I have my theories, but obviously Wiggins was concerned about my presence, so enlighten me."

"What?" said the boy, a look of confusion on his face.

"Whose house is it?"

"Oh, yeah, it's Steelfist Wasser's."

"The criminal?" I blurted out.

"Ah, Derrick Wasser," said Holmes. "The scourge of South London,"

The little tyke nodded. "'E don't use it much, but I seen some men there last week. And a cart went off south. Big fella driving it."

A wide grin grew on Holmes's face. "The game is certainly afoot, Watson."

***

"Derrick Wasser," I said as the cab made its way back towards Baker Street. "I know a little about him, but mostly through reputation. Supposedly he runs a gang in South London, but the police have never been able to find evidence to actually incriminate him."

"That is true. I've kept an eye and ear open for any connection to the man, and his organisation, but until now there's been little. This could account for how self-assured he has grown."

"Yes, over-confidence leads to imprudence. I do know that the bulk of his activities are within legitimate businesses. Any mention in the tabloids have always brushed these aside as merely fronts to his other ventures."

Smiling, Holmes added, "Ah, well, I tend to read between the lines. The most important factor is that Wasser controls the importation and distribution of cocaine and opium throughout most of South London. A very large part of his business enterprises, I understand."

"That must be the motivation behind the disappearance of Dr. Markey."

"I think that's part of it, but the question I have is: Why would a man such as Wasser risk so much just to remove a minor player such as Dr. Markey?"

"If Markey's stance against these drugs were to take hold, they could severely limit Wasser's business. Would that be enough motivation?"

"I know only too well the legality of the drugs of which we speak. I'm more than happy for their prevalence in society to remain, while they are seen as legal. If their legal status were to change, then I would need to seriously rethink my own stance."

"To that, I would be most happy."

Slipping me a wry grin, Holmes added, "Quite, but I could only think that Wasser's business would be pushed underground, and frankly, become possibly more profitable per transaction, though much riskier."

"So?"

"I can't understand why Wasser would pursue Markey with such finality."

"Who else stands to gain from Dr. Markey's disappearance?"

"Who indeed? Who indeed? I think that I shall have to cogitate on that for a time."

Holmes slipped into silence for the rest of our journey back home. I was tied up with patient visits for the rest of the afternoon, and by the time I returned, he was nowhere to be found.

It wasn't until morning that Holmes appeared and joined me for a light breakfast. His face looked drawn from lack of sleep, but his eyes were bright with an inner eagerness. Sitting, he quickly downed two cups of coffee while I read the morning paper, seemingly composing himself before speaking.

"Watson, we must make a journey this morning. Are you free?"

"Why yes, I've nothing till later this afternoon. Where are we to go?"

"Dorking."

"What? Dorking? Why in blazes do you wish to go there?"

"We shall be visiting a piggery."

***

I sent notes to my afternoon patients to inform them that I wouldn't be able to attend until the morning and hailed a cab for the two of us. It soon had us at busy Waterloo Station. No sooner had we alighted than the lean form of Inspector Lestrade stepped out of the bustling crowd and greeted us.

"Ah, Inspector," said Holmes, "Glad you could join us. I thought you might send an underling in your stead."

"I'm intrigued, Mr. Holmes, plus anything that can pin an actual crime, especially one of this heinous nature, on Steelfist Wasser, is well worth following up. I'm still a little peeved at the local sergeant for not investigating that house in Brixton, but they rarely enter the area unless they have strong cause to. If this pans out, I'll be having strong words with him."

"Indeed. At this stage, I'm still a little wary of admitting success. It is a long bow that I draw, but after dwelling on the facts we know so far, and the other information I found from the voices in the street, I believe that we'll find what we're looking for."

I was still quite perplexed, but hoped that Holmes would divulge more in due time. I didn't have to wait long, as he wished for the three of us to be in solitude before speaking further.

The trip to Red Hill took all of an hour. Holmes had me purchase tickets for a compartment where we could speak undisturbed during that time. It was there that Holmes explained all he'd learned overnight.

"Inspector, this Wasser fellow: What is the word at the Yard about him?"

"He's as bent as a centuries-old willow tree," spat Lestrade, taking a breath for a moment to compose his next words, "Trouble is, we have nothing on him. Everything points to legitimate business interests, but he's got so many fingers in the wrong pies. We know it, but we can't prove anything."

"Well, hopefully, I can help you out."

"What have you got then? Why are we heading away from London?"

"One of Wasser's legitimate businesses is a pig farm on the outskirts of Dorking."

"Just another of his many."

"Yes, but he only owns the one farm. Speaking with quite a number of my contacts last night, I discovered that there have been several disappearances over the last few years. Many seem loosely associated with Wasser, in one way or another. Those facts, and the evidence of the cart, and excrement-caked boots, gives me pause to believe that this particular farm is used for very despicable purposes."

Holmes went silent at that point, leaving me to wonder further on his words. I could tell Lestrade was agitated, but I found him that way more often than not when Holmes was being cryptic.

We were met in Red Hill by a carriage with two constables aboard. Lestrade had telegraphed ahead, seeking support in case it was warranted. The bumpy ride on to Dorking was thankfully quick, and we found ourselves alighting outside of a rather run-down farmhouse and into the midst of the most God-awful smell, one that I was sure my sensibilities would take months to forget.

The farm was anything but, by my estimations. It consisted of a ramshackle house with a single large pen to one side that contained several overweight pigs. Two smaller outbuildings stood behind the pen – probably storage areas or, given the presence of the pigs, a butchery or similar.

Without a word, Holmes started towards the pigpen, leaving Lestrade, myself, and the two constables a little dumb-struck. A shout from the front door drew our attention.

"Oi? What the hell are you doing?" asked the husky man standing on the porch. "This is my property!" He thrust his stockinged feet into a pair of boots and shuffled off behind Holmes.

"Excuse me, sir," yelled Lestrade, stopping the man in his tracks, "Might I have a word?"

"No, you might not!" he yelled back, trailing after Holmes. "What's that blighter doing?"

"That is Mr. Sherlock Holmes, and I am Inspector Lestrade of Scotland Yard. You are?"

Stopping, the man looked Lestrade up and down before saying, "None of your business. I don't need to answer to the police, I've done nothing wrong."

"Well, if you would just let Mr. Holmes finish his inspection, we'll see if that's the case."

"What? What the hell do you mean by that?" Looking towards Holmes, the man added, "He's got no rights to be on my property or looking at my pigs."

By now all five of us were walking towards Holmes, who was entrenched in his examination of the pigpen. As we caught up with him, I grimaced in disgust, he was virtually kneeling in a pile of muck at the side of the enclosure. He had rolled his sleeve up and was pushing his hand deep into an unmentionable mess. It was then he exclaimed and pulled his hand out. "A-ha! Watson, come here – I think this will be of interest to you."

As I sidled up to him, Holmes held up several teeth. I immediately realised that they were human incisors and molars. "Good Lord."

With a grim smile on his face, Holmes pointed past Lestrade and said, "Inspector, I think we should detain that man." I turned to see the heavy-set man waddling as fast as he could away from us. Lestrade nodded and within seconds the two constables had nabbed and taken him to the wagon.

Turning to Holmes, I asked, "How?"

"It's a well-known fact that pigs can eat virtually anything, including almost every part of a human being. Flesh, organs, bone – but they struggle to digest teeth. They are also quite clean in that they will choose a specific spot in their habitat to defecate." Nodding towards the wagon, he added, "Our farmer has been helpful by pushing all the pigs excrement into one pile – probably how his boots became so caked in it."

It's a well-known fact that pigs can eat virtually anything, including almost every part of a human being.

"My word, Holmes. Good work!"

Without another thought, I followed the group to the cart, thinking Holmes would join us, but when I turned to find him he had disappeared. Assuming he had simply gone off to clean up or find more clues, I watched Lestrade interrogate the man as he was loaded into the back of the wagon. As the policeman plied the farmer with questions, I noticed his hands. On the little finger of his right hand, he wore a stunningly fashioned gold Claddagh ring, the twin of which I had only seen the day before.

Pointing at the ring, I almost shouted over Lestrade, "That ring – where did you get that ring?" The man's mouth dropped open in a gaping expression. "I take it from your reaction that it isn't yours. I don't wish to cast aspersions, but you don't look like the type of man to outlay so much money on jewellery."

"I . . . I found it. I liked it. So I wears it."

"Quite," I finished, placing as much cynicism on my single word as possible.

"Good observation, Watson," said Holmes at my shoulder, making me jump in surprise, "The existence of that ring, which I'm sure is the mate of Mrs. Markey's, plus what I just discovered, will certainly lead to a conviction."

"What did you find, Mr. Holmes?" asked Lestrade.

"It seems that the owner of those teeth isn't the only person to have found their final destination in the stomach of these pigs. There are multiple human teeth amongst a pile of older excrement at the rear of the property, plus in a small shed behind the house, I found clothes and other items that could only have come from elsewhere."

Turning to the farmer, Lestrade raised his voice, adding a hint of a growl to it, and said, "You're going down, my boy, but you can make things easier for yourself if you tell us who you're working for."

The look of fear on the man's face almost made me sympathetic to his plight, but as he told us everything, my anger rose.

***

The journey back to Red Hill was quiet. I believe it was Lestrade's way of surreptitiously sweating the farmer for information. Instead of an outright attack of questions, he let the man stew in silence until he was in the Red Hill Station, where the questioning could commence. There his reserve broke, and he wouldn't stop talking.

His name was Walter Bacon, at first an unlikely name and possibly false, until he confessed that his family had been pig farmers for generations. A chance encounter at the Spitalfields markets had seen him form a partnership with Derrick Wasser. The gangster threw money into the farm, keeping it afloat. The return agreement was for Bacon to use the pigs to eradicate the remains of anyone Wasser sent him. The pigs were the tool. Bacon eagerly, and almost proudly, told of how they could remove almost all traces of a body within a few hours. Some of the bones, especially the skull, could be troublesome, but he usually burnt those in the incinerator at the back of the property. Lestrade made a note to return for that evidence.

When asked about Markey, Bacon was nonplussed. He admitted that he never knew who the people were that the pigs devoured. He simply removed their clothes and prepared them. When he added that he used his butchering skills, learned over many years, I gagged slightly at the revolting thought of poor Dr. Markey's fate.

When pressed about the house in Brixton, Bacon admitted that he was regularly called up to London to claim the bodies and transport them away. That house was one of several that Wasser seemed to own.

By the end of the interrogation, I'd certainly had enough, and I hoped that Holmes was satisfied. Lestrade seemed to be ready to jump aboard a train and arrest Wasser, until Holmes said, "You still only have this man's word, which I'm sure won't stand up too well under courtroom scrutiny. We know how Markey was disposed of, but the reasons are still unclear. I believe our next step is to catch Wasser talking with the true villain of this piece."

***

An early breakfast greeted us the next day. Holmes had been resolute that we needed to be ready for a timely exit in the morning and asked Mrs. Hudson to prepare a substantial meal to set us properly for the day's adventures.

Upon arriving back at Baker Street the previous afternoon, Holmes had quickly disappeared, leaving me perplexed, but thankful as I was rather tired and looked forward to a hearty repast and a quiet night in. My colleague arrived back just prior to me making my way to bed and announced that the morrow would bring quite a few surprises.

Precisely at nine o'clock, the doorbell rang.

"Ah, that would be Lestrade," said Holmes, standing and donning his coat and hat. I followed suit and was just buttoning up when Lestrade's footsteps stopped outside our sitting room door.

As he let himself in, he looked a little weary from the previous day's journey and said, "All right, Mr. Holmes, what's this all about then? I would have had Wasser under arrest yesterday, but your words said otherwise."

"As I stated, Inspector, it is all well and good to arrest this so-called businessman, but in the case of Dr. Markey, we need the catalyst behind it all."

"As mysterious as always," said Lestrade, a wry grin on his normally dour face. "I wouldn't have it any other way."

Parked in the street outside was a covered wagon, with two bobbies sitting on the trap. "Expecting arrests then, Lestrade?" I quipped.

"Always when Mr. Holmes is on the case."

Sitting in the uncomfortable rear of the wagon, we drove through the streets for several minutes before pulling to a stop. We climbed out and looked around the area. It had the same aspect as any street in Brixton or Lambeth. "Where the devil are we?" I asked. "Back in Brixton?"

"Camberwell," Holmes said, nodding towards a building down the street. It was two storeys high, in the typical Georgian style, with a pub on the corner and what looked like residential houses behind. "That is Derrick Wasser's main office. It's where he can be found most days, and by sending telegrams to himself and one other first thing this morning, I've orchestrated a meeting between him and his client." He shrugged before adding, "Or I have wasted my money."

As Holmes spoke, a hansom drew up outside of the building. "Ah – the former it seems!"

A podgy looking man with a balding head stepped from the cab and across to the entrance. Even from our viewpoint, I could make out the insistent beating of his fist on the door. As it opened, an animated conversation began between the man and an unseen person inside.

As soon as the bald man entered, Holmes set off. Lestrade, myself, and the two constables followed in his wake. Lestrade instructed one of the uniformed policemen to remain outside, while Holmes tried the doorknob. It turned easily. The tenant was too preoccupied to lock the door as he withdrew.

As we entered the dim corridor, the sound of an argument filtered up the hallway towards us.

"By God, Wasser, what is all this twaddle? You told me it was dealt with."

"It was Sir Benton, it was."

"Then what is this?" The sound of something slamming down on a wooden desk echoed out. "Arrived this morning. Says that Markey has been found. At your pig farm."

"I received the same thing. I've no word myself, but I think someone's playing us like fools. Nobody that goes to the farm is ever found again. Mr. Bacon is very efficient."

"Well, he better be. If word about this gets out, then I won't be the only one suffering."

"Don't worry, Sir Benton. If I feel any heat, then I certainly won't be alone in Wandsworth."

"What do you mean?"

"Remember, you need me a lot more than I need you. That money you get for keeping things smooth with the law is only good while the drugs are legal. I don't care either way. If I have to go underground, then so be it. Risks are higher, but so is the profit."

"Why you – I've made things much easier for you over the years! Threatening me isn't going to end well!"

"Well, if this Dr. Markey has friends, then maybe I won't need your help much longer."

"You blackguard! I wouldn't be surprised if this was all your doing!"

"Now don't be stupid, sir. Why would I damage my operations like this? I don't know who did it, but I'd like to find them."

"Well, in that case," said Holmes, stepping through the office doorway, "here I am."

"Who the hell are you?" asked Wasser.

"Sherlock Holmes at your service." Stepping aside, he continued. "And this is Dr. Watson, along with Inspector Lestrade and Constable

Conway of Scotland Yard. I think they'll be very happy to talk with you after you virtually confessed to the murder of Dr. Dermid Markey."

The looks on both their faces were priceless.

***

"So this Sir Benton McBrough – what was his motivation?" I asked Holmes, as we both sat down to a wonderful meal at a local pub. We thought it fitting to have a small celebration. Holmes had brought both a local gangster passing himself off as an upright businessman, and a corrupt politician to justice.

"For the last two nights, I have spent many hours scouring the backstreets of Brixton and Camberwell and Peckham, talking with many of my contacts and piecing together an interesting narrative." He took a sip from the fine brandy we had ordered before continuing. "Our fine upstanding politician, Sir Benton, was deep in with Wasser. They share interests in much of the drug trade throughout the south of London – a trade that would only continue while the drugs were legitimate.

"Sir Benton became scared by Markey's success in last year's election. The margin wasn't close, but it represented a change in the electorate's opinions of him. If Sir Benton lost his place in Parliament, his lucrative side business of supporting the drug trade within south London would be lost. Worse, if Markey's popularity grew and more politicians paid attention to his stance, then there was the possibility of a movement growing within the Government and the medical industry. Which could lead to a loss of illicit income on his part."

"Money," I sighed.

"Yes, Watson, money. There are seven deadly sins, as outlined in the theology. Whenever the other six fail to account for a motive, always rely on greed to provide the solution."

The Demise of the Painted Devil

I had known Mrs. Hudson for the best part of two years, the same period spent under her roof as co-lodger with my colleague and friend Sherlock Holmes. To that point, I had always found her to be calm, stable, and almost stoic in her resolve, with an extreme level of reverence and what could almost be called love for Holmes.

But it was that morning in the autumn of 1883, that I first saw her in a highly emotional state, making her even more human, and indeed humane, in my eyes.

"I'm so sorry, Doctor," she said from our doorway, her face flushed red, and her eyes almost brimming with the expectation of tears, "Is Mr. Holmes awake? I do need to see him. Urgently."

"My dear Mrs. Hudson. Whatever can the matter be? Please come in. Sit, I'll stir Holmes from his slumber." I moved back, to allow Mrs. Hudson gress.

"Oh, it's not for me. I have a friend downstairs. A long-time friend that I've known almost all my life. Her world is crashing down, and I didn't know where to turn."

"In that case, bring her up. I'll rouse Holmes while you do."

Nodding, she disappeared quickly. The sound of her feet on the seventeen steps leading down to the landing, echoed as she fled.

"What was all that about?" asked a voice still rough from recent slumber. I "I have no idea, Holmes. Mrs. Hudson was all in a tizz. Make yourself comfortable, there may be something intriguing in all this for you."

My colleague moved across to the table and sat. Helping himself to a cup of coffee and rubbing the final rime of sleep from his eyes. "I do hope this will be stimulating. I spent several hours, last night, stalking the streets of Soho, without any hint of interest from the criminal world."

I smiled to myself. Over the last couple of years, I had become accustomed to my friend's strange activities, but even then some of his more obscure doings always brought a touch of humour to my thought patterns.

I opened my mouth to ask about his recent undertakings but was stopped when our door opened revealing Mrs. Hudson with a matronly woman of similar age, whose eyes were red-rimmed from a former tearful state.

When her sight fell on Holmes, Mrs. Hudson sighed with relief. "Oh, Mr. Holmes, I'm so glad you're awake." Ushering in her companion, she added, "This is my good friend, Mrs. Sonia Wengert, widowed. We've known each other since school and kept in touch for all these years."

The other woman nodded her head slightly. A pained expression crossed her face, one that I translated as either sorrow or embarrassment at placing her reliance on a virtual stranger.

Holmes stood and moved across to the doorway. He took Mrs. Wengert's hand in his own and ushered the unfortunate woman into our rooms, showing her to a comfortable chair. I could tell the gesture was to place the woman in as natural a position as possible, so that she would be assured enough to relate her story as thoroughly as possible. "It is a delight to meet you Mrs. Wengert."

The woman blurted out, "Oh, call me Sonia."

Bowing his head slightly, Holmes said, "Sonia." With the woman ensconced in the easy chair, he added. "Now, a friend of Mrs. Hudson's is a friend of mine, Sonia. What is it I can do for you?"

"Oh, I'm so sorry to be such a bother, Mr. Holmes. I've heard so much about you. I never believed I'd need your help. No. Never."

"That is fine. Please tell me what troubles you."

In her own inimitable way, Mrs. Hudson found a way to help the situation as well, bringing a fresh cup of tea to her good friend. Mrs. Wengert nodded as she took the cup and sipped at the hot brew. Her demeanour relaxed even further until she was ready to tell everything.

"It's the lady," she said, "They came this morning and arrested her."

"The Lady?"

"Yes, my Mistress. Mrs. Smartwood. Mrs. Rowena Smartwood. I have been their housekeeper for quite a few years. Lovely people."

Holmes turned and looked at me, a questioning glance, with one eyebrow raised. I shook my head. I'd never heard of the woman.

"Why would *they*, and by *they*, I assume you mean the police." The woman nodded. "Arrest her? Did they say what she is accused of?"

"Yes, yes, they did. Murder. They said she murdered Mr. Smartwood, but that's impossible."

"My word," I blurted out.

Holmes shot me a withering glance. Stifling any further utterances. Turning back to the woman he asked, "Take me back to the beginning. Is there anything to tell before the police arrested Mrs. Smartwood?"

"Oh, yes, yes there is." Holmes waited while Mrs. Wengert took another sip of tea. Finally, she took a deep breath and began to relate her tale. "I would say that it started last night. The Master, Mr. Frederick Smartwood, went out to his club, or group, or whatever he calls it."

"A regular occurrence, I would assume."

Mrs. Wengert nodded. "Yes. He's been spending more time there of late. Anyway, on some nights he retires to the room in the basement, instead of climbing the stairs to the master bedroom. The Mistress is a light sleeper and is possessed of a delicate disposition, so he has taken it on himself to leave her be if he knows he will return late."

"Was there anything different about his return last night?"

"Yes. That's why I mentioned it. He is normally as quiet as a mouse, but on his return last night, he was louder. Clattering into some furniture in the hallway. Knocking over a hatstand. Then he clambered down the stairs to his basement room. Worried, I had sprung from my bed, afraid that the Master had hurt himself, and found the Mistress upon the ground floor landing before the basement stairs."

"He's not a drinker?" I asked.

The woman looked horrified. "No. Never a drop above the sociable. I've seen him partake of a sherry or two at dinner with friends, but nothing more." She took another sip of tea before continuing. “I've never heard anything like what happened last night. It was late. Just before he returned, I heard the hallway clock strike twelve.”

“What was Mrs. Smartwood's reaction?”

“Her face was a mask of fear. Like myself, she had never heard the Master in such a state. I lit a candle, and held it before us, as she pried open the basement door and we descended. The Master had flopped, fully clothed onto his bed. The Mistress moved over, prodding him slightly to see if he was alright.”

“He was asleep, I would assume,” said Holmes. “I don't wish to cast aspersions, but it does sound like he had imbibed.”

Holding up a single finger, the woman simply said, “I know what a drunk's reaction would be in most cases. My late husband was one for the drink, but this was certainly not it.” I noticed Mrs. Hudson nod at that, assumedly she well knew of the late Mr. Wengert.

“What happened next?” I asked.

“The Master virtually exploded in rage. As the Mistress laid a hand on his shoulder, he sprang up from the bed. His face, a mask of horror and rage. He lashed out, slapping the Mistress across the face with the back of his hand, before grasping her by the lapels of her dressing gown. The Mistress reacted in the same way I believe I would have. She slashed at his cheek with her nails extended. The pain drove the Master back far enough for the two of us to rush to the stairs and from the room. I locked the door, leaving the Master inside. For the next few minutes, we both cowered outside, listening for any response from within. When we finally felt safe, the tears flowing from both of us, I took the Mistress back to her bed-chamber, consoling her for all it was worth. We spent the next few hours in a fitful state of half-sleep because when the Mistress came down in the morning, she bore the darkened eyes of one who had not attained a good night's rest.”

“What did you do next?” Holmes prompted, once the woman has stopped for a moment.

“The Mistress knocked on the door and called out to her husband, but there was no response. After a few moments, she asked me to unlock the door. I did not wish to, but after all, it was her husband.

Even my own Wilfred would have been as calm as a lamb by then, so I did as asked, and followed her down the stairs." Visibly disturbed, Mrs. Wengert took another sip of tea. "It was so quiet. I lit the gas lamp at the bottom of the stairs, and both of us gasped in horror. The Master was on the bed, lying on his back, his eyes open and staring at the ceiling, his skin a strange pallor with a blue tinge. The Mistress ran to him and tried to shake him awake, but he would not respond. Touching his brow, she withdrew her hand in terror. He was cold, she told me. It was then I knew the truth. He was dead. When I said I would send for a Doctor, the Mistress nodded, a look of loss growing on her face."

Mrs. Wengert pulled a kerchief from her sleeve and dabbed at the edges of her eyes. The telling was taking a toll on her.

"Within half an hour, Doctor Gibbison arrived on our doorstep. I took him straight down, but as soon as he laid eyes on the Master he simply shook his head. I've known the good Doctor for many years, and he did not disappoint. He was professional but careful to preserve the Master's dignity. Finally, he turned to the Mistress and declared that he was indeed dead. When asked how, he simply said, that is something I will need to discuss with the police. It was then the Mistress fainted. With the Doctor's help, we managed to take the Mistress to her room, and I put her in bed, while the Doctor arranged for the police to attend."

"Who?" asked Holmes.

"An Inspector Lanner arrived not long after."

"Lanner," I said, "Didn't we come across him on that Blessington business?"

"Yes," answered Holmes, "Young, diligent, ambitious. What did Lanner make of the scene?"

"That's where I can't tell you much more. Once the Inspector arrived, he and the Doctor made their way downstairs, while I went up to attend to the Mistress. About a half an hour after, they both presented at the Mistress's doorway. She invited them in, as she had recovered a little by then. But, when the Inspector said that the Master had been murdered, she began to grow faint once more. When he said that he was arresting her for that murder, she again fainted dead away."

"The blackguard," I blurted out, "How could he accuse a young woman of such a thing?"

"Well," said Holmes, "That is for us to find out, isn't it?"

***

After reassuring Mrs. Wengert, and indeed, Mrs. Hudson, that we would get to the bottom of it all, Holmes and I took a hansom to Ealing Police station to meet our old acquaintance, Inspector Lanner.

Even though I was slightly enraged and looking for confrontation, and I noticed Holmes was quiet and serious, which I presumed to be hiding a demeanour similar to mine, Lanner was anything but. The constable at the front desk found the Inspector quickly once he learned of our names and past association. The Inspector was as I had last seen him, keen of eye, clean of face, with just a slight touch of world-weariness about him.

"Mr. Holmes, Doctor Watson, how wonderful to see you."

"Hello Inspector," said Holmes, keeping things professional.

"What brings you to Ealing? A little out of your way isn't it?"

"I've taken on a case. One that you should be quite familiar with. It has only fallen into my lap, and I hope it can be cleared up quickly."

"If you're onto it, then I'm sure it won't take too long," said the eager young police officer.

"It concerns a young couple, who live not far from here. He is a solicitor, working out of his offices on the Ealing High Street, and his wife. She has been accused of his murder."

Lanner's face grew slightly dark as he realised what Holmes was talking about. "The Smartwoods? How did you find out about that so quickly?"

"The housekeeper is an old acquaintance of my landlady. In honour of her, I have taken the case. Now, why did you jump so quickly to a charge of murder against the wife?"

"That was on the evidence at the scene. It was pretty cut and dried. The husband came home, intoxicated from some substance still to be determined. He struck out at his wife. She retaliated but left quickly. When he fell into a stupor, she returned later and finished the job."

"What?" I stammered, "Finished the job? In what way?"

"Strangled him. In his sleep. She's a slight thing, but he messed her up, and she did him in. Cut and dried. The Doctor, Gibbinson, agreed. The local coroner is due to make his own assessment soon, and then it will be the gallows. No other explanation. There was no inference of a break-in, no evidence of a third party. Even the housekeeper had no motive, so I ruled her out straight away."

"Preposterous," I cried.

"Come Watson, no need to get emotional. We must simply look at the evidence and determine the facts as they come to hand." Turning to Lanner, Holmes added, "I would like to view the body, but first I think it would be best to talk with Mrs. Smartwood. I assume she is here."

"Yes, happy to escort you. I know it seems a little extraordinary, but I can see no other outcome."

***

Lanner led the two of us into the rear of the station, where several cells were located. They had the air of another age and were dark, damp and very dingy. I felt for the fair lady who sat within one of these horrors.

A small room sat at the end of the corridor, past the row of cells. We were shown inside and waited until Mrs. Smartwood, her face drawn in terror, her eyes red-rimmed from hours of crying, was shown inside.

"If I could interview her alone, Inspector, just to remove any aspect of the fear of retribution that your presence may inject."

"Of course," said Lanner, withdrawing from the room, and locking the door behind him. I looked through the small window and watched as he strode away, leaving a burly constable behind to ensure nothing untoward occurred.

Holmes led the poor woman to the only chair in the room and sat her down. Hunkering onto his knees, so that he was at her eye level before beginning his interview.

"I am so sorry that you have been treated this way, Mrs. Smartwood."

"Who are you?" she asked between sobs.

"My name is Sherlock Holmes; this is my colleague Doctor Watson. I am a consulting detective, and your housekeeper, Mrs. Wengert, has asked that I investigate the event of your husband's unfortunate demise to determine the truth of the matter.

"I had nothing to do with it," she cried out through a veil of tears. "The police. That Inspector, he said I strangled Frederick. How could I?" Holding out her hands, she said, "I would never do such a thing. I couldn't even if I tried." She indeed had a pair of delicate hands that I failed to imagine could even grasp a man's throat, let alone strangle the life from him.

"I can understand," said Holmes, "So, we must find out as many facts as we can. Until I see your husband, I cannot determine the likelihood of your involvement. Having seen Mrs. Wengert, I can't imagine that she would be able to do such a deed either. To strangle the life from a full-grown man takes a great deal of strength." He stood up for a moment, I could see his expression change to ponder some fact and remained quiet for a while. "Can you take me through the events of last night and this morning?"

Mrs. Smartwood began to relate her version of her husband's return and demise. Everything matched almost perfectly to Mrs. Wengert's story. The only differences were the points about Smartwood's entry into the house. The woman before us having been upstairs, heard slightly different noises to the housekeeper who would have been on the ground floor and much closer.

When she had finished, Holmes stared at her for a good while, waiting I feel, to see if anything else entered her mind, before asking, "This club that your husband frequented. Do you know what it was? Or indeed, its location."

Shaking her head, a look of confusion crossed her face. "No. He was ever so secretive about it. All I know is that he kept a collection of clothes in the basement room, that he took with him. He went there a good two to three times a week. Sometimes even more. I do know that it wasn't a normal gentlemen's club. There was no drinking. No smoking. It was altogether strange."

"Your husband was a solicitor." She nodded at this. "Where did he study?"

"Oxford. He was born near Stratford, studied hard and moved on to study in Oxford. He started reading history and the arts but switched to the law when he realised there would be no money in the other disciplines. We met in his final year. He undertook a position at my father's firm in Oxford, gaining experience and grounding in the law before graduating and becoming a full-time solicitor. We moved to London not long after. That was over five years ago."

"No children?" I asked.

Mrs. Smartwood dropped her head. I immediately regretted the question, especially when she answered, "No. I'm afraid I am barren. That is one thing Frederick always wanted, but something I could never give him."

"I... I'm so sorry for even asking."

Holmes continued. "What has the Inspector told you about the state of your husband? Or at least, has he told you why you were arrested?"

"Yes. He said I strangled Frederick. That there were marks on his neck, and that the scratches on his face meant I had the most motive."

Holmes shook his head and pursed his lips. "Flimsy at best. I am sorry to have troubled you, Mrs. Smartwood, and I assure you I will get to the bottom of this and have you out of this horrid place as quickly as possible."

Spinning, he thumped the door, which brought the constable quickly. Within a few minutes, we had said our goodbyes to Mrs. Smartwood and were on the high street and heading for the nearby hospital.

***

"I cannot believe that Lanner would incarcerate that woman for such a crime," I said, as we walked, "I do hope you can have her out of there as quickly as possible."

"Not too soon, Watson, " Holmes said. I noted a change in tone, which struck me as concerning.

"You don't think she had anything to do with it, do you?"

"I believe that the chances are slim that a lithe woman, such as Mrs. Smartwood, would have the strength to strangle a full-grown man to death, but," he held up a finger, "Until I have examined all the pertinent facts and clues, I will not pass judgement on anyone. At this stage, we only have Mrs. Smartwood, Mrs. Wengert, Mr. Smartwood, or some unknown villain as our perpetrator. Or it is not a simple murder as Inspector Lanner would have us believe. Our next destination should provide us with further information."

A few minutes stroll later, we came to the entrance of the Ealing Cottage Hospital. A quaint building that served the local community for most of its medical needs and was the location of the only morgue in the area.

It took us but a few minutes to find our way through the building and introduce ourselves to Doctor Langham, the long-time coroner of the area.

"I haven't had a chance to start the autopsy on the poor unfortunate Mr. Smartwood," he said, leading us to the gurney upon which the object of our interest lay. "I knew this poor man, you know. Had need of his expertise only a few months back. Some documents needed drafting for a property I was purchasing. Precise, articulate, well-kempt. The sort of person you feel comfortable leaving your legal dealings in the hands of." Pulling back the sheet, to reveal Smartwood's head and chest, he added, "Now, just another lump of meat, poor blighter."

I quickly ran my eyes over as much of Smartwood's body as I could. His neck was bruised and appeared to have swollen, such was the trauma visited upon it. I still couldn't justify Lanner's accusations of Mrs. Smartwood. Her husband was a large man, possibly six feet in height, and of considerable build. Her tiny hands would barely stretch to half his throat, rather than be able to reach around and choke the life from him.

"What is your opinion, Doctor Langham?" asked Holmes.

"Oh, initial observations agree with Inspector Lanner's summation." He pointed to the discolouration on the neck. "Bruising on the throat, and rear of the neck indicates possible strangulation."

"By someone's hands or other?"

"There's no burning or tearing of the skin, so I would not think it was a garrotte or rope or the like. Hands? Yes, possibly."

Holmes bent over the corpse, and taking out his glass, inspected the bruising and discolouration at length.

"A woman's hands, perhaps?"

The coroner stopped for a moment, stared at the cadaver, then at Holmes. "I think I will need to reserve my opinion on that point until I have completed my examination," he said, a tone of authority creeping into his voice.

It was at that point that an orderly poked his head into the room and requested Dr. Langham's assistance in another part of the hospital.

"If you would excuse me, gentlemen, it seems I am needed elsewhere." Removing his gloves, he moved towards the exit but stopped. "I'm happy for you to observe the corpse, but please do not disturb it in any way. I will begin my examination forthwith, and the Inspector will be the first to see the report. It was a pleasure meeting you, and I bid you adieu."

Holmes continued to peer at the corpse's face for a few moments, before answering. "Thank you, Doctor, we will see to your request and not disturb Mr. Smartwood here. I would be loath for anything to interfere with your work."

As the coroner withdrew, Holmes waited for a moment before moving to the door and peeking outside. Turning back, he strode across to Smartwood's body and withdrew a syringe from inside his coat.

"What do you intend to do with that?" I asked, watching Holmes screw a needle in place. "Draw blood?"

"No. It's not blood I'm after."

I was shocked as Holmes proceeded to pull back the sheet, revealing Smartwood's lower body, and plunged the needle into the cadaver. Instead of blood, a large volume of yellow liquid filled the glass tube.

"Holmes," I cried, "What in the blazes are you doing?"

"I feel that there is one particular angle that may not be within the coroner's field of vision and wish to conduct my own examination."

Once finished, Holmes disappeared the syringe into his coat, pulled the sheet back over the corpse and hurried to the door. I followed quickly behind.

***

As we arrived at 221B Baker Street, Holmes virtually leapt from the hansom and vaulted up the stairway. I paid off the surprised driver and wearily trudged my way upstairs to find Holmes bent over his chemistry equipment in the corner of our parlour.

Rather than ask questions, I left him to it and stripping off my coat and hat, hung them away and proceeded downstairs to inquire of Mrs. Hudson.

As her friend, Mrs. Wengert, had returned home, I told our landlady of all we knew, which I admitted wasn't much, before she offered to prepare a light luncheon. Glad for any food, I thanked her and made my way upstairs again, to find Holmes preparing to depart once more.

"Lunch is about to arrive," I said, "Mrs. Hudson informed me that her friend has left, but I feel we should eat before any further journeys."

Looking once at the chemistry equipment, where two spherical flasks were now bubbling merrily away, the acrid smell of ammonia filtering into my nostrils, Holmes said, "Well, this will take some time, and we have at least one more stop to make this afternoon. So, yes, let us eat then be on our way."

"I don't suppose you could open a window, could you?" I asked, eyeing the darkening yellow liquid as it boiled away.

Sniffing once, Holmes nodded. "Yes, boiling urine isn't the most pleasant smell, is it?"

***

After a wonderful lunch provided by Mrs. Hudson, and I couldn't help wonder if the level of quality had improved given Holmes's assistance in the case of the demise of Mr. Smartwood, we caught a cab back to Ealing, stopping outside a modest two-storey house in Culmington Road.

"This is the address that Mrs. Hudson gave us, and it has all the hallmarks of an up-and-coming solicitor," said Holmes, examining the

Smartwood's residence. "Also, it would seem that Mrs. Wengert is the only servant. Thus, eliminating any others who may present as suspects."

Indeed, it was Mrs. Wengert that greeted us once we had rung the bell.

"Oh, Mr. Holmes, Dr. Watson, have you any news?" she asked, a look of expectation writ large on her face.

"Not at this stage, I'm afraid I have nothing more to add. I felt I needed to visit the scene of Mr. Smartwood's demise to ascertain any other facts or clues that remain viable."

The old housekeeper's face descended into a look of confusion.

"Mr. Holmes merely wishes to see where Mr. Smartwood died. There may be some hidden clue that can help."

"Oh, I see," said the old woman, "Well, you better come in then."

Mrs. Wengert led us through the well-presented and modestly furnished house and stopped before a set of stairs leading down into the basement. The door was wide open, as it probably had been since the coroner removed the body. Lighting a nearby candle, she bid us to follow her into the gloom. "Now, watch your footing. I'll light the gas at the bottom."

The stairs opened into a smallish room, which would normally be used as a storage area, or previously as a coal cellar, but had been cleaned up and converted into a bedroom. Once, the gas light was lit, I could make out the single bed that lay near the centre, with a free-standing cupboard, and a bureau against the opposite wall.

"You mentioned that Mr. Smartwood used this as a bedroom when he arrived home late at night from his club."

Mrs. Wengert nodded. "Yes, he didn't want to wake the Mistress, so would often sleep down here. Many times, we needed to rouse him in the morning to ensure he was on time for his morning appointments. At times, he did arrive home at the strangest hour."

Holmes moved across to the bed and hunched over to examine the linen closely. Pulling out his glass, he became highly interested in some tiny detail. "How often do you change the bed linen?"

“Oh, every morning after the Master had slept here. I don't know what he gets up to, but it would be in a right state and need to be boiled to remove the stains.”

Holmes murmured to himself as he straightened and moved across to the cupboard. Opening the door, he revealed all manner of brightly coloured clothing, not something I would have suspected a solicitor to possess. “I'm assuming this was not Mr. Smartwood's regular day clothes then?”

“No. I've never even looked in there. Mr. Smartwood was very insistent that I stay out of that cupboard.”

“Really,” said Holmes, “These may have played a part in whatever activities, Mr. Smartwood got up to at his club.” Closing the cupboard door, Holmes slid open the top drawer of the bureau. It contained several thick books and loose leafed sheaves of paper. Intrigued, I joined Holmes and peered down at the papers.

“Are they plays?” I asked, seeing the top sheets of several bearing the names 'Romeo and Juliet,” “Richard the Third,” and “Timon of Athens.”

“They do indeed appear to be,” answered Holmes, as he flipped through several pages. “Do you remember, Mrs. Smartwood mentioned that her husband was born near Stratford?”

“Now that you mention it, yes, I do.”

A wry grin came to Holmes's face. “From looking at these pages, I feel that he may have missed a calling in his home town.”

“What do you mean?”

“Well, with the newly established theatre in Stratford, which is dedicated to the works of the bard, he could well have found a career in treading the boards, rather than reading the law.”

“Quite, I suppose,” I replied, “I assume that's something you have often aspired to as well.”

Nodding, he added, “Well yes, but I have the advantage of plying my acting skills as part of my chosen career.”

Before I could add anything further, Holmes turned to Mrs. Wengert and asked, “Does Mr. Smartwood have a study or office upstairs?”

***

Unlocking the heavy door, Mrs. Wengert proceeded to ignite a small gaslight in the study. It was fully enclosed with no exterior windows, and each wall was lined with bookcases, overflowing with legal texts and other leather-bound volumes.

A large mahogany desk sat in the centre of the room, opposite a small fireplace that assumedly provided warmth during the winter months.

"The Master doesn't let anyone else in here. I only come in to give the place a quick dust and clean once a week. I know he's gone, but I do have reservations about invading his privacy like this."

"I assure you, Madam, that I will be circumspect in my investigation. I merely wish to track down Mr. Smartwood's movements, and as he is a professional I can only assume that he would have a diary with his appointments well documented."

Nodding, the housekeeper turned, and with one last look around the room, left.

Holmes took no time in moving to the desk and rummaging through the drawers, whilst I went to the bookcases and searched for anything that looked like a diary. "Aha," I cried at my success when I pulled a thick volume nestled next to several of the same and opened it to find calendar entries dating back several months. I moved to the desk and placed it down on the last page with records.

Holmes plonked a similar volume down next to it. As he opened the book we saw lines of figures. "A ledger."

"Yes. Should be just as important as the diary."

Scanning both journals, side by side, our first sight was the previous night's appointment. It simply read "WS."

"WS? Perhaps, William Shakespeare?"

"Good, Watson, good thinking."

I pointed to an entry for this evening. Again, it simply read "WS."

"Another meeting? Tonight?"

"I agree," said Holmes, "That gives us only a few hours to ponder what this club is about, and to cogitate on the evidence so far." Scanning the diary further back, the entries for "WS" occurred twice a week, until recently, when a third and fourth night had been added.

The earliest appointment with that moniker had been twelve months previously. "We must check with Mrs. Wengert and determine when Mr. Smartwood began his nightly sojourns to this group."

Scanning the ledger, I found a payment that tied in with the evening appointments. "Look," I said, pointing at the entry. "There's a monthly payment of a pound made to someone called Winduss. Winduss? Could that be a club contribution or similar?"

"My word," said Holmes, "I wonder." After a moment, he shook his head and added, "It couldn't be surely?"

"What?"

"Riley Winduss. One of the premier authorities on the plays of William Shakespeare. He has played all the greats, Hamlet, Lear, Othello, Macbeth. Directed several plays for the Lyceum as well but disappeared off the map a few years back following a dalliance with his Lady Macbeth co-star."

"What was so wrong with that?"

"She just happened to be the wife of the primary benefactor of the Lyceum Theatre at the time."

"Oh."

"If this is the same Winduss," Holmes mused, striding from the room, and pausing his sentence until we stood in the basement once more, "Then it could be that our solicitor from Stratford has taken it upon himself to live a long-held dream."

"Of what?"

Holmes dropped the diary and ledger on the bed and moved to the cupboard, opening the door to reveal the sets of colourful clothing once more. Smiling to himself, he withdrew one that was various shades of green, then another that was virtually nothing but a close-fitting cloak.

"Of being an actor?" Holmes added. "If I was to guess, I would say that these costumes are Puck and perhaps Oberon."

Confused, I asked, "Why would a respectable solicitor be engaging in such?"

"Oh, come now Watson. Many a dignified professional has dreams of the stage, or of some other creative bent. I trod the boards in college on many occasions. You have your writings, something I assume has always been a burning desire. Fortunately for you, these cases we undertake have given you a focus and outlet."

I pursed my lips, suffering a slight chastisement of my documentation of Holmes's adventures. "Where does that leave us then?"

"We just need to find where Winduss is holed up and pay him a visit."

"I still don't see how this has anything to do with Smartwood's death."

Checking his pocket watch, Holmes smiled. "For that, we need to pop by Baker Street once more." Snatching up the journal and ledger, Holmes headed out of the basement.

***

As we stepped into our parlour, I rushed straight for the windows and threw them wide open. The rank odour of Holmes's experiment lingered within the confines of the room. When I turned around, I found Holmes hovering over his chemistry table. I noticed the gas flames beneath both flasks extinguished.

"Your experiment finished then?"

"Why yes, Watson. I do apologise for the noxious odour but come and look." Moving back from the table, so that I could join him, he added, "I think you'll find this interesting."

Joining Holmes, I glanced down at the two flasks. One contained a yellow-brown substance clumped on the base, in the other a white residue had collected across the surface.

"Interesting, you conducted two separate experiments it seems. What were you trying to prove?"

"Ah, that's where you are slightly wrong. It was the same experiment, just two different sources of the primary substance."

"Alright, from the horrid smell, I can only conclude that you withdrew a urine sample from Mr. Smartwood's corpse. Why? I have no idea, as yet, but what was the second source?"

"I needed a control to ensure my hypothesis was correct, and my experiment was conducted correctly, so I used my own."

I wrinkled my nose in disgust, "Oh, Holmes."

"It seemed the most convenient source. It was either that or request a sample from you."

"Fair point. What was the experiment? What were you looking for? Smartwood died from asphyxiation, why investigate his urine?"

"From your extensive medical knowledge, what are the symptoms that come to mind when you consider arsenic poisoning?"

"Arsenic poisoning?" He nodded his head indicating I'd heard correctly. I thought for a moment. "The immediate effects are, cramping, nausea, muscle pains, diarrhoea."

"Yes. Immediate high-level ingestion or exposure will often then lead to cardiac arrest and death. What about longer-term exposure? Have you ever come across any cases or literature in that area?"

"It's not something that happens very often any more. Once the dangers of arsenic were identified in many common products, its use was stopped."

"True. There are records of long-term exposure resulting in sudden mood changes, delirium, swelling, and skin discolouration, especially around the throat and neck region."

My eyes grew wide as Holmes spoke. "My word, Holmes, are you saying that Smartwood died from prolonged arsenic poisoning?"

"Well, given the symptoms, I wanted to be sure, hence my surreptitious gathering of the urine sample. I didn't think it was something that the coroner would even contemplate searching for." Pointing at the two flasks before us, he added, "That's where this experiment comes in."

"What did you mix with the urine samples?"

"Magnesium Nitrate. It has been used of late to bond with the arsenic in urine to create arsenic nitrate, such as we find here." Holmes indicated the yellow-brown substance. "Smartwood's urine was filled with a high concentration of arsenic." Picking up the flask, he jostled it around, causing the flaky substance to break up. "A concentration this high could never have come from a single ingestion of the poison. Smartwood would simply have collapsed in excruciating pain and died straight away before the arsenic could be passed into his urine. This indicates that our poor victim has been exposed for quite some time. The poison accruing in his system until he finally succumbed." He replaced the flask on its stand. "I can only conclude that his inebriation of last night was the culmination of the poisoning, and the stress caused by his argument with his wife resulted in his body finally succumbing."

"The poor fellow." I almost choked on my next words, as I realised the importance of Holmes's findings. "But that means that Mrs. Smartwood is innocent." I turned to leave, taking two strides towards the door. "We must tell Lanner and have her released."

"Wait a moment, my friend, we have simply identified a probable cause of death. Before we can declare Mrs. Smartwood innocent, we must locate the source of the poison. The good inspector would still be quite prepared to lay the blame on his current suspect unless we can shed more light on the circumstances of Mr. Smartwood's demise."

Stopping I nodded, resigned to leave the poor woman incarcerated at Ealing police station for the time being. I hoped it wouldn't be for long.

***

The earliest entry in the diary, which luckily seemed to be the very first, included an address. Holmes had suggested that it may be Winduss's actual address, or where the club met.

The hansom stopped at the address on Park Street in Camden. The building was nondescript, with boarded-up windows, as if it hadn't been used for several years. "Are you sure this is the place," I asked.

"Oh, yes, Watson. You don't realise what this building is, do you?"

"No. A hangout for the destitute if anyone actually inhabits it."

"This, my dear Watson," Holmes said, waving one arm across the faded façade. "Is the Park Theatre, once known as the Royal Alexandria Theatre. It opened back in 1873 and hosted many wonderful productions through to the early part of this decade. Sadly, the owners had to sell up, and I believe it is destined to be demolished." He stepped up to the double entry doors. "I do hope it has retained some of its former grandeur."

The inside foyer would have appeared elaborate in its prime, but after several years of neglect, it was one step up from the back alleys of Brixton. A thick layer of dust covered the carpet and fittings. Vandals had broken in, or more likely walked in like the two of us, and broken or removed seats, counters, and anything that wasn't nailed down. "It has seen better days."

"Quite so. Though if someone were to rescue it, I'm sure it could be brought back to once again join other great London theatres."

"I'm afraid that is not likely. The group of men that bought this poor old place have their minds set on tearing her down within the next year or two."

We both turned to see an older gentleman, who I picked to be in his sixties, though his posture was as straight and true as any I had seen. As he walked towards us, I was struck by his impressively handsome face, untouched by wrinkles, but framed with a shock of steel-grey hair.

"Riley Winduss, if I'm not mistaken."

At Holmes's statement, the man stopped and slowly eyed us both. "Do I know you, Sir?"

"Like my knowledge of yourself, you may have heard of me. I am Sherlock Holmes, and this is my colleague Doctor John Watson."

"My word, to what do I owe this honour? Do you wish to join our little group? To relive your past successes on the stage?"

"You know of Holmes's past acting performances?"

"Yes, I do. It has been some years though hasn't it? There was a time that I caught as many university performances as I could, to recruit for my troupe. Now that I think of it, I should have approached you."

Holmes nodded, a wry grin and a twinkle in his eye, to which I presumed was his mind running through some of his memories. "The draw of the stage never leaves the soul. You will always find ways of revisiting it." Moving past Winduss, Holmes approached a large set of double doors and threw them open revealing a dark voluminous hall beyond. "This little group, as you called it, I presume you perform on the stage down here."

"Why, yes." Winduss floated past Holmes, firing up several gas lights inside the auditorium and casting a dull yellow pall across the area. "The new owners have allowed me to rent the place until they finally bring down the roof, so to speak."

"What is it that your group does here?"

"Ah, my boy, we explore all things concerning the bard."

"Shakespeare?" I asked, just confirming. My knowledge of the stage was far less than that of Holmes.

"Yes, yes. The one and only." We followed as Winduss strode down the aisle. He deftly climbed onto the stage and took up a position in the centre. To my eye, it seemed to be his natural habitat. "We read. We speak. We perform the plays of the bard."

"We?" asked Holmes.

"Men." He threw his arms wide. "In the spirit of the Elizabethan theatre, I have gathered a troupe of men together for the sole purpose of revitalising the Bard's work as it would have been performed in his time. The troupe contains only men. And there are only a few, so each actor plays several parts where possible."

"In full costume?"

"Oh, yes, with changes conducted at lightning speed, as would have been the case when these wonderful plays were performed before her majesty."

"Are there audiences?"

"Sometimes but always limited. We have had the odd occasion where members of the actors' families or close associates attend, but most of my actors prefer the solitude of an empty theatre."

"These men in your company, who are they?"

"Oh, we have many from all walks of life. From dustmen to scholars. Even a lawyer. All have a simple yearning for the stage."

My ears pricked up at the last occupation. "This lawyer? What was his name?"

"Oh, I couldn't. Most of the actors don't even know each other's names. When we are in character, we go by that name alone."

"Would it be a Mr. Frederick Smartwood?"

Winduss's jaw dropped open in shock, though I felt he was still in character and simply overplaying his role. “How? How did you know of Frederick's attendance?”

“Well, you may know me as an actor, but I am actually a consulting detective. Mr. Smartwood’s housekeeper has requested that I investigate his sudden and sad demise.”

This time Winduss's face became a mask of horror, though I wasn't so sure he was still acting. He dropped to the stage, sliding his legs over the edge, and sat, his head bowed and shaking. “Oh, my poor Frederick.” Growing silent for a moment, I half expected another explosion of emotion, but instead, he mumbled, “Who will play Caliban now?”

Not believing my ears, I felt compelled to accost the man. “Did you just ask who would replace Smartwood in your play?” I admit I was livid. “A man has died, and that’s all you can question?”

Lifting his head to stare into my eyes, he answered, “Of course, you’re right. I can worry about that later. How did he die? Was it sudden?” His answer did nothing to calm my unrest.

“The police say that it was strangulation, but I will present an argument to the coroner that it was indeed arsenic poisoning.”

“My word, poisoned, strangled. Who would murder poor Frederick? He was a lamb of a man. Such a wonderful actor. No part was too small, and he delved into each with all his soul. Even in the first readings, he would appear in full costume and makeup. Such commitment. I truly feel that within him was a sense of loss at pursuing a career in the law. His wish was a life on the stage, which was evident in his attitude and decorum.”

“Admirable, but like myself, he probably felt that life would not afford him the level of comfort to which he wished.”

“True. It is not a highly paid career. I do it just for the love. This little group is simply a sideline to pay the bills.”

“You mentioned that Smartwood appeared in costume and makeup on every occasion.”

“Yes. The dressing rooms are still intact, so the actors use them at their leisure.”

***

Within moments, we stood inside the large and once lavish dressing rooms. Now, simply a series of stalls for the actors to apply their makeup and store their costumes.

Winduss led us across to one corner and lit the gaslight above. “This was Frederick's spot. He had made it his own for quite a while now.”

Two costumes hung from hooks next to a large, stained mirror. Holmes took one look and said, “Ah, Caliban, as you have already alluded, and.” He ran his fingers across a more ornate costume of white silk and feathers. “Ariel, if I were to take a guess.”

“Very good, Sir. You know your Shakespeare. When I handed out the assignments, Frederick was extra effusive at being handed the dual roles of Caliban, the painted devil, and Ariel, the angel. He designed and had these costumes made at his own expense.”

Staring down at the makeup table, Holmes picked up a large jar and lifted the lid. It contained a thick white concoction. The pot looked as if it came from another age. The label had faded, and parts were sloughing off as the glue disintegrated. The jar itself was an opaque colour and reminded me more of ceramic than glass, while the lid was of the same material, simply sitting on top loose as opposed to a tight-fitting cork or rubber stopper.

“This makeup,” asked Holmes, “Where did it come from?”

“Again, that was something Frederick procured for his own use,” said Winduss, going quiet for a moment as he pondered. “He told me that he had found it in an antique shop in Stratford. I remember a bright smile on his face, as he said it was the same type of foundation used by the original Stratford Shakespeare players. I admit I did scoff at the notion, but he seemed genuine and proud of his find.”

“The original players,” said Holmes, staring at the pot of cream once more. “If that's true then this could contain an arsenic-based concoction. Something that was outlawed over a century ago.” He sniffed at the cream, then shrugged. “How long did Smartwood use this?”

“Oh, for well over three months.” Leaning in towards Holmes, Winduss nodded. “Yes. Over half has gone. It was full when he first showed it to me.”

Frederick was extra effusive at being handed the dual roles of Caliban, the painted devil, and Ariel, the angel.

"My word, Holmes," I said, "If he's been using this several times a week for months, then…"

"Precisely Watson, the arsenic would have leached in through his skin. That ties in with the white remnants I chanced across deep in the pores of his face when I viewed his corpse, and the stains upon his sheets." Holding up the jar towards Winduss, "Sir, I need to take this with me. The life of Mr. Smartwood's wife could depend on it."

"By all means, good Sir. But remember us here. As much as I am saddened by Frederick's passing, we could well do with another performer now."

"I will consider it," said Holmes.

I caught a slight glint in his eye and chastised him as we left. "Surely, you're not considering his offer of replacing Smartwood?"

"Why not? Caliban and Ariel are two of the more challenging roles in *The Tempest.* I understand the sorrow you feel at poor Mr. Smartwood's unfortunate death, but as they say, the show must go on."

***

It was four weeks later that I found myself once more in the auditorium of the virtually derelict Park Theatre. The main room was dimly lit, but the stage was ablaze with gaslights.

The Park Theatre Shakespeare troupe, as the esteemed Riley Winduss had decided to call them, was presenting their production of *The Tempest* to an audience of one. Me. Holmes had failed to tell me that they were performing, but Mr. Winduss had sent a telegram to 221B Baker Street with the sole intention of inviting me. I kept this from Holmes and snuck in while the preparations were underway. Luckily, Holmes was otherwise engaged, probably preparing his costume and makeup.

The day after our first meeting with Winduss, Mrs. Rowena Smartwood was released from Ealing station. Holmes, with myself in tow, returned directly to Baker Street and ran tests on the makeup that Smartwood had used. Within an hour it was confirmed that the makeup was the type outlawed over a century previously. It was riddled with arsenic, and users of an older age had dropped dead with great regularity before the authorities had finally outlawed its use.

Once the evidence was presented to the coroner, he, in turn, conducted his own tests on Smartwood's corpse and came to agree with Holmes's assessment. The cause of Smartwood's death was changed to long term exposure to arsenic, not strangulation.

Lanner’s reaction was one of suppressed rage at having his conclusions found to be incorrect. Reluctantly, he apologised profusely to Mrs. Smartwood and allowed her to leave. My final view of Lanner, was his crestfallen posture as he dropped his head and moped back into the bowels of the police station. Holmes’s only comment was, “Hopefully, he learns a lesson not to jump to the first conclusion, but to examine all the evidence and information presented. Only then, if the evidence doesn’t fit your postulation, re-examine all you know until your conclusion is irrefutable or you change it to fit the facts.”

Understandably, Mrs. Hudson was extremely effusive, showering both of us with thanks and later that evening as sumptuous a supper as I had devoured in many a year.

As I mused, the house lights dimmed, followed by the sounds of thunder and a remarkably effective flash of lightning.

“Boatswain!” the first actor called, and the play commenced.

The Adventure of the Great Wyrley Outrages

An adapted chronicle of an event from Arthur Conan Doyle's life.

It was a cold, crisp morning that saw me delivered unto the very steps of St. Mark's church in the tiny coal-mining town of Great Wyrley. I had an appointment with Reverend Shapurji Edalji, admittedly an odd name for that locale, but my understanding was he had emigrated from India many years before and converted from Parsee to the Church of England and taken on the ministry of St. Mark's.

I had long held the belief that our country could only benefit from the thoughts, opinions, and experiences of those born and raised from across the world. Reverend Edalji would be one such, and I hoped I could help he and his family in the matter that had come to my attention. Though I doubted if all my fellow countrymen held the same view, especially those whose lives were confined and entrenched in a tiny town such as this.

There was no one in the church itself, and I realised that at the hour of my visit, the Reverend would still be in his house at the rear of the property. A short walk found me before the modest house, and a quick knock brought the smiling face of my host to the door. "Mr. Arthur Conan Doyle, I am so pleased to make your acquaintance," said Reverend Edalji, his dark complexion broken by a wide grin showing pearly white teeth. Stepping aside, he allowed me entry and introduced his wife, Charlotte.

I was led to a small parlour, set with three places, and bade to sit, with the Reverend joining me, and Charlotte disappearing into the kitchen, I presumed. Within a moment, she re-joined us, placing a wonderful array of foods on the table for our breakfast.

"My word, I didn't expect anything this extravagant, so I thank you most humbly."

"Think nothing of it, Sir. You have expressed a wish to help our son, George, so nothing is too much trouble."

At the mention of her son's name, I noticed a sad look cross Charlotte's face. "I will do all I can to assist. His story is shocking and smacks of more than a simple misunderstanding," I said.

"Oh, you do not know the half of it," said the Reverend.

***

It had been when I read the headline *The Great Wyrley Ripper* that my initial interest in what became known as the *Great Wyrley Outrages* began. Four years earlier, in 1903, this quaint little village had become the centre of a series of horrid crimes. On numerous occasions, the residents would awake to find horses, cows, and pit ponies from the mines, mutilated and left to die in excruciating pain. Many were in such a state that their innards littered the clay soil, and the villages needed to put the poor animals out of their misery.

Great Wyrley became known as *the village of fear*, as the residents never knew what fresh horror may await them at the dawn of a new day.

From my reading, I realised that the local police were clueless. The attacks occurred in the dead of night, with the killer slashing the animals and leaving as silently as they came. No trace or piece of evidence was found that could conclusively lead to a single assailant.

The police issued orders for farmers to lock up their livestock, and for children to remain indoors after dark. Even with an increase in surveillance, the Ripper carried on with his deeds.

It wasn't until the 18th of August, when a young miner, Henry Garrett, was walking to begin his shift at the colliery and noticed a horse limping in a nearby field. His caring nature overcoming his desire to be punctual at work led him to find that the poor beast had been slashed. Raising the alarm, the villagers rushed to assist the animal, with the police soon pouncing on their only suspect, George Edalji, the Reverend's son.

***

"They put him away for three years," said the Reverend, his cup of coffee halfway to his lips. Replacing the cup, he shook his head in despair as the memories flooded back. "My poor boy, three years for crimes he didn't commit."

"Yes, I do agree with you. The whole trial was a sham. The evidence they presented was circumstantial at best. False at worst."

"He didn't even use a razor. George always attended the local barber, but the police didn't want to know."

The poor boy had suffered at the hands of the legal system. Something I was thoroughly disgusted about.

It had been chance that brought me into the story and convinced me to pursue the truth.

At the time of his arrest, George Edalji was forging a career as a solicitor in nearby Birmingham. Every morning he would make the journey to the larger town, only to return to the village in the evening. The police raided the vicarage where he still lived with his parents, finding a coat, supposedly with horsehair on it, a pair of muddied boots and a straight razor.

I hadn't established whether the police had sought legal permission to search the vicarage, or whether the Reverend and his wife had allowed it, having full faith in the constabulary.

George had been quickly arrested at his office in Birmingham, and then put on trial in nearby Stafford. The process lasted four days, with a jury finding him guilty of all charges after only fifty minutes of deliberation. He had been sentenced to seven years, and naturally, his career was destroyed.

Even though my interest at the time of the trial was purely in passing, minds more interested in the legal aspects of the trial took up the cause. Citing that the process was flawed, a petition was raised that gathered over ten thousand signatures. On presentation to the court, it was considered on its merits and George was released on parole. However, the spectre of guilt still hung over his head and barred him from practising the law, something in which he had spent years building up his proficiency and expertise.

By this stage, my own life had taken a dark turn. Touie, my darling wife, had recently died from tuberculosis. I was not myself, lost in guilt and despair, for while my wife succumbed to the dreaded disease, I had met and fallen in love with another. I know in my heart that Touie would never begrudge me a new love, but I could not shake the thoughts of betrayal within my own mind.

It was by chance that I happened upon George Edalji's letter amongst my usual sacks of mail from fans of the great detective. Reading his story, I realised taking up his cause was just the stimulant that my life required.

Writing to and meeting George at the Grand Hotel in Charing Cross was a tonic to my mind. Here was a man that had been wronged, by the very system I had supported for all my years. The system that my greatest creation reinforced throughout all of his dauntless exploits. George had read all of my novels and stories, and begged me, the creator of the world's premier consulting detective, to use his powers as if they were my own to prove his innocence. I have had many people write and tell me how much they love my stories, but there was something in George's appeal that piqued my interest.

As soon as I spotted George Edalji waiting for me in the hotel lobby, my heart went out to him. He was the only Indian in the room, a fact which drew several stares from other patrons and reinforced my thoughts on the matter, but it was the second pertinent fact that made me realise this man could never have undertaken such atrocious acts.

"He's extremely myopic," I mentioned to the Reverend and his wife. "When I met with him, he held his newspaper so close to his face that there was no other conclusion to be drawn. He confessed that he had read all of my stories but considering his condition I find that even more incredible."

"Yes. Sadly, our George does suffer with his eyesight. Something that tormented him for all those years in prison. Reading became his only relief."

"Before meeting George, I revisited the facts of the case. The night in question, the 17th of August was miserable. A virtual torrent ran through the county. In heavy rain, a man with George's eyesight would never have been able to cross the darkened fields safely."

"My word, that's true. George struggles to navigate the trip to the train station. I'm sure we told this to the police, but nothing came of it."

"I've also found, through my readings, that the killings continued after George was imprisoned."

Nodding his head sadly, "Yes, again another fact we brought up with the police, but by then they simply washed their hands of the incident. Some of the locals just put it down to someone copying George's acts."

I reached into my bag and drew out an old local paper that I had procured from the library. Turning to a particular article, I pointed at the horrid headline "Dark Oriental Killing Frenzy Stopped."

Charlotte gasped. The Reverend simply shook his head once more. "Yes. We have had to live with these lies and slanders for many years, even before George's arrest." He stood and walked from the room, returning momentarily with a handful of letters and placing them before me. "That article is mild compared to these."

I leafed through the letters and found myself shocked and disgusted at the contents. Each successive letter contained horrible accusations against the family, stemming from their conversion from the esoteric Parsee religion. They were accused of blood sacrifices and of virtually being part of some satanic cult.

"Did you show these to the police?"

"Oh, yes, many times. Ever since we started receiving them, which has been almost two decades now."

"How do you put up with this?" I asked, sliding the letters back across to the Reverend, and wishing to have nothing more to do with the filth they contained.

"I am a man of faith. I place my fate in the hands of God, and with that, I absolve these poor people of their sins."

I had to admire the Reverend's beliefs, but this was not something that could be swept away in the name of faith. A wrong had been committed and a man's future crushed.

Standing I said, "I have one more person to visit before returning to London, but rest assured I am thoroughly disgusted by everything that has occurred in this case. I will use whatever means I have at my disposal to see that justice is finally served."

With that, I bid the couple adieu and strolled back into town.

***

"Look, I don't care if he was blind as a bat. And I don't care what that Hindoo vicar says neither, he's just protecting his son. The evidence is clear. The little bugger did it. We arrested him, he was convicted and sent to prison. If a judge wants to let him out, then so be it. I done my job, and I won't be lectured to by some jumped-up little johnny that thinks he's a policeman just 'cause he had a few detective stories published."

I stared at Captain Anson, the head of the Staffordshire police, and took slow deep breaths to calm myself. This was the man that headed up the investigation that brought about the eventual conviction against George Edalji. He was a great beast of a man, and bull-headed in nature, and if I might say, not just a little racist.

It was becoming clearer in my mind that this entire affair smacked of ineptitude and incompetence, with a slathering of prejudice thrown in. Where little evidence existed, the police had fabricated, overlooked, or simply amplified what there was.

"Either the man is innocent and deserves exoneration and compensation, or he is guilty and deserves punishment," I thundered, my temper getting the better of me. "Your incompetence in this matter, Sir, has seen neither. But you have effectively destroyed his life and left him hanging by his thumbs in the eyes of the public."

"Pah," shouted Anson, "He's guilty. He wrote all those letters himself."

"Even those that arrived when he was merely twelve years old?"

"Then it was his father. No matter. His coat had horse hair on it. His boots were muddy. He had a razor."

"He has astigmatism. He can barely see one foot in front of himself. He could hardly navigate an open field on a dark and stormy night. As to the supposed evidence, all circumstantial and should have been thrown out before presentation."

The large man's face grew enraged. There was nothing further that could be gained from speaking with him. I simply left him to it and returned to London, convinced that a grave injustice had been played out.

***

I may not be the detective that I made famous, but I have my own abilities. Starting with an article in the Daily Telegraph, the name and story of George Edalji spread across the nation. Even appearing in the new world.

Keeping up my articles and protestations at this travesty for many months, I soon had others of my ilk on George's side. My friends J.M. Barrie, Bram Stoker and George Bernard Shaw joined my cause and lauded my articles far and wide.

So loud was the roar of disapproval, that the Home Office reneged and appointed a committee to look into the case.

Finally, after many months, they issued a full pardon to Mr. George Edalji, but no compensation.

This development angered me such that I pestered them continuously, making many enemies within the Office itself, and a lifelong enemy of Captain Anson. Neither worried me, my only concern was justice.

My harassment led to George's readmittance to the Solicitors' Roll, and with that he moved to London to begin practising law once more, never to return home to Great Wyrley, the town he had come to accept hated him simply for his heritage and appearance.

Although George never received the proper respect or remuneration for the court's bumbling, my pursuits found success with the establishment of what would become known as the Court of Criminal Appeal. In the future, this institution would allow those that could prove they had been wrongly accused and convicted of crimes, an avenue to have their cases revisited and hopefully, their verdicts overturned.

The entire affair left me with a resounding feeling of satisfaction and I found that my own bereavement and guilt were assuaged through my dedication to George's cause, for later that year I married my new love, Jean Elizabeth Leckie. We were fortunate enough to have three wonderful children and many years together.

I believe that Touie would have approved.

It was by chance that I happened upon George Edalji's letter amongst my usual sacks of mail from fans of the great detective.

The Body in the Box

"And who are you then?" asked Mrs. Hudson, staring down at the two filthy street urchins standing before her on the threshold of 221B Baker Street.

The taller one slid his flat cap from his head and held it close to his chest. "Tommy Bones, Ma'am. Wiggins sent me to speak wiv Mr. 'Olmes. 'E said we 'ad to use the bell, not charge in unannounced like."

"Good. I'll not have your like sullying up my house," Mrs. Hudson retorted.

Sitting in the parlour of the rooms that I shared with my friend Sherlock Holmes, I had just finished the day's papers and was a little lost for further diversion. When the bell rang downstairs, I felt the urge to investigate, but found Mrs. Hudson, our landlady, already addressing the visitors.

"What have we here, Mrs. Hudson?"

She glanced in my direction, barely hiding the slight look of disgust at the state of the two urchins on the doorstep. "These two are after Mr. Holmes. They are supposedly part of the riff-raff he pays to spy on half of London."

Looking through the doorway, I recognised Tommy Bones from a previous encounter, but the younger boy was a mystery to me. "What is it you want with Holmes, Tommy?"

"Good morning, Mr. Watson, it's little Nicky 'ere. I found 'im wandering around down near the river. 'E was senseless and kept muttering about a body in a box."

"That's Doctor Watson," Mrs. Hudson reminded the boy.

Dismissing the slight, I asked him to elaborate. "A body? In a box? Near the Thames?" The smaller boy's eyes drew slowly up into mine. He nodded but remained silent. I posed my next question to Tommy. "Is he one of the Irregulars?"

Shaking his head, Tommy said, "No, but I've seen 'im around. Pickpocket, 'e is. Runs with Solomon's gang."

"Oh," I said, "Marvelous, I'm sure Holmes will be delighted."

***

Quelling Mrs. Hudson's protestations, I brought our two guests up to the rooms that I had shared, for almost two and a half two years now, with Sherlock Holmes consulting detective. Tommy Bones was part of a group that Holmes called *The Baker Street Irregulars*, a rough and tumble crew of street urchins, that he paid to keep an eye and an ear to the cobbles and provide him with all manner of information.

Ushering Tommy and Nicky into our parlour, I was startled to see Holmes standing in his doorway. The dark shadows beneath his eyes indicated that he'd had another late night, probably prowling the back alleys of London in search of his next big adventure.

"What do we have here, Watson?"

"Tommy Bones has brought you something of interest, I hope. Little Nicky here says he found a body or some such." I bade the two boys sit on the settee, part of me hoping I could clean off any mess left behind.

Holmes strolled out, lighting a cigarette as he did so, and sat in the armchair facing the boys. I sat in the chair to his right. Addressing the small, frightened boy, he said, "Now, hello Nicky, I'm Sherlock Holmes. You've met my associate Doctor Watson, and it seems you know Tommy Bones, a long-time member of the Baker Street Irregulars. If Tommy has brought you to me, then you must have a tale of some intrigue."

Nicky's eyes flicked between me and Holmes several times while he seemed to build up his confidence. "I found a body. In a box."

"That must have been frightening."

"Yes, it was. I thoughts there'd be booty or somefin', but there was a body. I got scared and runs away, like. I don't knows what to do. Tommy founds me and says 'e knows a geezer."

Holmes smiled. "Yes, I would be that geezer." Pausing for a moment, he added, "Can you start at the beginning of your story, I don't think you simply happened on a body."

Nicky shook his head. "No. I didn't want nuffin' to do with no body. Just wanted the man's wallet."

"Ah, go on then."

His eyes grew wide. I could tell that he felt that little nugget of information might get him into trouble. It was Tommy that calmed him down. "Now, don't worry Nicky, Mr. 'Olmes knows what it's like on the streets, 'e don't care none about that stuff. You tell 'im what you told me."

His eyes flicking between Holmes's and mine once more, Nicky began. "I was down the docks like always. Lots of marks down there. Mr. Solomon makes us work the area. 'E says we blend in, like."

"Yes, there are many of your ilk down at the docks. I'm sure Solomon has a great many young urchins working in those areas. Shame really, most of them grow up to be adult criminals, and that's where I come in at times."

Nicky's eyes grew wide. "I don't want you coming after me, Mr. 'Olmes. I've 'eard o' you. You done put away loads o' geezers."

I had to smile at the fact this young delinquent was afeared of Holmes's reputation.

"Yes, well let's hear your story, then consider your future later."

"Right," said the boy, taking a deep breath. "It was only late yesterday. I was working down Smithfield way when I sees this geezer and made a move. 'E was all dressed up nice, expensive shoes an' all, and not paying much attention. Perfect mark, as Mr. Solomon tells us."

"Indeed, go on."

"Well, I sidles up to 'im. Does the bump and run, and ducks down an alley before 'e even notices. Finking I'd got some nice loot, I finds that I've only got a key and a scrap o' paper."

Pulling his hand from the pocket of his cardigan, Nicky held out the items. Holmes took each in turn and examined them.

"Hmmm. Looks like a Milner strongbox key. Tarnished and old, some scratches on the end, indicating it has been used recently." Placing the key on the table before him, he looked at the slightly crumpled paper, turning it which way and that, before carefully unfolding it and reading the writing inside. "Standard parchment, no watermarks. Hmm. An address in Limehouse, on Narrow Street."

"Yeah, I went straight there. Thought it must be important, could be some good stuff for Mr. Solomon." Nicky shook his head. "Nah, building was burnt out. Nothing left, 'cept the box."

"Box?"

"Yeah. Metal box. All black with soot from a fire. I almost left it but got curious. I wish I'd left it now."

"That's where the body was?"

Nicky's mouth quivered, and his eyes grew wide and distant. The hollow look of abject horror. He slowly nodded. "Yeah. That's where I found 'er."

"A woman?"

"No. A girl. About Tommy's age, from what I saw. I can still see 'er poor face lookin' up at me. All covered in blood. 'Orrible it was."

"My word," I said, "You poor little fellow."

It was at that point that Mrs. Hudson arrived at the doorway, with a tray of tea and biscuits. "Thought you and your, ahem, guests, might need some refreshments." We remained silent while Mrs. Hudson placed the tray down, and I doled out the tea. The two boys hoed into the biscuits like there was no tomorrow. Nicky had apparently recovered from the fear of his remembrance.

When all was quiet once more, Holmes pressed the young boy further. "What did you do next, Nicky?"

Shaking his head, he answered, "I don't rightly know, Sir. I must 'ave left. The next thing I knows is that Tommy 'ere took me aside, talked wiv me a while, then we ends up 'ere."

"Kept 'im wiv me all night, like," added Tommy.

"You didn't touch the body?" Holmes asked.

"No, Sir. I don't remember doing that."

"But you had the key and note?"

"I found them in my pocket. Must 'ave put them away when I unlocked the box."

"I don't suppose you thought about going to the police?" I asked.

Nicky drew back in terror. He shook his head, his eyes staring at me. "Not the bobbies. No. Never."

Holmes let out a slight chuckle. "I would be very surprised if a young urchin, in Nicky's trade, would seek out the constabulary." He grew silent for a moment, picking up the key and note in turn, before speaking. "I think you should continue to stay with Tommy, here. I doubt if the fellow you took these from would be able to tell you apart from any other child of the street, but it would be safer if he didn't have the chance. The man we are looking for is obviously involved in something nefarious, but I'd like to confirm everything myself before proceeding." Turning to the young Irregular, he added, "Tommy, can you inform Wiggins that he has a new member, temporary for now, but who knows what the future holds." Glancing at the younger boy, he asked, "Is that all right with you Nicky?"

"I don't know if Mr. Solomon will be 'appy."

"Leave Mr. Solomon to me. I know his story, and I'm sure he wouldn't appreciate the interest of my acquaintances at the Yard."

***

The journey to Limehouse took much longer than I imagined. There were a lot of carts and wagons on the roads past the tower, and the docks area around St. Katherine's that held us up for what seemed like ages.

By the time we were dropped off at the address on Narrow Street, I was bathed in sweat. The warm spring weather on that day in late May sapped the strength from my bones and brought out blossoms of moisture in my armpits.

Stepping down from the hansom, I studied the burnt-out hulk before me.

"This is recent," said Holmes standing to my left.

"How so?" I asked, examining the carcass of the two-story building, with its scorched brickwork and missing door.

Holmes pointed to the adjoining houses, each was attached to the burnt place, but seemed to be relatively unaffected by the conflagration that had besieged their neighbour. "The curtains on each of the upper floors of the adjacent properties are drawn back with the windows wide open. That suggests that they may have been affected by smoke and are airing out their rooms, but the occupants are not at home."

"What gives you that idea?"

"The windows and doors are shut fast on the ground floor. If the occupants were home, they too would be open. It would be a brave or desperate soul that would shimmy up to the first floor to gain entry." He peered closer at both houses for a moment, before smiling. "And the presence of broken bottles and glass lining the windowsills of both properties indicate a primitive, but a quite effective form of protection from would-be burglars."

"Devilishly clever."

Holmes turned his attention to the property before us. "Now, what have we here?"

The front of the property had been scorched and marked from the flames and smoke escaping from the conflagration inside but appeared structurally sound. A multitude of sooty footprints led through the doorway; I could sense Holmes's annoyance at the obliteration of any evidence that may have existed.

The door itself had been broken open when the Metropolitan Fire Brigade or some of the locals had attended to the fire. The windows however had survived but were blackened and restricted any view into the interior of the building.

Holmes stood on the threshold for a moment and stared inside. The light spilling in from outside was diffused due to the smoke-blackened windows, but there was enough to allow us to make out several details.

The front door opened into a small entryway with a sitting room off to one side through another doorway. Even from where we stood, I could tell that the fire had started in the parlour and raced through into the entryway. A line of black boot marks led to and from that room. The damage inside looked far less extensive than I had expected but was enough to make me concerned about the safety of the rafters and upper floor area.

"I assume you've noticed the origin of the fire."

I pointed to the side room. "In there. The scorching of the flames runs out towards the entrance but didn't advance down the hallway towards the back of the house."

"Yes. The floor is relatively unscathed the further one advances. These footmarks and water damage are from the firemen themselves.

So, most of the damage is limited to this room." He carefully stepped into the entrance, and moved to the doorway of the parlour, stopping for a moment before entering the room.

I followed and surveyed the scene of devastation. Even though it was limited to that one room, the fire must have burnt the majority of the furniture. The only piece left was a blackened steel box sitting in the far corner, its lid swung open revealing an empty, but almost pristine interior. The floor was a mess of black ash, mushed into a soggy pulp from feet and water. Some of the more intact pieces still glistened with moisture. "That's very strange. All the furniture has been burnt away, but that box remains relatively intact."

"And that is the box in question. It's a fireproof safe box, supplied by Thomas Milner. They are reportedly able to withstand the most intense of fires. As to the furniture, it's there." Holmes pointed to a pile of ashes and coals that surrounded the box. "Whatever furniture was in this room, was broken apart and piled around the box, before being set alight." Craning to look around the box, and then inspecting the insides, he added, "The miscreant attempted to burn the box, and its contents, which we believe to be a young girl's body, though we only have young Nicky's word on that."

And that is the box in question.

"It would seem strange to attempt to burn a fireproof safe box."

"Yes, which leads me to believe that the perpetrator either didn't realise that fact or could not stomach the burning of the body itself out in the open." Stopping, he scanned the area once more, stepping towards the small fireplace. It was blackened from soot acquired from both its operation and the fire in the room. He bent down for a while, before pulling out his glass and inspecting the area around the base of the fireplace. He shuffled away, before pointing at a dark patch on one of the hearthstones. "What do you make of this?"

I hunkered down next to him and stared at the blackened area. It appeared more solid than the smoke and soot stains affecting the other parts of the fireplace. "Something resting there melted, or something was spilt and dried, then burnt in place?"

"Or could it be dried and burnt blood?"

Squinting, I peered closer, before reaching out and prodding the patch. It had dried to a hard crust, but pushing at it, broke the hardened skin, causing flakes to break away. Holding my finger up into a beam of light, Holmes studied the flecks on my fingertip through his glass. "Hmm." He pursed his lips. "Inconclusive, but I wouldn't rule it out at this point. Could be that the poor missing girl was felled at this spot, bundled up into that box and set alight in the hopes of covering up the crime. Unsubstantiated at this point, but still probable."

Standing again, Holmes moved back to the box and pulling Nicky's key from his pocket, inserted it into the lock. It turned easily, triggering the locking mechanism. "Well, it is the owner of this key then." Replacing the key in his pocket, Holmes peered once more inside the box, murmuring as he studied the lining. "There's certainly blood or other similar stains in here. Dried now due to the heat from the fire, but not obscured. The rest of the box is dry, which indicates it served its purpose and kept the contents safe from the water used to douse the fire." Pushing his hand into the box, he exclaimed, "Aha, what have we here?"

Rising to his full height, he held articles in both hands. His left held two small strands of hair, the other a small swatch of fabric between his thumb and index finger. Rubbing the material between his fingers, he said, “Wool. Slightly poor quality. Grey.”

“Not a fashionable colour. Very workmanlike I would think.”

“If young Nicky found a body completely contained in this box, then I do not think the person was fully grown, more likely a child or teenager, as he said.” Holding the swatch of fabric up into the light, Holmes pulled out his glass and studied it carefully. “Hmm,” he murmured, “It is a very coarse weave. The type of material used in uniforms.”

“Military? Nurse?”

“Unsure, could even be from a school. Only someone who would be very reticent about speaking up would allow themselves to wear such a fabric. Even those in the military or medical services would baulk at this. But, as we know, the strict regimes of some educational facilities can dampen any type of protest.”

“That would fit if the victim were a child. As you said, the box is too small for a fully grown adult. But, where?”

“I can only imagine that the school would be in a more impoverished area, such as this one. There are several in the area. I would also think that it may be a residential school where the uniforms are supplied, rather than procured by the parents. These establishments tend to ensure that the costs are kept to a minimum. I think it would take too long to visit them all, I will first undertake some research before pursuing more information.” Looking at the tiny strands of hair, he added, “And this will need a closer inspection. It’s too dark in here, and I will need my scope.”

“Should we bring in Lestrade? He may be able to provide constables to take some of the load off your shoulders.”

“There's no reason as yet. We have no body and very scant evidence. The testimony of a small street urchin, one who dabbles in unseemly activities, would not be much to base a full police investigation on.”

“Hmm. Point taken.”

***

“Ah, Watson, be a good chap and put that down before someone gets hurt.”

I glanced down at the hand holding my service revolver, then over at the reason I had brought it with me.

The previous night had been a late one. No sooner had Holmes and I returned to 221B Baker Street than a message arrived for me.

One of my newly acquired patients had taken ill and I was forced to bid a hasty retreat to my room, before embarking on a call to the older lady and providing whatever ministrations she required. That little trip finished well into the darkness of night and found me back in bed long past midnight.

It was after only two or three hours' sleep, still in the early hours before sunrise, that I awoke and heard a noise from outside. Donning my dressing gown, I listened at my door, hoping that it was simply the fog of sleep that had dulled my senses. The sound continued. A slight creaking of floorboards and a rustling of papers.

Glancing at the crack beneath my door, I saw the flickering of candlelight beyond.

Creeping across to my footlocker, I drew my service revolver out, ensuring it was loaded and returned to the door. Breathing a sigh of relief when it opened with nary a creak or groan, I found a figure rooting around Holmes's desk and bookcase. The person was dressed in the shabbiest of clothing. From my viewpoint, I spied a torn and dirty overcoat that smacked of one from the slums or streets, possibly from the area we had visited only the previous day.

As I stepped forward, the figure stopped momentarily, and then spoke.

“Ah, Watson, be a good chap and put that down before someone gets hurt.”

“Holmes?”

The man turned. I expected my colleague, but spied instead a bent-backed figure, with a messy scruff of hair upon his head, a large bulbous nose, and the red-flushed cheeks of a heavy drinker.

“Who in the blazes are you?” I repeated, bringing my revolver back to bare on the figure, “And why do you sound like Holmes?”

A smile split the man's ruddy face, and he stood up to his full height, sloughing off the dirty coat, and suddenly taking on the form of Sherlock Holmes. “It's me, Watson. I would have thought you had become used to my disguises." He brought a hand to his face and quickly pulled away the face putty, and cheek fillers used to change his visage so remarkably.

My mouth dropped open as the dirty street dweller dissolved into my erstwhile companion. "Good Lord Holmes, I could have shot you."

"On that subject," he said, nodding at the revolver.

I gasped at the realisation that I still held the gun, cocked and ready to fire. Moving it away, I disarmed it and flicked on the safety, before popping it into the pocket of my gown. "Why are you dressed like that? And at this time of the morning?"

"Well, Watson, sometimes the best way to elicit information is to join in with the brethren of the street. I find that I can blend in much better in such a form, than if I were to appear as you would expect."

Shaking my head I added, "I still can't get used to this part of you."

A slight chuckle came from my friend. "Again, I have my ways, and sometimes they do pay off."

My interest piqued, I asked, "And?"

Turning back to the table, he pointed at a map of the Limehouse area. "As luck would have it, for us it seems, not for the poor unfortunate object of our hunt, a body was pulled from the Thames late yesterday afternoon. Down here." He pointed to a spot on the Thames, not far from the burnt-out house."

"Oh, no. Is it the missing lass?"

"That I don't know. All I could find out, from the street denizens of the area, was that the body was taken to the East London Hospital, they have a morgue there devoted to children."

"That's a tad sad if you think about it."

"Sign of the times, really. I didn't believe my disguise would be appropriate for a visit to the hospital, so I returned here to investigate other matters further."

"Such as?"

"Schools. I found that there are three residential schools for girls in the Limehouse area, with several more scattered further afield."

Pointing at a list before him, he added, "I've listed them here, for visitation later in the day."

Consulting our mantel clock, I said, "It's four in the morning, I do hope you will at least sleep before setting out once more."

A broad smile came to his face. "Well, I may not sleep much, but I can see no benefit in setting out before a hearty breakfast, and possibly a bath. Let us set a time of ten o'clock, shall we?"

Nodding, I turned sluggishly away and ventured back to my bed, hoping that Holmes would at least attempt to attain a higher level of silence during the remainder of the night.

***

The East London Hospital for Children was slightly more than five years old and still looked virtually new. It was set apart from the buildings around it and towered three storeys above Glamis Road. My understanding was that the benefactor previously ran the hospital from a nearby warehouse and bequeathed a large sum on his death, in 1871, for a new hospital to be built on the site.

As Holmes had stated, it was a sad reality that a hospital devoted to the health of children and their mothers would require a mortuary for when the outcome is not altogether positive.

A brief inquiry at the reception area found us led to the bowels of the hospital and let into a surprisingly bright room with gaslighting. Several beds lay along the far wall, each holding a small lump covered with a white sheet.

"So many children," I said under my breath.

"Yes, mostly from those areas that have less access to health care," said a voice from behind us.

Turning I saw a young man, whom I would place in his mid-twenties, dressed in a white coat over a neatly pressed white shirt and dark slacks. Even with his young age, he had the lines and shadowed eyes of one much older. I presumed it was from the stress of his work environment.

Looking us both up and down, the doctor continued. "I'm Doctor Robson, is there something I can help you with, or are you lost?"

Holmes replied first. "Pleased to meet you, Doctor, I am hoping we are not lost. I am Sherlock Holmes, and this is my associate,

Doctor John Watson." I noticed Holmes put particular emphasis on my title. I assumed it was to secure a professional bond with Robson.

He nodded towards me and smiled. "Ah, a fellow physician?" When I nodded, he asked, "And what can I help you gentlemen with? It is quite unusual for members of the public to be brought down here. Are you relatives of one of these unfortunates?"

"No. I am a professional consulting detective and have taken on a case involving a missing person, possibly a young schoolgirl from the Limehouse area. I believe that you have taken delivery of someone who may fit the description. I have scant information, but," reaching into his coat, he brought out a small envelope and removed the two clues discovered so far. "She is young, possibly early to mid-teens. With brown hair, possibly shoulder length, and wearing a grey woollen tunic or dress."

Robson's eyes grew narrow. "That's a remarkably precise description, on scant information."

"Why would you say that?" I asked.

Instead of answering, he crossed the room to one of the beds and drew the sheet back from its resident, stopping just below the neck. Immediately, I saw why. Lying on the bed, was the blue-tinged body of a young girl with dark hair, which clung to her head in knotted clumps, some sporting the detritus of the river.

"She was pulled from the Thames only yesterday. Down near the Limehouse docks. I put her age as about fourteen. Her hair is dark brown, hard to tell, but the length falls just below her shoulders. Her eyes are cloudy from the water but have a distinctive green tinge to them."

"Was she clothed?"

Nodding, Robson pointed to a small set of shelves. "Only just put the dress and shirt back there. They were soddened, so we dried them out." I noticed his nose wrinkle at a memory. "Still stink, though."

All three of us moved across to the shelves. Holmes at once found the tunic and compared the swatch of fabric to it. "Hmmm. The dress is a little stained, but the colour matches to a high enough degree. Any identification found?"

Robson shook his head. "No. She is as she was found. I performed a quick examination and found a wound on the back of her head. Serious enough to be the cause of her demise, or at least to have disabled her enough so that a quick swim was the end of her. I'd like to do a full autopsy, but we just don't have the funds, time or," he shrugged, "need. A young child such as this, found in the river, could be foul play, could have been a childish lark. The police won't be interested, so the administrators take the easy path."

"No autopsy?"

"No, and the strangest thing is, I'm sure she has been dead for a good week or more, but the presentation of her skin and flesh tells me that she was only in the water for a day."

Holmes nodded, a studious look on his face as he processed these new facts. "That is very telling, thank you, Doctor." Slipping his hand into his coat once more, he presented his card to Robson and said, "If anyone comes asking about the poor girl, could you please contact me?"

"Do you know what happened?"

"Not yet. Admittedly, an autopsy would tell us a little more, such as whether she inhaled water or not, but I'll have to do without it seems."

Robson placed a gentle hand on my forearm. "Please keep me informed. I see so many poor young souls come through here. It would be nice to see one find peace in the resolution of their demise."

Patting the hand, I added, "Of course. Again, thank you for your help."

***

Our immediate concern was to visit the schools that Holmes had identified from his research earlier that morning. I was immediately astounded by Holmes's knowledge of the Limehouse area. This was a situation I would find myself in, on numerous occasions over the course of our future association. Many schools are not listed on regular street maps of London, but Holmes appeared to have an almost encyclopaedic knowledge of their names and locations, even some of the uniforms they issued.

“There are three residential schools within a short distance from the burnt-out premises. In fact, all are within walking distance, which gives me pause for thought on the matter before us.”

“How so?”

“Even though my career as a consulting detective is relatively short, I have already borne witness to the worst depravities of the human condition. We were fortunate enough to have not shared poor young Nicky's view of the body in the box. Though from the scant evidence we have seen and been told about, this affair involves the probable death of a young girl, of school age, possibly a resident of a nearby school, whose remains were deposited within a fireproof strongbox, only to have a fire set in a probable attempt to erase that fact.”

“Yes, when you put it that way, very horrid. What of the house? Why was she there?”

“Ah, now there’s a question. There are several possible answers, the two most likely are that she was brought there of her own free will, or even against it; or that she was visiting someone. I’m leaning to the former, as the perpetrator had no real attachment to the property, given the fact they set a fire before fleeing.”

“Hmmm. It hinges mostly on the identity of the girl. Would the perpetrator have returned to remove her corpse?”

“Now there’s a question. Either he did or another was co-opted into doing so. Nicky mentioned a tall well-dressed man. That piques my interest, it may mean nothing, or it may mean everything.”

“Why?”

“Well, I must admit that to Nicky, well-dressed could mean anyone that isn’t living on the streets, but if the man were not of the same class as others from this area, what was he doing here?”

Our first stop was at the Northey Street School for Girls, a mere half-mile walk from the derelict house. Even before entering, we realised there was no need to go further. The students were enjoying their morning break and were milling and playing in the small, grassed area between buildings. Every girl wore the same uniform, a dark blue tunic, with a white blouse beneath. None, that we could see, sported a woollen garment bearing the same colour as the little grey swatch that Holmes held.

"Hmm. I know of two others, one of which will be of no use as well, for much the same reason. The Stepney girls' school to our North, is also known as the Greencoat School. Their uniforms are similar to these, but the tunics are a dark, bottle green. That leaves us with one more obvious candidate."

The Thomas Street Boarding School for Girls straddled the area between Thomas Street and the Limehouse Cut, a purpose-built canal built to connect the Limehouse docks with the River Lea.

In direct opposition to our previous destination, the favourability of this one was immediate. A group of girls, possibly as young as thirteen, exited from the main doors as we approached. All wore the same strict uniform, a grey tunic, with a white blouse beneath. Even from a distance, the tunic appeared to be made from a loosely spun woollen fabric, much like the piece that Holmes found.

"Hmmm," he said, "I think we have a strong candidate."

Stepping in through the front doors, we found a studious looking woman working alone at a desk behind a small partition. Within a few minutes of approaching her, we were ushered into the office of the headmistress, a stern and matronly looking woman in her fifties. The nameplate on her desk said, "Cordelia Smeekins," and her disapproving look told me that interruptions were not welcome.

"We are dreadfully sorry to impose on your time, Mrs. Smeekins," started Holmes.

"Miss," came a terse reply.

"So sorry, Miss Smeekins. I am Sherlock Holmes, and this is my associate, Doctor John Watson."

"Yes? And?"

"I am a consulting detective and am investigating the apparent disappearance of a young girl from a nearby Limehouse residence. We only have a few strands of hair, and this small swatch of material." He held up the piece of fabric. "A witness stated that the young girl was of school age, and this fabric appears to be similar to the tunics that form part of your uniform. These facts have led us to your premises. So, my question is, are any of your students missing?"

I'm sure Holmes saw it too, but a faint hint of trepidation crossed that proud, uncompromising façade before it flashed away once more.

Silence hung in the air for a good few seconds, before Holmes spoke again. "I do apologise, I'm sure if there are, you would have quickly advised the authorities and their parents, so silly of me to even presume." He started to rise, almost gaining his full height before Miss Smeekins bade him sit again.

"No. No, I should apologise for being harsh. Please sit down. I think you might be of some help."

Holmes sat down once more, remaining silent to allow Miss Smeekins time to regain her composure and continue. "As alarming, and indeed embarrassing, as it is, yes, one of our girls has gone missing. Now, this does happen quite often, but either their money runs out, or they find the streets of London a much more harrowing experience than they presumed and will generally saunter back after a day or two with their tails between their legs."

"But not this time?"

Miss Smeekins shook her head slowly. "No. The young lass left over a week ago. Slipped out in the early morning, well before breakfast time. None of the other girls saw her leave, and she only took the clothes on her back."

"Her school uniform?"

"Why, yes, as you've seen it is of the same colour as that piece of fabric, but that could be from anything, really." Holmes produced the small swatch of material, placing it on the headmistress's desk and sliding it across to her. Miss Smeekins picked up the piece of fabric and studied it, intently before nodding. "Hmm, yes, on second thoughts, this could definitely be from one of our uniforms." Sliding it back to Holmes, she added, "Forgive us, but the girls are only meant to wear these on the school premises or surrounds, so we aim for a hardwearing, but inexpensive material. I'm very disappointed, but not surprised by our Penelope."

"Penelope?" I asked.

"Yes." Miss Smeekins looked confused for a moment, "Penelope Burdett. Didn't I mention her name?" Dropping her gaze and shaking her head slowly, she added, “I’m sorry. This last week has been very upsetting. I do not enjoy having our students wandering about, so.”

“Would she have, perhaps, returned to her parents?” I asked.

“Oh, no, poor Penelope is an orphan. Her dear mother passed just late last year. The young girl has been beside herself. Changing from fits of grief to anger and back again. The awkward years are tough enough on young girls, but put this in the mix and it’s a harrowing experience. The girls reside here for much of the year, returning home during the holidays, but poor Penelope had to spend Christmas and Easter with us here. She was so distraught.”

Holmes brought the headmistress back to our inquiry. “Could you describe this Penelope?”

“Oh, yes. Fourteen years old, just this past February. Five-foot two in height. Brown shoulder-length hair. Slim build. Pretty much average, really. Her most striking feature was her eyes. Bright green.”

“Hmmm,” murmured Holmes. “The height and weight fit. The hair and eyes fit. And then there is that.” He nodded at the small piece of cloth. “It seems that we may be interested in finding the same young girl. Do you happen to have an address for her mother? Maybe there are other witnesses that may have seen her.”

“Oh, yes.” She reached for a thick ledger from within one of her desk drawers. After flipping several pages, Miss Smeekins said, “11 Narrow Street, Limehouse. But, as I said, the poor woman died almost six months ago.”

I gasped at the address, looking sideways at Holmes, he held his composure.

“Hmmm. That address tells us more than you are aware.”

“How do you mean?” the headmistress asked.

“I am sorry to inform you that we believe your student to be dead.” It was Miss Smeekins's turn to gasp. “The hair, I mentioned, and that swatch of cloth were found inside a steel strongbox in a burnt-out house, 11 Narrow Street, Limehouse, to be exact. It matches the uniform worn by a young girl, whose body was pulled out of the Thames yesterday afternoon.”

“My word, that poor girl.”

"We haven't informed the police as yet, but they will need to be involved soon. They will also need a positive identification, so if there is any way to find a relative or someone who knew the girl, then we need to pursue that avenue of inquiry."

"Or it will be I who must identify her, the poor thing."

"Yes, sadly."

"Sorry to be direct, but there was no father then?" I asked.

"No," she said, shaking her head and dabbing at the edges of her eyes with a kerchief. I was surprised to see such a matronly woman taken to emotion, but I could only imagine that Miss Smeekins looked upon her students as faux children.

"No other guardian?" I asked. Another shake.

Holmes thought for a moment. "I assume then that with no funds coming in to pay for Penelope's tuition, you would have had to terminate her residency here."

"No, not at all. Penelope's fees are paid through an intermediary. The funds appear in our accounts every year without fail."

"Intriguing, the mother set up a trust or some such?"

Miss Smeekins thought for a moment. "It never occurred to me before how she could afford it. Miss Lyra Burdett was a simple seamstress. As far as I know, she barely had two pennies to rub together, but that was never my business. As long as the fee was paid, I was more than happy to accommodate the young lass."

"Could I be so bold as to ask for the details of this intermediary? They may be able to shed light on a close relative."

"Ah for that, I will need to consult with my assistant." The headmistress rose and moved across to her office door, pulling it open so swiftly that her assistant spilt to the office floor. "So, Agnes, I presume you heard the request."

I stifled a slight chuckle as I watched the poor woman stand up and compose herself, before nodding. "Yes, Miss Smeekins, I have it right here." She hurried off, returning quickly, with another ledger. Ignoring both Holmes and me, she moved to the desk and opened it. Turning several pages, she pointed to an entry.

"Ah, that's right," said Miss Smeekins before writing the contact details onto a card and handing it to Holmes.

As he read, a small smile grew on his face.

"Pardon me, Miss Smeekins, but are the students able to contact people outside of the school during term time?"

The headmistress nodded. "Oh, yes, we're not some sort of prison. If a student wishes to send a message to a relative or someone else, then they can approach Agnes here, and she will arrange it."

Turning towards the assistance, Holmes asked, "Did Penelope Burdett attempt to contact someone recently?"

Agnes withdrew to her desk and shuffled through a pile of papers impaled on a bill spike. Eventually, she tore one off and held it up. "Yes, she did, I forgot all about it, but she sent a note to Mr. Cumbage," she said, nodding towards the card in Holmes's hand.

"I don't suppose you know what the message said, do you?"

"Oh, yes, Sir, it's right here." Her eyes dropped to the page. "Mr. Cumbage. I need to meet him. Tomorrow. Before school starts. Home."

"Do you know what date that was sent?"

Reading the message further, Agnes answered. "The twelfth."

"That was the day before she disappeared," said Miss Smeekins, "How could you have failed to tell me this, Agnes?"

"I do apologise, Miss."

***

"Who is Hyram Cumbage? You seem to know him, or at least know of him?" I asked Holmes, as I read the name on the card once more.

"I've not met the man, but I have come across his name in various dealings. He is a solicitor, but let us say that he specialises in practices that only stay on the right side of the law through plain good luck, rather than design. If he is involved, then I am forming more of a complete picture than I had previously."

Handing back the card, I nestled back in the seat of the cab and watched the streets of London pass by as we bumped our way through them. Within a few minutes we headed into Gossett Street near Shoreditch and the cab stopped before a small Georgian terrace with a sign outside that proclaimed it to be the offices of one, *Hyram Cumbage, Solicitor at law*."

The sole occupant of the office was a short, bald little man, with a strangely lined face that gave him the appearance of an apple that had been left in the sun for far too long. He sat behind a large, dark wooden desk and looked up from a pile of paperwork through extremely thick eyeglasses. “Can I help you, gentlemen?”

“Ah, Mr. Cumbage? Mr. Hyram Cumbage?” asked Holmes with an air of innocence that I could tell was drawn from his acting days.

“Yes? I’m at a loss, Sir. You know me, presumably from the name on the board outside, but I do not know you.”

Removing his hat, Holmes said, “I am Sherlock Holmes, and this is my colleague, Doctor John Watson.”

The scrunch-faced man's expression remained impassive for a moment until a look of confusion crossed it. “Sherlock Holmes? That name seems familiar, but I cannot place it or you.” Placing his pen back into its holder, he waved a hand and said, “Never mind. Please state your business. I am a busy man as you can see. If you are a new client, then have a seat. If you are selling something, then the door is behind you.”

“Neither I’m afraid. But, we have come about a client of yours.”

“Client? Whatever business you have with one of my clients is between you and them. So, in that case, please leave.”

“The client is Penelope Burdett.” A twinkle of recognition crossed Cumbage’s face. “Of 11 Narrow Street, Limehouse.” The solicitor remained silent. “You arrange the payments for her schooling at the Thomas Street Boarding School for Girls.” Holmes went silent and waited.

After a moment, Cumbage finally replied. “So? What of it?”

“Well, she contacted you only a week ago, asking to meet with, as she said, *him*.” Holmes held up the note that he had retrieved from Agnes. “Now, she’s dead.” Holmes dropped the bombshell and let its effect hang in the air for a few moments.

A stunned look dawned on the solicitor’s face. “Dead?” Cumbage said, his voice more of a whisper, his eyes staring into Holmes’s “When? How?”

“That is what I am trying to determine.”

"Sherlock Holmes. Now it's come to me. You're the private detective that has been circulating through Soho and Whitechapel for the last couple of years."

"And many other parts of London, to be honest, but yes, that is I."

"And Penelope's dead?"

"Yes. Sadly, she was drawn from the Thames only yesterday morning. The police have not been informed as yet, but they will need someone to identify the body. For my part, I wish to identify the reason for the poor girl's demise. To do that I will need your help."

"Well, I don't really know the girl, only by name. I simply manage her affairs."

"On, whose request?"

"I can't tell you that, I need to protect my client's identity and interests."

Holmes placed two hands on the solicitor's desk and leaned in, staring directly into the oversized lenses and through into Cumbage's eyes. "Would that be Lyra Burdett?" He remained still, the older man squirming but shaking his head.

"I don't know who that is?"

"That would be Penelope's mother. So, if you do not know her mother, then you must be working for her father?" I was intrigued.

The solicitor showed no outward signs, but Holmes began to smile. "Ah, yes, her father. Now, it would be very helpful if you could tell me his name."

"I can't."

"Hmmm." Holmes continued to stare into the man's eyes. There was no hint of malice in my colleague's actions, but the proximity of their faces was more than unnerving to the solicitor. "I understand your concern, Mr. Cumbage, so, it will need to be you that identifies the body of poor Miss Penelope Burdett."

"But, I've never seen her. I only act on behalf of …"

"Her father. Yes. What is his name then? We can inform the police and he can identify the body."

"I…I…"

"I'm sure that the police would be very interested in your other cases. Especially, young Malcolm Dalgleish." Cumbage's eyes darted down to the open folder to his right. "Doesn't he run with the Lambeth Lads? I hear he is under scrutiny over an assault and robbery that ended with the victim's unfortunate death. Only last Saturday night, wasn't it? That would be of interest to my friend Inspector Lestrade, I'm sure." Holmes lifted one hand and pointed to another file. "Or that one, Percy Renton. I know of him personally. A burglar working the Hamstead Heath area. Nothing of note, or at least nothing that has drawn any of his victims to me, but he has a reputation that has been growing down the East End of late. Inspector Bradstreet would find that information interesting."

Cumbage's face grew red, and I could see him visibly shaking. I started to worry that the man might have a turn and burst a blood vessel.

"Driesbach. Millard Driesbach. That's all I'm going to tell you. Now please, leave me be." He fell back into his chair, drawing deep breaths and fetching a kerchief from his breast pocket, which he used to wipe the beads of sweat that had burst from his forehead.

"Millard Driesbach? Hmmm." Turning away from the solicitor, Holmes added, "Come, Watson, a quick trip to Islington is required."

***

After a short side trip, the hansom took us north through the great metropolis.

"I've had my eye on Mr. Driesbach for quite some time," said Holmes as we approached the entrance to Liverpool Street in Islington. "He runs an importation business that sources furniture and artefacts from the sub-continent. Two years ago, I was requested to investigate a matter of several items that were brought into the country. Investigating Driesbach and two other businesses like his revealed nothing but led me to several dock workers who were intercepting the items and removing them before they reached the importation companies."

"But, you weren't convinced; otherwise, why would you still have Mr. Driesbach in your sights?"

"Quite so, even though I stopped the operation, I never found out who had been organising the smuggling from the sub-continent end?"

"Does this Driesbach know you, or anything about this surveillance?"

"No. No, I don't think he does. We've never met, but that may become useful."

For a man on the rise in business, Mr. Driesbach's premises were very quiet. The outer door opened into a small reception area, with a desk, which was currently unoccupied, sitting in the centre of the room. A coat rack stood near the main door holding several items, one particular coat attracting Holmes's attention. He moved across and studied the sleeves, before leaning in and sniffing the material. I was a little perturbed at his actions, but that was something I was becoming used to.

At opposite ends of the room, were two doors. Each sported a plaque with the name of the occupier of the room beyond. Holmes nodded towards the right-hand room, and we fronted the door, whose plaque said, "M Driesbach."

Holmes grasped the doorknob, before turning it and knocking at the same time. As he opened the door, he said, "Sorry to bother you Mr. Driesbach, but your reception area was unattended." Thrusting the door wide open, we spied a slightly startled man sitting behind a large mahogany desk. A virtual mountain of paperwork sat in baskets on either side of his desk, some of which he had been feverishly working through at the time of our intrusion.

"Who the devil are you? Where is Clarence?"

Rather than answer, Holmes strolled into the room, assuming an air of innocence. "I do apologise again, Mr. Driesbach, but the outer office was empty, I wasn't sure of any protocols in place to see you, so I sort of barged right in."

Confusion reigned on the man's face, but eventually, after looking the two of us up and down for a moment, he regained his composure. "Well, you're here now, what is it you want?"

"Ah, let me introduce myself, I am Sherlock Holmes, and this is my associate, Doctor John Watson. We have just come from a visit with Mr. Hyram Cumbage, whom you know."

With the mention of my name, I noticed his eyes flick from Holmes to myself, then return and linger on Holmes when he said Cumbage's name. It was those eyes that caught my complete attention. When they opened completely and caught the light, I realised they were a startling green colour. His hair was non-descript but did hold a deep brown tinge to it. His expression didn't change though, suggesting he was hiding his knowledge of the solicitor and feigning ignorance. Instead, he took a different tack.

"Holmes? I know that name, don't I? Though, I don't think we've met." Staring at my colleague for a moment, Driesbach seemed to search his memories before continuing. "Yes. You investigated those smuggling shenanigans down at the docks some years back. It seems I have to thank you for that; your intervention caused me to avoid a lot of unwanted attention and damage to my reputation."

He stood, reaching his hand across the desk. Holmes stepped forward and took it, shaking firmly. "No need to thank me, it was all part of the service I provided to my client at the time."

Releasing Holmes's hand, Driesbach sat down, a slightly relieved look on his face. "Well, again, I thank you. There was no need to visit, all that business is water under the bridge, as they say."

"Oh, that has nothing to do with why we are here. As I said, we have just come from the offices of Mr. Hyram Cumbage, a solicitor of slightly dubious reputation."

"Yes. So?"

"Mr. Cumbage was kind enough to help with our inquiries regarding a young schoolgirl by the name of Penelope Burdett." Only a slight movement in those green eyes, the lids opening somewhat, before relaxing once more.

"Who?"

Holmes paused, a sly grin lifting his mouth at the side. "Penelope Burdett. Fourteen years old. Slight frame. Brown shoulder-length hair, a similar shade to yours I think. Startling green eyes, almost identical to yours."

"What are you saying, Sir?"

He pulled something from his pocket, placed it on the desk and slid it across, pushing aside several sheets of parchment. "Penelope

Burdett. Killed, then squeezed into a steel strongbox, which can be opened with this key." Driesbach's eyes went wide as he stared at the key. Probably something he never thought he'd see again. "A strongbox that sits in the parlour of 11 Narrow Street, Limehouse." Holmes's hand darted into his pocket again, withdrawing the piece of paper with the address written on it. "The same address that is written on this paper. In a script very reminiscent to that which appears on the papers sitting before you on this desk."

"A key? Something scrawled on a piece of paper? What are you implying?"

"These items. Your striking resemblance to the young girl. Add to that, scorch marks and the smell of smoke on your coat. One last thing. How often does your man clean your shoes?"

"Well, I don't have a man. I do it myself, once every two weeks, why?"

"You have burn marks on the leather as well. Plus, some scuffing that may have come from leaving the scene of a fire in much haste."

"What fire?"

"Don't play the fool, Mr. Driesbach. Let me put it to you, that young Miss Penelope Burdett, is your daughter from a liaison many years ago with Lyra Burdett of Limehouse." Nodding towards a framed photograph sitting on a bookcase shelf behind Driesbach, Holmes added, "I assume that your current wife does not know about your previous dalliance and the issue that resulted."

The man turned and spied the photograph. With that, his entire reluctance to cooperate seemed to evaporate. He slumped back in the chair, staring at his desk while Holmes spoke further.

"To hide the fact of Penelope's existence, you employed Mr. Hyram Cumbage to facilitate the child's schooling, and deal with the money, keeping it all secret, as he is very good at doing."

Eyeing Holmes for a few moments, Driesbach's composure reasserted itself. "All right then, I admit it. It was before I was married, a stupid liaison with a woman of lower class down near the docks. I was stevedoring, working my way towards my own business. It was just another encumbrance that I didn't need at the time. I had no love for Lyra and no wish for a child at that time. So, I set them both up in that house."

"But Lyra died last year."

"Yes. I had hoped that would be the end of it, until Penelope left school, but…"

"She contacted you last week."

"Yes. With her mother gone, she wanted me to become her full-time family." He thumped the desk, shocking me, but bringing a smile to Holmes's face. "I couldn't have it. I've worked so hard on both this business and my marriage, to have this urchin bring down my reputation."

"But you did meet her."

"Yes. Last week, Wednesday I think, at the Limehouse place. She's fourteen. Old enough to start life. Without me. I offered her money. In exchange for her disappearing from my life."

"But she became angry. Went into a rage. A candle fell. The curtains caught fire. The place went up in a matter of seconds. I fled. I can only assume that she fled as well. When I turned back the place was engulfed. The brigade was already on its way. Their bells ringing through the streets. So, I returned home and thought no more of it. If I heard more from Penelope, I would deal with it at that time. With the money I gave her, I presumed she'd disappear from my life, and until you turned up, I've heard nothing."

"What a load of codswallop!" I cried out, incensed at the blatant lies of the man.

Holmes held up a hand to quiet me. "Patience Watson. Mr. Driesbach has told us his tale. We will get to the truth."

"That is the truth."

"Hmm. Perhaps, but it doesn't explain many things."

"Like what?"

"The blood, hair, and swatch of Penelope's uniform inside the strongbox, for a start. The strongbox that a witness said he found your daughter's body in."

"What witness?"

Holmes held a hand up towards Driesbach. "In time. The other inconsistency is the dark, dried pool of blood on the hearthstones of the fireplace." Driesbach went silent for a moment but kept his eyes on Holmes as he continued. "It is my conjecture, that during your, so-called, argument with Penelope, she fell, or was pushed, striking her head against the hearthstone, where she died or passed out. In your fear, you placed her body inside of the strongbox, locking it and taking the key."

I noticed Driesbach remain passive, but with his jaw clenched in anger. "Fanciful, but go on."

"You then set the fire, by breaking up the small sticks of furniture, but made one small mistake. The strongbox was extremely fireproof, a good old Thomas Milner. Penelope's corpse was preserved, only to be found days later by our witness, who procured the key and address note from your pocket or whoever you hired to retrieve the body."

"You keep mentioning a body." Driesbach's disposition moved from anger to assured. I sensed his appreciation of the situation was strangely calm, given the facts laid out by Holmes. "Where is this body? You've only mentioned finding a strong box with hair and blood, but no body, so I assume it was empty. Again, fanciful. Penelope took the money I gave her and escaped."

Holding up a finger, Holmes said, "Not so fast. True, Penelope wasn't in the strongbox, but she was found in the Thames yesterday. She is lying in the East London Hospital morgue, a sad figure left bereft of any chance to achieve adulthood through no fault of her own."

Driesbach muttered a curse under his breath.

"I can only assume that the person hired by your solicitor failed in your eyes. The police will no doubt see it differently."

Anger welled behind Driesbach's eyes. He stood slowly, pushing himself up with his balled fists pressed against the desk. "None of this should ever have happened. I was young. Stupid. Lyra was a single dalliance. A bit of fun on a Saturday night. How was I to know what would happen? Then nine months later, she found me. Showed me the babe. I only had to look into her eyes and knew she was mine." He moved from behind the desk and approached a nearby window that looked out onto the street. "I did what I could. There was no way I would have married the woman, I had already met my future bride, and nothing was going to threaten that."

"Yes, your bride is the daughter of another businessman, isn't she? I assume he has invested heavily in your company."

Driesbach turned to face Holmes. His eyes stared deep into my colleague's own. "Yes, but I have built this business. It is mine until I pay back the old man."

"What happened in Limehouse? Please tell us again. The truth this time."

As the memories filled his mind, Driesbach's haughty demeanour failed him. His shoulders slumped, and his eyes dropped to the floor. Slowly shaking his head, he confessed all. "A week ago, Cumbage sent me a telegram. Penelope wished to speak with me, in her mother's house. Well, my house really, but that's just semantics. She complained that she was lonely. She wanted away from the school. She wanted a family." He looked up. "I couldn't give her that." Indicating the photograph. "I have my own family. I promised her money, to help set her up, away from London where she could start afresh. She became enraged, knocked the money from my hand. Pushed at me. I…I…" He struggled back to his chair and flopped down. "I pushed back. She stumbled. Fell. Hit her head on the fireplace step. I was stunned. When she no longer moved. I panicked. I was worried that the neighbours had heard us, and would come and find me. I spied the old strongbox, something Lyra's father left her." Shaking his head, he added, "I know it was horrible, but I picked up the poor little thing and stuffed her in that box. I needed to cover my tracks and get rid of the body, so I broke some furniture and set the fire. It was only when I returned home that I remembered the damn box. For some reason, I'd kept the key in my pocket, and I recalled how proud Lyra was of that box. Strong and fireproof, she had said. Fireproof. The words rang through my head. I stupidly waited to hear any news that she had been found, but when nothing but a small account of the fire appeared in the papers, I set out for Cumbage's office, with the key and a note with the address. I wanted him to arrange for someone to retrieve Penelope's body and dispose of it. On arrival, the key and note were gone. Damn pickpockets. Cumbage said he would organise someone, but obviously, the old fool failed at that properly."

I studied the man, as he deflated in his chair. He was defeated. All the pent-up emotion and anger at the situation of his own making had taken its toll.

"Fourteen years. This whole fiasco has lasted fourteen years. I've hidden Penelope's existence from my wife for fourteen years. And now it's over, but not the conclusion I wanted." He looked up into Holmes's face, his eyes red-rimmed, with tears threatening to pour from them. "What happens now?"

Before my colleague could speak, the front door opened, and a familiar voice shouted out. "Holmes?"

"Well, that is for my invited guest to decide."

The office door opened and in walked Lestrade, a little flushed from his trip.

"I received your telegram. What in the blazes did you mean about a body in a box?"

***

That evening, ensconced in our parlour, with a small fire in the hearth to warm the still chilly nights, Holmes and I sat back ruminating about the adventure.

"What will become of Driesbach now?" I asked, sipping at my brandy.

"According to Lestrade, he is convinced that the girl's death was accidental, but it was the treatment of her poor body post mortem that will be the focus of his investigation. The father will definitely end up in Wandsworth; he made mistakes after all."

"I'm probably happy about that. It is one thing to sire an unwanted child, but it is another to simply wish that child out of your life, and then to turn your back completely on her such as he did. Shocking really."

"Yes, granted Mr. Driesbach had his reasons, they were fully selfish and the situation could have been handled in a much gentler and more moderate way. We all make mistakes, but it speaks to the character of the person on how they handle those mistakes. I'm afraid

Driesbach failed and will pay the penalty, not just in a penitentiary, but in his private life as well."

"Hmm. Yes, I think prison will be nothing compared to what happens on the home front."

"Quite so."

The Possession of Miranda Beasmore

"They are saying she's possessed – by a demon no less!"

"Preposterous!" I sputtered.

My good friend, Dr. Marcus Nefferson, sat back in his chair. "Any right-minded person would think so, yes." He sipped his coffee before adding, "But the Beasmores are so convinced they are bringing in an exorcist."

"Well, that should be intriguing," said Sherlock Holmes. A wry grin remained on his face as he took a long draw from his own cup of coffee.

"I simply don't know what to think anymore. My medical opinion has been thrown out in favour of the involvement of some sort of witch doctor."

"What brought all this about?" I asked.

Nefferson glanced my way, taking a deep breath followed by a sigh. "Yes, sorry, I jumped straight in without setting out the context." He drained his coffee, placing the cup back on its saucer with a slight clink. Leaning back in the chair once more, he began. "I have been the Beasmores' doctor since well before young Miranda was born. I have always found Julius and Claretha to be the most amicable of people, but extremely prim and proper to the point of priggishness. I generally have assigned the reason to their strong religious outlook. Both are avowed Roman Catholics."

"Intriguing," said Holmes. "That would be something that puts them at odds with the mainstream of Christian theology in this country, but one that I know is on the rise again after so many centuries."

"Quite, but I've never really paid attention to the fact until recently."

"Why?" I asked.

Holding his hands up to quell the questions and bring us back to his story, Nefferson waited until we both had the hint and then continued. “Miranda is central to this. Her parents’ obsessions comes later.” He took a deep breath and let it out slowly again. From that simple act, I could tell that the story had left his mind in a perpetual state of perturbation and remained silent while he continued. “Miranda was always a jovial and social child, but like so many of her generation, once the teenage years came upon her, that joviality left and was replaced by a dour outward attitude. Of late, she has been more introspective and has sought solitude and a life away from people. When she shunned even the weekly journey to Westminster on Sundays, the Beasmores approached me about Miranda’s condition. They attend mass at the Our Lady of Victories Church, and they seem very close to the priest there, Father Rammier – Morris, I think his first name is. I’ve met him on occasion at the Beasmore house in Kensington.”

“So very religious, which is no bad thing in these trying times,” said Holmes. “What does this Beasmore do?”

“Lawyer. For his clients’ defence, I think. Works out of an office in Belgravia. Anyway, I was dragged into this matter when Miranda’s emotional state became much worse. Claretha, the mother, contacted me when she couldn’t entice Miranda from her bed. I found the poor girl in a deep melancholy, bedridden and in a virtual delirium. She wouldn’t answer any of my questions, and any utterance made little sense. The mother said she had been like it for at least two days, and once had become very violent. All I could do was administer a powder to help her sleep. I could only diagnose a clouding of her consciousness, but I didn’t think it was the work of alcohol, as the girl is only fifteen, and her parents do not drink. There was something deeper that seemed to be troubling her.”

“When was this?” I asked.

“Almost a week ago. I left the poor thing, with every intention of returning the next day, but things as they may be, that didn’t happen for a few more days. By then the parents had decided to take matters into their own hands.”

“In what way?”

“When I returned, I was greeted by this priest, Father Rammier. He had the audacity to question my motives. When I said I was simply there to check upon my patient, he remonstrated me, saying that she was in his care now." Nefferson stopped for a moment, collecting his thoughts, and calming a wave of slight anger that had crept into his voice at this remembrance. "I know I shouldn't have, but I pushed past the pesky little man and headed for Miranda's room. What I found shocked me to the bone."

He stopped again. I was well engaged now, so prodded him to continue. "Go on. What is it you saw? How was the girl?"

"Nightmarish," he said, in a whisper, before raising his volume. "The young girl had been bound to the bed by her wrists and ankles. 'What have you done to her?' I shouted and, without turning to the priest, rushed to her side, freeing her right arm from its bond. Rammier grabbed my shoulder and said, 'No, she's too agitated!' I shrugged his hand away and bent towards the girl. Her eyes were closed as if she were asleep, but her breath came in short, ragged gasps. I leant in to examine her but failed to see the right-hand ball itself into a fist and fly at my face. The punch had more strength than I could imagine Miranda possessing and knocked me to the floor. Dazed, I sat up in time to see the priest replace the binding, with quite some difficulty as the young girl thrashed around, uttering curses and mutterings that I could nary understand. Finally, the priest turned to me and said, 'You fool! I warned you!' Feeling the pain in my jaw, I was almost in agreeance. Finding my feet once more, I looked down as Miranda strained at her bonds, eyeing us with looks of pure malevolence, and asked him how long she had been this way. He said that Julius had requested his attendance four nights previous, which was the evening of my last visit."

"Could you tell what was wrong?"

"No. This was a severe change in demeanour that was beyond my experience."

"Why was the priest there?" asked Holmes. "Surely a physician was the correct person to call upon."

Nefferson sighed. "That's where it gets very strange. As I mentioned earlier, the Beasmores are very religious. They have a predilection for calling upon God, and his servants upon this world, in times of need such as this. When the father, Julius, arrived in the room, he bade us both leave and join him outside. There he told me that my services would not be required just then. I was shocked. I protested, stating that the girl was obviously unwell and in a state of mind both harmful to herself and others. I suggested that she be taken to a sanatorium for the proper treatment. I was taken aback – Julius seemed to chuckle in mirth at my suggestion, before composing himself and saying that all was in hand. They had sent for someone that would be able to assist and cure Miranda of her ills."

"Really? Who?" I asked, surprised that a layman would be called upon, or even another doctor. Nefferson was one of the finest physicians that I knew of.

"An exorcist."

I laughed out loud, before stopping and calming myself. Even Holmes had a wry grin on his face. "An exorcist? This is the nineteenth century, not the Middle Ages."

"That was almost precisely my reply to Julius, but he was convinced. He stated without any hint of humour that they believed Miranda to be possessed by a demon from Hell."

"Preposterous."

"Yes. Any right-minded person would think the same, but the Beasmores are not of that mind. And this Rammier fellow simply re-enforced their view, and added his own take on the subject, hammering home all that the church said about demons and Satan and such." Nefferson dropped his head and shook it slowly. "I was raised to believe in God. I attended church throughout my formative years. I'll admit that once I became a man of science, my beliefs wavered, but I've never lost them altogether. But this, this devotion that the Beasmores have to their beliefs is beyond anything I've ever seen. Add to that their acceptance, without question, that whatever troubles young Miranda can be – and is – a demon . . . ."

"Hmm," murmured Holmes. "I can see that their position would put you in a very difficult situation. A physician, forbidden to help his patient because of some primitive adhesion to outdated religious doctrine."

"That is part of it, though the next part of my story will emphasise my concern greatly."

"Oh, there's more?" I asked. "Go on then."

"Yes. Two days ago, the exorcist arrived."

I shuffled forward in my seat. My interest had been piqued, but was now bordering on fascination.

"I can only tell you that I don't think I've ever seen another priest like this man. He flounced into the Beasmore residence like an actor entering the stage in the final scene of an Elizabethan farce."

"My word."

"Yesterday I attended the Beasmore residence, hoping to simply undertake one of my regular visits to appraise Miranda's condition. While still in the entranceway, there was a ring of the bell, and as soon as the door opened, this vision erupted into the place. He announced himself, with a thick Italian accent, as Father Ernesto Tinnerello. He was all flowing capes and scarves, not like the quiet and demure priest beside him. I found out later that he had been sent to England by the Vatican as part of a study tour, inspecting the ancient Catholic churches that had survived Henry VIII's purges. This gave me less impression of the man than his entrance. He did not seem the type to lead an archaeological or anthropologic sort of life.

"As I mentioned, he was the exorcist. Once the introductions had finished, I asked what his interest in the case was. He simply said that he had been asked to exorcise the demon and send it back to Hell. I must admit that I scoffed at the suggestion. It had been up until that point that I had merely seen the Beasmores' insistence on demon possession as some sort of sick fantasy, but with the appearance of Tinnerello, it was clear they intended on performing some form of rite to cleanse Miranda."

"And did this not worry you from a physician's standing?" I asked, appalled at the primitive nature of the goings-on.

"Of course it did!" Nefferson replied in a terse tone of voice. "I knew that I had to tread lightly. There was some form of mass hysteria in the house, but I strongly suggested that I should remain in case of any untoward medical problem arising. Julius almost showed me the door, but Claretha insisted that I be present, if not to provide medical assistance, but also to be assured that nothing untoward would occur."

"And what did occur?" asked Holmes.

"It was horrible." Nefferson leant forward for a moment and dropped his head into his hands. Holmes and I looked at each other before I stood and moved to the sideboard. Bringing back three glasses and the decanter, I poured us all a stiff brandy.

"I know it's a little early, but I feel you could be well in need of this," I said, offering the brandy snifter to my friend. Looking up, he took the proffered glass gratefully and downed the fiery liquid in one swig.

"Thank you, John. I think I needed that." I refilled his glass, before placing the decanter on the table and sitting down.

After taking a long breath, Nefferson continued. "Without a word or a whisper with anyone, Tinnerello requested access to Miranda's room. He was immediately led upstairs to the young girl. I followed in his wake, ensuring I wasn't restricted from entering the room, and huddled into a corner to give me as good a view of proceedings as I could. My worry was for the child, not the theatrical display that I was about to witness." Nefferson took a sip from his brandy. "Rammier assisted the exorcist, holding the other's satchel while several items were removed and placed on a table near the bed. I spied a leather-bound copy of the Bible, a glass bottle filled with clear liquid, and a large brass crucifix. My eyes fell on the girl. She slumbered, ignorant of the goings-on around her. My heart went to her, and I hoped that she would remain asleep through whatever would transpire. I was wrong."

I shifted in my seat and had to know. "Did they wake her on purpose?"

"I'm unsure, but the Italian moved to the bed and studied the poor girl for a moment or two, before leaning over and whispering. The effect was immediate. Her eyes snapped open, and a raging snarl rang out across the room. Miranda's eyes locked on Tinnerello, and a stream of abuse left her mouth that would make a fishwife blush. I spied her parents and noticed their faces aghast in horror, unsure whether at Miranda's words or the fact that she had said them in the first place."

It was horrible.

"Interesting. I'm intrigued how a young girl of such a delicate nature would come by such language," Holmes said, his face showing more amusement than horror.

"Indeed."

"What happened next?" I asked.

"The exorcist snatched up his crucifix and Bible and, holding them before him, extorted Miranda's sneering form with a stream of Latin. I haven't even heard the language since my school days, so all I could pick up were the odd word or two. Many references to God, to Satan, and such like."

"Did it have any effect?"

"Yes, but quite the opposite to what was expected, I assume. Miranda almost flew into a fit of rage. Her face became a snarling visage of pure hatred. Obscenities leapt from her mouth. As she strained at her bonds, I grew concerned that she might injure herself. I moved forward, but Rammier moved in front of me, blocking my way and holding a hand up to my chest. 'Do not disturb Father Tinnerello until he has finished.' I tried to push past, but the girl's father joined the little priest and grasped my arm, further restraining me. I felt that if I tried any harder things might turn ugly, so I relaxed and maintained my distance, gritting my teeth at the display before me."

"Good Lord."

"If only he had some say in it, but this was either the work of man – or worse," Nefferson added. "As Miranda thrashed and spewed her vile insults at the priest, he continued, expelling further monologues and prayers in archaic Latin, which only elicited more snarls and expletives. All at once, Tinnerello stopped and turned back to his satchel. Withdrawing some long-tapered candles, he lit them, filling the room with a pungent, but not unpleasant, perfume. I caught a hint of lavender and assumed that the Italian was attempting to elicit a soporific quality from the use of their odour. He placed the candles at various places in the room, before picking up the small glass bottle. Nodding towards me, he said it contained Holy Water, blessed by Leo XIII himself. The Beasmores whispered Il Papa under their breaths and crossed themselves. A strange display of devotion, in my mind."

The doctor paused for a moment, sipping from his brandy and taking a deep breath before continuing. "Whatever was in that bottle, it certainly had an effect. Tinnerello uncorked the bottle and poured a small amount into his palm. Placing the bottle down, he proceeded to flick the Holy Water across Miranda's form, whilst reciting another Latin prayer." Nefferson stared at Holmes for a moment. "What happened, I still can't explain. As the Holy Water touched Miranda's skin, white foam cascaded out of her pores. She screamed as if in pain."

"Did you intervene then?" I asked

"No," he said, his head hanging down in shame. "I know I should have, but I was so intrigued by the spectacle that I found myself rooted to the spot. The bubbling didn't last long, and soon the exorcist wiped the remaining water on a cloth and leaned into Miranda. He whispered into her ear and drew a small cross on her fevered brow. Within moments, she quietened down and fell into a slumber, much to my and her parents' relief. After a moment, Claretha asked whether it was over. To my disappointment, Tinnerello shook his head and said, 'No, the demon inside her is far stronger than thought: One of the major lieutenants of Lucifer's army – Pazuzu, or even Beelzebub. I am unsure. This will take much longer than I had planned. I may even require further assistance from Rome.' Julius stated that he didn't care. Any expense would be met."

I noticed Holmes's expression change at the mention of money. "Expense?" he asked.

"Yes. It seems that these things don't come cheap. The church is all well and good when the coffers are simply filled through the weekly services in their parishes, but these extra duties are costed separately."

"Do you know how much?"

"No. There were no figures thrown around, but I can only assume from Julius's stern look that it was not a small amount."

"Did you examine the girl afterwards?" I asked.

"Yes. She was sleeping deeply. I could almost have assumed she'd been drugged, but I never saw anything administered, so put it down to simple exhaustion."

"Quite so."

"Did you find out when the next session was to occur?"

"Why, yes. Tomorrow night in fact. When Tinnerello suggested tonight, I baulked and said that for the good of the patient she should be allowed to rest after such exertions. The parents actually agreed with me, much to Tinnerello's consternation."

"Good, good. Do you think you would be able to arrange for Watson and me to attend as observers? Perhaps state that you fear for Miranda's mental health after any repeat and would prefer if two of your colleagues could observe. Naturally we will assure them that we will not interfere in any way."

"I will try." He paused for a moment, his anger brewing slightly. "No, of course I will. I'm her physician. If this Italian fellow threatens the safety of my patient, then I will do everything in my power to stop it. You have my word. I will set off directly for the Beasmore residence, first to check in on Miranda, then to ensure that you are allowed access tomorrow night."

"Excellent." Producing a pen and notepad, Holmes asked, "Could you write down the Beasmore address and the time of the ritual, and we will meet you tomorrow night."

Nefferson jotted down the details before sliding the pad and pen across to Holmes, who read it quickly. My doctor friend rose to say his goodbyes but was greeted with one last question. "This Rammier – you mentioned that he had a close relationship with the family. Do you know if he is entertained at their house outside of his clerical duties?"

"Oh yes, the little fellow is there quite often. The Beasmores seem to draw upon his influence as if he can tap into the thoughts of God. As I have stated, I'm no atheist, but this over-reliance on not just the word of God, but also the word of the church, is disturbing to the logical mind."

"Indeed," I replied.

***

The sun had all but disappeared, bringing with it a late autumn chill, when I found Nefferson standing before the modest three-story Georgian terrace that was the Beasmore residence. The location of their home, in the well-to-do area of Belgravia, spoke loudly about their affluence, which surprised me even more given their reliance on the church for comfort and assurance.

"You didn't mention how well off this family was during your tale," I said to my friend.

Turning to take in the ambience of the house, he replied, "I suppose I hadn't thought of it. I'm fortunate enough that most of my patients reside in premises such as this."

"One wonders how many others take a special interest," I muttered, my mind awash with all sorts of nefarious villains that would be only too willing to take advantage of this family's prosperity. Bringing my thoughts back to the subject at hand, I asked, "Have you had contact with the Beasmores today?"

"Why yes. I performed my regular morning call to check up on Miranda's health and spoke with Claretha. I thought it more prudent to talk with the mother than the father, as he tends to be the more stubborn of the pair. Claretha was at first concerned at bringing in more strangers, but I posed to her that you and Holmes would be as discreet as possible, and would be there as observers, acting only in the direst of circumstances."

"Good. I haven't seen Holmes all day and do hope that he is circumspect in both his manner and garb." As I scanned the area, my concerns evaporated. Holmes strode down the street, resplendent in a morning suit with a matching overcoat, much the same as Nefferson and I wore. I'll admit that my profession isn't one to overdress, but my fellows and I do like to maintain a suitable level of attire.

"What ho, Watson!" Holmes said as he approached, nodding to Nefferson by way of greeting.

"Ah, Holmes, good. Any person on the street would see the three of us as colleagues attending to the same call-out."

"What story have you concocted for our beleaguered family, Nefferson?"

"To ease the concerns of our hostess, I've presented you and Watson as specialists in the study of the mind. Your attendance here tonight will be strictly observational, as part of a favour to me."

"Good," said Holmes. "I merely wish to witness this ritual – mostly to satisfy my curiosity before forming any opinions or producing any solutions."

"Do you wish to discuss what you've been up to for the last day-and-a-half?" I asked.

"At this stage, no. You should know that I'll only announce my findings once I'm fully convinced of the facts." I nodded, expecting exactly that answer. "However, I do have questions." Speaking to Nefferson, he continued. "This Rammier fellow – have you known him long?"

Nefferson nodded. "Only as part of my ministrations to the Beasmore family. He does seem to play a significant role in their lives. He's a regular visitor to this house, and I've found him here quite often now that my cycle of visitations has increased."

"But outside of this immediate circle, you know nothing of him?"

"True. Priest. Catholic. Moderately young. Nothing more really."

Holmes nodded and filed the information away.

"Why?" I asked.

"Nothing for now. Simply building as much of a picture of all the players as I can. The Beasmores? Julius, the patriarch? As far as I can tell, a righteous pillar of society. Lawyer. Well regarded amongst his peers. Money is all his, no inheritance. Puts all his success down to his diligent adherence to the Catholic faith and doctrine."

"Why yes, that would describe him perfectly."

"It's strange though that those who have the most faith are sometimes the same that have the most fears."

"Intriguing thought," added Nefferson.

***

Once inside, the pleasant atmosphere offered by the house's façade all but evaporated. Luckily, we were first greeted by Mrs. Beasmore who, armed with her prior knowledge, regarded both Holmes and me in an amicable manner. It was upon meeting Mr. Beasmore and the priest, who I immediately found to be extremely sycophantic to the former, that a chill grew in the air to such an extent I was surprised that clouds of vapour didn't appear any time a person spoke.

"Nefferson, I do not see the point of these gentlemen being here," said Julius Beasmore upon our introduction.

"Now, now, dear," said his wife. "I expressed you would have that exact opinion to the Good Doctor when he asked me. I, however, think differently. I would be much more comforted if we have someone here to assist in any medical emergency that may arise. Miranda has slept for two straight days after the last encounter with Father Tinnerello. She hasn't even spoken. I'm very worried about her."

"It's the demon," Beasmore rounded on his wife. "You know that as well as I do. The doctor has failed, it is now for the church to succeed where medicine cannot."

"And I completely understand, Julius, but I will be much more relaxed knowing that we have some of the very best medical minds on hand, in case of anything untoward." The emphasis that Mrs. Beasmore placed on indications of herself in that statement caused Julius Beasmore to wince, and I could immediately tell who held the most sway within the Beasmore family.

Eyeing all three of us with a stare that could have shot bullets, Julius Beasmore retreated up the stairs followed by the rat-like priest. It appeared that the exorcist had already arrived well before all three of us and was already in the girl's room.

"That actually went better than I thought," said Claretha Beasmore quietly, much to my surprise. "Julius does stick solidly to his opinions but will usually accept my advice, albeit begrudgingly." A wry grin came to her face. "He knows how to keep a happy house."

***

Entering Miranda's room, I was shocked to find the exorcist, resplendent in all black, except for the white dog collar of a priest around his neck, standing next to a sideboard. Nefferson had described him for us, but in person, he was even more of a presence.

"And who are these two fellows?" Tinnerello asked.

"My wife has insisted that these two . . . two doctors, I suppose," Mr. Beasmore struggled to name our fictional profession.

"Psychiatrists," said Holmes, stepping forward and offering his hand to the Italian. "Doctors Holmes and Watson at your service." The exorcist took his hand, shaking it lightly, a confused look on his face.

"Why do we need 'Sickiatrists'?" he asked, his accent slurring the word.

"I have no idea," said Beasmore.

"It was my idea," said Nefferson. "I am still Miranda's physician, and the last rite that you performed left me worried about her mental state. I asked my friends to accompany me here today, to determine if my worries have some foundation."

Waving us away and into the far corner, Tinnerello added, "Fine, but please stay out of the way. There is not much room in here, and I cannot be held responsible for you."

Holmes and I shuffled into the far corner and settled in to watch the proceedings. It was then my sight fell upon the subject of the evening's events. For a girl in her mid-teens, she looked a very poor figure in the bed. Her arms were tied up with soft material to the bedhead, and her feet likewise were bound to the foot. Even in that seemingly uncomfortable posture, she was fast asleep, but her eyes vibrated rapidly behind her closed lids. She was dreaming – a strange state given the description we'd heard from Nefferson. I had expected to see a snarling, violent creature hell-bent on eviscerating all within her reach, not the quietly slumbering form that lay before me.

It was then that a chill ran up the length of my spine. The day had been cool, but the temperature in that room was icy. Breathing out, I half-expected to spy a dense cloud of mist before my face. Glancing at the window, I noticed it was shut, but the external shutters were open. It may be that they had been open prior to our arrival. I rubbed my arms to get the blood flowing.

"The chill is strange, isn't it?" whispered my friend. Looking to my right, I found Holmes standing resolute, observing all the preparations that Tinnerello undertook. The Italian bent to his satchel, sitting on a small table, presumably brought in for that purpose. Out came the crucifix, the leather Bible, and a small glass bottle filled with a clear liquid, supposedly Holy Water. "Intriguing – this fellow must have a store of that Pope-blessed water."

"Why do you say that?"

"The bottle is full. I can only assume that he used copious quantities during the previous ritual."

"You are right," said a surprised Nefferson. "I remember the bottle contained only half that amount at the end of our last meeting."

The exorcist moved around the room, lighting four wax candles and filling the room with the thick but sweet odour of lavender, before picking up his crucifix and Bible and approaching the slumbering girl.

Holding the crucifix only inches above the girl's face, he began a Latin incantation in a low murmuring voice. "In nómine Pátris, et Fílii, et Spirítus Sancti. Amen." Finishing with a wave of the crucifix along the four points of the cross, leaving his hand in place at the lower point for a moment. I noticed the girl's eyes flicker before the priest began to incant once more. "Exsúrgat Deus et dissipéntur inimíci ejus: Et fúgiant qui odérunt eum a fácie ejus." A low growl emanated from the girl, with her eyes flickering as she began to wake. "Sicut déficit fumus defíciant. Sicut fluit cera a fácie ígnis, sic péreant peccatóres a fácie Dei." The girl's eyes snapped open. A terrified look crossed her face as if waking from a dream into a nightmare. She pulled tentatively at her bonds, a questioning glance at each of her hands. "Miranda!" the exorcist snapped. The girl's eyes locked onto his face.

The Italian's voice became deep and commanding, he barked what seemed to be an order. "Quisquis hanc puellam regit, me aspice! Derelinquamus!" The effect was immediate. Miranda spat a stream of abuse at the priest. I picked up a few words – most sounded like Latin, but I couldn't be sure. She thrashed at her bonds, straining at each in turn. I stepped forward, afraid she would cut herself. Holmes placed a hand on my chest, restricting my advance. A quick glance at his face was met with a shake of the head.

"Let us observe," he whispered.

Tinnerello repeated the phrase. I listened intently, but my knowledge of conversational Latin was very rusty. I did pick up words for "eyes" or "sight", and for "leave" and "girl". I could only assume that it was a command aimed at the supposed-demon to withdraw. Instead, Miranda snarled and snapped, hurling lines of abuse, some in Latin, some in English, at the exorcist. After goading the demon with the same phrase once more, and receiving nothing but a foul stream of swearing, the Italian moved back to the small table, placing the Bible and cross down before retrieving the bottle.

Pouring some of the Holy Water into his left palm, he approached Miranda. "Virtus Christi urget te!" he shouted, before flicking the water at the girl, repeating several times and receiving the same responses. Screams came from the girl as if she was driven to agony by the water's touch, and the white bubbling of some effluent flowed from Miranda's pores as the water splashed across her delicate skin.

I cried in anguish, looking from the girl to the parents to my friend. Holmes stood stock still, his hand resting beneath his chin, one finger extended up to his cheek, taking in every detail that could be drawn from the performance before him. When no change appeared in his attitude, I meekly turned my attention back to the outrageous display before me.

The effervescence on Miranda's skin had dissipated, and Tinnerello was back at his table. He wiped the Holy Water off his hand before stepping back towards the girl, who lay with her eyes closed, breathing heavily after her exertions.

The exorcist bent close to the girl, whispering in a voice so low that I could barely hear anything he said, and certainly unable to make out the words. The girl's breathing calmed. With his right thumb, Tinnerello drew a cross upon Miranda's head before touching her top lip and chin. Miranda seemed to slip into a deep sleep, almost immediately.

Rammier stepped up next to his colleague and assisted in clearing away the tools of the trade. Sneaking a glance at Holmes, I hoped to see evidence of his opinion on the matter. He remained resolute, his eyes glancing at the supine figure of the girl before returning to the two priests.

***

"Well, what did you make of all that?" Nefferson asked.

We stood by the street, outside the Beasmores' front door. Holmes remained quiet, thoughtful. "I'm simply shocked," I said. "I don't know what was more concerning – the strange and awful language coming from that girl. The rage she showed as she struggled against her bonds, or simply the pain that she showed as the ritual went on." I took a breath, still struggling with my own emotions after such an occurrence.

"I agree," said Nefferson. I've never seen someone lose their mind so rapidly, without any form of external stress. Unfortunately, I cannot have her committed unless her parents consent to it. The explanation of possession is all we have at this stage, until I have an actual psychiatrist examine the girl and declare her insane."

My anger welled as I remembered the pain that the girl had suffered during the exorcism. "I'm livid. How can any parent even conceive to allow their child to be subject to such as we saw? Surely after this, they will only be too happy to have her taken somewhere appropriate where she can be treated for her condition. As loathe as I am to admit it, we may have actually witnessed a truly supernatural experience, in which a young girl has been possessed by a demon from the depths of Hell," I said, shaking my head slightly at my own realisation, "but this is not the type of care she should receive."

"Well, I do agree, but as I have explained, Miranda's parents are staunch in their beliefs. I went almost as far as begging them, but my pleas fell on deaf ears. It was all I could do to ensure I was on hand in case anything untoward occurred that threatened the safety of the girl."

"I find it barbaric. Ancient rituals to solve a problem that cannot exist. And to no effect. As you heard, Tinnerello stated that he needs to perform the rite again, as per the doctrine."

"So what happens then? If the third time does not work? Do we simply fob this off as a supernatural problem?"

"What say, you Holmes?" Nefferson asked my colleague.

"I have read of so-called cases of devil possession in some esoteric texts associated with the church, and this had all the hallmarks of such." Smiling a wry grin, Holmes added, "But I will continue to gather all the evidence I need, in order to eliminate every contrary angle. I never dismiss anything, however improbable."

"Foolishness!" huffed my medical friend.

"Do not be hasty to judge," offered Holmes. "I have been presented with many unnatural events, all of which have been found to have their origins in the perfectly normal. There are many elements to this case which may go against that, but there are also numerous probable answers to every uncertainty."

"Then I do hope you discover them quickly."

"Fear not. Even from what I have seen so far, I have severe doubts as to the authenticity of these claims of demons. Let me dig further over the next day or so."

"Should we attend the next ritual?" I asked.

"Oh, yes. I believe that is paramount to the investigation. If there are no mystical causes behind all this, then I would hope to have discovered the causes before this so-called Italian exorcist continues with his unearthly practices."

"Good," said Nefferson. "I'll ensure that you are allowed witness to the supposed 'final' rite. I caught glances of Claretha's horrified face, and I'm sure she is as worried about Miranda's health as she is about her soul. Julius, on the other hand, may be a more delicate matter, but he does defer to his wife on most domestic matters, so that should be fine."

"We shall meet here at the same time in two days, then," said Holmes, and with that, we strode away to find a hansom.

***

All through the next day, my mind kept replaying the perplexing series of events that we had witnessed. I longed to discuss them in detail with Sherlock Holmes, but was drawn away by a call from a patient and didn't return until later that evening. By then Holmes was nowhere to be seen. I could only assume that he was investigating some matter or another.

In fact, we didn't cross paths again until the next morning where, upon rising from my bed, I came downstairs and found him engaged in several experiments at his chemistry table. As I sauntered across the room, I noticed the bubbling flasks and a small pamphlet on the edge of the table. It was an advertisement for some sideshow in the East End. I gave it no mind and turned my attention to the experiments.

"Good morning. What do you have there? Need I ask?"

Turning, Holmes smiled at me in his enigmatic way and nodded, indicating the bubbling mixtures before him. "You can and you should. These flasks contain several items and chemical compounds drawn from the room – and person of one Miranda Beasmore."

"What?" I said, astounded and fully showing it upon my face, I expect. "How? How did you retrieve those?"

"Ah, well. Let us say that I may have needed to bend the rules of engagement a little. It appears that young Miranda's parents have a habit of visiting their church of an evening. By chance, as I stood outside the house, observing as much as I could from without, I saw them leave. The house itself went rather dark and silent, the servants having retired, so I took the opportunity to enter and make my way to Miranda's room. She was well asleep, probably sedated from one of Dr. Nefferson's tinctures. Having memorised the room during our encounter, I was able to avail myself of samples of the supposed Holy Water, and other possible chemicals used in this play."

"Really? What have you found?"

"I've identified nothing so far. I will require further analysis until I can be completely satisfied."

"As always," I added, "so I shan't rush your examination."

"You may find me missing this afternoon," he explained, "so I will meet you at the Beasmore residence tonight. I have several other avenues to follow up before we attend this final exorcism."

"Very good," I said. "Where else have your investigations taken you?"

Another smile. "Oh, but that would be telling before I have confirmed. I won't suppose on things until I have the evidence and facts before me."

Nodding, I stated, "Yes, I know that, but sometimes I like to be included in the picture."

A slight chuckle emanated from his angular mouth. "Oh, you will be my friend, you will be."

***

"Have you solved it, Holmes?" asked Nefferson. His face seemed more drawn from worry than on our previous meeting.

"I believe that I'm very close. I would like to see this ritual at least once more to satisfy myself on a few salient points."

"Good. Well, let's hope it is only the one time. I stayed up all last night with worry over the health of that poor girl. She has barely spent an hour awake over the last week. Either I've administered powders to help calm her down, or the stress of these so-called exorcisms have sent her into deep unconsciousness. Sleep is good for the body and mind, but like anything, too much can have dire effects."

"On that point, have either of you brought your medical bags?"

I shook my head. I hadn't due to the pretence that we were observers and doctors of the mind, not physicians. To my relief, Nefferson nodded and showed us the satchel that sat behind him, obscured from view.

"Never leave home without it – especially when I visit this place."

"Good, good. I think we may need some of your stimulants once the rite has been performed."

***

As we entered Miranda's bedroom, the atmosphere became even chillier than the ambient temperature of the room would suggest. Tinnerello, Rammier, and Julius Beasmore all regarded us with piercing stares but begrudgingly bade us enter and move to the same corner as we occupied on the previous evening. Claretha remained in the doorway, her eyes locked with her husband's, in a provocative stare waiting for any resistance to our presence. When he turned away from her look, I knew we would receive no further anguish from Julius.

It was the Italian that voiced his annoyance, but also his reluctant acceptance. "Well, we have an audience once more. Fine. Please, again, do not interfere or make any sound. This third execution of the ancient ritual of exorcism will either rid our beloved Miranda of the foul demon within, or we will lose her forever." Pointing an accusatory finger at us, he added, "It is upon your shoulders how this will progress." I thought long and hard about a response but decided that discretion was the better part of valour and remained silent.

The exorcism routine started as it had the night before. Four candles were placed around the room and lit, filling the area with the almost overpowering and cloying perfume of lavender or some such flower. The girl, Miranda, was silent, still bound by her soft restraints and lost to a deep sleep. It was only when Tinnerello leaned over and whispered in her ear did her eyes flicker open in that same stunned and disoriented way.

It was only as the priest approached with his crucifix and Bible, invoking his Latin chant, and his voice grew louder did Miranda's demeanour change. Within seconds, she went from wild-eyed fright into full-on raving demon-child, sprouting all manner of vile curses and snarling and snapping at the priest as if she was a bound animal, not a young girl.

As the priest droned on, the girl's manner remained. Curses and snarls filled the room, followed by cries of pain as the Holy Water was splashed across her skin, resulting in the same effervescence and bubbling as the previous night. On the final invocation, Tinnerello grasped Miranda's snarling face, holding his hand across her mouth and nose, while repeating a Latin incantation. Finally, the girl's eyes closed, and she fell back into a deep slumber.

Silence fell once more upon the room. The only sound came from Tinnerello as he returned his items to the satchel.

It was Claretha that broke the peace. "Is that it? Is the demon gone forever? Will my little girl return to me?"

The Italian shrugged. "I tried to stare into her eyes and see the demon's soul leave, but there was nothing, so I do not know yet. She will rest. I shall return in the morning and perform the last test. If all is well, she will be herself. If not, then I shall consult with the church to determine the next course of action."

"And how much will that cost?"

"What was that?" Tinnerello asked, turning towards Holmes, the source of the question.

"I simply asked how much this next course of action would cost?"

"I don't think that is any of your business," said Rammier.

"That is true, but I understand that the Roman Catholic Church does not charge the members of its congregation for such services as exorcisms." Turning towards Julius Beasmore, whose face showed an expression of surprise, he asked, "How much has Senor Tinnerello requested from you, sir? Five-hundred pounds?"

"A thousand," stammered Beasmore. "But I don't care how much I pay, as long as my Miranda comes back to me, whole and unblemished by this unnatural interloper."

"Ah," said Holmes.

"It is not for me," said Tinnerello. "It is simply to cover my trip to England and the tools of my trade." He looked once at Beasmore, who nodded, then with one last glance at Holmes, Tinnerello turned to consult with Rammier.

I noticed Holmes whisper to Nefferson, who reached for his medical satchel and within moments handed something to my friend. The detective immediately moved across to the bed and sat down next to the reclining figure of Miranda. He unscrewed the lid on the small bottle Nefferson had handed him and held it beneath the sleeping girl's nose. Within a few moments, her eyelids flickered and opened.

"Welcome back, Miranda," Holmes said.

"What are you doing?" shouted Tinnerello, rushing to the bedside. "She needs to rest! The demon has plagued her mind. We need to keep it silent."

Miranda looked around the room, her gaze resting on each person in turn, a confused expression growing on her face.

Her mother stepped forward. "Miranda?"

"It isn't her!" shouted Tinnerello. "It is the demon! Your daughter is in there, but the fiend controls her."

Holmes rose and stepped back. "I apologise for this, my dear girl, but . . . ." He took a deep breath and then repeated one of the Latin phrases Tinnerello had said during the exorcism. "Quisquis hanc puellam regit, me aspice. Derelinquamus." Every person in the room gasped as Miranda, once again, turned from a mildly confused teenage girl into a snarling animal, spouting curses and swear words at all and sundry.

"What are you doing?" shouted Tinnerello. "You have awakened the demon. The girl is in grave danger."

"Is she though?" said Holmes. He bent close to Miranda's snarling face and spoke another Latin phrase. "Angelus dormies somnum!" Immediately, Miranda slumped into a deep sleep.

I expected Tinnerello to shout at Holmes once more, but his face was a mask of shock. "How do you know the rites of exorcism? You are not an ordained priest. It is blasphemy for a layman to repeat those phrases!"

"Except that they do not belong to the rites of exorcism, do they?"

"What?" said Julius Beasmore. "What do you mean by that? We've all heard them said here over the last few days. The Father has spoken perfect Latin, and you've seen the effects they have had on the demon within my dear Miranda."

"Ah, yes, that is true, Mr. Beasmore. We have all heard some Latin phrases," said Holmes, pulling a small leather-bound volume from within his jacket pocket. Holding it up, he asked Tinnerello, "Have you seen one of these before, Father?" The priest stood still, unmoving. "You should have. Especially given your station in life." Thumbing through the volume, Holmes added, "This is a copy of the De Exorcismis et Supplicationibus Quibusdam. The book which outlines the actual rituals of exorcism, sanctioned by the Roman Catholic Church. I obtained this copy from Cardinal Manning. You would know him as the Archbishop of Westminster. He was very interested in my story about a priest from Rome undertaking exorcisms in the London area."

As I turned to face the priest, I noticed Tinnerello edging towards the doorway. As he reached out for the doorknob, another hand slammed against the door jamb and stopped it from opening. Claretha Beasmore's face was stern, her posture showing an inner strength that belied her slight frame. "I think you should stay, Father. I'd like to hear more from Dr. Holmes. I'd also like to hear an explanation in your words as well."

The supposed Italian's expression dropped. He turned meekly and stood, summoning up as much courage as he could to face his accuser.

"Go on, Doctor," said the Beasmore matriarch.

"It seems there is no record of a Father Tinnerello working here in London – but we shall get to his identity in a moment."

"I knew he was an imposter," said Rammier.

Holmes turned to face the little priest. "I don't think you should be trying to cast an image of innocence, Father. Westminster didn't have any complimentary words for you either. In fact, they were extremely interested to hear that you were also involved in this little escapade as well."

"But – but I . . . I – " stammered Rammier, before closing his mouth lest he put his foot further into it.

"What in the blue blazes is going on here?" cried Julius Beasmore, his face flushed red with anger. "How dare you come into my home and accuse men of the cloth of some egregious act for which you have no proof." He stepped towards the bed and indicated his sleeping daughter. "My daughter is ill – has been for weeks! We have all seen with our own eyes that she is possessed by a demon – a demon that this man – " He pointed to Tinnerello. " – recognised and hopefully has vanquished through the words of the Lord."

"Julius!" snapped Claretha. "Quiet! Let the man speak."

Julius Beasmore's expression changed to abject fear at his wife's voice. I was most impressed at the hold she had over him, though I did feel a little hint of pity for the man. He was mostly bluff and bluster, but was firmly held under his wife's thumb.

"Can you explain what has gone on, Doctor Holmes?" she asked.

"I will also identify myself. It's a good time for it. My name is Sherlock Holmes, as you know, but I am not a physician. I am a consulting detective. Doctor Nefferson requested my involvement, fearing that your daughter might be subject to ill-treatment as part of these rituals." He indicated to me. "This is my colleague, Doctor John Watson – an actual physician, but of the body, not solely of the mind."

He looked from face to face, biding his time and taking in the expressions each before continuing.

"Now, what has gone on here is a charade. Nothing more, nothing less. Your poor daughter has been subject to manipulation of the mind by these two loathsome scoundrels."

"What?" asked Julius. "But Rammier here is a priest. He has been one of our closest confidants for years."

"No doubt – but sometimes even the most pious of men can become tempted by the lure of a better life. Is that not right, Father?" Holmes stared at Rammier, who remained silent, his expression fixed.

"To the ritual played out before us: I'm afraid that this little affair has been ongoing for quite some months. Your daughter's attitude has changed of late, is that right?"

"Yes," said Claretha, "she has grown ever more sullen and withdrawn ever since she turned fifteen."

"And you have relied on Father Rammier to console and confide in her, as part of his representation of the church, is that right?"

"Yes. He has been a true comfort to not just Miranda, but all of us as well."

"Is that right, Father?" Holmes directed his question at the quiet priest. "Or have you been preparing Miranda all these many months for this final denouement of your plan?"

"What do you mean?" blurted out Julius.

"It was all his bloody idea!" said Tinnerello, pointing at Rammier and suddenly losing his accent and revealing one of a much broader East-End origin.

"Oh, I already know that, don't I, Father Rammier?"

The little priest's head dropped as he realised the game was up.

"What are you going on about?" asked Julius. "This is all very confusing."

"Let me explain, then. Father Tinnerello here is a mesmerist. In fact," Holmes stepped towards Tinnerello, "you are better known as 'The Amazing Ernesto'. Isn't that, right? Mr. Ernest Sinister, formerly of the Casartelli Circus from Italy, after spending many years performing in Astley's Amphitheatre, here in London." He slipped the small page I had seen on his chemistry table from his pocket and unfolded it. Nefferson glanced at it, reading quickly.

"I don't believe it," cried Nefferson. "A bloody circus act?"

"Yes. Sinister here was expelled from the Italian circus about five years ago and ended up back in London. He has made a name for himself in the East End as a small-time act in some of the music halls. That is where I believe you may have seen him, Father Rammier?

Was it about six months ago? A few weeks before Miranda's emotional state began to surface?"

The priest looked up momentarily before dropping his eyes once more.

"Good Lord!" said Beasmore.

"Ah, yes, I think so," continued Holmes. "After observing Sinister's act on several occasions, Father Rammier conceived his idea. You trained the priest in mesmerism, well enough to seed some vital phrases into poor Miranda's mind. Isn't that, right?"

The mesmerist's face was a mask of grief. "I . . . I didn't know what he was going to do? He promised me money, I . . . I never thought we would hurt anybody?" Sinister dropped his head and stared at his feet.

"This is impossible!" cried Beasmore. "My Miranda? The snarling – the cursing. The rage!"

"All implanted in her mind by Father Rammier. It took a second viewing of their act to deduce the phrases and actions, but I feel I have most of them worked out. I brought Miranda out of her sleep with the use of some smelling salts from Doctor Nefferson's bag. Then the phrase I said out loud was one of those that triggered Miranda's delirium and rage. The second was the one used to put her back to sleep. I didn't however use the ether that Sinister has administered as the last part of the ritual, I didn't feel it was required."

"But – but – the bubbling on her skin from the Holy Water!" asked the girl's mother. "Surely, that must be demonic?"

"Ah, now that was clever." Holmes moved around to the bed and pulled a small flask from an inner pocket. "You could not fail to have noticed the lighting of the heavily scented candles that preceded the ritual. That was to mask three significant odours. The smelling salts to rouse her, the ether to subdue her, and this."

Holding up the bottle he uncorked it and dripped several drops of the liquid on Miranda's exposed flesh. Immediately, it began to bubble and sizzle on her skin.

Beasmore groaned.

"A simple chemistry trick. Miranda's skin was prepared with a concentrated solution of sodium bicarbonate. This is vinegar. The acid hitting the alkaline results in the bubbling as we can see. A harmless reaction, except for a minimal amount of heat, but when dressed up as Holy Water splashing onto the skin of a demon-possessed girl, quite a striking effect. The vinegar would have stung our nostrils if it hadn't been for the lavender scent on the air."

"Quite so. This whole affair has been, actually"

"That's quite devilish," said Nefferson.

"And the room's colder temperature?" I asked.

"Frozen carbon dioxide – dry ice – packed into the false priest's bag. It caused enough of a temperature difference that, in that atmosphere, it felt noticeable."

I started to ask another question when the front doorbell rang. A smile grew on Holmes's face. "Ah, Watson, could you? They are right on time."

Within moments I returned with Lestrade and Bradstreet in tow. They were accompanied by a dour-looking man in his fifties, dressed all in a black cassock, with a white priest's collar.

"Ah, good. It's a little crowded, but can you please join us. Bishop Althorp?," Holmes indicated the man in black. "This is Father Rammier. I think you'll be wanting to ask him a lot of questions."

The bishop stared down his nose at the little priest. His anger was palpable. He pivoted towards Julius. "Firstly, I think I will talk with Mr. and Mrs. Beasmore and offer the full apology of the Catholic Church."

***

"I do hope that the poor girl will regain her senses. Nefferson has had her committed to a sanatorium for the time being, until all this clears from her mind," I said, as we relaxed in the sitting room with late-night brandy and cigarettes.

"Yes. She will need complete rest, and hopefully, Lestrade can pry out of Rammier and Sinister all the phrases they used on the poor girl. Sinister seemed amicable to helping, but Rammier proved himself far more nefarious than his unwitting accomplice."

Nodding, I added, "Well, I'm certainly glad that you unearthed a solution grounded in reality. I am a little sorry that I even entertained the idea that the poor girl was possessed by a demon, but her mental downfall was so sudden and so complete that I couldn't easily fathom any other answer. I can understand why the Beasmores gave it so much credence."

"Some people, no matter their station in life, do sometimes need the comfort of the spiritual realm to make sense of what happens to them in the real world." Holmes took a sip of brandy, a slight grin on his face in response to my own beliefs.

"Bravo. Yes, I am impressed that you approached the matter without any thought of giving credibility to the demon possession angle." I took a drink, before settling back and musing. "I know that over the years, you have been presented with many intriguing cases, supposedly exhibiting some form of supernatural origin, but have always found a rational explanation. Surely there must exist within your mind something that longs for the day when you shall be proven wrong and be presented with something that seems impossible and otherworldly and does indeed exist in the realm of the unknown, and no matter how much you examine it or all the clues you unearth in the quest for knowledge, nothing can drag the solution into a logical and sensible conclusion. Am I right?"

Holmes's face grew stern. I noticed him pause and gaze at me for quite some time before he uttered a single word answer in response.

"No."

A Matter of Tainted Honey

Almost every day since I chose my retirement, I have found myself giving thanks for my decision. Towards the end, the cases that found their way into my attention had become bogged down in their tawdriness. Very rarely did anything occur that was either a challenge or of interest to me. Indeed, I found, on many occasions, that I simply undertook an investigation, as a way, to assuage some shred of guilt that may arise if I said no.

Eventually, I left London and all the unwanted attention that my presence there attracted. The simple life I assumed, maintaining my property, on the Sussex Downs was a much more welcome existence.

It is true, I did miss John and Mycroft. Sadly, John died only this last year, which concluded with my last journey to London. I stopped in on Mycroft, but with his wonderful mind suffering, he barely knew who I was. Travel of that distance is almost beyond me now, so I doubt that I will ever set foot in the great Metropolis again.

Life is not the same as it was. Certainly, it is not the romantic world of the "great detective" that John described in his stories. I have undertaken cases over the intervening years, but no longer do they present at my door from a cavalcade of wanting souls; instead, I simply find myself in the presence of a need. Much like that Catholic priest that I crossed paths with many years ago. He never seemed to seek out any adventures, but they continuously found him. Interesting man, with no idea of the deductive arts, instead using a simplistic knowledge and understanding of the human condition to solve his cases.

Yes, life is much more enjoyable in its simplicity. I have my bees, after all.

Ah, the bees. It is they I live for now, but it is they that were the genesis of this tale that I have decided to commit to paper. More for my own purposes, but also as I no longer have the luxury of my good friend's attentive documentation skills—though at least this story will be recorded correctly, not over-embellished like John was wont to do.

As anyone who knew me would understand, I couldn't simply follow the system used by others of the apiarist bent. The harvesting of honey was a highly destructive event, which left many of the worker bees dead or distressed to the point that they wouldn't last long at all. After many years of studying these marvellous creatures and their instinctual lives, I invented a new way of retrieving the product of their endeavour. A simple redesign of the honey containment system, linked to inbuilt plumbing enabled the honey to be harvested from outside of the hive, with minimal disruption to the inhabitants.

The product could be collected in jars, and with a final straining of any collected debris, was ready for consumption. In fact, in most cases, the filtering step was wholly unrequired but was used as a precautionary measure. I engaged a local carpenter, presenting him with my rough drawn plans which piqued his curiosity markedly. Over several weeks, he endeavoured to create working examples of my designs to the functional level that we both agreed upon. His wonderful realisations now sit on my property, home to thousands of bees.

My allotment wasn't large compared to others in the immediate area, but it allowed me to position hives in three corners of the property, enabling me to conduct a comparative experiment of sorts. Given that the field surrounding my house was devoid of flowers or plants other than a short type of gorse, I could assume that my worker bees would need to fly further afield to procure the nectar they require to produce the miracle of honey.

It is that little experiment that initiated this adventure.

Towards the middle of September, I regularly undertake the last harvest of honey. The colder weather heading into late autumn and, of course, winter, leads to less activity amongst the bees, and naturally, fewer available sources for their required nectar.

On that lovely autumn day, I completed my honey collection, returning to my cottage with several jars of golden liquid. Careful to ensure that each set of containers was separated according to the location of the hives, I set them aside until the next day when I would finalise my processes. I liked to separate the honey into smaller jars that I would then distribute amongst my contacts in the nearby town. Part of my experiment was to test the flavour and quality of the product from each of the three apiaries.

Though sometimes I did miss the familiarity of having John around, I didn't feel the constant need for close human contact. Giving pots of honey to many locals was for a perfunctory purpose and generally involved paying for services provided or was part of the end of a bartered exchange. My housekeeper indulged in a love of honey by taking most of my produce, resulting in a satisfactory return through a higher level of service.

When she saw the newly harvested produce, her eyes lit up in expectation. I, however, quelled her eagerness by suggesting that the honey should sit for a few days, and be decanted into smaller portions for distribution.

It was no small expression of disappointment that bade me farewell that night, though I would have thought she would be fine to wait as she had taken a large portion of my product over the previous few months. My bees worked tirelessly, but even they had their limits.

After a rather perfunctory supper, prepared and left behind by my housekeeper, I settled in for an evening of reading. My young protégé from London had sent down a copy of his dissertation entitled "*An examination of the Cthulhu Cult and others*." I must admit, like any other religious doctrine or cult, I found the motives of the members to be somewhat lacking in reason. By the time I had read the paper several times and added comments and corrections, I realised the time had moved well past eleven.

My nocturnal pursuits were well within my past and I rarely found myself still awake after ten o'clock. Even though I am generally a good sleeper, my dreams were filled with strange images and impressions. Of an island, devoid of human occupation, but home to a towering presence, which sat unformed on the periphery of my mind's eye. Of devotees to the presence, which prostrated themselves in obeyance at the feet of their god, wrought in stone but impossible in its depiction.

Shaken awake by an event within my dreams that culminated in my essence flying through the void and suddenly succumbing to gravity, I rose from my bed, blinking several times to clear my mind of the images and thoughts. I'm not one to regularly dream or to have nightmares for that matter, but the vivid visions still spun in my head and seemed to refuse to leave.

Reaching for the glass of water on my bedside table, I quickly drained the last dregs, but still felt slightly parched.

It was as I carefully shuffled towards the kitchen—my legs are not as they were in my youth and require much time before the knots and tensions ease enough for them to carry me confidently—that I noticed the radiance.

I had never seen such a sight. A phantasmagorical display of light bled across the kitchen. It didn't illuminate as much as almost *eliminate*. Colours danced upon objects, at once shimmering upon their surface, and then causing the item to almost disappear as if the reflection was consumed and sent into a void of darkness.

I stopped on the threshold and stared, half imagining that the events playing out were still a part of my recent nightmare, whilst deeply examining the reality of the situation. The lights, or colours, which flickered across the walls, floor, and objects in my kitchen, seemed to be from the boundaries of the visible spectrum. When directly spied they could not be discerned, but when seen from the periphery of my vision showed in a starker contrast, whilst continuing to defy any attempts at focusing on them.

After what seemed like several minutes, I tore my eyes from the light show and scanned the room for the source. It was then I noticed the jars of honey that I had harvested the day before. Two sets of jars were dark, hidden in the shadows, with the barest hints of that magnificent colour display reflecting across their glass surface. The set of jars to the far left, however, was pulsating with the colours. One moment, brightly shining from within, the next seeming to disappear from this reality to virtually hide outside of the same plane of existence.

I picked up one jar to study it closer, the colour immediately leaching out and consuming the space around it. Brightly illuminating my hand, before forcing it to withdraw from view before my very eyes.

Taking the jar, I shuffled across to my small dining table and sat, placing the honey before me so that I could examine it further. I have no recollection as to how long I sat there, but must have fallen asleep, as the next moment I found myself awakening to bright sunshine bleeding in through the partially closed curtains. Looking around, I found that the world had righted itself. The light and colours of my kitchen and all it contained were as normal as could be. Even the jar before me sat in silent indifference. The light from the morning sun shining through the bright, golden honey cast a yellow pall across the white tablecloth.

Had I imagined everything? Was it all just a strange dream, carrying on from the nightmare I had suffered?

Unsure and annoyed at my confusion, I made my way back to bed, intent on snatching another two or three hours of sleep to settle my mind before undertaking any investigation.

***

I awoke to the sounds of clinking and clattering crockery as my housekeeper moved around in the kitchen. Bright light filtered in around the edges of my curtains leading me to deduce it was well into the morning, a fact confirmed by my bedside clock. Groggily, I rose, donning slippers and a dressing gown, before snatching up my walking stick to support my aching hip and shuffling out to the kitchen.

My housekeeper had prepared a sumptuous repast which made my stomach growl in anticipation, even though I had no thoughts of hunger that I could remember.

"Ah, Mr. Holmes, so glad you've decided to join the world of the awake," she said, spying me out of the corner of her eye.

"Alas, I had a fitful night's sleep. My mind was plagued with strange dreams. One was especially vivid, and I thought it was as real as you or me, but now I'm not so sure."

"Well, these things can't be helped. Have some breakfast and put your mind at rest."

Nodding, I poured a cup of coffee, sipping it before anything else. The brew was strong and delightful. Within a moment I could feel myself growing stronger and ready for the day. Dropping two slices of toast on my plate, I quickly applied butter and reached for the jar of golden honey. Pleased with the spread, I quickly munched down on the toast. Almost immediately I coughed and spat the horrid-tasting mess from my mouth.

"Good Lord," I cried, snatching my housekeeper's attention.

"Mr. Holmes, are you all right?" she asked, rushing to the table, and fussing over me. It was as if I had snatched up a burnt brand from a nearby fire and chomped down upon it, filling my mouth with the taste of ash and soot. I downed some of the steaming hot coffee to remove the horrid flavour from my mouth and stared first at the toast then the honey. It was then I realised that the pot was one of the larger collection jars, rather than the smaller ones I use for storing the honey for general consumption.

"This jar of honey?" I asked, pointing at the container, "Where did it come from?" The answer was already clear, especially once I pivoted and glanced across at the newly stocked shelf used to store the freshly harvested honey. The jars from the north-western hives numbered one less than their counterparts from the others.

"It was already on the table," my housekeeper confessed. "I presumed you had left it there for your breakfast."

Nodding, I squinted at the far corner. In the soft shade, I was sure I could see a glistening in the other jars. A shimmering of light and colour that brought back all the memories of the hours from earlier that day.

I realised it hadn't been a dream.

***

The horrible taste of ashes had come from the honey. I tempted fate once more, dipping a finger into the pot and licking the viscous liquid. The foul taste of cinders was there. Finishing two more cups of coffee and some more toast with marmalade, I finally cleansed the horrid taste from my mouth. Fatigue still tugged at my bones, wishing me back to bed or to at least lounge in my comfortable chair for the rest of the day, but an inner purpose filled my senses.

Donning my protective clothing, I ventured out to the northwestern corner of my property. Unless I was mistaken, this was where the tainted honey had been retrieved. The sight that beheld me was ghastly to my apiarist's eyes. Dozens of bees lay dead on the ground beneath the hives. Carefully bending to one knee, I examined them closely. They were not the regular colourful black and yellow that I was used to. Instead, they were grey, or at least covered in a thin coating of some grey material.

"Perhaps it's ash?" I thought to myself. I picked up several corpses, one after the other, to discern whether they were covered with soot, but nothing rubbed off or left a trace on my fingers. The insects were indeed discoloured, or de-coloured, as the effect seemed to be that the hue of their carapace had lost all hint of their normal appearance, instead receding into that ashen palate.

Unlocking the roof of the hive, I peeked inside, expecting a lively mass of insects, only to stare in silent horror at the dull, grey mess within. All were dead, lying scattered about the floor of the hive, with dozens stuck to the wax of the honeycomb, as if they succumbed whilst working away. Each hive showed the same devastation within.

Turning the honey release crank and opening the valve resulted in a grey-tinged effluent of thick liquid seeping out. It possessed none of the golden, translucent honey that I had collected only the previous day. Instead, it was a viscous slurry of opaque grey.

Shaking my head, I scanned the area to the north and west of my property. My only thought was that the bees had visited some tainted or poisoned plants in that general area. They had brought the disease or, perhaps, fungus back with them and infected the rest of the hive and even the honey itself. I wished to investigate, but was not dressed for an excursion, and had no solid idea of where to head.

Convinced that there was nothing more to examine, I shuffled back to my cottage. My hip was smarting with my short journey and would need to be rested if there was any chance for a trip beyond the confines of my property.

Back inside, I went straight to the honey pots from the previous day. Bringing them into the light, the once-golden colour of the honey inside had vanished, replaced with a dull, grey sludge-like liquid. All three were so tainted.

"My word," said my housekeeper, "What have you got there, Mr. Holmes?"

“Strangely, this was golden honey only this morning. Something has afflicted the bees, the hive, and now the produce. I’m afraid it looks like you may not be gifted as much as would be normal.”

“If it’s all that colour, then I’m more than happy to miss out.”

Picking up the other two jars, I trudged back out to the hives, wishing to leave all the evidence together. I was of a mind to burn the lot. Hives, bees, and honey included; but thought better of such a rash act. I wanted, no, I *needed* to uncover the reasons and get to the bottom of this terrible situation. I may still yet need to examine everything again.

Once more I returned to my cottage, taking to my easy chair after placing a small ceramic bottle filled with hot water against my hip, in an attempt to relieve the growing pain. I must have dozed off, as I awoke when the shadows had begun to creep into the parlour. Glancing out of the westward-facing window, I could see the sun dipping below the horizon as evening took the land in its grip.

My housekeeper had prepared me some dinner and left it on the table covered with a cloth. Sadly, it was cold, as due to my napping, I had missed luncheon and found myself famished. Though the cold meat and bread provided a substantial amount of sustenance and I found myself vigorously improved.

Pouring myself an after-dinner brandy, I stepped outside and lit a cigarette. If my housekeeper had been in attendance, I felt sure I would be lectured on my habit, with labels such as *disgusting* and *horrid* heading my way.

Sitting on the small chair I had positioned for just such a night, I gazed across the fields towards the dark expanse of forest to the northwest. It had not been my intention to look in that direction, but I could only assume that my subconscious mind issued those commands.

The night was clear, and with the lack of any moon, was as black as pitch. Sweeping my sight across the dark tree line, it was as I turned away from one area that a trace of light was left upon my sight. Staring back at the spot, I could barely perceive anything untoward, but as I moved my eyes away, I saw it again.

The events of the dark early morning came back to me. The colours and radiance from the tainted jars of honey. That leaching of light from the surrounding area, mixed with shades that did not belong in the visible spectrum but from the peripheries. It played out as a subtle contrast to the darkness surrounding it, far off in the nearby woods.

I thought for a moment whether the journey was beyond me but banished such views. I was still Sherlock Holmes, and there was no Mrs. Hudson or John Watson or even Mycroft to temper my enthusiasm or sense of adventure. Only the frailty of my own ageing body, but that was mine to control and ignore.

***

The darkness had set in fully by the time I donned my coat and hat, snatched up my walking cane, and headed out my front door. Noting the gloom of the night, I filled my hand-held lamp with kerosene and lit it. The lamp would at least light my way, showing up any holes in the roadway, and assisting me if I needed to thread my way through any part of the woods.

I followed the road to the corner of my property and turned north, heading towards the area where my stricken beehives sat, and the dark woods which appeared to be the source of the strange colours and lights.

I had only a passing reference to, and indeed interest in, my neighbours on the northern boundary. They were a queer family, keeping very much to themselves, but engendering rumour and gossip amongst the denizens of the nearby town. By my recollection, their name was Gardner, with the patriarch known as Nahum, living with his wife and three sons on a plot of land where they grew vegetables and raised sheep.

I didn't consider that the Gardners had any hand in the cause of the strange colour, only that what I had seen came from the direction of their land. I hoped to contact Nahum or his family to see if they could help to determine what had infected my bees and turned the honey to ash. I feared that whatever it was could spread wider, affecting all my hives, and making many more of the surrounding farms inoperable.

I knew from previous walks that there was a thin track leading off from the main road and heading into the dark woods. This path, I understood, led to the Gardner property. Within a few minutes of trudging along the road, I spied my poor hives full of ashen honey and dead bees. Not long afterwards, I found the pathway into the forest and lifting my lamp peered into the gloom that shrouded the track. Small pinpoints of light shone back but disappeared almost as quickly.

Wildlife. Foxes perhaps?

The track that plunged into the darkness was overgrown to the point that a wagon or cart simply couldn't make the journey. I did not know much of the Gardners, but I did know they ran sheep or goats on their small holding and took some to market, from time to time, in the nearby village. Presumably, they drove the animals on foot.

As I moved on, pushing back a particularly thick set of branches that I was surprised hadn't been exorcised from the pathway by any regular users, I noticed a small clearing to one side. Shining my lamp across the area, I spied a lush patch of round-headed rampions, known as the *Pride of Sussex*. These flowers could be found all over the countryside and were the main source of nectar for my hives.

Normally the flowers were small, around an inch across. These, however, were almost three times that size. The bushes were almost as large as a good-sized rose bush. With no other facts to hand, I simply put their existence down to the good soil of the wood, nourished with centuries of leaf litter.

A scrabbling noise to my left had me spinning. My lantern caught sight of something large and grey disappearing into the underbrush. The strange colour of the animal stayed in my memory well after it had gone. It was much larger than a squirrel, the only grey-coloured animal I could picture. I pushed the thought away, allaying my concern that it was possibly a stray cat or dog.

Turning back to the pathway, I noticed a yellow light filtering through the thick brush. Within another twenty yards of overgrown trail, it became clearer. I squinted into the darkness, trying to make out more details, but would have to wait until the woods grew thinner.

Finally, I stepped out into a cleared area that ran all the way to the farmhouse. It was a modest place, a simple stone cottage with a high roof that sported a single window at one end, presumably a second level or attic. A light burned in the lower floor windows, which indicated that someone was at least home. The property itself lay over a larger area than my own, but in the dim light where I stood, I could see nothing moving.

Silence sat over the area like a shroud. There was no immediate evidence of the livestock that I understood lived here.

Wishing to conserve the fuel in my lantern for my return journey, I turned it down, diminishing the yellow glow around me. That was when I noticed the aura playing in the air about the well.

The memories from the early morning encounter with my honey jars came flooding back. Those same colours that sat on the periphery of the visible spectrum flourished about the small stone structure. The light, or absence of light, reached out of the well, like the tendrils of some great cephalopod. From a distance, I edged myself around the well, staying clear of the perceived reach of what I had started to refer to internally as *the colour*, for no other reason than I needed to give it a name.

Turning up my lantern's wick, I swung it gently across the ground. The yellow glow struggled to illuminate anything, as the very brightness seemed to be sucked into a void of darkness by *the colour*. What I could see of the ground appeared to be devoid of all hue, and simply showed the same ash grey I had seen in my bees and hives. As if not only the life had been drawn from the plants and grass, but all evidence of any tint or lustre.

Halfway around the well, I saw the most devastating evidence that something was awry. A crater, for it looked less like a hole that man or animal could have dug than the impact of some great object, lay beside the well. Dirt and mud had been thrown up onto the flat earth surrounding the channel, the stones of the well cracked and broken, with several having fallen into the waters inside. The strange and perturbing glow of *the colour* emanated from the hole, almost creeping across the ground rather than radiating out like any normal light source.

I felt drawn to the well, to look inside and view what I imagined was a broiling morass of colour, light and that strange negative glow that accompanied it. Stepping forward, I leaned heavily on my cane. The long walk and the moment of standing still had inflamed my hip, making progress difficult. As I closed in on the circular wall of the well, I strained forward to spy inside, my mind intent on investigating, but ignorant of any possible danger.

As soon as I peeked over the edge, I knew it was a mistake.

The waters of the well swirled in a miasma of colour and light, with the eye of the vortex devoid of both and exhibiting that negative emptiness that sucked at all around it. Staring into that eye was like staring into the void. I felt something pull at my mind, coaxing and coercing me to join, to enter the abyss and become one with *the colour*. And like many who have stood at the edge of a precipice, I felt that call of the void and teetered on the brink of simply vaulting over the wall to fulfill the summoning.

If not for the sudden cry from the house, I may not be here to tell the tale.

Glancing towards the source of the sound, I became aware of several grey-coloured mounds lying in the mud to the side of the house. I was desperate to investigate the cry but fearful of what these objects may be. I shuffled across as quickly as my pained legs would allow.

Holding the lantern out before me, I quickly realised they were the corpses of several sheep. Their white wool was a mottled grey, like the ashen shades of the grass and the fur of the animal I had seen in the woods. Their faces were contorted into all manner of agonised expressions, with lifeless eyes that shone not from my lantern, but from *the colour* in the well.

There was nothing I could do for the poor beasts, so I turned my attention to the house.

The door was unlocked and opened on creaking hinges to reveal a modest and functional kitchen and dining area. Plates lay used on the table, caked with the rotting remnants of food. Others were stacked high in the basin, pleading to be washed. The fire had died in the hearth, leaving a chill across the room. The embers were cold. It had been a long time since the fire went out.

The evidence of recent human occupation caused a feeling of wariness to rise in me. The cry, I had heard only moments ago, had not been repeated, but I could only deduce it had originated somewhere in the house.

As quickly as I could, I searched the ground floor rooms. Two bedrooms were empty, the bedclothes on the four beds unmade indicating use, but not for how long. Given the state of cleanliness of the bedding, I decided not to test for warmth. I knew that the house had five occupants, so the existence of four used beds was not surprising.

With the ground floor vacant, I decided to trudge up the stairs to the attic room.

It was less of a room and more of a storage area. Crates, boxes, and old furniture littered the area, but no obvious signs of human habitation. Until I spied a strange heap of blankets in the far corner of the room.

As I approached, holding my lantern out before me, the heap moved, emitting a cry of despair.

"Away. Stay away. No light, it burns," it said.

Shocked, I stopped and turned the lamp down, dimming the light. "Nahum? Nahum Gardner?" I asked.

"Gone. He gone," the figure mumbled. Its voice was muffled and malformed. Every utterance seemed a struggle.

"Mrs. Gardner?"

"'es. Me."

"Oh, my dear," I said, approaching but receiving terrified cries in answer. The poor woman pulled the blankets above her head and backed away as far as she could into the corner.

"What has happened? Did your husband do this?"

"No," she croaked. "The colour. The well."

"I can get you help." I turned to leave, but she cried out again.

"No. No time. Must help Nahum."

Spinning back, I asked, "Where is he? What's happened?"

"Out. Will be back. Not himself. None of us is."

Confused, I needed to know about their children. "Your boys? Where are they? Are they safe?"

A thin ash-grey arm slowly extended from the pile of blankets, pointing towards the far wall. "The well. They now live in the well."

Live in the well?

My mind raced back to the terrifying sights I had seen down that well. Although brief, I felt that as I stared into that void, a veritable unknown universe stared back at me. Flashes of images crossed my mind. Of immense depths of despair, filled with nightmare creatures of unfathomable size and shape. Such a glimpse of horrors almost unimaginable could only come from the effects of some mind-bending substance leaking from that well.

Is that what this is?

I had by my own hand tried many drugs and tinctures, but none had ever affected me in this way. There was something more, almost other-worldly about *the colour's* influence on the human condition—not just the mind, but the flesh. Had its manipulative sway buried itself so deeply that the body itself reacted, or was there more to the radiance? A disease embodied in the luminosity, which preyed upon the body as well as the mind.

Shaking my head, I thought of the case in hand. One person was missing from this equation, and in my experience, people didn't generally just disappear down a well of their own free will, especially young men.

Stepping closer to the woman, I asked, "Did your husband do this? Where is he?"

The woman shuffled back, feet and legs pinwheeling beneath her as I moved forward. The topmost blanket caught on her foot and was dragged down, revealing her face for the first time.

I stopped, shocked.

By my calculations, Nahum Gardner and his wife were barely in their mid-forties, but the poor unfortunate woman lying on the floor before me looked positively ancient. Her skin held the tones of pale grey that I had seen in those nearing the end of their life after nigh on eight decades. Her eyes beseeched me, their iris colour all but gone, the pupils clouded as if Mrs. Gardner was afflicted with advanced cataracts. She threw an arm across her face to shield herself from the lantern, the sudden movement resulting in her skin splitting and revealing a long rent down her arm that bled forth a dark and putrid fluid.

"Stay away," she screamed, "Keep away, the light."

I stopped advancing, bringing my lantern back and shielding it behind my body. The woman had undergone some horrible trauma and I cursed myself for causing her any further harm in my haste for answers, but that wound needed attention.

The thudding of heavy feet on the steps, drew my attention, spinning me around to face the newcomer, obscuring all concern for the poor woman.

I could only guess it was Nahum Gardner. Like his wife, his skin was dank and sallow, sporting an ash-grey complexion with the consistency of congealed lard. His eyes were dull and watery, devoid of iris colour, and any spark of intelligence. The folds of skin hung from his cheeks, as if ready to slough off and drop to the floor. His clothes told of life for a man once powerfully built, but now hung in limp folds from his desiccated frame.

Gardner took one look at me, then at his cowering wife, then back at me.

"What you do?" he screamed, pointing to the corner. "You hurt her?"

Before I could plead my case, he struck out with the axe he held. The blade narrowly missed my head but knocked the lantern from my grasp. It somersaulted through the air, spraying the kerosene across the floor, before impacting on the hardwood and exploding in a fireball that spread tendrils of flame across the room and into the far corner.

More screams pierced the night as the fire leapt onto the pile of blankets containing Mrs. Gardner. She stood for a moment as the blaze engulfed her. Those frail arms flailed wildly as the inferno consumed her shrunken body. Gardner cried out in horror, ignoring me, and rushing to his wife.

"No, don't," I cried to his deaf ears.

The effects of *the colour* had stripped all sense from his being as he threw his arms around his loved one, joining her in the conflagration. They fell in a heap amongst the flames that quickly leapt up the walls and into the dry, ancient wooden beams.

There was nothing I could do for them. They were gone the moment they both caught fire. All I could do was save myself and bring back help.

Turning, I shambled towards the staircase, coughing on the thick smoke that filled the room. Halfway to the ground floor, my hip failed me, causing my legs to tangle and pitch me down the remaining steps. The last I remember was the black embrace of darkness filling my mind and leaving only the memories of *the colour* swimming across my mind's eye.

***

Light flooded across my vision as I blinked the sleep from my eyes. Groggily, I glanced around and realised I lay on my bed.

A dream? Was it all a dream?

After much effort, I sat up on the edge and looked down at my clothing. I was still fully clothed. Mud streaked my pants and caked my boots. I smelt smoke and looked around expecting some conflagration to have taken hold of my room, but realised my clothes were saturated with the odour of fire.

It was real.

Standing unsteadily, my hip burst into a rage of agony and threatened to buckle and send me to the floor. My walking stick leaned against the foot of the bed. I snatched it up and used it to take the weight from my ailing leg as I made my way from my room and into the kitchen.

It was evident that my housekeeper had arrived, as the table was set for breakfast. I noticed a smaller pot of honey had been placed. It caught my eye for a moment and found me examining the golden liquid for any hint of *the colour*. When nothing showed, I turned away and shuffled towards the kitchen window.

All thoughts that I had dreamt about my previous night's adventure were washed away the moment I spied the column of thick smoke rising from the woods in the northwest. The Gardner place was indeed afire.

I felt the need inside me grow. The need to know what had happened. How I had returned home. The need to retrace my steps. The need to see if there was any help I could offer.

As I stepped towards the rear door, I was brought up short by a voice behind me. "Look at the state of you." Turning, I saw my housekeeper standing at the doorway of the kitchen with a bucket of water and a scrubbing brush. "I figured it was you who tracked the mud into this house. What were you up to last night? Tramping all over the county?"

"I…" A single word with a gesture towards the window was all I managed before being cut off.

"Yes, horrible that. The Gardner place. Been aflame all night. I heard the engines rolling through the streets before I came here."

I took one more look at the smoke. "I need to return."

"From the looks of you, you're more in need of a change of clothes and some breakfast."

***

Taking my housekeeper's advice, I broke my fast and redressed in another set of outdoors clothes. It was then I noticed the scrape on my shoulder, a bruise on my forehead, and a tender spot on the rear of my head. I could only presume I had suffered these during my tumble down the stairs. I was wary that my loss of memory may be a symptom of some cerebral contusion, but without the guidance and concern of a nearby physician, ignored the infirmity and pledged to struggle on.

Stepping outside I first noticed that muddy footprints led to my rear step. In my delirium, I had trekked across the fields, soaked with evening dew. Switching to sturdy waterproof boots, I followed the trail of stamped grasses, surprised that I was able to make such a journey in the state I presumed I had been in.

The trail led to the small dry-stone wall that surrounded my property. There I noticed some stones had been dislodged, and a smear of mud graced the top. Presumably, I had climbed or stumbled over the wall; a large area of compressed grass on the house side indicated that I had fallen, and possibly lain in a dazed state for some time.

Once on the road again, I retraced my steps from the previous evening and found the narrow trail that led to the Gardner residence. In the full light of day, it presented as a pleasant walk in the woods, rather than the dark journey into the terror that I had faced on the previous night.

Carts had plied their way along the track, churning up the dirt and mud with new ruts, and tearing the overhanging vegetation. Within minutes I came, once again, upon the clearing that led to the property.

The house was a burnt-out shell. The soot-darkened stones held together through sheer force of will rather than any advanced building techniques. The roof was gone, only showing blackened beams that looked more like the rib cage of some long-dead creature. Three carts were arrayed before the property, with many men milling around.

With shock, I saw that they were drawing water from the well and carrying buckets of that vile effluent across to the house to douse any remaining cinders.

I must warn them.

Spying the local senior constable, I shuffled across the damp ground to where he directed some of the men.

"Bower, you need to stop those men."

The young policeman turned and beheld me, a slight look of confusion drew across his face. "Mr. Holmes? What are you doing here?" He searched the area behind me. "Did you walk? At your age?"

"One thing at a time," I replied. I realised I needed to construct a tale that wouldn't paint me as some sort of madman. Even though I felt that *the colour* was the catalyst for all this calamity, it still fell to the actions of man. "I still undertake evening walks for my health, young man." I tried to sound more authoritative than annoyed. "Last night, I heard a scream come from this area. I tramped down the pathway and found the house lit for the evening and heard cries issue from the upstairs window. There I found Mrs. Gardner in a sorry state. As I tried to assist her, Mr. Gardner returned home and flew into a rage. My lantern was knocked from my hand and was the cause of this conflagration. I escaped but tripped down the stairs. I awoke this morning in my bed but have no memory of how I arrived home."

"My word. Do you need a doctor?"

"Perhaps, but that can wait. It's the well I'm more concerned about. Before I was attacked, Mrs. Gardner confessed that her three sons are in that well. I can only presume that Mr. Gardner put them there."

Just as I was extolling my fears, a voice cried out from the direction of the well. We turned to see several men gather and point into that pit. Images filled my mind of the despair that I witnessed in that deep void. The shouting and gesturing of the gathered men were more alarm than anguish. As Bower and I moved towards the group, I heard the cries more clearly.

"There's a body."

The policeman stopped and stared back at me. I simply nodded. Barking orders to clear the way, he strode to the well and stared into the darkness below.

The next few hours were a new bustle of activity as the three bodies were retrieved. One of the men, who knew the family quite well, pointed to each in turn and named them as the three missing sons. Sadly, my intuition was correct. Each corpse sported a deep wound to the head. The type of wound that a blow from a sharp axe would make. With Bower's consent, I searched the remnants of the house and found the axe head lying alone in a pile of cinders. The handle had all but burnt away. Two constables assisted in my search, discovering both Gardner parents lying huddled together, all life stripped from them by the fire.

Bower was satisfied that Nahum Gardner had lost his mind and perpetrated the crimes. The cause of his madness was listed as unknown.

"You noticed the dead sheep and the greying grass?" I asked.

Nodding he put it down to an unknown disease or similar. I pointed to the waters of the well as the source of all the family's ills.

"I believe it comes from there. If you stop and sense the atmosphere, it is almost palpable. Whatever invaded that well, whether from the skies or the land, has left its mark upon the ground and inhabitants of this area."

"What should be done?"

“I think a team of scientists should examine the waters, but once they are done, it should be filled in so that nothing more drinks of that foul effluent.”

Nodding, he added, “Fair enough. I do not know of any other family members that can lay claim to this land, so we can act in good faith to protect the citizens of this county.”

“Good,” I nodded. I was fascinated by what the well may contain, but the part of me that had become more focused on self-preservation wanted that foul pit covered for all posterity.

As the shadows drew long, I welcomed Bower’s offer of a ride back to my cottage. I had more pains in my joints and muscles than I could count and needed a long, hot bath, and dinner.

***

Nothing gave a conclusive solution to what invaded the Gardners' well. A team of scientists came from London University to excavate and examine all that could be discovered, but once the well was drained and the stones removed, all they found was mud.

I kept up to date with their progress through frequent visits and interviews, but nothing much was recorded or published. One fellow from Oxford suggested that the hole that I discovered was possibly caused by a meteor strike, or some such, due to the smooth sides of the trench leading into the shattered wall of the well, and the fact that all the bricks were inside. But the object that caused it refused to be found. By the time they had finished, *the colour* had all but disappeared from the area. On the few night-time visits I made later, only the merest shimmer could be seen. Once the area was filled in, and the house levelled, I stopped my visitations completely, merely passing the start of the pathway on my regular strolls. Even that entranceway, into the madness I had witnessed, eventually became overgrown, and disappeared from view.

However, the effects of that strange *colour* were still evident. The land around the well and across the entire Gardner property never recovered. Nothing grew. The area was silent. Devoid of birdsong or the rustling of animals in the woods nearby.

The plants that I could see from the road, showed the same strange signs. Incredible growth at one stage, then that pale-grey lustre that signalled their imminent death, and finally a crumbling away to dust.

Nothing gave a conclusive solution to what invaded the Gardners' well.

The intrusion upon the woods and adjacent land had been gradual, but slowly, inch by inch, it stretched out, gripping more of the area in its grasp. A sluggish, creeping death to all around it.

The authorities were unalarmed. I alerted them to the effect on the surrounding woodlands, but my pleas attracted little more than a nodding acknowledgement. I fear that the days when my authority stood alone are well and truly past. I'm seen more as a doddering old fool than the sharp-minded detective of my youth.

For myself, I burnt the affected hives and made sure that any new ones were placed well away from that accursed corner of my property.

The slow grey death that appeared to inch ever onward would take some time to reach my boundary. I have written up my findings and observations. This commentary is a testament to that fact. I have tried to tell my tale, only to have it fall on deaf ears. My only hope is that I do not see the day that *the colour* arrives at my doorstep and, like poor Nahum Gardner, consumes all that I am and all that I have been, for I fear the loss of my mind most of all.

Little Boy Lost

I must admit that my day, in fact my week, had lapsed into a series of tedious menial chores around the inspectors' room. I was jealous of the others; all were out on calls. My cases were all tidied up, the culprits locked away, the paperwork done. I sat at my clean desk, working up the courage to just pick up my hat and coat and head home for the day, but a sense of duty kept me in my seat.

As luck would have it, Commander Ennis stepped in, scanned the room, and locked eyes with me.

"Bell," he said, waving at me, "My office, now."

Not needing to be told twice, I leapt to my feet and hurried after the boss. Even if it was just to pick up his tailoring, I was up for the task, so bored I was. It wasn't anything that dismal.

Arriving at the commander's office, I cleared my throat to announce my arrival. Without even looking up, he waved toward a nearby chair and said, "Bell, sit. This is important."

As I sat, he viewed the sheet of parchment in his hand, before turning it around and sliding it across the desk. Picking it up I scanned the page. It was an incident report. A missing person.

"Do you know Reginald Huxley?" the commander asked.

Thinking for a moment, I replied, "Businessman. Horses or something? Word on the street is that he's not as clean as his appearance and circle of friends would suggest." A slight nod of the head agreed with my assessment. "I've also heard he has been included in the Queen's Birthday honors list. OBE or a Knighthood or something?"

"Yes, well done. While not always above board, Huxley has convinced someone high up and will receive a knighthood in the next round, and a possible Lordship in the future, if he plays his cards right. He has connections, and it shouldn't surprise you that the commissioner is one of them." Nodding at the paper, he added, "That's why this is important."

I quickly read the document. The name Benedict Huxley appeared as the missing person. My eyes grew wide as I read the birthdate. "My word, his son is missing? Seven years old? Huxley would be beside himself."

"Yes. He was straight onto the commissioner. The boy only went missing this morning."

"Where?" I read the description at the bottom of the page. "Leicester Square? Empire Theatre? What was he doing there?"

"Theatre or some such. It's not written there, but it seems the boy didn't want to see Peter Pan. Scared of pirates or something. Threw a fit and dashed off. Huxley and his man chased after the boy, but he disappeared."

"Do they know which direction?"

"Toward Soho. I've had uniforms scouring the place for the last few hours." He sighed. "Nothing. Not a sign."

"There's no description of what he was wearing. Only his fair hair, and brown eyes. Four feet tall. Not much to go on."

"He was last seen wearing one of those twee sailor's costumes that are popular for young boys at the moment. I wouldn't have my son caught dead in one." The commander stopped for a moment. "Hmm. Probably not the best turn of phrase; don't repeat that."

"It sounds like looking for a needle in a haystack. Do we have any other ideas? Has he been kidnapped? A ransom note, perhaps? Or is he simply lost in that devilish area of London?"

The commander shrugged. "Nothing. My only hope is he turns up in a day or two. Little blighter." A sneer formed on his lips. "These rich folk don't treat their children properly. Spoilt. A good whack around the ears would have sorted him out, and all this would have been avoided."

I was a little gobsmacked at that remark but could understand the commander's attitude. Legend has it he was brought up on the streets of the East End. A rough and tumble boy that turned into a hard man. Lucky for the city of London, he turned to the law instead of crime. I folded the report and, grasping it in my right hand, stood. "I'll start at the theatre district and work my way toward Soho. I know a few contacts in the area that keep their eyes open, so hopefully, they have seen the boy."

He was last seen wearing one of those twee sailor's costumes that are popular for young boys at the moment.

"Good man. I'll send someone to assist when they get back in. There are a few uniforms still circling. Use them if you need to."

"Very good, sir." With that, I left.

With my coat on and hat in hand, I headed out into this great city of ours.

By the time I arrived at the Square, it was early evening. Outside of the Empire, a large crowd had gathered for the evening performance. I made a quick hunt around the area, questioning as many of the theatre staff as I could, much to no avail. Most hadn't been working that morning, only starting their shift in the mid-afternoon. Accepting those facts, I used the knowledge that the family had last seen Benedict racing off north in the direction of Soho.

I set off down Wardour Street, stopping at each stall and shop to ask the keepers. Most were annoyed at being asked once again, it seems the bobbies had already covered this ground. It wasn't until I came to Shaftsbury Avenue that I finally had some luck.

A young flower girl, working the crowds, told me she had seen a lad of the same description; he'd crossed through the lines of carts on the avenue and hurried on up Wardour Street. Slightly relieved to have more or less confirmed his direction, I plunged into Soho, fearful that the boy had come to harm from one of its many miscreant denizens.

Working the streets around Soho for what seemed like several hours, I received a few hints that there was a boy of Benedict's description in the area that morning, but nothing definite. As expected, most of the public wouldn't talk to me, and those that would were suspicious more than helpful.

By the time my stomach was rumbling from lack of food, I was almost despondent. The child had indeed vanished, and nothing I could think of was going to bring me closer to finding him.

Over the next two days, I checked all my grasses, but none had seen anything or knew any more than me. Quite depressing, really.

The only avenue left was to seek the aid of my associates. I'm new to Scotland Yard, I can't hide that fact, and have only been an inspector for the last two months. Luckily, I was a constable on the city beat, so I know the Soho area well. The problem is I don't have much sway with the other inspectors but have formed a bond with Lestrade and Bradstreet.

***

"So, that's what brought me here today."

My eyes flicked from one man to the other. Holmes sat forward slightly, his elbows resting on his knees, his fingers steepled, supporting his long aquiline face, with one index finger extended up his cheek. Watson sat back, a cup of tea held in his hands, a slight trail of steam curling upward from the cup toward his face.

"Lestrade and Bradstreet hold you in the highest of esteem. They suggested this meeting."

"Yes," said Holmes, "It is often that both your colleagues make their way to our parlour, as have you. Generally with some trivial exercise in deduction, but sometimes with a nugget of pure intrigue that prompts me to assist them."

"Oh," I said, perceiving from Holmes's somewhat frosty response that I was at a dead end here as well. I began to rise. "I'm sorry for wasting your time."

Holmes cried out. "Oh, don't misjudge my answer as some sort of dismissal. I was merely cogitating on the problem."

"Yes, you must excuse Holmes's sharp retorts," Watson chimed in, "He doesn't mean to appear rude; it is simply his way."

I sat back down, slightly relieved.

"Now, I must also apologize, I can only offer you the barest assistance. Watson and I are due to leave on the first train in the morning. We are headed to the west. A Roman Goddess or some such has disappeared."

Confused, I stammered. "A Roman Goddess?"

"Statue," added Watson. "Gone missing. Someone stole it from the excavations going on in Bath."

"Regardless, I am intrigued with your case." Holmes stared at me for a moment. I could almost feel that I was being sized up, that every facet of my being was under examination. "It's only been two days? Am I right?"

"Yes. Without a word."

"No ransom note? No correspondence of any kind?"

"That's correct."

The great detective waved his index finger in the air. "That tells me that this was more opportunistic than planned."

"How so?"

"If someone knew that they were kidnapping the Huxley boy, then they would have sent a ransom demand immediately. If nothing has been heard of in three days, then either the boy was kidnapped under some other pretence, or…"

He trailed off. By the dour look on his face, I could tell that his lack of words meant more than any of his other utterances. My heart sank. "Dead, you mean?"

Holding out his hands to diminish my fears, he added, "One must not rule anything out. Until we have evidence to the contrary, the boy is as good as alive." He stood and stared across at a collection of thick notebooks, brimming with loose sheaves of paper.

I drew a heavy breath. It had occurred to me at that point that the lack of any word for several days could mean the worst, but I had dismissed it, preferring to think of a more positive outcome.

My anguish was disturbed by Holmes stepping across to his collection and pulling down a thick volume. He strode to a nearby table and plonked the tome down, opening it with a slight creak and leafing through the pages. I noticed many newspaper clippings, some fixed to the book, others threatening to slip out as the pages were turned.

"Aha," said Holmes, causing both myself and Dr. Watson to find our feet and join him at the table. The tall man pointed at a single news article, the headline of which read: *Second Boy Missing.* "I remember reading about this occurrence a few years ago."

I focused on the article and quickly read the account. The printed date was missing, but someone, Holmes I assumed, had written the date on the top of the cut page. It was the same month, but four years previous. Two boys of about seven years of age had disappeared in the Soho area. The page turned again, and Holmes pointed at another newspaper cutting. This one read: *Little Boy Lost.* Another child had disappeared.

Holmes quickly turned and retrieved another volume. Flipping through this he found similar articles relating to children, this time two boys and a girl, lost in the Soho area. The clippings were only two years old.

"I think I can go back even farther, but now looking at these again, I can see that every two or three years, a few children go missing. Soho seems to be the center of this activity."

"Why? Or should I say, who would do such a thing?" asked Watson.

"That I don't know and have never had the impetus to investigate. Children in that area disappear all the time, so individual reports only raise sadness and a vague interest, but now, looking at them, they begin to resemble a pattern of behavior."

"But Benedict Huxley wasn't a typical Soho child."

"No, that's why more attention will be paid to this series of events. From the unfortunate disappearances of these children mixed with poor Benedict's fate, a whole new light may be thrown upon this."

"So you will help?"

Shaking his head, he said, "No, as I said, I cannot at the moment, but I will offer assistance from afar." He smiled and clapped me lightly on the shoulder. "This is your affair. One that I believe may be the making of you as an inspector."

"But I'm still none the wiser."

"Ah, but you are. Much wiser." Holmes indicated the folders. "Before you are several instances of the same crime. They may or may not be related, that is for you to investigate, but if they are in fact part of a string of crimes, then you will have unearthed something far greater than just a simple kidnapping." Holmes must have seen the vague and, frankly, overwhelmed look on my face. A broad grin crossed his visage. "Never fear, Inspector, I may not be able to attend to this matter, but I have many others at my service who can be of assistance."

He snatched up a calling card and wrote down an address on the back. Handing it to me, he said, "Now, please find yourself at that address tonight at seven o'clock. My associate will make himself known to you." Stepping back, he eyed me up and down before adding, "And please wear something a little less policeman-looking."

***

The sun had dipped behind the surrounding rooftops of Leicester Square when I positioned myself in the growing shadows beneath the Lyric Theatre's alcove. Studying the passersby, I felt oddly out of place. I had, as Holmes suggested, worn clothes not befitting of a police inspector. They were old, dirty, and a might smelly. I felt almost like a tramp or beggar and wouldn't have been surprised if a copper or two were thrown my way. I was shocked from my musings by a voice to my right.

"I thought Mr. 'Olmes told you ta dress less like a copper?"

Turning, I found myself looking into the dirt-streaked face of a young street ruffian. His eyes showed a world-weariness well in advance of his years, but still with the bright sparkle of youth in their depths. His assertions seemed correct, compared to the disorderly state of his dress, I presented as a well-to-do man about town.

"Inspector Bell, I presume," he said in hushed tones. When I nodded, he continued. "I'm Wiggins. I'm with Mr. 'Olmes's irregulars. 'Elp 'im out once in a while. Keep a keen eye on the streets, and keep me ears open, know what I mean?"

"But you're barely in your teens."

"I'll be fifteen next September. I been around, don't you worry about that." His head darted from side to side as he eyed the area. "Now, you got a problem, don't ya?" Staring at my face, he smiled. "Little boy lost. Maybe got 'imself snatched off the mean streets? Yeah?"

I nodded.

"Well, I've seen some nasties prowling around that might fit your bill. Come wiv me." The boy led me down the street and into the shadows of an alleyway next to the Empire. We stopped and he pointed across Shaftesbury Avenue. "Look."

A small boy, in filthy and torn clothes, wandered along the street. With cap in hand, he looked up at the stream of people, begging for pennies or coppers. Most of the adults passing by ignored or stepped around to avoid him. The odd coin dropped into his hat and was immediately snatched out and pocketed.

"That's little Paulie. 'E's one of the irregulars. We don't do the begging, it's just a cover."

"Well, what's he doing then?"

"Fishing. Just wait and see if we can 'ook somefin'."

The shadows deepened while we stood there, silent, watching, waiting. After almost an hour, my will began to ebb, and the frustration grew. As I said, "This is pointless," Wiggins held up a hand.

"Look. Got 'im."

A tall, well-built man stopped by Paulie and tossed a silver coin into the hat. He dropped to one knee and began to converse with the boy. I couldn't make out the gist of their conversation, but as I stared, the face became familiar.

"Freddie Hoffhines," I whispered.

"Yep," said Wiggins, "I seen light-fingered Freddie around 'ere a lot. Don't know what 'is interest is in kiddies, though. Bit suss either way."

I began to move, but Wiggins put a hand on my chest. "Sorry, Inspector, not trying to be familiar, but let's wait, right?"

I stopped, glanced at Wiggins, and then looked across at Freddie and Paul. After another minute of conversation, Freddie stood and took the young boy by the hand before leading him off down Shaftesbury Avenue.

"Now," said Wiggins, stepping from the shadows and taking off after the pair. He looked around and clicked his fingers, before pointing at the pair ahead of us. Several filthy street urchins appeared from nowhere and kept pace with us. "More eyes can't 'urt."

As Freddie and his hostage barrelled along down Shaftesbury Avenue, I noticed the little boy looking around, making eye contact with the cohort of street children before turning back to play his part. I assumed he was simply assuring himself that all was going as planned.

When they turned left down Charing Cross Road, Wiggins and I crossed the busy avenue, snaking our way between carts and hansoms, before catching sight of them once again.

"I need to catch Fingers and have a quiet chat with him," I yelled to Wiggins, above the cacophony of voices, horses, and squeaking carts.

"You'll get your chance, Inspector. Pretty soon, I reckons." Within moments, Wiggins was quite right.

Ahead of us, Freddie and Paulie stopped for a moment before crossing Oxford Street and heading up Tottenham Court Road. As they passed an open gap between buildings, Paulie tore his hand from Freddie's and ducked into the darkened alley. Freddie hollered in surprise and raced after the little boy.

Seconds later, Wiggins and I arrived at the entrance. In the darkness, I could just make out the two figures at the other end. Freddie the fingers had his hand raised, ready to strike the small child. "Do as you're told, or you'll get worse."

The small boy cowered away and cried as the taller man's hand descended.

"Fingers. Stop." My cry foiled his plan and halted the blow. The petty thief's face was aghast in fear as he turned toward our two shadows in the entranceway.

"Who? Who's there?"

I moved forward, closing the distance between us before announcing myself. "Inspector Bell. Scotland Yard. You're nicked."

"I done nothin'. I's just helping this lad up. He… he fell down like. Tell him, Paulie."

"Wouldn't have anything to do with you snatching him off the street, would it?"

"Now, why would you say that, officer? He was lost. Destitute. I was simply helping him find a new home." His expression relaxed, replaced with a cocksure grin.

"Just doing your civic duty, I take it."

"That's right. I'm a conscientious sort, I am. Like to help out my community, I does."

"Just like you helped a little boy a few days ago. Blond. Blue-eyed. Wearing a dark blue sailor suit? Ring any bells?"

A flash of worry crossed that face before the same grin returned. Shaking his head, Freddie said, "I don't know nothin' about no little sailor boy. I only got back to town yesterday, trust me."

"I wouldn't trust you as far as I could throw you. What say you, Wiggins?"

"'E must 'ave a twin brother, Guv'nor. I seen 'im around at least a couple a times over the last few days."

"Have you a twin brother, Freddie?"

"Oh, you mean Eric. Yeah, he's been around. Spitting image of me. I can give you his address if you like."

Shaking my head, I said, "Don't sell me a dog. You don't have a brother. I would know." I must admit, I lost my nerve a little at that point. Grabbing Freddie by the shirt front, I slammed him back against the nearest wall, went nose to nose with him, and said, "Stop lying to me. What were you going to do with this boy? What did you do with little Benedict Huxley? You've got me mad as hops, so you better start talking, or you'll start hurting." I waited to let that sink in a bit, before asking, "Who are you working for?"

Like the typical little weasel that I knew he was, Freddie's gums went flapping straight away. "I don't know who it is. I just delivers 'em to the boss at 10 o'clock. He's there every night. If I've got one, I hands 'em over and gets a crown, if not, then I don't. It's good work. Easier than working the streets."

Looking into that man's face, anger welled inside me. "What's the address?"

"It's the corner of Wigmore and Harley Street, up north of Cavendish Square."

"I know the area. Who is your contact? What's he look like?"

"I don't know his name. Big man. Bald head. Smokes a cigar, or at least always smells like it."

Sneering into that face one last time, I let his shirt go. The petty criminal almost collapsed to the ground. I grabbed him once more to keep him upright.

"I can go now, then?"

“Don’t be stupid. I might have some more questions.” I pulled out my police whistle and gave two long blows. The high-pitched noise echoed down the little alleyway. Wiggins was smart enough to head for the entrance to the alley to keep a look-out for any passing bobbies. After a few moments, I blew again. When Wiggins started waving his arms, I knew the local constabulary was on its way.

When two blue-clad bobbies appeared, I dragged Freddie with me toward them. They were taken aback at the sight of the two of us, and I could see by their faces they expected trouble. As one started to draw out his truncheon, I said, “No need for that, constable. I’m Inspector Bell of the Yard.” Thrusting Freddie forward, I added, “This miscreant has been done for kidnapping and worse when I think of something. Get him to the cells at the Yard. I’ll be along later to interrogate him further. If you need a contact, give them Commander Ennis’s name. I was assigned by him.”

The last I saw of Freddie Hoffhines was his wide-eyed stare as the two bobbies carted him off. Turning to Wiggins, I fished out a crown from my pocket. I hoped I could be compensated from petty cash at the yard, but if not, the street urchins’ help had paid dividends aplenty.

“A pretty good pay for a couple of hours work,” I said, handing over the coin, “Thanks to you and your irregulars, I think I’m on the right track.”

The coin disappeared from sight quicker than a bride’s nightie on her wedding night. Wiggins smiled and said, “We’ll keep an eye on you until you’ve finished with your investigations. I promised Mr. ’Olmes.”

With that, he turned and mirrored the coin, vanishing into the crowds of Tottenham Court Road and leaving me all alone amongst the sea of people.

***

By the time I walked to Cavendish Square, it was edging past nine-thirty. I pressed on up Portland Place, skirting the meeting spot, by one street. At Weymouth, I turned and kept as close to any shadows as I could find as I shuffled down toward Harley Street. A quick look at my pocket watch revealed it was now quarter of ten.

Only the north-eastern corner possessed a gas streetlight. It threw a relatively small circle of light across the cobbles. I stopped up short and sneaked into the shadow of a nearby doorway as I spied a rotund, bald man, dressed in a thick coat to ward off the evening chill, leaning against the wall just on the edge of the circle of light.

When he blew a thick cloud of smoke into the air, surrounding himself in a noxious pall, I knew this was the man Freddie Fingers had described. My task now was simply to wait until the allotted time came and went, then follow the man, hopefully back to his paymaster.

After what seemed like an age, he finally moved. The cigar end dropped to the ground and was crushed under his heel, and with no further attention to it, he spun and turned up Harley Street. I peeled myself from my hiding spot, my muscles and bones groaning after spending a long time still in the cold and headed across Weymouth Street.

Joining the man on Harley Street, I was thankful for his shining scalp and lack of headwear. Even though the street attracted only a few people at this time of night, it was dimly lit, with large expanses of darkness between streetlights. I was several seconds' walk behind the man but found he disappeared from time to time, only to emerge into the light like a shining beacon once again.

My pursuit led me down Marylebone Road, onto Hamstead Road and into the backstreets near Camden Town. I could hear the *whoosh* of a late-night train pulling into St. Pancras station off to my right, which told me it was now close to eleven o'clock, but I couldn't confirm the time with my pocket watch due to the darkness of the area.

The portly man's journey ended when he stopped before the open doors of a large stable, before entering. Keeping to the shadows, I edged closer to glance at the goings-on inside. A large, covered wagon sat just inside the doorway. Two draught horses were hitched to it. Their coats were bright and glossy, they stamped and snorted with impatience.

Just as I was starting to cross the narrow street, two strapping young lads of perhaps twenty years appeared and stepped up onto the buckboard. With a shout behind them and a flick of the reins, the horses started forward, gaining traction, then pulled the cart from the shed. They turned right and headed north to who knows where. The only clue that was left to me was the stamped name on the side of the wagon: *Stepson and Co.*

I couldn't place the name, but it was the high-pitched cry that caught my attention as the cart drew away. I could swear it came from beneath the covering on the rear of the cart but couldn't confirm as the horses trotted off before the cry was repeated. After a moment, I simply thought I'd heard one of them whinny, and put the memory aside.

From my position, I noticed the fat man step into the dim circle thrown by a lone gaslight inside the stable area. He blew out another cloud of cigar smoke and stepped out to watch the wagon disappear down the street. The *clop* of the hooves and the *squeak* and *squeal* of the metal-covered wheels faded into the distance.

Staring at the man, I stopped myself from striding across and confronting him. All my evidence was hearsay from Freddie's mouth. I needed something solid, or else my investigation was going nowhere, and I was back to just a petty thief and a possible charge of kidnapping.

Sneaking across the narrow lane, I sidled up to the wall of the stables — avoiding any glances from the cigar-smoking man — and edged my way around the dark corner. A small passage led past and around the building, soon bringing me to an open area with a low fence that must have been used to exercise any horses while they awaited their duties.

The yard was empty but led to the rear doors of the stables. Vaulting the fence, I landed in a damp patch, soaking my boots and soiling my lower legs with filthy mud. Cursing under my breath, I squelched through the effluent and made my way to the rear wall of the stables. A feeble light filtered out through a single window, spilling onto a small pile of refuse.

Sneaking a glance at the rubbish, I was shocked to find several assorted articles of clothing. Curiosity snatched my attention but paid off in spades when I found, nestled under several filthy items, a dark blue sailor suit. I had evidence, circumstantial at best, but enough to enter the premises and confront the bald man.

Finding a door nearby, I unlatched and drew it slowly open, grimacing at the prospect of any squeals from the hinges. Once inside, I crept through the darkened stalls until I found myself in the open area that accommodated wagons as they were loaded and fitted with fresh horses.

The portly man still stood at the entrance, a cloud of smoke billowing around him as he finished off his cigar. Surprise was on my side.

Stepping silently across the straw-strewn floor, I reached out and grabbed his shoulder, spinning him on the spot, and said, “Oi, care to explain this to me?” I held up the sailor suit so he could get a good look at it.

My surprise tactic worked; his face was a mask of shock, but it quickly turned to anger as he glanced at me. “Who the heck are you? Get your filthy mitts off me.” He tried to pull away, but I tightened my grip.

As I started to ask more questions, another voice spoke from the gloom outside in the street. “What’s all this then?”

We both looked at the owner.

A young constable stood mere feet from the stable’s entrance. Another not far behind him. “Heard there was a disturbance in this area, so we headed here. Seems we were just in time. Now gentlemen, care to answer my question?”

“Constable,” I said, “Good, you can help me. I am Inspector Bell, of the yard. This man will be helpful in my inquiries.”

“What?” said the fat man. “You’re no more a policeman than I am. Look at you! Filthy street scum, that’s all you are.” He struggled, and I let go of his shoulder, rather than cause any more concern in the constable’s mind.

“Oh, we know who you are, Inspector. A little birdie told us all about you.” I smiled, imagining that Wiggins or Holmes had a hand in this fortunate turn of events. Turning to the other man, the constable added, “As to you, sir? Please answer the inspector’s questions, or else we’ll have to ask you to accompany us.”

The second constable pushed past us and began to search the area.

"What are you doing? You have no right. This is ridiculous. I… I…." His bluster faded quickly as he glanced across our stern faces, before facing me. "All right. What?"

"This," I said. Thrusting the sailor suit into his face, I asked, "Wish to explain how it got here?"

"Filthy piece of cloth. Probably blew in off the street. I dunno any more about it."

"It resembles the clothes that a young boy who disappeared from Soho two days ago was wearing. My inquiries have led me here."

The man shrugged. "As I said, I dunno."

"Freddie Fingers Hoffhines? Name ring a bell? Skinny. Dark hair. Shifty-looking fellow. Know him?"

He shook his head. I wasn't taking his indifference as fact. "Then why do you wait for him to turn up every night at 10:00 o'clock at the corner of Harley and Weymouth Streets? I saw you there tonight after he'd told me you'd be there."

Shrugging, he said, "Dunno. I was just out for a walk, Officer. Sometimes I like to stand and have a cigar. It's not against the law, is it?" He smugly glanced across each of our faces, a small grin on his own.

"No, you've got me there. All right, Stepson and Co.? What do they do?"

"Dunno. We provide them with fresh horses when they come to London."

"Where from?"

"Umm. Newcastle, I think?"

I thought for a moment. "That's a long journey. What did they have in the back of the wagon?"

"I don't know. Again, we just do horses. Cargo's their business."

"This could be interesting, sir." The second constable stood behind, holding a ledger out toward me.

Nodding, I took the book and flipped through to the last page. An entry stated the name on the wagon, plus four straight lines, with a fifth that had been crossed out, a figure of five hundred sat next to the lines. The other entries in the ledger were of a similar nature, but with much lower figures and only single or double lines.

"Care to explain this entry then?" I asked, shoving the book under his nose. "What do the four lines mean?"

"Horses. Two in. Two out."

Looking around the empty stables, I said, "So, then, where are the other two horses? The wagon left with two, therefore there should be two somewhere around here. The yard out back is empty, as are the stalls. Plus, why is one line crossed out? An invisible horse?" Pointing to the second figure, I said, "Is this the payment? Five hundred pounds? Guineas? Crowns? Means a lot of money, especially just for fresh horses."

"This is a bit interesting," said the second constable. Turning, I found him holding four pairs of boots and shoes. One pair was a very expensive pair of soft leather shoes, the others mostly scuffed street boots. All were child-sized.

The fat man's face dropped. I sneered into his shocked expression. "Okay, I think you've got some explaining to do."

***

"And what did he have to say for himself?" Commander Ennis asked, his eyes red-rimmed from lack of sleep.

I stood before his desk, rigid from a sense of duty and fear. After all, I was the reason he now sat at his desk in Scotland Yard, several hours earlier than would be normal.

The two bobbies had helped organize a wagon to take Will Duchini, the hefty proprietor of the stables, onward to Scotland Yard for additional interrogation. I stayed behind for another hour, mostly to examine the building further, but also to let Duchini stew in his own thoughts until I returned to question him.

From the rubbish pile outside, I withdrew three more sets of clothing. Nothing matched the quality of the sailor suit, possibly worn by Benedict Huxley, but all suggesting they were owned by boys of a similar age. Seven or eight years, I deduced.

From the lack of horses in the stables coupled with the ledger the young constable had found, I drew a picture that the stables acted more as a waystation than a full-time provider of horses. They simply procured the animals from a nearby stable in St. John's Wood, rather than hold any stock, or they simply housed the customer's animals until they were rested and ready for a return journey.

Duchini, it turned out, merely managed the business, but I couldn't find the owner's name amongst the paperwork on hand. After another half an hour of fruitless searching, I left the stables, dousing the gaslight as I went, then headed to the high street where I caught a passing hansom back to Scotland Yard.

The stable manager, his forehead sporting many beads of sweat, but his face impassive and calm, sat quietly and unperturbed as I entered the dimly lit interview room. I dropped the clothing and shoes, with as loud a thud as I could, onto the wooden table, sorting them into their probable sets before stepping back and watching Duchini's face as he stared at the items.

"Four children. Around the ages of seven or eight. Why would clothing that should be adorning the bodies of four children be hidden in a pile behind your stables?"

He stared up into my face, that unconcerned look drilling into my eyes, and shrugged. "Some geezer's probably dumped them. We don't have any security, not needed."

I leaned forward. "Did you kill them? Is that your thing? Killing little boys?"

"No." Duchini's face screwed up in disgust. "What do you make of me? That's horrid, that is."

"What was in the wagon that left just before I found you alone? Was it the owners of these clothes?" I watched his eyes widen slightly. I reckoned I was onto something. "What does Stepson do with them?" The eyes darted to one side. I'd seen that in others trying to hide their lies before. Linking Stepson with the missing boys meant something more than I knew. "They were heading to Newcastle, yeah? What do Stepson and Co., do in Newcastle that has them come to London on such a regular basis? Seemingly to take little boys back with them?"

His head twitched slightly at that point.

I smiled, then leaned back from the table, rising to my full height. "Yeah. You probably shouldn't keep such detailed records." I brought out the ledger and flipped several pages toward the front. “Two years ago, about this time of year. Stepson. But there’s five strokes and only four hundred pounds.” Placing the ledger down on the table, I stood with my arms crossed, staring at that pudgy face, trying to read his thoughts. “That just happens to coincide with a bit of nastiness down the East End about two years ago. A young boy went missing. About seven years of age. Could be nothing, as you say, but that seems strange to me. I wonder if I could find anyone that knew of another four boys going missing?”

Duchini blinked several times but was otherwise unfazed.

“I do know of one person that will be concerned about one of these boys.” I pointed at the sailor suit. “These clothes belong to Reginald Huxley.” My suspect’s eyes widened at the name. “Yeah. That Reginald Huxley. Now, he seems to be a fine, upstanding citizen and all. But,” I tapped my nose for effect, “there are rumors. Rumors which suggest that maybe some of his business rivals have come to grief in very mysterious ways. He has some very powerful friends, though, and funny enough those rumors amount to nothing. But so do many of his more antagonistic adversaries.” I let that sink in for a moment. It was well known around the traps that Huxley was a force of nature in business, and with such a reputation came the myths that he was extremely ruthless in all aspects of life. “What do you think would happen if he found out the name of someone linked to his precious son’s disappearance? Now, I would think that even if there was no evidence, he might want to dig a little deeper himself. Know what I mean?”

Finally, that smug look dropped from Duchini’s face, replaced by an abject look of fear. It seemed that the rumors of Huxley’s dark side ran deep through the bowels of London’s underbelly.

“I… I don’t know what happens to them,” he stammered. “I just hands them over. Every coupl’a years or so.” He shrugged. “They’s just street kids, like. Nobody’s gonna miss ’em. I don’t fink they come to no harm.”

“But one of them wasn’t a street kid, was he?”

A slight sneer appeared on Duchini’s mouth. “If that wooden spoon Freddie had done his job proper then I wouldn’t be here.”

"You're right, but that doesn't change the fact that you are. Now it's up to you: I can let you back out into the streets — but I might have to send a telegram before I do — or you can stay at her majesty's pleasure for a while longer. Your choice." His eyes widened once more, his mouth curving down and looking almost fish-like in his fear. "Now, who was behind all this?"

He dropped his head and mumbled. "Stepson. I don't even know who Stepson is, really. They sends a telegram. Then we rounds up the kiddies. They load 'em up and away they go. Done deal. No questions asked. Nothing for another two years."

"How long has this been going on?" I tapped the ledger. "This only goes back two years."

Playing his eyes across the closed book, Duchini said, "About four years. I've only been there for the last five, so don't know if anything happened before like."

I leant forward and stared into Duchini's eyes for almost a full minute. He pulled back as far as the straight-back chair allowed, his eyes darting left and right to avoid mine. Finally, I said, "You disgust me. Selling children off to some unknown people, for God knows what purpose. I won't let you walk the streets; there's a place for you on this Earth, and you will rot in there. When you depart, there is a place in Hell for you to see out eternity."

Before he could answer, and before my anger got the best of me, I left.

"Stepson?" asked Ennis, his tired voice slipping into an accent that I couldn't quite place but suggested a northern origin to it. "I know that company." He stared up into my face and continued. "You'll need to go to Newcastle. Stepson is a family business, been running a colliery in Whickham for as long as I can remember. Nothing big, but if I recall correctly, the patriarch of the family passed on about ten years ago. His sons were ruffians, always getting into mischief around town. They'd be in charge now. No idea what they want young children for." He shook his head and almost shivered in disgust. "And I don't even want to imagine too hard."

"How do you know about them?"

"I'm from Newcastle. Born and bred. Led the Newcastle station for ten years before the wife wanted to see the bright lights of London, so found myself here. I've had many run-ins with those Stepson boys over the years; look after yourself." He pulled out a sheaf of paper and dipped a quill in his inkpot. "I'll inform the local constabulary that you're on your way. If you hurry, you might be able to get the first train out of King's Cross." Sliding the paper across to me, he added, "Give this to the sergeant. If my telegram doesn't arrive, it should do the trick."

I snatched up the page and read it before folding and securing it in my jacket pocket.

"Thank you, sir. I won't let you down."

He caught my eye with a softer expression on his face, which spoke of reserved admiration. "No, I don't think you will. If fact, you've already begun to prove yourself. Well done, and keep it up." Reaching into one of his desk drawers, he brought out a wooden box. Unlatching it, Ennis opened the lid and spun it around. Inside sat a revolver lying on a bed of red velvet. "This was mine during my time in the Army. Take it, just in case. But," he held up an extended finger, "don't go turning Newcastle into the wild west. This is just for protection. And I want it back."

***

"So, what are we looking at?" I asked.

Constables Magaw and Chumber, under Sergeant Onken's direction, had brought me out to the Stepson and Co., coal mine.

I had arrived at the police station in the early afternoon, six hours after leaving King's Cross on the first train of the day. Sergeant Onken had been expecting me. I found him sitting in his office with the commander's telegram before him.

As I entered, he said, "Inspector Bell, I presume." A long conversation on what had brought me all the way to Newcastle ensued, with Onken very interested in every aspect that appeared to point the finger at the Stepson brothers.

"Nasty pair, them Stepsons," he had repeated on several occasions, finishing with, "I will give you every help you need if it means bringing those two to justice. I've never been able to pin anything on them."

An hour later, Magaw, Chumber, and I headed out from the center of Newcastle in the hopes of reaching the Stepson mine just before knocking off time. That journey found us on a hill overlooking the mine's operations. I had never seen such in my life and, to be honest, was a little disappointed given some of the stories I'd heard about the complexity of such an endeavor.

The set-up was simple, with a large mine entrance dug into a small hill. Massive wooden beams shored up the ceiling and sides of the entrance, and from the activity we noticed, this was the only real entrance into the deep tunnels below the ground. A small rail track extended out from the entrance, which was serviced by mine carts carrying loads of freshly dug coal to waiting horse-drawn wagons. The familiar sign of *Stepson and Co.* appeared stamped on the side of each cart. They had the same look as the one I'd seen in London — except for the lack of a covering — and each was equipped with four horses to draw the heavier load.

"What are those two buildings?" I asked, pointing at the two structures sitting just below us, about fifty yards from the mine entrance. Both were of a similar size, with curtains over the windows stopping my prying eyes from peering inside.

"Management, I suppose," said Magaw. "Don't rightly know."

"Lunchroom?" suggested Chumber.

I realized these two weren't the brightest prospects but was still pleased they were here in case I needed an extra pair of hands or two.

"What time is knock-off?" I asked, just as a loud, deep whistle blew, followed soon by the cheery sounds of the men, their faces encrusted with black coal dust, as they made their way from the mine and deposited their picks, shovels, and helmets into a small shed near the mine entrance, before walking off toward the township of Whickham.

"Hey, there's Smithy. I thought he was up at North Shields," said Magaw.

"Nah, they gave him the sack after that time he got half rats and took on the entire White Horse pub," replied Chumber.

"Oh, that's right. Bloody lunkhead. Now he's ended up here. Can't fall much lower than that, I suppose."

"Why?" I asked, suddenly drawn into their conversation.

"We've always had our doubts about this place, ever since old Stepson died, though that was before our time. The sergeant doesn't think things are proper like here. About six years ago, they sacked a few miners and suddenly started making more money. Something's not quite right in that."

"Hmm. You don't say."

Turning back, I noticed the cavalcade of miners leaving the pit had dwindled to a trickle. Then I was shocked by the next group exiting the darkened entrance. A cluster of boys. About twenty in all. I couldn't directly tell their ages, but their height suggested that they ranged from about seven to around ten or eleven. They were led by two brawny men and shepherded into one of the buildings.

"Those children? They looked far too young to be working the mines. I thought they had to be over ten before they could even start?"

"Yeah, that law's been in since the middle of the century, hasn't it? Kiddies that young should be in school. Though didn't do nothing for me. I was working the pit from eleven. Didn't join the police 'til I was twenty," said Magaw.

As I watched the last of the children enter the building, I decided I needed a closer look. "Come with me, but be quiet," I said to the two uniforms as I stood and made my way down to the side of the nearest building, the one that now housed twenty young boys.

Sidling up to a rear window, I tried to peak through, but found a flimsy curtain pulled across. Voices filtered through from within. A mix of high-pitched young voices and the gruffness of an older one.

"When can I go home? I miss my mummy," cried one of the children.

"This is your home now. Your mummy doesn't want you no more," came from one of the men. Immediately a soft crying issued, probably from the original child. "Shut up," was followed by a slap and shout of pain. "The rest of you listen up. You're here now. You work, you eat. You don't work, you don't eat. If you don't eat, you'll die. So you better work."

More crying issued from several voices.

"Bugger this, I'm off." The thumping of work boots across the floor, followed by a final order. "Look after them. Any complaints, deal with them in the same way. If any try to escape, then we have plenty more coming. Now, I'm gonna eat and wait for the wagon." A muffled acknowledgement was followed by the creaking and slamming of a door. Footsteps carried on across the gravel.

I moved to the corner and watched the receding figure of a large man head across to the other building. Whispering to Magaw I asked, "Do you know him?"

"That's Markus Stepson, the younger of the two. Right nasty piece," he answered.

I nodded thanks. Pointing at Chumber, I said, "Stay here and watch the one inside. You know how to whistle?" When Chumber nodded, I added, "Whistle if he comes out, but keep hidden. It'll distract him and give us time to get to cover. Magaw, you're with me." I stood and started moving toward the second building, keeping to the shadows as much as possible.

Luckily, the window on this building was open, with the shade drawn aside. Peeking in I saw the large figure of Markus Stepson spooning stew from a large pot into a bowl. He moved across to a table and sat heavily, pulling the cork from a beer bottle, and downing a large swig before setting his attention to the stew. He ate without ceremony, scoffing the stew and washing it down in a rapid progression that hinted more at accomplishment than enjoyment. Finished, he sat back and drained the last of his beer, before belching his approval.

"That was horrible. Still, hit the spot, but would prefer to be at the pub. Damn it, Michael, why couldn't ye get someone else to meet ya?" I glanced as far around the room as I could, convincing myself that he was speaking only to himself. The big man picked up a small piece of paper on the table and peered at it intently. I could only assume he struggled with reading or needed glasses. "Four more? We ain't got beds for four more. Some will have to share, then." He stood up and pulled a pocket watch from his pocket, nodding as he checked the time. "Got a bit of time afore you get here." He picked up the dishes and bottle and disappeared from sight for a moment. All I could make out was the clatter of the plate and spoon as it was deposited in a nearby sink. Moments later, he returned with another bottle, sat, and leaned back, putting his feet on the table.

It was time to move. I didn't have much of a plan but hoped I could confuse him enough. I caught Magaw's attention and nodded to the front of the building.

***

"Who in hell are you?" Markus Stepson's face was a grim vision of anger. He stood as we entered, rising to his full height, which put his eyes several inches above both mine and Magaw's.

"Mr. Markus Stepson?" Not waiting for a reply, I added, "I'm Inspector Bell of Scotland Yard, this is Constable Magaw. I believe you may be able to help me with my inquiries."

"What damn inquiries? I got nothing to say to no coppers. Get off my property, afore I gets annoyed."

I held up my hands in a pretence of peace. "I'm here looking for a young child that has disappeared from a wealthy London family. You may have seen him nearby."

"What?" Stepson's face screwed up in confusion. "What are you talking about? This is Whickham, you're hundreds of miles away from London."

"Ah, fair enough. I just thought that since you appear to be harboring several boys that are much too young to be working in the coal pit, you may have seen him. Are any of those boys from London?"

His eyes darted to the open door and across toward the other building, before returning to me. "Don't know nothing about London boys. These are from the local area. Parents have all sent them here to work. Nothing dodgy here."

"Oh, that's all right then. Sorry to have disturbed you." I turned and stepped toward the doorway, before stopping and glancing back. "Do you mind if I take a quick look and have a chat with the boys? They might know something."

"Don't you do no such thing."

"Oh, sorry, I thought you said everything was aboveboard. I really do insist. I've travelled all this way and feel that I do need to talk to those boys. If you are worried that I might upset them, then I can have a few more constables here in another hour if you like. Wouldn't want anything untoward to occur, must protect the young boys. I'm sure the local sergeant would like to be involved, too. I shan't be long."

As I turned away once more, I heard the sound of glass dragging across wood. Looking back, I saw Stepson holding the bottle of beer in his right hand. He raised it, ignoring the final dregs dribbling from the mouth. "I don't think you should do that. In fact, I don't think you should be here. If you don't leave quickly, I will need to help you." As he took one step forward, Magaw and I stepped away from each other to give ourselves room.

Holding my hands up, I said, "Now, now, Mr. Stepson, this is a little untoward. I'm simply investigating if any laws have been broken."

"Don't care about no laws," he yelled, stepping forward and swinging the bottle at me.

Years of patrolling the East End taught me all I needed to know about pub brawls. I stepped inside the swinging arm and thrust my hands out at Stepson, catching him in the chest and arm. His forward momentum caused him to lose balance, and he crashed into another small table with chairs set around it. As luck would have it, he caught the full brunt of the edge of the table to the back of his head. The result was a mess of twisted man and very used wooden furniture, but at least he was no longer a threat.

Bending down, I felt for his breath and pulse. "Alive. Good." Looking around, I said, "Need some rope. Check that little tool shed across the yard."

While Magaw was gone, I dragged Stepson's bulk up onto one of the sturdier chairs. I had brought a set of handcuffs, so snapped them around his thick wrists and looped the chain through an opening in the back of the chair. With the rope Magaw found, I bound him thoroughly not only to the chair but to some pipes leading through the wall of the room. If he woke, he'd need to bring a lot of items with him.

Crossing to the table, I quickly read the piece of paper that had drawn Stepson's attention. It was a telegram, signed off "MS," and stated that they would arrive around eight o'clock. Pulling out my pocket watch, I found it to be just past seven o'clock.

"We've got an hour. Next is the man watching the children. Play it nice. No violence, the poor little buggers have probably been through enough."

***

The other man, Peter, was much more compliant than his colleague. As soon as we stepped into the room, he threw his hands up in surrender. The look of shock on the children was priceless. Many realized that we were there to help them and the looks of joy that crossed their faces lifted my heart.

Magaw took Peter away, locking him in the employee's dining room, after handcuffing him to a chair. He assured Magaw that he'd play nice, that he was only doing what he was told. I held my suspicions but would sort it all out later. Magaw stayed just outside the building to ensure that there were no attempts at escape.

I was barraged with questions and stories from the children. As I had suspected, they were a mix of locals and from farther afield. They told tales of kidnap. Of being dragged from their hometowns and ferried across the country to this place. Of punishment, if there was any rebellion against their masters. Of being forced to work in the pit. Tiny tears ran down their coal-grimed faces, revealing the soft pink skin beneath. My heart bled for these poor unfortunates, whilst my anger grew at the demons that had orchestrated this vile trade.

Scanning their little faces, I struggled to judge their ages, but none looked much older than ten, the legal age to begin working the mines. They told me they were tasked with crawling through the tiny tunnels, of dragging the coal trucks up from the deepest parts of the mines. It became clear as we talked. The smaller children were key. The pit had been dug with them in mind. Using their size to keep the tunnels small. The other upshot being they were slaves, unpaid, with no need to maintain their health or even report any accidents or deaths.

My mind reeled. Questions pounded my consciousness. What of the adult workers? Did they know? Did they care?

It was as I pondered my next steps that the wagon pulled into the yard outside.

***

As soon as the covered wagon came to a full stop and the two burly men dropped to the ground, the constables and I appeared from the dark. The driver looked almost identical to the unconscious man inside the nearby building.

"Michael Stepson, I presume," I announced, drawing his attention.

"And who would you be? Where's Markus, that idiot?"

"Markus is unable to join us. I am Inspector Bell. Scotland Yard."

Even in the soft light bleeding from the dining room, I could see his face turn into a scowl of intense anger. "Bloody copper," he spat, "What do you want?"

Raising my voice, I said, "Actually, I'm here investigating the disappearance of a young boy from London. Name's Benedict Huxley." Then all hell broke loose.

A high-pitched voice came from beneath the rear cover. "Here. I'm here."

Huxley turned to his colleague and shouted. "We're done. Davo, run." The other man did as he was told, pursued by Chumber.

Turning back, Huxley noticed me on one side and Magaw on his other. Instead of fleeing, his hand dove into his pocket and brought out a long-bladed knife. The light flashed off the shiny surface. I backed away, bringing my hands up in protection. "Don't do anything stupid, now, Huxley. This won't end well."

The big man towered above me, but I held myself resolute, withdrawing my hands and dropping my right into my coat pocket.

"You ain't takin' me down. I've done time, not again." He raised the knife and came at me. My hand closed around the revolver in my pocket, my finger slipping through the trigger guard. As the knife sliced down toward me, my finger squeezed. The deafening roar was met with a confused look on Huxley's face. A dark stain grew across his shirt. The knife dropped to the hard earth, followed by its owner.

My heart pounded, as my chest rose and fell, rapidly dragging air in to calm my senses.

"Blimey. Good shot," said Magaw, his face a mix of shock and glee, and his eyes fixed on the smoking barrel. "Do they give you one of those when you become an inspector?"

***

"Good work Bell," said Commander Ennis, a slight grin hiding behind his normally gruff expression. "Young Benedict is back with his very appreciative parents. I hear that the criminal world in London is just as relieved."

"Yes, and we are tracking down the parents of the other twenty-three children. Dreadful business it was."

Ennis picked up a small sheaf of papers, reading the front page. "So, this went on for six years? That will solve a lot of missing children's cases… well, those that were reported anyway."

"Yes, that was the main problem. They preyed on street urchins from London, Newcastle, and as far as Manchester. No one missed them or reported them gone. Then the poor mites were put to work pulling the coal trucks up through the tiny narrow passages deep down in the mines. The Stepsons thought it was a great way to cut costs. The law states that only children over the age of ten can work in the mines, but in the Whickham mine a ten-year-old child was normally too tall to fit in the passageways."

"What of the Stepsons?"

"Michael died from the bullet wound thanks to your gun."

Ennis stared down at the freshly cleaned revolver and closed the lid. "Never thought this thing would see service again," he said, putting the box back into its drawer.

"Markus confessed to everything. He'll be going away for quite a while. Several others were in on it, he grassed on them to save his own skin, but the local judge wasn't too lenient. Most of the other workers just thought the kids were there legally. I sat in on a few interviews but couldn't see anything untoward."

"Very good. Very good." Staring down at my report, Ennis asked one last question. "How on Earth did you piece this all together? You started on the streets of Soho with the flimsiest of leads, only to end up in Newcastle with a tale that you can dine on for years."

"I can only confess that without the help of one Mr. Sherlock Holmes and his cadre of street urchins I would never have gone farther than the streets of Soho. I dropped by to thank him for all his help, but his housekeeper mentioned that he is once more out of town."

Standing, Ennis extended his hand, shaking mine firmly.

"Well done, Inspector. You have outdone my expectations, and I look forward to watching your career with keen interest."

"Thank you, sir."

Leaving his office my heart was filled with immense pride. Since stepping into the inspectors' room, I had always felt out of place, but that feeling had been washed away. This was my home, and I truly intended to add my name to the list of great policemen that had sat in this place over the years.

"But he was hanged last week, wasn't he?" I asked.

"Yes. Yes, he was. The yard quickly found him guilty, and the judiciary executed rapid justice."

"Well, some might say it took the yard too long to find the fellow, in the first instance. He avoided detection for a good three months. In that time, he supposedly dispatched four young girls," said Holmes.

"That is true, so why didn't you become involved earlier then?" asked our visitor, sitting back with a slightly smug look on his face that I found quite disconcerting. I watched him study my colleague for quite some time as Holmes formulated and delivered his answer.

"The series of disappearances was confusing at first. Poor Patricia Sherlin and Ashlee Dickson went missing about two months apart. Miss Sherlin had visited a relative in North Feltham before leaving on foot to return to her house in Twickenham. The relative reported her missing a few days later when she failed to show up at home. Ashlee Dickson lived in Richmond but had been visiting her lover in Hatton. Even though her husband reported her missing there didn't seem to be a connection until the lover came forward, but that wasn't until after the assailant had been hanged. It was only when Carmen Finos, and then your poor unfortunate wife, disappeared within two weeks of each other that a pattern finally emerged."

"How so?"

"I read about both disappearances in the paper. They included a detailed account of the last known location of both girls."

"Hounslow Heath?" our guest asked.

"Yes. Their last known locations were near the boundary of the heath. The acquaintances that had reported both missing, stated they were headed through the Heath to their respective homes. The dates were odd. Wednesday evening, two weeks apart. Reading the report about your poor wife, it was then that I remembered the disappearance of Miss Sherlin. It occurred on a Wednesday, some two and a half months before your wife. The trajectory of her journey led her straight through the Heath. At that stage, I knew nothing about Mrs. Dickson."

"What did you do?"

"I journeyed to the Heath and began an inspection of the area. Sadly, the police had completely despoiled the location by the time I visited. But there was something about both the location and the timing that intrigued me."

"Yes?"

"There were personal items found scattered amongst the trees near the entrances to the cemetery."

"They would be very high-traffic areas, surely? They could have been anybody's."

"True. But the police found several items that were identified as belonging to the last two girls. I was able to find the locations very quickly. They were set back from the pathways through the heath, leaving the assailant almost unfettered by any casual witness."

"Horrible," I stated, imagining what such a man may have accomplished.

"Quite. Searching further afield, I found two more such areas, where the detritus of misadventure had accumulated. Ribbons, kerchiefs, such things."

"That was where you found my wife's purse?"

"Yes. The fact that there was still money in it, negated the Police's view that the assailant was simply a thief."

"I was surprised when it was returned to me, as well. Though the result of his actions was no less disturbing."

"True. It was after reporting my findings to the constabulary that I became quite despondent."

"Jones?" I asked.

"Yes. Inspector Athelney Jones was heading up the investigation. When I presented the locations and items that I had found, signalling a possible connection, he simply scoffed at my suggestion."

"Though, he changed his mind a week later."

"Yes. Taking matters into my own hands, I set up a nightly watch for any activity within the Heath. Ensuring that my fellows kept an eye on the four entrances to the area; I joined them for much of the time as well. Given the two latest victims had been at the same entrance, I stayed there for several nights."

"But you went one step further, didn't you?"

"Oh, yes, and that's what led to his arrest." Holmes smiled and sipped his coffee. I could tell that he was delighted with the outcome. "I asked one of my associates to find a suitable young lass to act as bait for my trap. The traffic through the Heath had been light leading up to the second Wednesday since your wife's disappearance. The young lady, Meredith Torresdale, dressed in common street clothes, as a shop worker would wear, and sent on several journeys through the Heath, closely shadowed by myself and my associates. As luck would have it, we hooked our catch."

"I remember that night well," I said. I had been at the other end of the Heath but was as prepared as Holmes.

"The assailant, a rough-looking fellow by the name of Homer Bodkin followed Meredith into the Heath, skulking in the underbrush and almost bumping into me at one stage. As he passed by, I followed closely, treading carefully so as not to arouse his attention, and just as he stepped onto the path behind Meredith, his arm raised with a blackjack in his hand, I called out to him."

"My word, if you hadn't seen him, he would have brained the poor girl."

"Yes. Sadly, I think that is how he subdued his other victims."

"What happened then?" asked Sir Delmar.

"He stopped. His arm raised and turned ready to defend himself, but I had predicted that my quarry would possibly resist and held my revolver towards him, at the ready. He simply dropped his weapon and stood staring at me with suppressed animal rage, while one of my associates ran off to find a constable."

"And that was the last you saw of him, wasn't it?"

"Yes. In contrast to Inspector Jones's attitude, his bobbies were alert to the possibility of a connected series of disappearances, and several arrived on the scene. Bodkin was dragged off."

"How did they connect him to my wife's disappearance?"

"Luckily, an old friend, Inspector Bell, you remember him, don't you Watson?" I nodded. "At a later date, Bell confided in me what had occurred once they'd arrested Bodkin. Apparently, Jones took the assailant into a small room and applied a very enthusiastic level of interrogation. Throughout, Bodkin remained tight-lipped. Not a word came out of him until Jones mentioned that things could go badly for any of the man's relatives if he didn't give them information. That seemed to crack his resolve. He not only told them his name, but his address, and pleaded with them to leave his mother alone. Once, they agreed that they wouldn't contact his mother, he shut up once more, and didn't speak another word, even when led to the noose."

"How very strange," I said. "I thought they'd had determined that he had a hand in the disappearance of all four women."

"Oh, that they did, but only once they visited his house. It turned out that Bodkin liked to keep mementoes of his victims. It was in his house in Hanworth, that they found a small box of items." Nodding towards Sir Delmar, he added, "That is where your wife's wedding ring was found. Plus, a single item that was further identified as belonging to each of the other three missing women."

"But there were more objects, weren't there?"

Nodding, Holmes added, "Yes. Yes, there were. The police are quite confused. They undertook an examination of other missing persons, but none could be found that fit the same details as the four in question. The extra objects were taken and shown to several known relatives of missing women, but none were identified." He shrugged. "Whom they belonged to remains unknown. And the last part of this mystery is still to be solved, which brings you to us today, is that right Sir Delmar?"

Sir Delmar's eyes took on a look of sorrow. "If you ask me; the judiciary was too swift in his execution. They should have waited."

"Sometimes justice can be too swift, but you are here now, and obviously in need. What is it you wish from me?"

"All I want is to find Ryann once more. To give her a fitting place amongst her family, but that horrid man never admitted his crime, or where he hid their bodies. Now that he's dead, I'm afraid that it is too late, and we shall never know the truth."

Holmes steepled his fingers for a moment and cradled his chin upon them, thinking for a moment before responding. "It may well be, but one should never give up until all hope is truly gone. You want me to discern the location of where this miscreant took your wife's body? Now, that is a challenge well worth my attention."

"Holmes! A little decorum please."

"Forgive me, Sir Delmar, I do like a challenge and can sometimes forget myself."

"Do you believe you can find her?"

"I can only follow the clues to the best of my abilities. It has been several months, I hope things have not become too cold, but I shall see what I can do."

Sir Delmar stood, taking Holmes's hand in his and shaking it gratefully. Without much more than a thank you and goodbye, he hurried off. I was astonished at the speed of his withdrawal. "How peculiar? As soon as you agreed to assist, he couldn't be gone from here quick enough, and his demeanour changed completely."

"Yes. He was an odd sort, but it could be due to his grief."

"Perhaps, but do you believe you can track down his wife's remains? As you said, it has been several months. I'm sure the trail has grown cold, if not positively arctic."

"We shall see," Holmes said, picking up his cup and taking a long draw.

***

"Mr. Holmes, so good to see you again." We turned to see a very enthusiastic Inspector Bell striding towards us. He threw a hand towards my colleague and shook Holmes's with undisguised revelry. "I'm so glad you contacted me with the key to tracking down this villain."

"Think nothing of it, Bell. If Inspector Jones had allowed me to interview this Bodkin fellow, then we may have closed the case earlier on without the need for heavy-handed tactics."

Bell couldn't suppress a slight sneer. "Yes, I believe it too." Shrugging, he added, "I'm trained to believe that my superiors are always correct, even when my thoughts belie that reasoning."

"A fair call, too," said Holmes. "Still, we can only do what we can do."

Holmes turned to discern the villain's house. A modest two-story semi-detached in Curtis Road, Hanworth. Such a place showed no evidence that it had harboured such a nasty piece of work.

"What did this Bodkin do?" I asked, my knowledge of the case extended only as far as the number of missing girls and the identity of Homer Bodkin.

"Grave digger," said Bell shrugging. He pointed down the road. "Itinerant, it seemed. Hounslow cemetery is that way." Turning he indicated another location to the east. "The borough cemetery is over there. The blighter would simply turn up from time to time and see if there was any work available. He was a large man and good at his work. The pay was cash in hand. No questions were ever asked."

"None of his workmates knew him, I suppose?"

Shaking his head, Bell replied, "Not that we found. But we didn't really need to delve any deeper. After you helped us catch him and Inspector Jones teased out his name and address, it was simple".

"As you told me, the incriminating items were in the house. Was that all that your colleagues investigated?"

"Yes. Once we established that some of the items belonged to the missing women, the process went swiftly. The newly appointed Director of Public Prosecutions caught wind of the case and the prosecution had it rushed through to trial. If I was to make a judgement, I would say he wanted to justify his promotion."

Holmes stood with one hand under his chin, listening to Bell and contemplating the final part of Bodkin's journey. "It is possible, but with such flimsy evidence, I'm surprised."

I finally piped up. "I'm more intrigued by how an itinerant grave digger could afford a house such as this. Also, why has it not been cleared out and reoccupied?"

"I was surprised too," said Bell, "So, I looked into that after I received your telegram, Holmes. It seems that this Bodkin fellow wasn't all he seemed. He owns the house. I have no idea how, but it was paid for about two years ago. The notes on the case, show that the neighbours thought he was a quiet chap, kept to himself, but had been here for all of those two years."

"Very strange," said Holmes, "For most of that time he lived here, keeping to himself. Then all of a sudden, he is linked to the kidnap of four women, and possibly to their disposal. It was a long bow drawn that led from assault, possible kidnap, to murder."

Bell nodded towards the house. "Yes, it was all in there. The jewellery. Items of clothing. He seemed to have kept them as mementoes it seems."

"Yes, one of those types." Holmes exhaled in a disheartened way. "There seem to be more and more of late."

"London is growing. Attracting all types from across the country and worldwide even." Bell shrugged. "I suppose it keeps us both in a job."

"Yes, unfortunately, both our talents will always be required." Holding out a hand towards the house, Holmes added, "Shall we?"

"What is it you're after in here?" asked Bell as they approached the front doors. He quickly extracted a key from his pocket and opened the door leading into the entry foyer. A set of stairs rose before us, with another door leading into the lower-floor apartment to our right.

"I have been asked to find the remains of one of his unfortunate victims. Lady Benware."

Bell's mouth dropped open in shock. "Surely there's no hope of that? Bodkin is dead. All knowledge left with him at the end of the noose."

Holmes shrugged. "Perhaps, but Bodkin already proved himself a creature of habit by retaining the little mementoes for each crime."

"Very well, it was unfortunate that you weren't given access to the house before. My men and I combed through it, but once we found the trinkets, Jones believed it was all the evidence we needed. We picked our way through this house, but there's nothing to indicate what happened to the victims. In the end, we simply closed it up and haven't been back since. We traced a next of kin and notified them but haven't had any further contact. I was surprised we still had a key," said Bell, "Follow me." As he climbed the stairs, he added over his shoulder, "Though I think you'll be as perplexed as we were by what you'll find inside."

I certainly was. When Bell unlocked the front and pushed it fully open, struggling against something on the other side, I had my first glimpse of the place and gasped in shock. It was a madman's paradise.

The door opened onto a reception room, though there was no chance that anybody could have received guests in that space.

Bodkin was a hoarder, it seemed. The room was full of newspapers, books, bottles, and items of detritus possibly taken from the streets or from other sources. A single chair sat between mountains of newspapers, almost like a throne amongst gothic columns. A small table sat before it.

Pointing into the room, Bell said, "The only furniture in this room is that chair and table. Over to the right is the bedroom, with an attached bathroom. There's no kitchen, or if there was, it's been taken over by all this."

"You mentioned that you found effects from the victims. Where?" asked Holmes.

"Lying on the bed, all laid out nice and neat. It is as if he placed them there in readiness for the next piece from Miss Torresdale."

"Ah, quite possibly. He liked to collect it seems. Perhaps, he also liked to adore his prizes."

"I'll leave you to it. Not enough room for too many folks in there." Bell stepped back allowing Holmes and I to enter.

He was correct. The area was almost claustrophobic. Piles of newspapers formed corridors along which you could shuffle. On the other side were piles of other detritus of all sorts. Amazingly they were arranged in an almost clinically neat array. In one corner, a collection of bottles in wooden crates, stacked on top of each other. In another, a pile of boots and shoes heaped in what appeared a disordered mound, but on examination turned out to be matching pairs arrayed in ordered layers.

"This is incredible and disturbing all at the same time," I remarked.

"Yes. I must agree. It would have made a fascinating study of this man, Bodkin's mind. An animal, no doubt, from his pursuit and probable dispatch of those young women, but one possessed with some innate desire to collect, store, and order all manner of debris."

Holmes pushed ahead of me, turning, and entering the bedroom. I realised that I would only damage the scene, and possibly get in his way, so stopped where I was and observed him from afar, ensuring I was ready to assist if called upon.

To amuse myself, I looked at the stacks of newspapers. The ones nearest to me were a mix of London papers, the Morning Post, the Times, and the Chronicle. Sifting through the ones on top, I realised that they dated back several years. "Holmes?" I called.

"Yes," came a slightly agitated reply.

"How old was this fellow, Bodkin?"

A slight pause before Holmes replied, "Forty-five. Why?"

"Oh, nothing, yet." I moved along the corridor of newspaper stacks, reading the dates and finding the papers, as I would have guessed, stretched back for over ten years. The very last piles were even more intriguing. They were all piles of *the Devizes and Wiltshire Gazette*, with publication dates of over ten years previously. "He's from Wiltshire," I blurted out.

"Yes. Yes, he is," came Holmes's answer. "Well done, Watson. How do you come by that fact?"

"The papers. He has them from Wiltshire, over ten years ago."

"Well, that sets the scene, doesn't it? This pattern of behaviour is nothing new then. He must have moved up to London around that time but couldn't bear to part with his possessions. Presumably, he brought them to his own house after he purchased it."

When Holmes fell silent once more, I moved closer to the chair. From the piles of more recent papers surrounding it, this seemed to be where Bodkin read the papers that were such a strong part of his life. Two were simply stacks of local London papers gathered over the last few months before his death, but the pile to the sitter's right held more copies of the Gazette. Curious, I picked up several issues and scanned the dates. It took a moment but finally a picture formed in my mind. There were groups of two- or three days' worth of copies, each from the first week of the month.

It was then I realised that the dates coincided with the dates that we knew girls had disappeared from the area.

"Holmes?"

"Yes, Watson." Came the reply after a moment. "Have you found anything of worth?"

"There appears to be a system to these newspapers. Bodkin had gathered copies of the Devizes and Wiltshire Gazette on the days after the four girls disappeared."

Turning to speak more clearly in Holmes's direction, I was startled to find him hovering over my shoulder. He studied the dates of the newspapers as I flipped through them. "One would think," he said, "That this Bodkin journeyed to the Wiltshire area, on the day following each of the girls' disappearances."

"He hails from Marlborough." The voice from the doorway rattled me for the second time in several minutes. "Sorry," said Bell, "I was wondering how you are getting on."

"Watson has found a significant piece of information that may give us a possible location for Bodkin on the days following each disappearance. If he came from Marlborough, perhaps he has relatives there?"

"That's where his mother lives, I think. Elderly. The yard didn't need to bother her. The local constabulary kept her informed of proceedings here in London. She never appeared at the trial or execution as far as I am aware. Bodkin's body was buried in the Wandsworth cemetery. I was surprised she hadn't retrieved the key to this place, to at least have the place sold off."

"Have you found anything in the bedroom?" I asked.

"Oh, yes, and it may interest you, Inspector." Holmes turned and moved into the other room.

As we joined him, Bell gasped. "Good Lord. Are those?"

"I believe so." Holmes had placed a small, lockbox on the bed, its lid lay open possibly not unlocked by the key, but something my colleague held in his deep pockets. An array of jewellery, and other articles associated with the fairer sex, lay scattered across the bed covers. "I don't wish to surmise without more evidence, but it would be hard not to conclude that Homer Bodkin's activities did not only begin a few months ago."

"That is disturbing."

Moving to the bed, I scanned the items and picked up a kerchief. It had a small amount of dirt on it as if the item had fallen to the ground for a moment. There was also a distinct chemical smell about it.

"Ah, you smell it too, Watson?"

"It's not ether, possibly embalming fluid?"

"I believe so. I'd like to investigate further, but given Bodkin's employ as a grave digger, he may have used his position to appropriate these trophies."

"Perhaps that explains his actions. His desire for these trifles accelerated to the point that he couldn't simply wait for the opportunity at his workplace and took matters into his own hands?"

"Hmmm. That may explain a lot."

"That is very disturbing," said Bell, his face screwed up in disgust.

"Much about this affair is disturbing." Turning to Bell, he added, "It may be worthwhile speaking with his employers to determine if there are any graves that have been disturbed post-internment."

"By that you mean, did he dig anyone up?"

"Precisely."

"Oh, that would be truly terrible."

"It may not have been Bodkin's pattern of behaviour, but any such inclination on his behalf may shed light on his overall behaviour."

"Fair enough, I will do so once we have left here. Is there anything else you wish to investigate?"

Holmes scanned the bedroom once more, before stepping into the reception room. "There is one thing that intrigues me about this space."

"What?" I asked, always alert when my friend was fascinated by something, his cognitive processes were a world of their own.

"There's no kitchen." He turned, pointing to a small table in the far corner of the bedroom, nestled against the bathroom wall. A small brazier sat atop it. "That seems to have acted as his cooking area. Water came from the bathroom, and that simple stove was used for heat." Holmes turned, surveying the reception area once more. "But this is a purpose-built apartment, not simply a conversion of the upper floor bedrooms of a previous two-story house. I wager that if we were to investigate the premises below, it would be a virtual duplicate of this place."

His eyes fell to the floor, scanning and studying the dull, well-worn wooden planks. I followed, noting several dents and scratches weaving their way between the piles of papers. Dropping to his knees, Holmes ran a finger along a rather deep set of ruts worn into the wood.

"What have you there, Holmes?"

"Something heavy has been dragged…" Running his fingers along the marks several more times, he added, "Nay, wheeled along this path. These tracks are evenly spaced as if a heavily laden trolley or some such was moved along here several times. The tracks overlay each other but are of uniform width. The depressions are the same."

"It must have been quite heavy to do that?"

"Heavy or rather compact. The weight of a human being, compressed into a small area, dragged on something with wheels, could conceivably create such dents."

"A human being?" stammered Bell, "Do you think the women's bodies are here?"

"Unsure," murmured Holmes, eyeing off the path of the tracks as they wound their way between what I now saw as lines of newspaper stacks. He followed the tracks until they stopped before a tall set of shelves filled with all manner of bottles, cups, and jugs.

Hunkering down before the shelving unit, Holmes drew his finger along the path left by the indents. "Hmm," he murmured, before standing and running his hands all across the shelves and up and down the sides of the unit. "Aha," he exclaimed, as an audible *click* echoed out from the wall. Holmes pushed the shelves, revealing a room beyond. "I think I've found the missing kitchen."

A damp, almost putrid smell wafted out of the newly opened doorway. "My word," I said.

Within a moment, Holmes found and lit the gas light inside the dark room. As the glow covered the area, I gasped in horror. The room no longer resembled a kitchen in any way. A strange-looking table sat in the middle of the room. One end was higher than the other, all four edges had raised borders, and there was a hole in the centre at the lower end. "That looks similar to a …"

Holmes cut me off. "Yes, an autopsy table. Or more correctly, a mortician's table."

"What?" asked Bell.

"A mortician's table. Look around." Holmes pointed at the other items in the room. A trolley sat against the wall. Large bottles sat on the lower shelf, and on the very top sat an array of medical tools including a trocar, a large syringe, several lengths of rubber tubing, scalpels, twine, and needles. Another shelving unit held more bottles and jars, with spare instruments. Several thick books on the shelf below.

"What do you make of it, Holmes?"

"First impressions are that someone, this Bodkin most likely, wished to undertake training in the mortician's arts." Pointing at the table, he added, "this is where the work was undertaken. The blood drained into that bucket below the exit hole and probably poured down the sink that has been left intact." He then turned and pointed to an object in the shadows of the far wall. "The remains were then placed in that steamer trunk for removal."

Stepping across to the trunk, I found it lying against the wall. A pair of steel wheels were affixed to one end. Their width was about half an inch, matching the grooves we found on the wooden floor outside. "Can I open it?"

"Yes, only by the handle, I'd like to examine the edges to see if there are any clues there.

Doing as Holmes suggested, I recoiled at the putrid smell from within. "Good Lord," said Bell standing by my shoulder.

The trunk was simply a standard steamer trunk, but the interior had been lined with what looked like leather and coated with pitch. I could only assume to make it watertight. The odour it exuded was of the foul stench of rotten carrion.

"Hmmm, seems to have been used to cart around the remains." Holmes, drawn by the smell, had appeared at my shoulder and was clinically assessing the interior of the trunk.

"Not the missing women, surely," said Bell, "That would be horrid."

Moving closer to the trunk, Holmes peered inside and all around making various murmuring sounds before answering. "It is quite possible. The size of the trunk and the width of the wheels, indicate that this is the item that has made the deep grooves in the floorboards outside." Looking down I noticed that this area was tiled. "The trunk is definitely large enough to hold a body if it was compressed enough to fit."

"Oh, those poor girls."

"Quite. The smell is especially indicative of decaying human tissue. Perhaps there was a little blood seepage, or the bodies were further decomposed leaving traces inside. The pitch would have stopped any leakage, very clever. Bodkin may not have cleaned it out thoroughly after it was last used."

"That's horrid," I said, peering into the dark interior of the trunk. "But why go to all that trouble? And where did he take the bodies?"

Using a pencil pulled from his pocket, Holmes gently eased the lid closed. "There." He pointed at the luggage stickers adorning the lid of the trunk. There were several scattered across the surface, all from the Greater Western Railroad, as identified by the letters G, W and R. The station names Swindon, Marlborough and Paddington were stamped on the tags.

"To Swindon and Marlborough?"

"Yes, so it seems. The train from London goes to Swindon, with a change to the south line heading to Marlborough." Pointing to a chalk mark on the lid of the trunk, he added, "These letters, MLB, possibly confirm a side trip to Marlborough, probably on an omnibus when the connecting train wasn't running. With his insistence on heading towards Marlborough, it must be a connection to his mother or a coincidence that he visited regularly but took his trophies with him."

I grimaced in disgust. "Oh, that is abhorrent. Why would he do such a thing?"

"I believe we may need to visit his mother to find out." Turning to Bell, Holmes asked, "Was Bodkin found with any money on him?"

"Not that I know of, why?"

"Well, I know this place is quite untidy, but in an almost ordered way. I did not find any stores of money or bank account books of any sort. Bodkin's employment would have been purely on a cash basis. Though not very high paying, a diligent man could earn a decent living. I can only assume that given his ownership of this house, he had a store of money at his mother's house."

"With his mother, perhaps."

"Yes. That would explain his trips back to Marlborough. It just seems that at times over the last few months, he took extra luggage with him."

***

Bell suggested that we stop in at the local police station to obtain Mrs. Bodkin's address. He had been in communication with Constable Kennith Todman on several occasions. As we left, he offered to send a telegram to Todman and announce our imminent arrival. Holmes agreed and asked if transport around Marlborough could be arranged.

The train to Swindon left quite early, which gave us little time in the morning for a decent repast. Mrs. Hudson, as always, outdid herself and provided a light breakfast before the sun had even broken the horizon. I dined whilst waiting for Holmes to appear, and with a quick slurp of coffee, he was striding from the house and onwards to adventure.

The connection to Marlborough was several hours away, so we left the platform to seek out an omnibus but were surprised to be greeted by a police carriage, with a young, smiling constable standing beside it. As soon as we exited the station, he excitedly waved towards us and shouted Holmes's name.

As we approached, he shook Holmes's hand and said, "Pleasure to meet you Mr. Holmes, you look exactly as Dr. Watson describes in his stories." He quickly shook my hand and added, "I get the Strand brought down from London. It's very expensive, but I first read one of your adventures on a trip east and couldn't wait for the next story to appear. And now you're both here in the flesh, it is indeed an honour."

"I assume that you are Todman, then?" asked Holmes. "Bell must have announced our arrival as he suggested."

"Oh, yes, sorry, should have introduced myself. Yes, I'm Constable Todman, please call me Kennith or even Kenny if you like."

I smiled to myself. Thanks to my stories, Holmes was garnering notoriety and reputation amongst the public, and obviously, the constabulary. It seemed that would be of great advantage in this case.

Once we were settled on the buckboard, instead of sitting inside the prisoner wagon, Holmes asked, "Mrs. Bodkin. Would it be possible to meet with her?"

Todman's face went dour. "Oh, that won't be possible, I'm afraid."

"Why?

"I'm afraid she passed on. A month ago."

"That would be only a week or so after her son was hanged."

"Yes, I'm afraid the doctor believes she died of a broken heart."

"Hmm. That's very disappointing," said Holmes, showing no sign of empathy. "Would it still be possible to visit her home?"

"I suppose. I've brought the keys, but upon thinking further, I'm a little hesitant. It doesn't seem right to intrude on that poor woman's home."

Holmes began to show a slight level of annoyance. I girded myself thinking I may have to mediate. "I do agree. It could be seen as improper, but I understand that Mrs. Bodkin had no other relatives. From her death, one can only surmise that she was deeply devoted to her son and would want all this nasty business to come to a satisfying conclusion so that the relatives of her son's victims can have some seek solace in giving the victims a proper burial."

Todman thought for a moment whilst concentrating on the road ahead. Finally, he added, "Yes, you are right. Inspector Bell did not mention your intentions, just that it related to the Bodkin case, but if it is to bring this whole detestable matter to a close then I think it would be best."

I breathed a slight sigh of relief.

Within half an hour, we reached the little community of Marlborough, a very old market town that swelled in population once a week when the markets were held. As I pondered upon Marlborough's history, we crossed over the high street, one of the widest in the land, used on those very market days to house all sorts of stalls and temporary shops selling all manner of wares.

Constable Todman drove the cart onwards, soon leaving the bustling community and heading into an area dotted with small allotments that were probably maintained by some of the store holders themselves. The road carried on southwards out of town and passed by the local train station. If our timing had been different, we would have alighted from that spot rather than Swindon, cutting the time required to sit in a bumpy horse-drawn cart, to which my rear end would have much favoured.

Within another few minutes, we drew up before a small, neat cottage, sitting on a modest acreage with some vegetable plots and a small flock of goats milling around in the rear paddock.

As the three of us alighted from the wagon, I was taken by the proximity of the dark forest beyond the property's borders. The trees were thick, casting an almost impenetrable gloom not far from their edge.

"Impressive, isn't it?" asked Todman.

"Quite. It is rather rare that we come across such an imposing wood."

"That would be Savernake Forest, then?" Holmes asked, already knowing the answer, but confirming it for me.

"Yes. I've spent many a wasted afternoon tracking down some lost wanderer in that place," said Todman in a dismissive tone before opening the gate and heading up the small gravel path to the front door. Holmes strolled after him, leaving me to ponder on the forest for a moment before I hurried to join them.

Todman spoke as he fished for the keys to the Bodkin house. "I'm the only constable that comes here, that's why I have the keys, and I don't think anybody else has been in here since Mrs. Bodkin passed. There are no relatives that we have found so far. We have been trying to keep the few friends she had away until the proper next-of-kin is found."

"Are they a little too eager to gain access?" I asked.

Todman nodded. "Yes. If they managed it, the place would be stripped of anything useful or valuable before the day was out."

"Has the owner not stepped forward?" Holmes asked.

Confused, Todman turned and said, "No. Mrs. Bodkin owned the house. As far as I know, she had owned it for years. Rumour has it that she came from money. Quite a bit of money, in fact. Has never had to work. Neither has her son. Though he did undertake employment from time to time. As I understand it was more to pass the time than for money."

"That would explain how Bodkin bought that house in London," I said. Holmes nodded.

"What sort of jobs did he undertake," asked Holmes.

"He moved away about ten years ago, but supposedly he helped out at the local cemetery. He was a big fellow, so may have enjoyed flexing his muscles with gravedigging and such."

As Todman moved towards the small set of steps, Holmes halted him. Dropping down and examining the stone slabs. Running his fingers along the edge, he examined the traces of stone dust on his fingertips, rubbing them together and murmuring to himself.

"What have you found, Holmes?"

"The edges of the steps have small chips out of them. As if something heavy was dragged up them."

"Could it be normal wear and tear?" asked Todman.

"Could be, but these steps are as old as the cottage. Hundreds of years in age and made from immensely strong stone. Suffering all sorts of weathering. Any chips would be infrequent and be smoothed over after a few seasons of rain and wind. This damage seems to have occurred recently, and over several occasions, as some are sharp and recent, while others are slightly smoothed."

After a moment, he stood and allowed Todman to climb the short flight. Opening the front door, a small draft of stale air escaped past the policeman. I smelt or rather tasted the sweet tint of rot on the breeze, hinting that something had been left to decay within. While

Todman and Holmes moved into the saloon, I followed my nose. Soon, I found the culprit, a small bowl of fruit had been left to moulder on a shelf in the small, but functional kitchen.

As I picked it up to take it outside, my eyes were drawn to the painting affixed to the wall above. It was a landscape depicting the wondrous colours of the forest, possibly the one nearby. The striking feature was a massive oak tree that dominated the centre of the painting. The artist had captured the tree in a particularly colourful display when the light must have hit the autumn leaves and shone across the area. Leaning in, I noticed a simple signature of two initials, VB, and a two-digit year that, if correct, was ten years ago.

Moving through the kitchen, I found a key ring hanging from a hook near the rear door. Finding the correct key, I quickly unlocked it and deposited the bowl of rotten fruit outside. It was there I saw the forest in all its glory. The sun was beginning its descent into the evening, and the rays shone across the colours of the late autumn foliage, bursting into iridescence much like the painting inside.

Gaping in awe, I swept my gaze across the area. The forest dominated the view, broken only by a small stone outer building on the far edge of the property. It was possibly a utility shed, housing the tools used to tend the small vegetable plots. A pathway led from the forest up to a small gate in the rear fence of the Bodkin property, not far from the shed itself. From where I stood, it seemed to be a completely natural trail, having been cut from many feet walking the track over many years.

Returning inside, I noticed another room to my left. Inside, I found some blank canvases, tubes of paint, an easel, paintbrushes, and a pallet. A single unfinished canvas sat apart from the rest. It depicted the view I had just witnessed and was in the same style as the other painting.

The artist lived here.

I pondered on the initials and remembered that the mother's name was Velia. Velia Bodkin. VB.

Impressively talented.

...my eyes were drawn to the painting affixed to the wall above...

Navigating the house in search of Holmes and Todman, I found several more canvases, each depicting forest scenes, and each signed with a simple VB and two-digit number.

Holmes found me staring at one of the paintings. “Startling, aren’t they?”

I could only nod in agreement.

"It seems our accused murderer had a rather creative mother."

Turning towards him, I asked, "How?"

Holmes simply shrugged. "The signature. It is not very common to find someone with a first name beginning with V. Add to that the second letter, plus the number of paintings lining these walls, and the conclusion forms itself.

Again, I could only nod in agreement. "Yes, and there are some artist's paraphernalia in a room at the rear with a single unfinished canvas. Have you found anything else to lead you further?"

"Yes. Todman is poring over the clues as we speak. I came to bring you to Bodkin's room to observe."

Unlike Bodkin's rooms in Hounslow, this bedroom was neat and tidy, and almost bereft of anything out of the ordinary. I stood in the doorway and scanned the room for a moment before looking at Todman who inspected what lay on the bed. Staring at the objects of his fascination, I was filled with the impression of familiarity. There, spread out was another collection of objects that could only have belonged to a woman, or as we had seen, a group of women.

"Are those?"

"Yes," replied Holmes. "They were already arranged on the bed. They've been there a while as there is a fine layer of dust covering them."

"What would Bodkin need with all this?" asked Todman, picking up a small kerchief, bringing it to his nose and sniffing. "Perfume. Definitely belonged to a woman." Finally, his eyes opened wide. "These are from his victims, aren't they?"

"Yes, but given the number, I feel that his infatuation was not limited to London."

"Do you think he murdered some local women?" Shaking his head for a moment, Todman added, "I don't remember any missing persons of late?"

"I'm surprised he simply left them out on his bed."

"Ah, that has me confused as well." Holmes stood pondering the arranged trophies, his head resting on his hand, with his index finger extended up his cheek. "I wonder. There are eight individual items.

All left out as if for viewing by Bodkin himself, but his movements mean that he wouldn't have been here for at least two months prior to his capture. Which means that these items would have been covered with almost four months' worth of dust."

Turning, he whirled from the room. I watched him leaning over and examining the various items of furniture in the adjoining room. He disappeared through a nearby doorway, and I could hear him moving through the house with a flourish. Finally, he returned moments later, a wry smile on his face.

"All right, Holmes, you obviously have drawn some conclusions, what are they?"

"Our matriarch."

"Mrs. Bodkin?" asked Todman. "What about her?"

"I believe that it was she that arranged these items on display. The level of dust covering them matches the layer of dust covering the furniture around the house. From all evidence, the poor woman was a fastidious housekeeper, and would never have allowed dust to build up. Hence, what we are seeing has accrued since the poor woman's demise, about one month ago."

"Are you saying that she put these here?" asked Todman, pointing at the bed. "Why?" He went silent for a moment. "She knew?"

Nodding, with that sly grin widening, Holmes added his next observation. "There are eight items. Indicating eight victims. I think we may find some of them are indeed from the four London victims. That kerchief for instance." Todman looked at the item in his hand, holding it out to display embroidered initials, P and S on it. "That possibly belonged to Patricia Sherlin, the first London victim. As to the other items, I have no idea at this stage, but I truly believe that if you return to the station and investigate you may find some disappearances from over ten years ago, perhaps longer."

"When Homer Bodkin lived here?"

Holmes nodded before turning to face Todman. "How did Mrs. Bodkin die?"

"Um, well, the local doctor suggested natural causes. His idea of a broken heart was taken a little lightly at the time."

"Was an autopsy done?"

Shaking his head, the young constable added, "No. I think after all that had happened, the doctor and the senior sergeant wanted to let the poor dear well alone and have her put to rest as quietly as possible."

"A tad careless," said Holmes, a slightly gruff tone to his voice. "Can you at least tell me where she was found?"

"Oh, yes. Follow me." Todman led us from the bedroom, through a small dining room, with a wooden table and six chairs.

Holmes stopped. "Interesting," he said, looking down at a single key, laying at one end of the table. The same thin layer of dust lay across the table and the key. It had obviously been placed there before the old woman died. "I won't touch this yet, but I believe we need to investigate whatever this key unlocks."

Continuing, we reached the back door, which I had used only minutes earlier. Todman ushered us outside, striding past us, and stopping about twenty feet from the door. There sat a small, cobbled area, with a table and two chairs, which had a magnificent view of the forest. The type of spot that would be wonderful for taking morning and afternoon tea.

"I wasn't here at the time, but a neighbour came by to check on Mrs. Bodkin. They found her lying here upon the cobbles. She had been painting, as far as I am aware. By the time the doctor and I arrived, the neighbour had put away the easel and painting equipment, leaving just the poor unfortunate woman."

Holmes scanned the area, staring at some of the plants along the rear wall of the house, before stooping down to examine the area. Pulling a kerchief from his pocket, he reached under the table and picked something from between two cobbles. As he examined the find, I piped up. "What have you there Holmes?"

"A small sliver of ceramic. And it seems that the table has moved slightly, there are scratches on the cobbles, I believe that Mrs. Bodkin may have nudged it as she became bewildered and fell. A cup or saucer was knocked from the table and shattered. The kindly neighbour seems to have been a little too overanxious and cleared away the mess, removing a possibly vital clue."

"Why is it a clue?"

Still examining the shard, he said, "I'm not convinced that Mrs. Bodkin died from purely natural causes. Did you notice the plants along the rear wall?"

Todman and I both glanced in that direction. A small line of green stemmed plants, with small white flowers lined the wall of the cottage.

"What are they?" the policeman asked. "I've seen those flowers on the edge of the forest. Never really understood what they were."

"Hemlock," replied Holmes. "Relatively harmless if handled carefully, though best to wash your hands thoroughly afterwards, but deadly if ingested."

"What are you suggesting?" I asked, a strange set of questions rising in my mind. "She took hemlock?"

"Possibly." Standing, he strode back to the rear door and entered. We found him rummaging around the kitchen. "Aha," he said, spying a small box beneath the sink that held some items of garbage. A small China cup lay in pieces within the box. Picking it out and laying it on the counter, he compared the sliver to the broken cup and nodded. "This appears to have been the cup in question. It has the discolouration of dried tea on the inside. I'd have to run tests to determine whether it was hemlock or not, but for now, that is relatively immaterial to the case, other than providing more evidence that the poor woman was distressed and wished to have this whole grisly mess behind her, in more ways than one."

Placing the cup pieces back into the small bin, Holmes replaced his kerchief and washed his hands. I took that to mean he was more than sure of what was consumed from that cup. Turning he asked, "Watson, you mentioned that you found an unfinished painting."

Nodding, I took him through to the small anteroom where the canvas sat. A wry smile appeared on his face as he studied the artwork. "Can you bring the easel," he said, stepping past me and heading back outside. I followed with the requested item and set it up on the cobbled area where Holmes had stopped.

Placing the painting on the easel, and adjusting it slightly, he stepped away before looking back.

"What do you see, Watson?"

"I see that little outer building, plus the forest behind it."

"Yes, and the little path that meanders from the rear wall to the edge of the forest."

"Oh, yes."

"What does it mean?" asked Todman.

Rather than answering, Holmes disappeared into the house once more, returning a moment later and striding past the two of us and heading for the little building. We hurried after him, catching up as the key that I recognised from the dining room table was inserted in the door lock and turned without resistance.

I braced myself, half expecting another carnal display as that seen in Hounslow, but the shed was just that. A shed. It contained all manner of gardening implements, along with sticks of unused furniture, covered in dust and cobwebs, plus various boxes, and crates full of bric-a-brac.

"Well, that's a little disappointing," I said, half-chuckling to relieve the tension.

"Not in the least," answered Holmes.

"Why?"

He pointed to some implements to our left, a spade, a shovel, and a pickaxe. They rested against the near wall, their handles were relatively free of dust and webs. Holmes picked up a long-handled shovel and turned it over. The blade was covered with a thick coating of yellowish-brown dirt. A pair of thick boots sat next to the pickaxe. Replacing the shovel, Holmes retrieved the boots and turned them over. The soles were caked with dirt of various shades, from the yellowish-brown to dark brown and almost black.

"The different shades of dirt on these boots hint at the wearer stepping through the various layers of dirt to be found in this area. The dark brown dirt would be near the surface, receiving a fresh layer of leaves and plant matter over the years, which breaks down. The yellowish dirt is found much deeper, around four to five feet. The shovel has been used to dig down to that level, far deeper than would be required just to tend to these vegetable patches."

"For what purpose?" Todman asked, before stopping, his eyes growing wide. "Oh, you don't think?"

Holmes nodded. "Very much so, at this stage. The poor unfortunate missing girls, I'm afraid."

"How can you be so sure?" I asked.

"Mrs. Bodkin. I feel that it was all too much for the poor dear. She could only be a good mother to her son while he was alive, sharing his horrid secret. When he was finally dispatched, she still couldn't bring herself to directly tell the authorities, so she staged a little deception herself in the hopes that someone would see."

Todman gave voice to his scepticism. "But where are the girls? Not in the forest? I know you are very clever, Mr. Holmes, but surely you don't think you can find them there, in all that acreage?"

"Ah, that's where Mrs. Bodkin has been even more clever. Did you notice how many items there were?"

"Eight."

"And how many paintings?"

Todman counted in his head. "Seven?" He stopped for a moment, his mind ticking over. "No." His eyes almost bulged out of his head. "Eight."

"Precisely. This last painting," Holmes pointed back towards the easel, "Was to set the scene for anybody that had the mind to look."

"What now?" I asked.

Holmes picked up the spade, handing the shovel to Todman and the pickaxe to myself.

"We go for a stroll in the forest."

As we began to set off, Holmes stopped, handing his spade to Todman and hurrying back into the house. He returned moments later with one of the many paintings in his hands. He had removed it from the frame, making it much easier to carry. Holding it up to show Todman, he said, "Do you recognise this location, Constable?"

Todman stared at the large tree in the centre of the painting for a moment, before nodding. "Yes. The townsfolk call it the cathedral oak." He glanced up towards the forest. "In fact, it's not far from here." Hefting his implements, he headed towards the little gate that led out of the yard.

***

Even though Velia Bodkin was quite the artist, the painting didn't do the cathedral oak justice. There was nothing else to give any perspective within the painting. The tree itself looked at least ten yards in girth and towered well over twenty-five yards in height. The late autumn had turned the oak into a wonderful golden hue, making it stunning in the late afternoon sun.

Todman and I both admired the scene and watched Holmes. My colleague moved around the area, with the painting in his hands. Studying the tree, then the painting, and then moving. He eventually stopped and held the artwork up before him, lowering it from time to time as he adjusted his position slightly until he was satisfied.

We strode across and stood behind him. As expected, Holmes had found the exact place where Mrs. Bodkin had stood to paint her vision. There was a certain artistic licence used to depict the scene, but she had been rather accurate. Stepping to one side, I viewed the vista before us, trying to work out what it was that Holmes found so fascinating.

"Do you really think there's a body here, Holmes?"

"From what I've seen at the house, I believe that Mrs. Bodkin has left us clues from beyond the grave. Possibly as a way of tracking down the poor unfortunate victims of her son's evil crimes. There are exactly eight paintings. Each depicts a forest scene, mostly with a large, impressive tree in them. Four of them are dated this year. Three of them are dated from ten years ago, and one is from eleven years ago."

"That's a very long bow to draw," said Todman, his scepticism on full display. "And how on earth could we find them even if they are here? There's nothing in the paintings that indicates a grave or anything. There are no markers that I have seen around the area, so how do we prove your theory correct?"

"Except, there is that." Holmes pointed to a spot on the far side of the tree. I looked, but all I could see was a patch of thick grass, its colour a deep, rich green.

"I don't understand," said Todman, squinting and straining to look in the direction Holmes indicated.

It was then I noticed the grasses nearby were far less lush and a much lighter colour the further they grew from the middle of the spot. Glancing at the same location on the painting I noticed the grass was depicted as uniform across the area.

"I think I do," I added. "The grass, it's much lusher than shown in the painting."

A wry grin came to Holmes's mouth. "Well done, Watson."

"Care to explain," said Todman.

"I read a recent study on the effect of decomposing bodies on nearby plant life. The nutrients escaping from the corpse cause grasses, plants and trees to almost explode with life, explained Holmes, as he strolled across to the verdant area of grass. "What we see here, could be the last resting place of one of the poor unfortunate victims of Homer Bodkin."

"Are you sure?" asked Todman.

"Not completely, but every indication points to that explanation."

"So, how do we find out?"

Taking the shovel from Todman's hand, Holmes said, "We dig."

***

"The least we could have done was to seek out a change of clothes," I said to Holmes as I reclined in our parlour chair and sipped at my brandy. "I was filthy once we returned to the cottage."

"Oh, pish, Watson," he replied. "You were able to borrow a change of clothing until yours could be cleaned."

"Yes, but they were the murderer's clothes. And besides, he was a large man, and they were far too loose."

My colleague smiled broadly, sipping his brandy, and taking a deep draw from his cigar. He blew out a long line of smoke before adding, "I didn't want us to lose momentum. If we had returned to the town to ask for more men, it would have been another day lost."

"Fair call, I suppose. Still, the look on Todman's face when his spade struck something solid beneath that lush grass was priceless. When we unearthed the object and found it to be poor Miss Dickson, he was a total believer in your skills."

"Yes, again, that was an advantage. It rattled the young policeman so much that he rallied enough troops to have the other seven corpses found and exhumed before the next night fell. Effectively, wrapping up the case within twenty-four hours, and providing solutions to four others that he didn't even know about."

"I'm still intrigued. How did you expect to solve this one when you took on Sir Delmar's request."

Holmes sipped his brandy, deep in thought for a moment. "Unsure. To be perfectly honest, I was simply fascinated by the opportunity. I was a little wounded by Athelney's dismissal of my original offer of help further and thought this may provide a chance to prove him wrong. As I cogitated on it, I became less sure of myself and the mountain I had to climb." He replaced his glass and drew on the cigar, continuing as another waft of smoke was blown out. "It was only when I saw the evidence at Bodkin's apartment, and then the paintings created by his mother, that I held out any hope at all. If not for the assistance of the poor unfortunate widow, then all would have been for nought."

I nodded. "Yes. I figured as much, but to give you your dues, I don't think there would have been much likelihood of anybody else putting the clues together and finding those bodies."

"Sadly, no. Our Mrs. Bodkin was clever, but I think a tad too clever. It was as if she protected her son, at the same time being horrified by him, and then wanting his crimes unearthed but only on the off chance that the right person came along."

"And an off chance that was."

"Quite so."

He raised his glass and said, "To the assistance of the Wiltshire widow, may she now rest forever in peace."

"Here, here." Taking a sip of the wonderful brandy, another thought occurred to me. "I am a little distraught, however, with the actions of our benefactor in this case."

"Ah, yes, Sir Delmar." Holmes nodded for quite a while before adding, "It would have been hard not to pick up on his dismissive nature upon viewing his wife's corpse."

"Yes. It was as if our finding of her body was not his main preoccupation."

“Agreed. It was those items associated with her, that took his attention the most. When presented with the objects found on her person, his eyes grew increasingly wide, as if something he sought was not there.”

“And then he asked about other things, describing that gold, heart-shaped necklace in almost precise detail.”

“Yes. I feel he would have almost strangled Bell if that had been kept as evidence in the case, rather than being returned to him on the spot.”

“I had that impression as well. Do you know why?”

“No, but I studied all the items at one time or another, and that little pendant held a scrap of paper within.”

“Anything of note?”

“A four-digit number. That is all.”

“Strange. Do you have any idea for what?”

“No. No, I don’t. Could be part of an address. It could be a combination of a lock. It could even be the number for a safe deposit box. Could be anything, really.” Drawing on his cigar once more, and letting the smoke drift forth, he finished with, “But, I do believe we may be drawn into yet another adventure on the back of that simple scrap of paper, and its contents.”

“Hmm. Hopefully not immediately,” I answered, draining my glass, and reaching for the decanter.

A Death at Stonehenge

The flames erupted, licking at the dry straw and wood, which caught fire immediately. Within seconds the twenty-foot tall statue of a man, a traditional wicker man, was well alight from head to toe. A blazing pyre that lit up the night sky all around us. Turning, I stared across the area at the accompanying bonfire that blazed brightly on the other side of the stones.

"A truly magnificent sight isn't it?" said our host, Sir Edmund Antrobus, the last in a long family line that claimed ownership of Stonehenge and the land upon which it stood.

"The fires, or the stones themselves," asked Holmes, glancing from the flaming wicker man to gaze at the tall stones of the henge, now bathed in the light of the orange flames.

"Both I suppose," chuckled Antrobus, "I suppose I get a little jaded by the sight of the henge. I see it almost every day. But, the druids only gather here twice every year. Beltane and Samhain."

"Samhain would be a little more dour and quiet though, I presume?"

"Oh, yes, they do like to celebrate the coming of summer, and May is generally such a nice time of year." Glancing around at the gathering he smiled. "This is a larger gathering than in previous years." He pointed across at the line of tents erected outside of the perimeter of the stones. "They've come for a number of days, this time."

The smell of roasting meat wafted across my face, causing me to involuntarily salivate at the imagined taste. "They have a suckling pig on a spit, it seems."

Holmes turned to glance at the line of tents, squinting to make out any details. A large fire was ablaze in the encampment. A large man stood by a fire, turning a spit threaded with two pigs. "Hmm. From the smell, I agree, but the breeze is coming from the direction of the wicker man. Still, it's not a strong wind, so that would account for the overpowering smell of the roasting pig."

I shrugged and turned back in the direction of the wicker man. There was something primaeval about staring into a blazing fire. The dancing flames told a story all their own. Stories that impinged on the instinctual memory and took one back to simpler times filled with working and hunting during the day, and sitting by the fire eating the day's catch and preparing to repeat it all the following morning.

Shivering at the thought of eschewing the conveniences of modern times and applying myself to such a lifestyle, I turned my attention to the gathered druids as they moved amongst the stones of the ancient henge. It was they who really wished for simpler times. Everything about the evening was in celebration of Beltane, the ancient festival proclaiming the onset of summer and the day on which all the cattle were driven back out into the fields. From what I knew, the burning of effigies and bonfires was to invoke the spirits to bring protection to the cattle and to the people.

In those olden times, the winters were harsher as the population had little or no protection against the cold. Modern building techniques, clothing and heating were only a distant dream. The cold of winter was a far greater killer than the heat of summer, and the people celebrated in earnest every time the warmth returned to their land. They thanked the Gods and spirits for their benevolence.

Such primitive times.

Holmes's voice broke through my reflections. "Shall we, Watson? The hour grows late."

We bade adieu to Sir Edmund; Lady Anne; and their eldest daughter, Louisa; and headed to the small dog trap we had procured for the last couple of days. The dark was intense on our journey, but within an hour we found our way into Amesbury and proceeded to our lodgings for the night.

***

The morning of the second of May broke bright, with a slight haze in the air. Looking out the window of my second-storey room, I took in the fresh beginnings of that spring day and breathed in a lungful of the clean country air. My nose twitched at the slight tinge of wood smoke on the breeze.

Glancing to the west, I noticed a thin grey haze spreading out from over the horizon. That way lay Stonehenge, so I could only imagine that this was the last vestiges of smoke from the wicker man and the bonfire. I smiled at the memory of the previous night. A joyous celebration of the coming summer formed from the ancient superstitions of a dying religion. A festival that had, so far, avoided subjugation into the more mainstream celebrations of Christianity.

A sudden knock at the door shook me from my reverie. "Watson, are you awake? Come downstairs as soon as you are able."

Within a few moments, I joined Holmes in the main bar of the pub on the ground floor. He was deep in conversation with a man in his mid-forties. From his attire, he appeared to be a working man. He wore a weather-stained coat and hat, with knee-high waterproof boots that had seen a lot of adventure in their time. His face showed the deep colour of someone who has spent a lot of his life outdoors.

"Ah, Watson, good man." Holmes motioned me to join them. "This is William Judd; he is the gamekeeper to Sir Edmund and oversees the entire Antrobus estate." I took Judd's proffered hand and noticed the callouses that lined his palm. I surmised that this was a man well-used to working hard.

"Doctor," Judd said, shaking my hand warmly, but retaining a slightly disturbed expression on his face.

"Judd has hurried to find us. It seems that both our talents may be of use."

"I think so," the gamekeeper said. "I've not seen the likes of this for many a year. Horrible it was."

"What has happened? Is it Sir Edmund?"

"Oh, no," he said. "We found a body. Well, what's left of a body."

"Where?" Now my attention was alight.

"At Stonehenge. In the ashes of the wicker man."

***

"Ah, you'd be Mr. Holmes and Dr. Watson?" asked the young constable as we approached the scorched earth where the remains of the previous night's celebration highlight lay. "Thank you for coming. I'm Constable Petteway, from Amesbury, and I hate to admit it, but this is a little out of my usual depth."

"I assume you've sent for an inspector?" asked Holmes.

"Yes, sir, the nearest one would be in Salisbury, so if he's available, he should be here within the hour."

Stepping closer, Holmes surveyed the area but kept to the unsullied side of the scorch marks. The wicker man had burnt well into the night it seemed, and collapsed in on itself, the straw and sticks burning themselves out overnight. All that remained was a conglomeration of ash and coals. And the body. Well, it could really only be called a skeleton. From where I stood, the poor unfortunate had been set upon by the flames, leaving only a charred collection of connected bones.

"When you're finished, I'd like to check the body, Holmes."

"All in good time Watson. I don't wish the site to be any further ruined by extra feet."

It was as expected, but I had hoped for a little more leeway. I waited patiently as Holmes traversed the perimeter of the scorched patch of earth. He stopped, and scanned the area intently, moving to and fro, whilst carefully watching his footfalls. I noticed he became very intrigued by some marks in the turf, following one set away from the ashen ground, before turning and retracing his steps. His eyes then followed a similar set of tracks that moved into the scorched area.

"What have you got there, Holmes?" He held up a finger to silence me for the moment, scanning the ground and prodding it in various places. Finally, after what seemed like an eternity, he stood and motioned towards me. "Watson, please come and let us look at this poor unfortunate."

Hurrying across the scorched ground, I joined Holmes in the centre where the blackened body lay. He stood, simply staring down at the corpse, his hand resting along his jaw with one finger extended up his cheek. A typical pose indicating deep thought.

Studying the body, I tried to determine the heat that would be produced by the wicker man fire. I estimated it to be greater than a thousand degrees. A flame so hot that it should burn through skin and flesh, but not bone. This was evident in the corpse. All that remained, on show, was the blackened skull, with scant tendrils of crisply burnt muscles keeping them together.

All that remained was a conglomeration of ash and coals. And the body.

Looking down the length of the body, I was surprised at the resilience of the person's clothing. His thick woollen coat had been scorched and still showed wisps of smoke rising from the heavy fabric, which was mostly intact, but had obviously provided some protection to the flesh beneath.

"Male," I observed out loud, which received a confirming nod from Holmes. "The coat seems to have protected his chest area. The trousers didn't." In fact, his trousers were burnt away, as was most of the skin and flesh of the legs, except for the thick leather boots.

"What do you make of the remaining attire?" asked Holmes, pointing first at the coat, then at the charred remains of the jacket and shirt beneath, then finally at the thick boots.

"I'd have to strip them off to get a good idea, but they seem to indicate someone who understood the cold and damp of the countryside, but who maintained a certain social presence. It looks as though he wore a daytime frock coat, with a dress shirt, and possibly a cravat, but that has burnt away. The outer coat is similar to the style of Inverness that you prefer." To this Holmes nodded.

"The boots are obviously an addition for venturing into the countryside. One would suggest that this man was dressed for a social visit, but fully aware of the cold and damp of the outdoors."

"I agree. What are those?" I pointed to several holes in the front of the coat. Dropping to a knee, and wincing as the cold damp of the ground seeped into my trouser leg, I strained to focus on the damaged area of the man's chest. "Has he been shot?"

Pulling his glass from an inside pocket, Holmes deftly bent forward and examined the holes more closely. "They penetrate through the inner fabric as well, and possibly into the man's chest. I could make out three, and they are too regular to be bullets unless the culprit was an incredible marksman. Another thing to check when we have this body in a more sanitised environment."

"Should we have him moved as fast as possible? I can only imagine how the cold and damp will be affecting my examination."

"Not yet, I wish to finish examining the area. Did you notice his posture?"

Looking at the body within its surroundings, I saw what he meant. The body was in a slightly crumpled arrangement. He was on his back, with one arm thrust behind, and one leg curled up under the other at a strangely unnatural angle. "He wasn't placed like this?"

"No, I can only imagine that he fell from a moderate height, landing feet first, before collapsing as if he were a rag doll."

"He was dead before that. Otherwise, he would have fought against the flames, and we would have heard screams last night."

Nodding, Holmes replied, "Yes. From what I can see of his location and posture, he was interred in the wicker man, prior to its immolation."

"Murder?" asked Petteway.

"Very likely," said Holmes, "and this makes it even more interesting." He strode to the edge of the scorched grass and pointed at the track nearby. Following him, I found the object of his interest. The area showed a myriad of ruts, but a single pair could be made out running across the top of all others.

Turning to the gamekeeper, Holmes asked, "Judd, do you know when the wicker man was constructed?"

"Oh, yeah, it took them a week. Finished it about four days ago, and just left it. Nobody's been near this area since then. Only those that walked over to make sure everything was ready for the burning."

"So, these tracks were possibly made in the last few days. There are fresher hoof prints as well. And these," he pointed at two smaller ruts in the grass and dirt that led into the scorched area but were then covered in blackened ash.

"What are those?" asked the young policeman.

"I would think that someone dragged a body along this way, up to the wicker man." He turned and walked quickly to the body. Grasping one of the man's boots and carefully turning it to reveal the heel. Dried mud flaked off of the rear of the boot, but a build-up could be seen above the sole, pressed into where the leather joined it.

"Hmm, he may have simply stood in a damp mud patch."

"True, but as always it isn't one piece of evidence, it's the overall picture that it forms.

“And what do you make of this?” Holmes motioned towards the soul of the right boot. It was caked with dried and slightly burnt fibrous matter. I leaned in closer and noticed a slightly pungent smell above the odour of ash and smoke.

“Manure?”

“I suspect, though I’d like to analyse further.”

“But this is the country. One has to walk only a hundred yards without paying attention and you would likely walk through something similar.”

“All too true, Watson.” Turning to Petteway, Holmes called out. “Constable, is there anywhere sheltered that this poor unfortunate can be taken? The good doctor and I need to examine him further, but this is not the most appropriate location.”

The young policeman strode over, wincing at the sight of the burnt corpse. “Oh, I’ll never get used to that.” Composing himself, he continued. “We can probably take him to Amesbury Hospital. I can send for an ambulance or mortician’s carriage. Should only take an hour or two.”

Judd piped up. “If you’d like, we can probably use the coach house in the stables back at the Antrobus estate. The master hasn’t had the need for a coach for quite some time, and it’s used for storage mostly at the moment. It’s only two miles away.”

Nodding, Holmes added, “Constable, I think we should send word to the local coroner and have him ready to receive this poor unfortunate. In the meantime, I’d like to take you up on that offer Mr. Judd.”

As both men moved off to make arrangements, I asked Holmes what he was thinking.

“I’m still unsure, at this stage, Watson. Everything points to murder. The wounds to the chest. The concealment in the wicker man. First, I’d like your opinion on the manner of death, before the body succumbs too much further.”

“Very good.”

***

The Antrobus estate was relatively modest, given the area and the lands it encompassed, but as we had found from meeting with Sir

Edmund, he was rather down to earth and not given to the grandeur and ostentation of others of his ilk.

The stables were impressive though. The building was larger than many a grand house in London. The main doors were open revealing two lines of stalls filled with horses, and a large open area used for grooming and exercising the animals out of the weather.

Judd drove the dog cart towards a set of doors to one side of the open area. Whilst he hopped off and opened up the doors, Holmes and I picked up the poor unfortunate corpse and followed him into the large room.

He had sent word ahead, and his underlings had quickly tidied the area, pushing loose crates and odd pieces of furniture off to the side. A table had been constructed with saw horses and a long plank of wood. It was a simple, but serviceable area in which to closely examine the body. I hoped that an autopsy or any invasive examination would not be required, as I wouldn't feel comfortable performing such in this environment. I expressed my reservations to Holmes who simply nodded and said, "I fully understand, Watson. I too hope that we shall reveal most of what we need by a cursory examination."

With the poor man deposited on the long makeshift trestle, I began a more thorough investigation. Scanning every inch of the corpse before undertaking anything more invasive. "Can I have your glass, Holmes?" Leaning in I focused on an area at the front of the poor man's forehead. The skin and flesh had burnt away, leaving a blackened patina of ash, but I could see a tiny crack in the bone. Handing the glass to Holmes, I asked, "What do you think? Did the fire do that? Or was it pre-mortem?"

Holmes joined my examination of the area, and after several murmurs of thought, stood up again. "There's no other breaking of the bones, nearby, so I can only suspect that the poor fellow was struck at this point, cracking his skull. Not enough to kill him, but certainly enough to incapacitate him."

"Why do that if the assailant were only going to stab him, anyway?"

Shrugging, my friend answered, "To that, I'm unsure at this point."

Moving down the body, I carefully peeled back his coat and remaining garments. Surprisingly, the thick woollen coat had protected his chest quite well. The flesh was dried, and shrunken through the heat of the fire, but had avoided any devastating burns. The wounds in the man's chest were of immediate interest. They were on his right-hand side, with two holes protruding deep into the flesh between the man's ribs, but a third wound was merely a deep rent in the skin and muscle, as the penetrating object had been deflected by the sternum. From the damage to the flesh, it appeared they were made from a blow angling slightly upwards.

"Intriguing," said Holmes, leaning in with his glass and studying the edges of the wounds as closely as he could. "Do you agree that it is a single wound?"

"How so?"

Pointing at the two on the left, my friend added, "See the way the skin on the left of the puncture is relatively cleanly cut but is torn to the right. As if the object was thrust in and then pulled sideways. It's the same on the sternum. The rent seems to start at the left and runs to the right. As if the man were stabbed with a three-pronged item, which was wrenched to the right before being pulled out."

Studying the wound myself, I had to agree. It was messy, but if the man had been stabbed three times with a single-pronged instrument, then each wound would be completely different. These appeared to have been caused at the same time, and then the extra damage subsequently occurred in one fell act.

"What would have caused such a set of wounds then?"

Scanning the area, a wry grin came to Holmes's face. "I think we are in the perfect place to find out."

Turning, I spied the object of Holmes's interest. Lying on top of several wooden crates was a selection of gardening and other implements used in husbandry. One stood out in particular, a fork with three tines splayed out from a central pole. I recognised it as a simple pitchfork, and the shape indicated by the points was almost a direct match to the horrid wounds in the burnt corpse's chest. Holmes crossed the room and retrieved the implement, bringing it back and holding the pointed end several inches above the man's wounds.

"It's not an exact match, but this type of implement could well have made these."

"I agree. That one has a crack in the handle, possibly why it's been dumped in here."

"Quite so."

I was about to ask Holmes whether we should search for another when a bellicose voice rang out from the entrance to the room.

"My word, Holmes, what have you got there?" We turned to find Sir Edmund Antrobus standing in the doorway. Not waiting for an invitation, he strode in and stood next to the body. A mixed look of horror and disgust on his face. "By Jove, where did that fellow come from?"

"Your man hasn't informed you yet, then?" asked Holmes.

"I'm sorry, sir, I couldn't find you," came Judd's apologetic voice from the entrance. "This poor man was found in the remains of the druids' wicker man. Under the circumstances, this area seemed to be the ideal spot to undertake this examination, so that we could determine who it was, and how he died."

Glancing from Judd's face back to the corpse, the landowner took a deep breath before solving the first mystery. "Well, it's that archaeologist fellow, isn't it?"

"Archaeologist?" I asked.

"Yes. Hollian, I think his name was, Wesley or some such. Been bugging me for weeks about the henge."

"How can you tell?" asked Holmes.

"The boots, mainly, good solid pair of leather boots. Crafted in London, no less. And that coat. Thick, woollen coat, you'd need it out here. He was staying in a tent up near the henge. A man would freeze if he didn't have something like that to keep him warm." Scanning the body once more, he added, "Not much else left of the blighter. Must have been a damn fool to get so close to the wicker man that he'd catch fire like this."

"We think there may have been foul play," said Holmes.

“What?” Sir Edmund’s voice rose several levels. “Foul play? Here? Why? Who?”

“Of that, we aren’t sure. The corpse displays some wounds that were possibly the cause of death, only the coroner will be able to tell us that, but it appears that the wounds were caused by one of these.”

“A pitchfork? Good Lord. In my stables?”

“Well, we can’t ascertain that, sir, only the indications of the type of weapon.”

His face beaming red from a mix of anger and horror, Sir Edmund turned on his gamekeeper. “Judd? Judd? Where is that layabout Soutter? Get him in here to explain himself.”

“I…I haven’t seen him since early yesterday, sir.” Judd then disappeared.

“We are also unsure, Sir Edmund, if these wounds occurred here. The poor man was found at Stonehenge, so he could have been killed anywhere and delivered there at any time after the wicker man was erected.” Holmes described all that we’d seen at the henge, and the reason for us bringing the poor man back to the coach room.

Sir Edmund started to speak but was cut off by Judd returning with a look of horror on his face. “You might want to come and see this.”

***

The terror-stricken gamekeeper led us into the main room of the stables and headed straight towards a stall at the far corner. The horses whinnied and stamped as our group passed through. I realised they would be more used to the quiet of a single stablehand tending and preparing them for use, not a group of relative strangers hustling through their home.

As we reached the entrance to the stall, Judd stopped and pointed. “I looked in each stall for Soutter, but came upon this.” He shook his head. “I can’t tell if the blood is his, or someone else’s, but …” As his voice trailed off, Holmes held out an arm to stop anyone else from entering the stall.

I knew that he meant no offence, but simply wanted to preserve the scene for inspection. Unfortunately, Sir Edmund became slightly flustered at the treatment. It was obvious he was not one to be denied.

"What is the meaning of this?"

I placed a gentle hand on our host's arm and added, "Holmes means no offence. He simply wants to study the area while it is still preserved." Glancing into my eyes, the older man nodded and stood still, moving back slightly to give Holmes room to work.

It was a well-proportioned stall and had obviously been vacated only recently. The straw was a mess of horse droppings and had been stamped by moving hoofs crushing many of the hay stalks almost to a powder. It was the obvious signs of violence that attracted all eyes. A three-pronged pitchfork lay in the straw. The tips darkened with a substance that slightly glistened in the dull light. The spatters and the small dried pool of the same coloured substance brought a slight feeling of dread to my mind. When Holmes moved across, hunkered down and drew his glass, I felt compelled to ask. "Blood, Holmes?"

"Very likely," was the terse reply.

The offending implement lay near a barrel of water, pushed up against the side of the stall. Holmes studied the barrel, before moving to his right and examining a hook attached to the wooden wall, then the floor, concentrating on a pile of horse droppings, and then a shovel lying in the messy straw nearby.

Finally, he stood, standing for a moment with his chin resting on his hand. I kept my silence, knowing that he was cogitating on the evidence before him. Building all manner of possible scenarios in his mind. The silent deliberation was broken by Sir Edmund. "Well, Holmes? Anything?"

My friend turned slowly. No anger on his face, just a look of confidence. He had formed an opinion. Nodding, he said. "I have a picture of the events, but I believe we will need to find the other witness to this fiasco, to truly understand."

"Was it that pitchfork?"

"Yes," Holmes hunkered down and pointed to the tines. "There is a lot of blood on these two prongs, but barely any on this one. That would seem to match the wounds on the corpse." Standing he pointed to the hook on the wall. There is some blood, and possibly skin on this hook. It could be the cause of the broken bone at the front of the dead man's skull."

"Anything else?"

Indicating the horse droppings and straw beneath the hook. "There may have been a scuffle. Someone seems to have stepped into and possibly slipped on this manure."

"The remnants on the sole of his boot?"

"Precisely." Stepping towards the rear of the stall, he pointed at the discarded shovel. It still held some remains of droppings on its face. "There was a second man, possibly this Soutter fellow, working away. The corpse, this archaeologist, probably met with him. They seem to have scuffled." Stepping to his left, he added, "The dead man hit his head and was then impaled on the pitchfork." He stood for a moment and studied the second implement's location once more. "Something doesn't seem right though. Hence, we should seek this stable hand of yours, Judd. His testimony may shed more light."

"But, if he was the culprit, surely he'll just lie about it all."

Holmes smiled and nodded. "Ah, yes, but as we have seen many times before, old friend, liars always come undone when their stories are picked apart."

I could only silently agree. As one, the group turned to follow Holmes, but all were brought up short as a high-pitched scream arose from outside the stables. We rushed towards the source and found the landowner's lovely young daughter standing before the open coach room. One hand was on her mouth, the other pointed limply towards the corpse. She swayed on her feet, threatening to topple into a faint at any time.

"Louisa," shouted Sir Edmund, racing to the lass's side. She took one look at the older man's face, her eyes closed and it was only his good reflexes that stopped her from crashing to the straw-covered ground.

***

"That...that was Wesley." Louisa Antrobus sat, slumped in an overstuffed armchair.

Sir Edmund, an obviously diligent and proud father, had carried the poor girl into the house. Placing her in the armchair in the corner of the ground-floor parlour. It was well-ventilated, and she began to come around quickly.

After checking her breathing and overall well-being, I draped a moistened cloth on her forehead to alleviate any fever in her brow.

Her eyes flickered as she came fully awake. Her slightly delirious speech continued. "Those boots and that coat. I saw him only two nights ago. Is he?"

"Yes. I'm afraid he is dead, dear."

"Oh, my." She threatened to faint once more. I asked Sir Edmund to step back and give her some air, waving another small cloth to fan her face and hopefully keep her awake.

Holmes, who stood a ways back, staring intently at the girl, his hand resting on his chin, with the index finger extended up his cheek, waited until Louisa was fully aware once more before speaking. "Can you remember where and when you last saw Wesley?"

The young girl's face turned towards my friend, her eyes adjusting as if she had only just realised he was there. "Who are you?"

"I am Sherlock Holmes. I've been asked to investigate the fate of poor Mr. Hollian."

"Doctor," she sighed, "He preferred to be called Doctor."

Nodding, Holmes said, "Can you remember where you last saw the unfortunate Doctor?"

"He came by two days ago, in the early evening. Asked if I would like to take a walk with him."

"He was courting you?"

Her eyes grew wide at that question. Her head snapped towards her father, whose expression was one of confusion. "Was he?" Sir Edmund asked, his voice gruff.

Nodding, she said, "Yes. He had made his intentions clear that he wished to ask for my hand. He had planned to approach you, father, at the earliest convenience."

"Were you in agreeance with his advances?" asked Holmes.

A tear formed in her eye and ran down her cheek as she turned towards my friend. "I could see that his station in life would have given me all that I could want. But …"

Holmes waited for a moment. When Louisa left the sentence open, he finished it. "But there was no love there?"

She dropped her head. The sound of her sobbing echoed out across the quiet room.

"There was another?"

The slight bobbing of her head while she wept, indicated acknowledgement of the question. Sir Edmund's voice rose, slightly tainted with fury. "Not that damn stableboy? I told you to stop seeing him. Worthless layabout."

The tears flowed accompanied by the louder sounds of open crying. "I tried, but …"

"I assume the beau in question is this Soutter fellow?"

Sir Edmund nodded and turned to Judd, mumbling, "You should have dismissed him."

Judd's face was a mass of guilt and confusion.

Holmes interrupted. "Regardless, where would this fellow seek refuge? If you haven't seen him for two days, then we can only assume that he is guilty, or at least feels guilt for the death of Doctor Hollian."

"He's not local. Comes from Somerset, probably fled back home after he dispatched the poor Doctor," growled Sir Edmund.

"No," came a quiet peep from the distressed woman. "He wouldn't leave me behind. Even if he killed Wesley, he'd want to take me with him, or at least say goodbye."

"Nonsense," cried her father, "the scoundrel has killed someone. He'll be miles away from here."

"And there is a cart missing. I noticed it earlier," added Judd.

"Damn," said Petteway, "We'll never find him."

Pulling a kerchief from her sleeve and dabbing at her eyes, Louisa Antrobus raised her face towards us. She scanned the group of men before her with the shrewd eyes of a woman in love and bent on protecting her man. "He is more of a man than any of you. If he did this deed, he would not run. He would hide and come back for me, and we would return to his home in Somerset. This he promised me. I know you would see him hang, but I won't have his name muddied without proof."

"The proof is in the carriage room," Sir Edmund scoffed, "What more could there be?"

"I know Bryce. He is big. He is tough, but he is kind and gentle. He would not kill."

"This is your heart talking, not your brain," said her father. "If he would not run, then where would he be?"

"The Red Lion."

***

"That's our dogcart," Judd said as we pulled up in front of the quaint little Wiltshire pub.

It was a two-storey public house. With white-washed walls and a thatched roof that was as tall as the top storey, windows poked from beneath the overhanging thatch indicating rooms on the second floor. Two chimneys let out a stream of smoke; the place was being heated in readiness for the expected clientele.

Dropping from the constable's wagon, Judd strode across to the cart. Seeing that there was no horse attached, he disappeared around the rear of the building, returning a moment later. "Good, Bessie's been put in the stables round back. I was half afraid that Soutter had got rid of her or something."

The five of us headed into the pub. The darkness within caused me to blink several times to adjust my eyes to the lack of light. A burly man, with short-cropped hair, and a grizzled appearance thanks to a three-day growth of beard, stared at us from behind the bar. He put down the glass he was drying and addressed Judd.

"You're here for Bryce then?"

Even Holmes was surprised by the question, but Sir Edmund was first to ask. "How do you know that?"

"He's been holed up here for two days now. Drinks himself into a stupor then I takes him upstairs and he collapses on his bed, wanders down and does it all again. He's never done this before, but he's paying, so I figures it's about a woman or some such; frankly, I don't care, but he's upsetting the other patrons."

"How so?"

"Muttering into his beer. For hours."

Holmes chimed in. "About what? If I may ask?"

"Nothing much. Just confusing angry talk. Something about someone called Wesley and someone else called Louisa. I was afeared he'd killed or hurt someone but din't want to put the law on him. He's a good bloke. Known him for years. Wouldn't hurt a fly."

"Well, he's certainly hurt someone this time," Sir Edmund said, his voice full of vitriol.

Holding up a hand towards Sir Edmund, Holmes suggested, "Perhaps, you should stay here, Sir Edmund. Let Petteway and me handle this." The older gentleman looked at the hand and then into the earnest face of its owner.

Slowly, his ire subsided and he nodded. "Fair enough. I'd only throttle the foozler."

***

At the top of the stairs, Holmes stopped for a moment, examining the area before continuing on. I was intrigued but decided to wait before asking. His simple reply, many hours later, was to see if any of the windows had been unlocked or opened whilst we had been downstairs. Holmes wanted to ensure that our quarry had remained in his room and hadn't absconded; in short, Holmes wanted to determine whether our quarry had prepared the windows in advance of any need to escape.

We stopped at the second door, the one the publican had indicated. Petteway led the procession, rapping on the door and announcing himself. "Mr. Soutter, please come out. It's Constable Petteway of the Amesbury precinct."

After a minute or so, with no reply or sound of movement inside, Petteway tried the door, finding it unlocked. Careful not to fall into some trap and come to harm, the young constable pushed the door inwards, whilst remaining outside the room.

The smell that emanated told us why Soutter hadn't answered. He'd obviously had a skinful before falling into his room and collapsing on his bed. "I don't think he even shut his own door, last night."

"I agree," said Holmes, "It may prove difficult to arouse him."

And it was. After applying all manner of rousing techniques, such as slapping his cheeks, talking loudly, and moving him about, we almost gave up. Our actions attracted the attention of the group downstairs, urging Judd and Sir Edmund to the second floor to join us.

Holmes became slightly disgruntled and retrieved a small cup of water from the bathroom. "I'm loath to do this, but it's either gain his assistance now or put him in the lock-up to sleep it off until later. I'd rather finish my investigations sooner."

Without any ceremony, Holmes indicated for us to move aside and simply threw the contents of the cup into the sleeping man's face. The effect was immediate. He gasped and sat bolt upright, his eyes springing open and blinking at both the flood of water and the flood of light. "What in blazes is going on?" he yelled out in surprise before he finally focused on those standing around him. "Oh." Soutter's face dropped into an anguished grimace as he spied the policeman. Rather than try to bolt from the constable, he held out his hands, ready to be placed in handcuffs. "I didn't kill him. I didn't even touch him. Well, not until after he was dead."

Drawing attention to himself, Holmes placed the cup down on a side table before returning to the bedside. "I'm intrigued, Constable, shall we dispense with the handcuffs until we've heard more from Mr. Soutter, here?"

"Fine with me," said Petteway, "I didn't come prepared for an arrest, don't even have any darbies on me."

Standing before the stable hand, Holmes drew himself up to full height, forcing Soutter to look up at him. "Now, Mr. Soutter."

"Bryce," the man said, "My father was Mr. Soutter."

"Bryce," Holmes continued a small wry smile on his lips. "You mentioned that you didn't kill him. Who didn't you kill?"

"You mean you don't know? Why are you here then?"

"We know, but I'd like to hear the story from your lips before we reveal our knowledge of the situation."

Soutter looked confused before he dropped his head and thought for a moment. "Hollian. Wesley Hollian. Or as he liked to throw it around, Doctor Wesley Hollian. Though I don't think you should be able to call yourself Doctor just 'cause you dig up old bones."

"Yes, he was an archaeologist. How did you know him?"

The stablehand lifted his head, his eyes watery as if on the edge of tears. "He's been hanging around for weeks. Doing something out at the henge." Nodding towards Sir Edmund, he added, "The Governor gave him access and let him set up camp. I don't need to go out there, so have kept away."

"But you crossed paths it seems."

"Yeah. He's become a right nuisance. Always dropping by to see Miss Louisa. Unannounced, like. Not real proper."

"Do you feel that way because you have intentions for Miss Louisa?"

Soutter let out an involuntary chuckle. "If only. Sure, we've become close friends, but she's a lady, I'm just ..." He glanced at Sir Edmund. "I'm just a nobody. I try, but I know I could never live up to the Governor's expectations."

"Too right," answered the landowner, receiving a stern look from Holmes, but ignoring it.

"Go on."

"I know Miss Louisa would just love to leave the estate with me, but I've got nothing but hope. Hope that I can work hard and save, and then buy us a little place out west where I'm from. And then this city boy turns up and tries to whisk her away from me."

"So, Hollian's attention for Louisa angered you?"

"Well, yeah, but not enough to do him any harm. Besides, Louisa didn't like him at all. She called him a jumped-up little toad and only put up with him to please her father."

"He had much more to offer than you, my boy."

Rather than answer his boss and incur further wrath, Soutter went quiet.

"So, what happened in the horse stall?"

"I was working away yesterday morning. Miss Louisa wanted Bessie fixed to the cart for a trip at lunchtime. I got to it early, so's I could do my other jobs and hopefully drive for her. So, there I was working away. I'd moved Bessie out into the mounting yard. I wanted to clean out her stall. I goes in with my trusty pitchfork…"

"Trusty all right," snapped Sir Edmund, before a squint-eyed look from Holmes shut him up.

"Leaning it against the water barrel, to keep it out of the way, and went about scraping up all of Bessie's doings. I wanted to sweep out all the straw and bring in a fresh bale of hay. Then he showed up."

"Hollian? The archaeologist?"

"Yeah. He'd done an all-nighter. You could smell it on him. He kept going on about how he was gonna take Louisa with him to London. How I couldn't hope to have her. He was nasty. Swearing and all sorts. I don't know what he'd been drinking, but he wasn't fit. Kept staggering and swearing, and when I just ignored him, hoping he'd get fed up and go away, he took a swing at me."

"Interesting."

"Yeah, but he weren't no boxer. Missed by a mile, but that was the end of him."

"Why?"

"Well, he sidles up like, and does a passable roundhouse with his right, but he steps in a pile of Bessie's doings. He slips, then overbalances and topples forward. Straight into the bridle hook. I can still feel it meself." Soutter rose a hand to his forehead in remembrance. "He cracks his head good. Blood sprayed out and he sways like he's about to pass out. I dropped the spade I was holding and tried to get to him, but he steps back, slips and spins to the left and falls forward." He paused for a moment, taking a deep breath. "Straight onto the pitchfork, then he fell to the ground next to the water barrel. I reached down, but he's already dead. Blood everywhere. I pulled the fork out and tossed it aside. Nothing. No groans. No breathing. Dead as a doornail."

"What did you do next?"

With eyes wide in terror, and tears sliding down his cheeks, Soutter went on. "I panicked. A dead gentleman. I'll be in a noose in days. I snatched him up. Threw him on the back of the dogcart, hooked up Bessie and went out to the henge. All I could think was to get rid of the body. I pulled the cart up near to the wicker man and stashed the silly bugger inside. I just hoped he'd burn away, and nobody would know. Stupid I know, but …"

"And then you came here?"

"Yeah. I was scared. I came to the Red Lion and just drank myself into a stupor. I remember climbing up to my room. I slept, then went down and drank again. I think I passed out downstairs. Old Sherwood must have dragged me up here. And now you show up."

Turning to look at Petteway, he added, "You can take me in, but I din't kill him. It was a horrible accident. I can still see him lying on the floor of the stables. I don't know how the fork stuck him. I've been thinking about it. It was just resting against the barrel. It should have fallen over. He should be alive."

"What a load of codswallop!" said Sir Edmund, obviously not believing a word of Soutter's story. "I didn't like that Hollian fellow much, but I will see you swing, my boy."

The constable turned to Holmes. "He's told you everything. I should take him in now."

Holmes nodded. "Yes. I think that's best. He still needs to sober up fully, so he may have something else to add when he has."

As the distraught stablehand was led away, he turned to Holmes. "I swear I didn't do it. I've thought long and hard, and everything points to me, but I swear. All I ask is that you tell Louisa goodbye for me."

Sir Edmund followed Petteway and Soutter from the room, leaving Judd, Holmes and myself behind.

"What do you make of it all, Holmes?"

"Watson, I'm not fully convinced of his guilt. Something has been disturbing me."

"What's that?"

"Well, from what we saw, Soutter was working towards the rear of the stall. That's where the spade holding some manure fell. Where it lay, the pitchfork's tines were pointed towards the same area that is towards where Soutter was working."

"So?"

"It means that either as Soutter attacked him, the archaeologist spun around a hundred and eighty degrees before he fell, or Soutter stepped around to attack him from the other side and Hollian simply fell over."

"I follow, but don't understand how you could tell whether either happened."

"It's the straw. It was messy from the horse treading over it, but for two grown men to have played out such an event, the straw would have been disturbed by their feet."

"Maybe Soutter messed up the straw afterwards?"

"Perhaps, but he'd have had to use his feet or hands. The spade was used. The pitchfork was covered in blood. Also, the pooling of blood on the ground indicated that the straw hadn't been disturbed. And why would he do that, instead of cleaning up all the evidence?"

"So, what are you saying?"

"I feel that there is credence to Soutter's view of the events. What I need, is to return to the scene and study it with a new eye on the details."

***

Judd had us back at the Antrobus estate within half an hour. Once the gamekeeper had harnessed old Bessie to the dogcart, the three of us squeezed into the lone seat and were away.

As we pulled up outside the stables, Holmes leapt down and headed to the rear stall. His mind was as active as his body in pursuit of the entire story of the events that had played out. Joining him, I took in the scene once more, still unsure of what had happened, but I couldn't shake the idea that the stable hand was guilty of murder.

Holmes stood stock still towards the middle of the stall and stared at the area around him. It was as we had left it. The shovel, still with some of the horse's manure on the blade, lay near the rear. The pitchfork lay towards the front, the head pointed towards the rear of the stall, with blood darkening two of the tines. A dark pool of blood stained the floor near the water barrel. Smears of the dark liquid ran away from the pool but stopped abruptly after a couple of feet. The straw was stained with it and messed up as if the body had been dragged away and then picked up.

My friend stooped for a second, examining the pitchfork, but the handle, not the head. Standing, he then moved to the barrel, and ran a finger around the topmost ring, nodding as he did so. Glancing along the wall next to the barrel, Holmes dropped down once more, running a fingertip across the wood and murmuring to himself.

It wasn't until he stood once more that I aimed to quench my own thirst for knowledge. "Anything, Holmes?"

Turning towards Judd and me, a slight grin crossed his face. "I think the stable hand was telling the truth."

My eyes grew wide. "How? How do you come to that conclusion?"

"It was something that Soutter said early on. He mentioned that he leant the pitchfork against the water barrel."

Judd piped up. "That's a normal thing to do."

"Is it though?" Holmes swept a hand along the wall before us. "The sides of this stall have hooks attached at regular intervals. They are used, as we can see, to hang ropes, bridles, reins, etc. I would think that most workers would use them to lean their implements against, to hold them out of the way."

"Fair enough, but sometimes …"

"Yes, sometimes, expediency outweighs logic. Soutter leaned that pitchfork against the water barrel." Pointing to a spot on the barrel, he added, "right here in fact. When the poor unfortunate archaeologist slipped after his attack on the stablehand, he struck his head against one of these hooks, he then turned and collapsed against the water barrel. Normally, that would just be uncomfortable, and he'd have hurt his chest, but with the pitchfork leaning against it, he drove the tines of the fork deep into his chest." Moving around the barrel, he pointed. "There are blood spatters here, and more running down the sides." Pointing at what I now saw as a slight dent or abrasion on the topmost band of the barrel, he said, "There's a slight bend in the metal, indicating that something of great weight was forced against it." He moved around once more and pointed at the shaft of the fork. There's a fresh cut in the handle, probably from where it was forced against the band of metal. And here." He moved and hunkered down, clearing away some loose straw and showing a small knot hole in the wooden board. The edge was slightly scuffed, showing clean wood rather than the rest of the hole surrounds that were caked in dirt and muck. A small scuff mark led away from the knot towards the barrel. "It appears that the end of the handle scraped along the floor before it jammed into this knothole and stuck fast."

Standing again, he picked up the pitchfork, and gently placed the end of the handle into the knothole, before leaning it down onto the barrel. Everything fit like a glove. The scored cut in the handle sat directly on the dent in the metal band. The deadly tines pointing upwards, ready to receive their next unfortunate victim.

"My word," said Judd, "That's incredible."

"As you can see, I think Soutter was telling the truth. The poor Doctor Hollian died from a horrible series of accidents. Partly caused by Soutter propping his pitchfork against the barrel, but mostly from Hollian's own actions in attempting to strike at your stablehand."

"So, he's innocent?" Judd asked.

"Of murder, yes, I think so. I would present my findings and the evidence to the magistrate, but it would serve to have Petteway visit once more and see for himself."

"But you think there's more," I said.

"Oh, yes, there's the matter of moving and attempting to dispose of the corpse."

"He won't swing for that, will he?" asked Judd.

"I doubt it, but the law doesn't look favourably on such acts. He may serve a few years if the magistrate feels he should."

"Oh, the poor blighter. He was simply out of his mind in fear," I said.

"Seeing him at the pub, I can truly believe he was. He certainly wasn't rational or he would have come back to clean up this scene and erase all trace of the accident and subsequent crime."

"He's a good man. A damned good worker. Can you put in a good word for him?" asked Judd.

"I will present the facts as I see them. Again, it comes down to how the magistrate sees it as well."

***

"Six months. I still feel that was a little harsh," I said, offering Holmes a snifter of brandy. A small fire burned in the grate and threw an orange light across the parlour. We had only just returned from the trial in Amesbury and finished a solid meal prepared by our wonderful landlady.

"Yes," said Holmes, sipping his brandy before placing it on the table beside him. "Still, it could have been much worse. The magistrate did seem intent on a conviction. He mentioned that if I hadn't presented such a compelling case that he would have called for at least a manslaughter charge to be brought against Soutter. That would see him in prison for up to twenty-five years. As it was, the charge of interfering with a corpse was all he could bring."

"True. I still feel for the fellow. He wasn't in his right mind. I tried to give the magistrate that indication. Even after I went back to the lock-up and talked with Soutter, he still wasn't quite right. Not sure he'll ever be. A damn strange occurrence, and one that will haunt the rest of his days."

"Quite, so. A sad state of affairs, and mostly from no fault of his own."

"Just a simple accident."

"Many a person's life has been crushed by such."

Nodding, I took a drink, welcoming the warmth of the liquor as it spread through my midriff. "What of the Antrobus family?"

"Sir Edmund seemed almost gleeful at the result. To him, it meant the object of his daughter's affection was out of the way for a good period of time. I doubt if Soutter would be returning to the estate once his sentence was served."

"Again, poor fellow."

"The young Louisa will recover. Her heart will mend in time, or her father will arrange another suitor to distract her."

"That is the way of that part of society. True love is never the goal."

"Yes. I'm so glad it doesn't affect us in any way."

"Speak for yourself. I'm still young, and if the right woman comes along I would be more than happy to pursue her and see how things play out."

I noticed a twinkle in Holmes's eye as he smiled. "And good for you, my friend. I wish you all the best on your hunt."

The Adventure of the Flustered Theologian

"Hello, can I help you?" I said to the slightly dishevelled man standing just outside the entrance of 221B Baker Street. I had been cooped up all morning, writing and revising some notes on several of my patients, and simply wished to take in the early afternoon on that sunny, but chilly May day. Opting for a stroll, I decided to head outside. As I opened the door, I startled the man before me as he was reaching for the door knocker.

He simply gaped for a moment, allowing me to study him. He was well-dressed in a dark grey morning suit, with a white shirt and matching tie. Over this, he wore a thicker woollen coat with the emblem of the University College of London. Even from where I stood, I could feel the slight chill in the air, but it wasn't enough to offset the impact of the heavy coat and the man's excess activity. Beads of sweat were evident across his wide forehead and receding hairline, indicating a hurriedness about his demeanour. One, I could only presume, that had brought him to our door.

"Doctor Watson," he finally stammered out. "Do you not recognise me?" Pausing, he looked at his hands for a moment. They trembled slightly as if revealing some inner turmoil that distressed him so.

Staring into that reddened face as the beads of sweat broke ranks and ran in rivulets down his face, I searched my memories and my eyes widened as his identity finally dawned on me. "Professor Rozee?" The unannounced man was none other than Wendell Rozee, professor of theological studies at University College, hence the emblem upon his coat. "My word, what has brought you to me in this state?"

"I am so sorry to intrude on you like this, I was hoping that I could infringe upon Mr. Holmes's time and explain a sorry situation that I find myself in."

“Certainly, old man, come in and take off that coat. You look positively distressed.” As I ushered Rozee inside, Mrs. Hudson appeared in her doorway.

“Is everything all right, Doctor?”

Turning to my housekeeper, I said, “Sorry to disturb you, Mrs. Hudson, this is Professor Rozee, come to see Holmes. If you have time, would you be so kind as to bring coffee upstairs? The good professor seems to have overexerted himself in an attempt to reach us.”

“Certainly Doctor. I’ll be up in a jiff.”

As Mrs. Hudson vanished inside, I ushered Professor Rozee up the flight of steps to the rooms I shared with my erstwhile colleague, and the object of Rozee’s visit, Sherlock Holmes. Halfway up the stairs, Rozee stopped, pricking an ear up at the melody floating down towards us.

“Mendelssohn, if I’m not mistaken,” he said.

I listened for a moment and caught the snatches of music. Nodding, I said, “Yes. From the *Leider ohne Worte*, I believe. Holmes must be in a good mood. He transposed the piano to violin and has become quite accomplished at the piece.”

“I agree. It is quite elegant.”

Not wishing to break too quickly into Holmes’s humour, I quietly opened the door to find him standing before the windows, bowing away happily. Without stopping, he called over his shoulder. “Didn’t get very far on your walk, Watson. And you’ve brought someone with you. A guest? Or perhaps a potential client?”

Without missing a beat, he continued to play, until the piece reached its natural conclusion before moving into the next opus. Stopping, he gently placed the violin on its stand and turned to face us. Moving across he stopped a mere yard away and studied the professor.

“Ah,” he said, after a moment, “University College. I can see by the emblem on your coat. A lecturer, doctor, or possibly professor. Medicine, or maybe even theology. You have an urgent need to see me, so this wasn’t a social visit.”

The professor stood with his eyes wide, and his mouth hanging open. “Yes. But, how? I?”

Holmes moved in and picked up the man’s hand and shook it. “Quite elementary. You present as someone unused to walking the streets, hence your thick coat on this somewhat chilly, but sunny day. Your suit is from Elias Moses and Son, I can tell by the cut and stitching. They’ve grown quite a lot of late and are specialising in a single style of suit offered at a reasonable price. Their customers are not the higher payers like lawyers and doctors but aimed at the middle tier of the professional demographic. Teachers, accountants, and the like. Of late, the University College has forged a deal with Moses to outfit their staff. You have a slight bulge under your shirt, which hides a large piece of jewellery of some sort. From the shape, I concluded it is possibly a crucifix, hence the nod to theology. I thought medicine, only because of your familiarity with Watson here. I heard your conversation on the stairs. As to your haste, you are red in the face, with sweat, so have toiled to arrive here. Plus, your shoes have suffered several scuffs, meaning you weren’t paying a lot of attention to your feet as you hurried along.”

“Remarkable.” I grabbed at Rozee’s elbow and moved him to the settee. Anybody that had undergone one of Holmes’s assessments, generally needed to recover afterwards.

“Let me introduce, Professor Wendell Rozee, Holmes. And yes, you have outdone yourself. I met the professor at a medical seminar at University College last year. He was there by invitation, having been a medical specialist earlier in his career.” I turned to confirm that fact and received a curt nod from Rozee. “But, of the last few years has taught theology.”

It was at that point that Mrs. Hudson entered the room with a tray holding a coffee pot and three cups. Placing them on the small table, she withdrew and returned with another small tray holding several biscuits and petit fours.

“Thank you, Mrs. Hudson, you’ve outdone yourself as always.”

“Doctor,” was the only reply before our landlady withdrew downstairs.

I played mother and doled out the coffee, before sitting back with my cup to indicate to Holmes that the floor was his. He didn't disappoint.

"Now, Professor, as I have already mentioned, this visit was not a social one. What is it that I can do for you?"

Rozee sipped from his coffee, which seemed to stir his attention back to the subject at hand. "It's about one of my students. He's gone missing, and I'm very worried about him."

"What is the name of this student?"

"Lionel Turnquist."

My eyes grew wide, and I noticed Holmes even allowed his stoic demeanour to slip for a moment. The name was familiar to us both, or at least the surname was.

"Turnquist?" asked Holmes. "Not the son of Lord Lindsay Turnquist?"

"Yes. The one and the same."

"Good Lord," I expelled, failing to stop myself.

The professor did not fail to notice that we were both acquainted with that name. "I assume that you are aware of Lord Lindsay's fate, then?"

It was hard not to have become conversant with the poor man and his wife's demise. The news had been writ large across the broadsheets for several days. Lord Lindsay Turnquist was one of the owners and managers of Fortescue Prospecting and Mining. They specialised in coal and copper mines in the north of England and were reputed to be one of the largest and most profitable mining companies in Great Britain. Over the last couple of years, they had expanded their operations onto the Continent, and it was there on a tour of Eastern Europe, supposedly in search of new claims and areas to mine, that the Lord and his Lady met their fate.

"That was a horrible accident," I said.

"Yes. It was barely a month ago, in early April that they boarded the steamer Mariupol on a trip through the Sea of Azov. My understanding is that they were heading for Volgograd and would be docking at Rostov-on-Don in western Russia to continue by train, but they never made it."

Holmes finished the tale. “The Mariupol sank while in deep waters. If I remember correctly, there was only one survivor.”

“Yes, not much is known about them. The news that came to the University didn’t identify them. As far as we know it certainly wasn’t Lord or Lady Turnquist.”

“How is the boy taking it?”

“He’s always been a sullen, studious fellow. This has hit him hard, I feel. His demeanour has been even more withdrawn, his interactions full of a morose attitude.”

“You mentioned that he has disappeared.”

“Yes. It’s the middle of our busiest period of study, but he hasn’t shown up to lessons for the last two days. Nobody has seen him since last weekend, it seems.”

“Could he be simply seeking solitude to bereave?”

“Possibly, but it’s been a month since his parents perished. He only returned to school a fortnight ago and I have been helping him catch up on his studies. As I have said he was sullen and brooding, but the impression was that his parents’ passing was not the main reason.”

“What do you think was?”

“As the eldest son, he has had more responsibility thrown upon his shoulders than many a full-grown man could cope with. Suddenly, he has an estate to manage, and a major corporation to run, and he must take his seat in the House of Lords. The boy has only just turned nineteen, I’m more than afraid that it is all too much for him.”

“There was a sibling, if I recall correctly, couldn’t he take up some of those duties?”

Rozee’s disgust at the mention of the Turnquist sibling was all too obvious. “Hmff,” he muttered, “Jasper Turnquist. That wastrel isn’t worth anyone’s time, or money. My true hope was that Lionel would simply turf the layabout to the gutter. It would take away more of the pressure on his young head.”

I noticed Holmes move forward, his chin resting on his steepled fingers as he stared into the professor’s face. I’d seen this posture before and knew he was sizing up the man’s concern. “Professor, one last question, and please tell me with all honesty, where do you think Lionel, or should I say, Lord Lionel, has disappeared to?

The professor dropped his head for a moment, before wiping his brow with the back of his hand. When he looked once more into Holmes's face, there was nothing but an almost fatherly concern on his face. "I truly do not know, but I do know Lionel. I've known him for many years, even prior to coming to University College. In fact, it was through my intercession that he rejected his father's wishes to attend more business-oriented studies, and to take up his passion for theology. He's a good boy. Dedicated, studious, thoughtful, and kind. Everything that would make him a great Lord of the House and a benevolent manager of any size business." He took a deep breath before finishing, "I don't think he's gone off on some soul-seeking adventure; I truly believe there has been interference of some sort. My only hope is that he has come to no harm and is safe."

Holmes remained silent for quite some time, putting the professor, and indeed me, on edge a little. Finally, he drew his head back from his steepled hands. "You certainly have your convictions over this matter – that I cannot dispute. I haven't heard anything from you though, which makes me believe that Lord Lionel has done nothing more than gone off to seek solace in his own mind."

I started to interject, as I believed that there was more to this than met the eye, but was stopped when Holmes held up one of his long slender fingers to silence me.

"But I have recently received word that somebody broke into the offices of Fortescue late last night." A slight smile crossed his lips. "Your tale of the disappearance of the Fortescue heir and that of the break-in occurring so close together piques my interest somewhat. I was mulling over the facts as you returned, Watson. I had hoped for longer, to let the music clear my head and set me to thought, but your return has proven just as invigorating." Picking up his cup, he drained the last of the coffee and refreshed it from the pot. "For now, I think it best if you give me a little more background about Lord Lionel's disposition, and then we'll press on with our investigations."

***

"Shouldn't we be investigating the break-in first?" I asked, a little astounded that Holmes chose to journey to the University College dormitory where Lionel Turnquist roomed.

"When I said that I had just received word, I meant that one of my informants had dropped a note into 221B earlier this morning. My appearance at the office may prove to be a little premature, as the note suggested that my informant had overheard two of the more well-to-do members of the staff speaking. Unless they engage with the constabulary, there is not a lot I can do without putting a dent in my network. I have sent word to have more of the management staff surveilled, so hopefully, we will gain more insights as the day wears on."

He paused, just as the hansom pulled up outside of the main building of the college. "As to our other matter, it seems we are here."

We quickly strolled the path running between the beautifully manicured lawns and entered the main building. Professor Rozee had gone on ahead and met us in the main foyer. He looked slightly less ruffled and had even sloughed off his coat, in favour of a teacher's robe.

"Ah, wonderful, I'm afraid I have class soon, but I can lead you to the western dormitory." Bringing his hand from an inside pocket, he brandished a dull brass key. "Even managed to convince the caretaker to lend me his access key. It opens every dormitory room."

"Useful," said Holmes. I'm glad we hadn't been left in need of Holmes's lock picks. It would have looked a little odd if we'd been caught breaking into a student's room.

Following Rozee through the halls, I was delighted to see that the college building was spotless and showed no signs of age. Having only been established in the early seventies, it wasn't overly surprising, but also with so many young men and the odd woman striding its halls, I had expected some level of decline.

We stopped outside one of the many identical dormitory rooms, and the professor inserted the key. The unlocked door swung open, revealing a stunned young man sitting at a desk by the window. "Oh, dreadfully sorry, Edison, I had expected you to be in class."

The shocked man blinked twice, before finally replying. "Um, professor, I…I had a free period. I was trying to catch up on my mathematics." His brow creased as a hint of anger grew behind his previously stunned expression. "Hang on, what are you doing breaking into my room?"

"Again, sorry, Edison. I've brought Mr. Sherlock Holmes and Dr. Watson here to investigate Lionel's disappearance. Gentlemen, this is Edison Harvelle – Lionel's roommate and long-time friend."

At the mention of Lord Turnquist's name, the young man's demeanour changed. His eyes grew wide, and he stood and turned towards the other side of the room. "You've found him?"

"No, sorry." Rozee stepped into the room and placed a hand on the young student's shoulder. He was obviously distraught at his roommate's disappearance.

"I do hope nothing has happened to him. These last few weeks have been a desperate time for him."

"What has his disposition been like?" asked Holmes.

Edison turned towards Holmes, a forlorn look on his face, and I swear I could see tears forming. My only thought was that these two men were somewhat close, as only good friends can be.

"Silent. Solemn. Morose even. His parents died, you know, how should he feel?"

"That is only fair, plus I can only assume that the extra burden of taking over the family business must have weighed heavily on him as well."

Shaking his head, Edison added, "He didn't want to do it. Never once mentioned assuming his father's place. He had always hoped his brother would do it, but even I could see that was never going to happen."

"You know his brother?"

Anger bloomed on Edison's face. "Oh, yes, that detestable lazy pig of a man. I've known him for as long as I've known Lionel. He was always his mother's favourite. Spoilt to the point of rotting. While Lionel spent his days bettering himself with education, sport, and other pursuits, Jasper did nothing except serve himself."

The professor spoke up. "I shouldn't say this, but I understand that Marjory always wanted Jasper to take over the company. Lindsay wouldn't have it. Though that is only conjecture."

"Did you know the parents well, Edison?" I asked.

Shaking his head, the boy replied, “Not socially, only as the parents of my friend. They were always kind, but sort of stand-offish. Lionel was always a little strange around them. Formal. Always referred to his father as Sir, never Father or Dad. I think it was their way.”

“But you don’t like Jasper?” Holmes asked.

Again, that bloom of anger. “No. Such an oaf. I can only hope that Lionel turfs him out of the family house. He should learn to walk on his own two feet.”

Looking at Holmes’s face, I could tell he wasn’t receiving any facts, only impressions. He was never one for gossip unless it contained information he could use. He turned away from the young student and looked at Lionel’s side of the room, studying the contents of his bedside table. “I can only assume that young Lionel’s fascination with theology extended from a religious upbringing.” He pointed at the ornate wooden cross, with silver Jesus affixed to the wall above the bed, before pointing at the well-thumbed copy of the bible sitting beside the bed.

“Oh, the Turnquists were far from religious. Lindsay wouldn't have a bar of anything like that,” said Rozee. “Lionel's interest came from his studies.”

“Yes,” added Edison, “I’m not the slightest bit religious myself, and I’ve never understood how Lionel became so enthralled with Christianity.”

“Some say that one turns to religion to fill the void left by other wants in their lives,” said Holmes, almost absentmindedly as he ran a finger across the embossed cover of the Bible. The professor and his student looked a little confused at the statement. I decided that Holmes was possibly relating to the formality of Lionel’s interactions with his parents.

Edison stood, breaking the pause in the conversation and stepped up next to Holmes. “Is that Lionel’s bible?” He reached down and picked up the small leather-bound book, flipping it open to the first page which contained a dedication to Lionel from someone called Father Brown. “It’s his all right. Strange, he reads from it every night and rarely ventures anywhere without it.”

"Do you know this, Father Brown?" Holmes asked, pointing to the dedication.

The young student shrugged. "No. He's not from the college. Possibly from the local parish, perhaps." As he placed the book back on the nightstand, a small slip of paper slid from between the pages and floated to the floor. Edison bent and collected the page, opening it as he did. "Well, this is strange."

From my position, I could see a line of numbers scrawled on the paper. Holmes took the paper from Edison, an eyebrow cocked as he read the numbers several times. "I can speculate as to their meaning, but without further evidence, I'm afraid only the owner would understand these." He passed the page back to the young man, who folded and inserted it back into the book.

Stepping away, Holmes moved to a cupboard at the foot of the bed. "Is this Lionel's?" When Edison nodded, he opened the door, revealing it almost overflowing with clothes.

"For all his good traits, he wasn't the most fastidious when it came to keeping his wardrobe tidy."

"Would you know if anything is missing?"

"Couldn't say, but there doesn't seem to be any fewer items than normal."

"Why does the lad's wardrobe interest you, Holmes?" I piped up, wondering at the relevance.

"Well Watson, I'm trying to deduce whether our young Lionel went on a pre-planned trip with some forethought, or simply vanished. It would seem that he hasn't packed any clothing for a trip, and, as Edison here said, he rarely leaves without his Bible."

"Ah," the young student held up a hand, with a single finger extended, "I should point out that Lionel will often travel to the family home with only the clothes on his back. He has everything he needs there, including another copy of the Good Book. That said, his coat is missing from the rack." Raising a hand, he pointed to his coat hanging on the back of the door.

Diverting the conversation back to the Turnquist estate, Holmes asked, "Where is Lionel's family home exactly? It must be reasonably close."

"Yes. Hertfordshire. Just north of Barnet."

"Do you have any idea whether he had planned a trip home?"

"Of late, he has been disturbed by his brother's behaviour. Only fair, as I said, that man is a bit of a mess, and with their parents' death has become even more detached from reality. Lionel may have simply gone off to see him."

"Without telling you though?"

"That has been the strange part of this. I've never known him not to tell me, or at least one of the professors, that he would be gone for more than a day. I presumed that's why Professor Rozee brought you here."

"When was the last time you saw or spoke to Lionel?"

"Sunday morning. I awoke just as Lionel was leaving for, what I can only presume was the early service in the chapel. I called out to him but didn't get a reply. He was still out when I left a couple of hours later for an early luncheon date. I can give you the names of my rendezvous partners if you need them."

With a wave of a hand, Holmes said, "Shouldn't be necessary, but thank you."

"When I returned later that afternoon, the room was empty. I'll admit that I had imbibed a little too much and had a nap. I awoke in the early evening, ready for supper, the room was still empty, but I thought nothing of it. We don't spend a lot of time in here, especially on the weekend."

"When did you first grow concerned?"

"Monday morning. There was no sign of Lionel when I awoke. I checked back during my first break, but still no sign of him. That's when I went to see Professor Rozee, just to find out if there had been any word. It was more to do with whether I needed to pick up any assignments for Lionel."

"I hadn't heard anything either," said Rozee. "That concerned me enough to begin further investigations. The chaplain had last seen Lionel on Sunday morning. None of his teachers had seen or heard from him all day. There was nothing reported at the administration building. He had simply vanished from the confines of the college."

"It's Thursday now, no one has thought to send word to the Turnquist estate?"

"Oh, yes, I did that on Monday afternoon. I sent a telegram to the manor asking whether Lionel had visited in the last two days."

"Any reply?"

"Oh, yes, I received notification from Jasper on Tuesday morning." Reaching into his pocket, Professor Rozee retrieved a small slip of paper and handed it to Holmes. I spied over Holmes's shoulder the two-letter word on the return telegram, with the name of the younger Turnquist sibling beneath.

It simply said, "No."

"Well, that's a rather curt reply," I said.

***

"Lionel didn't attend service on Sunday morning or confession afterwards. I was slightly worried about his absence, but I presumed he had pressing business elsewhere, what with his parents' untimely death and all."

I could see that the priest's words had piqued Holmes's interest. "When was the last time you saw the boy, then?" he asked.

"Not since Wednesday last week. He came to me during the day. His head seemed to hang heavy. At the time, I supposed he was simply downcast from the weight of his choices and the duties thrust upon him. The company. The lordship."

"Was it?"

"Strangely no, it was his brother. He asked to speak in private, so we withdrew here." We sat in Father Lunney's private chambers at the rear of the college chapel. "I made tea, but he hardly touched it. He confessed to confusion over his brother's fate, or rather what part he should play in his brother's future."

"In what way?"

"Well, Jasper is well-known as an indolent, layabout, having hung on to his mother's apron strings for the best part of his life. The boy has no means outside of the family upon which to draw his future. Legally, Lionel has no reason to keep him to the manner to which he is accustomed. But, as the Good Book says, blood is thicker than water."

"Did the brothers get on?" I asked.

The old priest turned at my voice and shook his head, a slight look of sadness upon his face. "No. No, they didn't. I don't think they have ever been that affectionate towards each other. Well," he shrugged, "from what I know in my conversations with Lionel. I did have the pleasure of an invite to dinner at the estate on one occasion." A slight shudder escaped from him. "It was a very formal, and chilling affair. Lord and Lady Turnquist were amiable, but I could tell they had been put out by Lionel's insistence on inviting me there. And the younger lad, Jasper, was simply a horror. He acted like a spoilt teenager, even though he was eighteen, only a year younger than Lionel. He complained about the food. He complained about being at the table. He had no compunction in complaining about me to my face. A most repellent boy, for I won't call him a man."

"Interesting," said Holmes. "You mentioned that Lionel had questions about what actions to take with this Jasper."

Nodding, the priest said, "Yes. To cut him off altogether, or to set him up in his own home and simply give him an allowance. Without the parents there, I don't believe Lionel would want Jasper anywhere near him, such is their relationship."

"Intriguing. I think I need to meet with this Jasper fellow."

***

Flagging down a modestly maintained brougham on Euston Road, we headed north to Barnet along Holloway Road, and then onto the Great North Road. Within half an hour we had left the more closely packed buildings of central and outer London and found the countryside to be dotted with small, but growing villages. Barnet itself presented as a delightful little village, with a stately old stone church as its centrepiece.

As we turned into the long driveway that led to the Turnquist estate, a beautifully presented black growler, with matching jet-black stallions, passed by at high speed. Exiting the estate, the driver pulled at the reins forcing the carriage to the left and cracked his whip, exciting the animals and eliciting huffs and neighs as they accelerated away.

Well, someone's in a hurry.

"Well, someone's in a hurry," I remarked, receiving a nod from Rozee and nothing from Holmes, who continued to stare after the diminishing carriage.

Asking our driver to wait for our return, the three of us alighted and headed towards the large ornate doors of the manor house. Professor Rozee did the honours of knocking, in the hopes that at least his familiarity with the family might diminish any negative response from Jasper Turnquist. The door was opened by an ancient butler who bore the demeanour of someone bearing the weight of the world upon his shoulders.

"Ah, Jenkins, wonderful," said Rozee, "I do hope you remember me, Professor Wendell Rozee, from University College."

The old man blinked several times at the teacher, as the wheels of confusion turned within his head, and finally nodded. "Yes. Yes. You, I know." Turning his gaze on Holmes and me, his head shook slightly, and one long gnarled finger was pointed at both of us. "You, I do not know."

"Ah, this is Mr. Sherlock Holmes and Dr. John Watson. We wish to speak with Lord Lionel."

At the mention of the older Turnquist brother's name, the old butler's eyes grew wide and full of fear. His head turned to glance over his shoulder, before turning back towards us. "Um…Um, the young Lord is not here. Hasn't been here for quite a while. I haven't seen him, honest, I haven't." Out of the corner of my eye, I noticed Holmes smile slightly before resuming a stoic non-expression.

"Is young Jasper home then? I'm here on college business and need to find young Lionel. He may have had word from his brother."

Realising that he could attend to this, the butler resumed a statelier manner. "Um…yes, he's in the downstairs parlour. Please come in." Stepping back, he allowed us entry.

Sloughing off our overcoats, we hung them on hooks in the nearby anteroom. As I hung up my coat, I bumped the one next to it revealing a flash of colour on the right breast. Pulling the coat away from the wall I made out the red, black and blue insignia of the University College. Showing it to Holmes, I said, "Strange that young Lionel would keep a spare college coat here."

Rozee chimed in, "A spare? That's rather unheard of. Students receive a supply of uniforms at the beginning of the year. Only one coat is ever issued. Most students can't stand to wear them off campus, let alone store a spare at home for some reason."

"Students tend to have a more reactionary mindset and reject the doctrines and policies of their schools once away from the campus, so yes, if I were to conjecture, I would say that the coat has been left here. We didn't see a twin at the dormitory, which means that Lord Lionel is either still wearing it, or this is his only college coat."

Turning back towards Jenkins, I spied his wide-eyed expression once more, before he snatched it away and resumed the appearance of a docile butler. I made a mental note to ask Holmes about it.

As Jenkins led us through the ornate corridors, Holmes stayed level and plied him with questions. "I can only assume that you were in the employ of the late Lord and Lady Turnquist."

"Yes. Such a sad state of affairs," the old butler replied, slowing to a crawl as he heaved a sigh at the mention of their name.

"Sorry to drag up such emotions. How has the rest of the house staff been affected?"

Suddenly, the butler's demeanour changed completely. "Not many left. Up and left, if they weren't fired on the spot. The new master isn't one for so many staff."

"You mean Lord Lionel?"

Stopping, the butler's face became confused. "Oh, no. The Lord has put his brother in charge of the house, or so the story goes from Master Jasper's mouth."

"Have you heard such from Lord Lionel himself?"

"Oh, no, but who are we to question the young master?"

"Indeed."

Jenkins started to walk at his slow shuffling pace, once more, muttering slightly under his breath. I thought I heard him grumble about his old bones, and what was to become of him. It was Holmes again, who broke through his hushed proclamations.

"We were passed by a black carriage as we arrived. Can you tell us who visited?"

"Oh, that was Mr. Vassiniotis. The old Lord's, and I suppose the new Lord's, business partner. Strange name. Strange fellow. Greek, I think."

"Was he after Lord Lionel as well?"

The old butler stopped again, a confused look crossing his face. "Oh, no. Why would he come here to look for Lord Lionel? He was here to visit with Master Jasper." With no more to add, Jenkins shuffled off towards a large set of double doors.

"Intriguing," muttered Holmes.

"Why would this Vassiniotis fellow be visiting with Master Jasper?" asked Rozee.

Holmes simply held up a finger to silence the professor. The coincidence had triggered a thought pattern in his mind, I'd seen this attitude before.

We all went silent, as Jenkins knocked on the doors, opening one and speaking to someone on the other side. I could make out Jasper's name, and then our names. After a moment, the butler pushed the door open, turned and spoke. "The Master will see you but has professed a wish for you to dally no longer than a few minutes. He is a very busy man."

Staring at the old butler's face, I was hoping to see a suppressed smile or laugh on his face, but all I found was a look of resignation. Once we moved inside the room, I could see why.

Professor Rozee's description of Jasper Turnquist's attitude was not enough to prepare me for the reality of the young man. He was a large, bloated specimen of a man. Barely in his late teens, his girth was impressive for one so young. His skin suffered from post-adolescence, peppered with acne and pimples. The evidence of his diet made it no surprise to my doctor's mind.

He lay on a settee, propped up on several cushions, and was encircled by several small tables that held a large selection of plates covered in the remains of piles of sweet treats. His mouth was surrounded by the remains of several of the cakes, and the front of his shirt was sprinkled with crumbs.

Popping one more cake into his mouth, Jasper chewed whilst eyeing each of us in turn. His small piggy eyes darted from face to face. Finally, he spoke, letting out a small shower of cake fragments. I grimaced within, hoping my disgust did not show on my face.

"And how may I help you, gentlemen? As it's you, Professor, I assume you've come in concern for Lionel? How is my brother?"

"You haven't heard from him then?"

"Why would I? He has his studies at the university; I have a house to run."

"He's disappeared. I've asked Mr. Holmes and Dr. Watson here to assist in finding him. Our first port of call was to ask you whether you had seen him of late."

Shaking his head, Jasper replied with a negative, reaching out for another cake and popping it in his mouth.

Holmes took over the conversation, adding a robust tenure to his voice. "That's a strange state of affairs. Your brother left without packing any clothes, which made his family home the most probable destination."

Through another mouthful of cake, Jasper replied, "What can I say, he hasn't been here."

"Then why is his college coat hanging in the boot room?"

"Don't know. Has he got two of the things?"

"Unlikely, he either left it here by mistake on his last visit or …" Holmes left the sentence hanging, prompting a reply from Jasper, whose expression changed slightly as suspicion grew within him.

Shrugging, he replied, "He's not here. Hasn't been for days. I'm not my brother's keeper, you know." A smile grew at that comment, as his eyes darted towards the professor. I glanced Rozee's way and saw his eyes narrow at the biblical reference.

"No. That has always been Lionel's job," he added a hint of vitriol in his normally calm voice.

"And Vassiniotis, what business did you have with him?"

"Sylvester? He was looking for Lionel as well. I must say, my brother has attracted a lot of attention of late."

"You know Mr. Vassiniotis closely enough to be on first-name terms then?"

Jasper hesitated for a moment, before recovering his thoughts. "Ah, I've known him for a while. Mostly through my father's business dealings. I always called him Uncle Sylvester, but that seems a little tawdry now that I'm an adult."

"Indeed. Did Mr. Vassiniotis mention the break-in at the Fortescue company headquarters?" Holmes went quiet, inducing a heightened level of silence upon the room, punctuated only by the sounds of Jasper munching on more cakes. I noticed a slight widening of Jasper's eyes at the break-in comment, but he quickly regained his composure and continued eating.

Finally, the younger Turnquist brother spoke. "Is there anything else, gentlemen? I am a very busy man."

Withholding a chuckle at the young layabout's confidence in himself, I joined Holmes, when he turned and moved from the room.

Rozee said one final word to Jasper. "If you see Lionel then, have him contact me in the first instance. He is now the head of your family, regardless of your role."

"Will do. Now run along," was the dismissive reply.

As Jenkins led us back to the foyer, Holmes asked whether we could view the study. The old butler hesitated. "I don't think that would be appropriate."

"It may help us determine Lord Lionel's whereabouts. I can assure you we will be discreet. You may have heard mention of a break-in at the company headquarters. If someone were looking for an item there, but didn't find it, they may turn their attention to this house. Your security may be threatened."

"Nothing like that has ever happened here before." Nodding, Jenkins added, "All right then." He turned down another corridor and brought us to a large, padded leather door. Turning the latch, he opened the door and let us enter. "Excuse the mess, the maid left us not long after the mistress's passing. I've tried to keep up with the rest of the house, but not many have been in here since."

The mess that Jenkins referred to was simply the accumulation of dust on the desk and bookshelves that lined the walls. The shelves held all manner of files, books, and rolled maps. Scanning the spines, it became evident that most of the books were geographical in nature, with others relating to mineralogy. They were all connected to Lord Lindsay's business and hinted at how his fortune had grown through his own sheer efforts.

"An impressive collection. One, the geology and geography departments at the college would be very interested in possessing," said the professor.

"I'm sure Lionel may be amenable to that position; I can't imagine his interests lay in this arena."

Ignoring the books, Holmes headed straight to the desk. It had barely been touched in the last couple of months, assumedly since Lord Lindsay was last in attendance. Stepping closer, I spied the thin layer of dust across the surface but was surprised by several small lines drawn across the surface, possibly by fingers.

"Jenkins," I asked the butler, "who has been in here since the poor unfortunate Lord Lindsay departed for Europe?"

"The young master, Lionel, came in not long after we received the awful news, but I think it was more to lament his father's passing."

Nodding, I turned back to see what Holmes thought. "Oh, and Mr. Vassiniotis. He stopped in just after he met with Master Jasper." Even Holmes paused and looked towards the butler.

"That's a fairly vital piece of information that may prove fruitful," he said, "Do you know what this Vassiniotis was after?"

"No. He's been in here before when Lord Lindsay was in attendance, so I didn't think much of it."

A barely concealed flash of annoyance came to Holmes's face; he brushed it aside and stared back at the desk. It was as he reached for a small pad of paper, that I noticed the change in the depth of the dust layer. "That's been moved," I said.

"Yes, as well as those documents. They've been rifled through. Also, the drawers have been opened. The handles are free of dust. Did you notice the type of paper?" Holmes pointed at the pad. It seemed familiar, and then a flash of memory came to mind.

"Is it the same type as we found in Lionel's bible?"

"I believe so." Reaching for a pencil from the collection at the top of the desk, Holmes preceded to shade in the top page of the pad. Almost immediately a negative image of the line of numbers we'd seen in London appeared. "Ah, ha!"

"My word, Holmes, it's those numbers again. What does that mean?"

"I can only assume that this was the last thing that Lord Lindsay wrote on this pad of paper. Something that he then gave to his son, who kept it in the one place he knew would be closest to him at all times."

"Do you know what they are yet?"

"I can only suspect." Tearing off the page, he scanned the rest of the room, before nodding to himself and striding across to a far bookcase. Running his hands along the edge of the shelves, I noticed a small grin appear on his face, followed by a tiny *click*. A portion of the bookshelf opened outward, revealing that it was indeed a false panel, covered in the cut-down portions of several books, all of the same height. Behind the panel was a small wall safe.

"Quite clever that, Holmes."

My colleague held up the page near the dial and spun it several times, lining up the numbers with those on the paper. Another significant *click* rang out. Holmes turned the handle and dragged the heavy, metal door open. Inside were several piles of papers. He removed the piles and brought them to the desk.

"I don't think the master would be very pleased with all this," said Jenkins.

"I will be quite careful. I wish to examine these only to determine what knowledge Lord Lindsay needed to bestow upon his son before leaving for Europe."

The documents were mostly title deeds and other legal paraphernalia, with names of places in both Great Britain and Europe on them. "Ah, ha!" Holmes exclaimed, holding up a thick document bound in red ribbon, and a small, folded paper. Several words were written in Cyrillic on the outside of the bound paper.

"Is that Russian?" I asked.

"I can only assume, or some other Balkan language." Tapping the unfolded page, he added, "This makes more sense." It was a map with a large body of water to the bottom left. Several towns were indicated on the shores, each titled with Cyrillic letters. "My Russian is only fairly passable, but if I'm not mistaken that is the Sea of Azov."

Pointing to one of the towns and then another, Holmes said, "This would be Mariupol, and this is Rostov-on-Don."

Further inland, a large circle had been added in red ink, with the name of a nearby town translated to Shakhty. The Cyrillic word next to the circle, Шахты, appeared on the front of the document tied in ribbon. Another paper was a letter featuring the name of the Geological Society of Britain. From where I stood, I could only make out the large figure of 10 million in a sentence mentioning coal.

"What do you make of it, Holmes?"

"I can only really assume until we have this document translated if that is required, but given Lord Lindsay's business, and his recent trip to Europe, culminating in his, and his lady wife's, demise at this very location, it would appear that he was visiting a newly acquired mining site in Russia." Picking up the single sheet letter and reading, he added, “One that the Geological Society has estimated contains upwards of 10 million tons of coal. A very profitable site indeed.”

“Do you think this has any connection with his son’s disappearance?”

Tapping the documents before him, Holmes replied, “I think that all depends on who knew about this.”

“What do you mean?” asked Rozee.

“Jenkins mentioned that the Fortescue business partner had visited just before us. There is evidence that somebody has rifled through the drawers, and it would seem out of place for young Jasper to have done that himself, as his attitude seems to be one of indifference.” Folding the business contract and retying the string, Holmes added, “The biggest conundrum is whether this Vassiniotis knew about Lord Lindsay’s purchase and whether it was personal or part of the company’s business.”

Gathering up the documents and stepping back to the safe, he shut them inside, spinning the safe’s dial and ensuring it was locked. After shutting the false panel securely, Holmes moved to a nearby bookcase and began examining it.

“Should we not be off after this Vassiniotis fellow?” I asked.

“All in good time,” said Holmes, “There is more that we need to investigate.”

As I was about to ask another question, Jenkins shuffled in, a confused look on his face. “Pardon me, gentlemen, but I feel that I should ask you to leave.”

“Has Jasper requested this?” asked Rozee, with a tone that sounded quite aggressive.

Turning to the professor, the butler replied, “Well, no. He left. In quite a hurry. Without another word. Took the little buggy we keep for trips into town. I’ve never seen him so agitated and animated, for that matter. So, I’m a little confused. Without the master here, I probably should usher his visitors from the house, but part of me doesn't want to.”

“That’s quite all right, Jenkins, we have almost finished here. We’ll see ourselves out in due course.” Bending down and scribbling something on the small notepad, before slipping off the sheet, Holmes stepped towards the butler, took his arm, and started to lead him from the room. "If you give me a few minutes, I believe there is something you can help us with, and then we'll be gone."

"As you like, sir," said the ageing manservant before he left, followed by Holmes.

My colleague returned a few moments later, followed by the butler. He headed directly to the bookcase that had taken his attention before Jenkins's arrival. "Now, Jenkins," Holmes began, "You've been withholding some information from us, haven't you?"

The butler's eyes grew wide as he raised his head to stare at Holmes's back. "I…I was only following Master Jasper's commands, sir."

"Instead of the presumed wishes of your actual master, Lord Lionel?"

"I was confused. Master Jasper was put in charge of the house, therefore in charge of me."

"Yes, but Lionel pays the bills, doesn't he?" Holmes turned with a wry grin on his face. "This is the way into the cellar, is it not?"

It was my turn to be confused.

"What are you blabbering about, Holmes?" asked Rozee, just as perplexed as I.

Holding up a single finger, Holmes reached under one of the shelves, straining for a moment, before smiling confidently. "Ah, here it is." A resounding *click* echoed out from the bookcase, followed by a slight *scraping* as Holmes stepped back, drawing the hidden doorway with him. The bookcase hid a stairwell that descended into a stygian abyss beyond.

"How in blazes did you figure that one out?" I asked.

"Simple," came the reply. Pointing at the floor, he continued. "You'll notice the slightly curved scratches on the floor, plus there is a small, dried puddle of what I believe to be soup. I surmised that, like the safe panel, this bookcase was a hidden door. I only had to find the trigger." Glancing at Jenkins, he asked, "I can only assume that you spilt some soup as you opened the doorway one night."

"I…I simply forgot to clean it up. I have been so busy, and I am so tired."

"Why was he taking soup through this doorway?" Then it dawned on me. My face must have shown utter astonishment. "No. Lionel's not down there, is he?" I turned towards the old butler; he hung his head in shame.

He mumbled under his breath. "I'm too old to find another position. I didn't want to be sacked. I did all I could to make him comfortable."

***

Jenkins led the way, brandishing a three-armed candelabra. He carefully climbed down the stone steps leading into the darkened cellar. We later learnt that Lord Lindsay's study was once an anteroom for the kitchen staff, these steps leading down to a now disused root cellar.

At the bottom of the stairs, Jenkins lit several paraffin lamps that had been arranged, giving a yellow glow to the area. I gasped when I spied the soon-to-be-anointed member of the House of Lords, lying on a makeshift cot in one corner. He was unconscious, with his hands and feet bound to the frame of the bed. A small tray with a bowl of soup sat on the ground nearby, the soup untouched.

"What in the blazes has been going on here?" I cried out, more from astonishment than fear, as I ran to Lord Lionel's aid. A quick examination revealed that he was in relatively good health, possibly suffering from the chill in the cellar, and groggy from the administration of some form of sedative. Ether was my guess, a crude way to subdue a person but effective.

My eyes fell on the butler, who looked on the verge of tears. "They threatened me. Said if I didn't help, then I'd be cast out into the street, or worse."

"Who threatened you? Jasper?" asked Holmes.

Jenkins shook his bowed head. "No. The master doesn't have the bottle. It was that Vassiniotis scoundrel. I've never trusted him. In his private times, the old Lord never spoke of him politely. Always referred to him as a necessary evil. Ever since his Lordship's untimely death, the fellow has spent a lot of time at the house. Searching for something. I think it was when he found the safe that he began to bring Master Jasper into his plan. Nobody knows the combination."

“That’s when they decided to kidnap poor Lionel here?”

“Yes. I overheard them talking a few days back. The Greek fellow reckoned that Lord Lionel had the combination.”

“Why not just use a safecracker?” I asked.

Holmes added “I think that’s what they did at the company headquarters. As I’ve said there has been no police involvement and my source didn’t have much in the way of details, but if I were to surmise, Lord Lindsay would have had a similar set-up at his company’s premises. A personal safe that held documents, just like the one upstairs. It’s a very good safe, a Chatwood. Hard to crack without damaging the contents. I can only presume that Lord Lindsay chose a similar model for his office. Would take any good yeggman a few hours to crack it. That was probably their next avenue, but they would need to have Jenkins, and the cook, out of the picture for that time.”

Joining me at the bed, Holmes stared down at the unconscious man. “But first, it seems, Vassiniotis wanted to drag any information he could out of young Lord Lionel here. I can only assume they hadn’t managed it so far.”

“No, he was in a rage, to begin with,” said Jenkins, “Especially at his brother. I’ve never seen him so angry. That was two days ago when he first arrived back here. I could hear his cries from upstairs. I almost left to fetch the police, but those two thugs that Mister Vassiniotis brings with him stopped any chance of that.”

Holmes tapped his pocket in a reflex action. I realised he’d brought his revolver. He caught my eye, and I nodded. Experience meant I never left Baker Street without one of the last souvenirs from my time in the army.

“Watson, would you have anything that can speed up Lord Lionel’s re-awakening? I feel we should move him upstairs and out of these dank quarters as soon as possible.”

I realised that I had left my bag upstairs, and made a hasty exit, returning moments later with a small vial of smelling salts. The rank odour from the glass container had the young Lord, snorting and coughing within seconds. Holmes and Rozee released his bonds, and we soon had him sitting up and blinking away the deleterious effects of the ether.

He sat for a long moment; his head hung low as consciousness returned. Finally, he snapped his head up and shouted, "Jasper."

"He has gone off, presumably to contact his partner in crime."

Lionel glanced from face to face, a deep look of suspicion on his own, until he saw Rozee. "Professor? What the devil are you doing here?"

"I came to find you. Your disappearance was very out of character, and so I grew concerned." Indicating Holmes and me, he added, "I have brought Mr. Holmes and Dr. Watson, who have been key to finding you down here."

Lionel tried to stand, but his head still suffered from the anaesthesia and his legs gave way, dropping him back onto the cot. Holding his head, he mumbled, "I'll have the law on that rotter."

Taking that as a cue, Holmes asked, "Who drugged you, and brought you down here?"

"Sylvester Vassiniotis, my father's treacherous business partner. My father always warned me about the cad. I took his advice, but even that proved useless."

"What happened?"

"I received word on Sunday morning, from Jasper. He wanted to see me." Holding his head for a moment, he took a deep breath, supposedly collecting his thoughts. "It was chilly, I remember that. The telegram came while Edison was still asleep. I left straight away and caught a cab on the high street. Jasper was in Father's study. Strange for him, he hates the place. Then that scoundrel entered with his two ruffians. I became slightly concerned, but it was my house, why should I be afraid? Stupid that."

"What did Vassiniotis want?"

"He rambled on about some mine in Russia that my father had purchased. Said it should be half his. To be perfectly honest, I have no idea what the fool was talking about. All I know is that Father's trip to Europe was a holiday, mixed with scouting a couple of potential mine sites. Sylvester raged on about somewhere called Shakhty. I've never heard of the place. That's when he went crazy, ranting about my father's deception, and suddenly, his goons grabbed hold of me and dragged me towards the bookcase. Vassiniotis pulled open the hidden panel and pointed at the safe, screaming at me to open it. I said I had no idea how to open it, and I don't. Father gave me the combination just before he left, but it's in my Bible back at the college. I don't even know what's in that safe."

"It's where your father kept the deeds for his new mine, well your new mine, it seems. This Greek fellow was correct, though unless he can prove that company funds were used to purchase it, I don't think he has any legal right to it."

"Father did mention he had been setting up a sort of legacy for Jasper and me, but he never went into the details. I simply presumed he'd added something to his will or was going to bequeath us a significant amount when we came of age."

"From the papers that we found in the safe, the amounts will be significant."

Lionel shrugged. "My plans have never involved a lot of money. I only wish for a simple life, that's why I started to set up a fund for Jasper to take over the house." His face grew dark again. "With his betrayal, I may rethink that."

"I can only assume that they drugged you when you refused to help open the safe," said Holmes.

Lionel nodded. "Yes. The last thing I remember was a wet cloth over my face and the stink of chemicals."

"You've been unconscious for two days. I thought the worst," said Jenkins. "I'm so sorry Master Lionel. I didn't know what to do."

"It's all right, Jenkins. None of this is your fault. It's that vile blackguard and my stupid brother." He tried to rise once more. This time steadier on his feet. "I need to call the police. You said that Jasper isn't here? Has he gone after Vassiniotis? That won't do well if they find us here."

"No. We have some time to prepare, but I think it would be best if you were to remove yourself until fully recovered. Leave any physical business to Watson and me. Jenkins should stay with you as well." Turning to the ageing professor, he added, "And you too, sir." Rozee nodded with a look that stated he understood.

***

"What about calling for the police?" I asked.

"When I left with Jenkins, I took the opportunity to send our driver on a little task. If all goes well, they should be here in time."

With the others out of the way, we quickly prepared the cellar, placing a bolster under the thin blankets on the cot, and arranging the stained pillow and some others procured for the effect. They looked like a person resting on the bed in the dull light of a candle flame.

Leaving the cellar in complete darkness, we hurried up the stairs and closed the fake doorway. The only places to hide were behind the curtain, and directly behind the door as it swung inwards. Holmes chose the door, nestling up against the bookcase and drawing his revolver. I mimicked his action and nestled behind the curtain, holding them in such a way as to leave a small gap to peer through.

And there we stood, in silence, for the best part of half an hour, until the sound of crunching gravel filtered into the house as a heavy carriage made its way up the drive, followed by a smaller cart. I guessed it was Vassiniotis in his growler, and Jasper in the family's dogcart.

Within moments, four sets of feet tromped through the front door and down the long wooden corridor towards the back of the house where we hid. A deep voice barked orders and questions, with another more insipid voice answering.

Then I saw them. Vassiniotis wasn't the commanding presence, I had expected. He was a rather short, squat figure, with a shock of black hair, and a dark complexion enhanced by the dour look on his face. He stormed into the study, with Lord Lionel's submissive brother behind him. On their tail, followed two powerfully built men. The bodyguards. Both had the swarthy look of Greek extraction, so probably they had followed Vassiniotis from his homeland.

The businessman headed straight for the desk and lit the candelabra we had left for such a purpose, before heading to the bookcase. He was well-acquainted with the mechanism and had it swinging open within seconds.

Turning to his henchmen, he said, "Stay up here in case that bumbling butler interrupts us." They nodded and held their position.

As Vassiniotis and Jasper descended into the bowels of the house, I noticed the study door swing silently aside and saw Holmes bring his revolver out and nod towards me. I followed his lead and stepped quietly from my hiding spot.

We trod gently across the floor until we each stood behind one of the guards. As one, our left hands clamped on their mouths, with the revolvers pointed at their temples. "Hello, gentlemen. We are slowly going to exit this room, all right?" Holmes said. The thugs trembled slightly, in a mix of fear and agitation, but nodded meekly.

Pushing them before us, we stepped from the room and found the closet chosen for this purpose. To ensure they were unable to interact, one by one, we forced their hands down into their pants and tightened their belts as a precaution. When they were safely locked in the closet, Holmes shouted to the professor, who came downstairs and sat in a chair, we had placed before it, with a loaded rifle procured from the old gamekeeper's shed outside.

Speaking softly, but loudly enough for the two thugs to hear, he said, "I'll keep the gun trained on them. Any noise and I'll fire."

"Please, only fire in the direst circumstances," I said, receiving a wry smile from Holmes and a nod from Rozee.

Upon re-entering the study, we found Vassiniotis and Jasper Turnquist standing before the open doorway to the cellar. The stocky Greek man's face was red with rage. "Where is he?"

"Ah, Mr. Vassiniotis, I believe," said Holmes, receiving a snarl in response.

"Who the blazes are you?"

"I am Sherlock Holmes, and this is my colleague, Dr. Watson. I can only assume that you are Lord Lionel's business partner, Sylvester Vassiniotis?"

"I thought they'd gone. Their carriage, it wasn't out the front," said Jasper, his face a mask of horror.

"Holmes? Not that bloody busybody that helps the police out?"

"I prefer consulting detective, but yes, I can only presume that you've heard of my actions."

"What are you doing here?"

"A Turnquist family friend was concerned for young Lord Lionel's well-being. I offered to assist. It seems I was needed after all."

"He owes me. His father stole from the company. From me."

"I'm sure Lord Lindsay was far too well-heeled to need to stoop to thievery, so what exactly did he steal from you?"

"Half a coal mine. In Russia. Worth millions. I want what's mine."

"Well, surely if company funds have been used to purchase something of that value, then the accounts will all be transparent and all of the directors will receive their rightful share. Can you prove that this coal mine was purchased through the company?"

Vassiniotis's face went blank, his eyes grew wide. "Of course, I can."

Holmes held up his hands to settle the matter. "Well, there you have it. A simple solution. You should organise to meet with Lord Lionel and his accountants. I'm sure if there are any deeds or receipts of the purchase, they can be produced, and you can thrash out the details like gentlemen."

Silence descended for a moment.

The Greek businessman thought for a moment before nodding and striding towards the study door. Jasper took one look at Holmes, then Watson, before hurrying after him.

"However, there is the matter of Lord Lionel's drugging and kidnapping. Of course, that cannot be overlooked."

Both men stopped in their tracks. Vassiniotis slowly turned, a sneering grin on his face. "What do you mean? He's not even here. I haven't seen him for weeks."

"We both know that is a lie."

"Who cares?" The Greek shouted to his henchmen. "Stavros, Giorgi, get in here. I have rubbish for you to take out." Several muffled shouts were followed by thumping from the cupboard down the hall. A loud rifle *crack* echoed into the study, stunning Vassiniotis. "What the hell?"

"Oh, I hope he didn't shoot one of them," I said, "Can I go check?"

"Wait a moment, Watson."

"We have your men in our care, Mr. Vassiniotis." Holmes drew his revolver from his pocket, letting the businessman's eyes find it. "Now, it might be best if you forget all about evasion. The police will be here soon and would wish to speak with you."

At that moment a call went up outside. "Holmes? Where the devil are you? Who's this fool with the rifle?"

"Ah, that would be Inspector Bell now."

The air blew out of Vassiniotis's bravado, his shoulders deflated, and his head dropped. "Damn."

***

"So, if Lord Lindsay bought the title to the mining operation with his own funds, what does that mean for his two sons?" I handed Holmes a brandy, before taking my seat and settling back. We had spent the rest of the afternoon with Lord Lionel and Professor Rozee, establishing the facts behind the Russian mining operation and Lord Lindsay's intentions.

"Well that all depends on what happens to the Fortescue company. Vassiniotis is looking at a decent stint in Wandsworth, after which he will probably be deported. He doesn't hold British citizenship and kidnapping a member of the House of Lords may not be seen as the best way to obtain it. Whether that means he will forfeit his part of the company or whether Lord Lionel can purchase it is another matter. As for the Russian mine, well that is Turnquist family business, and will probably be split between the two sons." He sipped his brandy before continuing. "Now, whether they will be able to act as brothers given Jasper's betrayal, is another matter. Lionel may simply buy out Jasper's share, which will mean the boy has something to keep himself secure with, once he returns from Wandsworth, or they will come to some business agreement."

"Or Lionel will simply sell off his share. He insists that he only wants a simple life of study and research."

"Well, that may be the way. It is for him to decide."

"At least he wasn't harmed. I had my fears that something awful had happened to him."

"With that sum of money involved, that is a fair assumption. In the end, I'm just glad that I could be of assistance."

Picking up the bottle of brandy, I read the Cockburn and Co. label, with the date of eighteen sixty-five written on it. "And this little present was a nice reward as well. A twenty-year-old bottle of brandy is not something to cough at."

"Very true, my friend, very true." Holmes took another sip. "Plus, the nice retainer that Lord Lionel has given me for any future services has made it all worthwhile as well."

The Case of the Trepoff Murder

"Hello, Mrs. Hudson."

"My word, Dr. Watson." The look of surprise and glee on my old housekeeper's face made my journey to Baker Street already worth my while. "It's always nice when you visit."

"I've just finished with a patient nearby in Dorset Street, and felt I simply had to make the time to drop by."

"Oh, very good to see you as always, how is married life treating you?"

I knew I smiled widely at that point. "I am so happy, Mrs. Hudson. Mary is the light of my life." I began to extol the virtues of my new world, but I realised I must have carried on for quite some time because even someone as delightful as Mrs. Hudson couldn't disguise a need to retreat back inside. Finally, I stopped talking and took a breath.

Without missing a beat, Mrs. Hudson brought Holmes into the conversation. "His nibs is upstairs, he'll be so glad to see you. It's been ever so quiet around here without you, and I do worry when that happens."

"Let me see if I can't bring him out of any ennui he has allowed to settle over him."

My hostess stepped back and disappeared into her room, possibly preparing some refreshments for us. I watched her vanish, before turning my attention to the seventeen steps that separated me from my former lodgings and climbed.

Standing on the landing before Holmes's door, I stopped and drew breath for a moment. In all honesty, I was unsure what I would find behind there. When I had vacated Baker Street a small part of me began to worry about leaving Holmes unattended, and in my quiet times, I often pondered what he was up to.

Bucking up my courage, I knocked.

“Come on in, Watson, there’s a good chap.” Only slightly shocked, I turned the knob and stepped into my old life. The rooms looked almost the same as when I left. There were quite a few more files, folders, and papers scattered around, a hint that Holmes had been occupying his time, but hadn’t been overly concerned with maintaining a modicum of tidiness.

Smiling, as I found my good friend reclining in his chair by the window, and smoking a pipe, I said, “Good morning, Holmes, still as sharp as ever.”

“Yes, Watson, having heard you traipse up that flight time and time again, it was hard not to recognise it once more.”

“Very good, I would expect nothing less.” Shrugging off my coat, I hung it on a nearby hook and strode across to greet Holmes, throwing my hand out and shaking his effusively. “I had a gap in my day, and was nearby, so thought I’d take the chance you were in.”

“No worries there. I have kept myself quite active. When I’m not on a case, I continue with my research into all things.” His face showed no signs of any boredom, but I could detect a slight waver in his voice, which told me his story was not always the way. There was no evidence of his other distractions. No sign of his little Moroccan leather case in the immediate vicinity, which lifted my heart slightly.

I sat down in the vacant chair next to his own and breathed a sigh of relief. Nothing really to do with Holmes, just a sudden overwhelming feeling of tiredness from my morning’s activities and a dire need to rest my feet.

“If I was to suggest, I should be the one concerned about you. Our adventures never left you in such a breathless state or is it that you lead a more sedentary existence in your own house and practice, which has left you slightly bereft of fitness.”

“Perhaps,” I said, a smile playing on my face. The familiarity of the room penetrated and brought a type of warmth to my body as well as my mood. “I will admit that I have not had the need for rigorous excursions of late. Something that my body probably misses more than my mind.”

“Oh, I’d like to think that you miss the stimulation of our adventures, if not the intrigue and danger.”

Chuckling, I replied, “You might be right.” Changing the subject from myself to Holmes, I added, “Speaking of your past adventures, I spent a few nights collating my notes, and came across a memo to myself from a while back that mentioned some of your adventures abroad without me. I never had the chance to ask, but you visited, what was it? Sri Lanka? Holland? Ukraine?”

Leaning back in his chair, Holmes steepled his fingers and thought for a moment. “Ah, yes. That was a while ago, but I did have the opportunity to journey to some far-flung places, all work, no real pleasure, though.”

“I know you, Holmes, your work is your pleasure. Though I would have loved to join you on some of those adventures. What were they for? Holland was for the Dutch Royal Family, wasn’t it?”

"Ah, yes, now that was a matter of some delicacy, and I'm afraid I'm bound to keep my silence on that one. I do apologise, I know how much you love to document my cases, but for now, there are many high-level aristocrats who would react quite dramatically to any word leaking about that one." He touched his nose with his forefinger. "In time things may change."

It was at that moment that the parlour door opened, and Mrs. Hudson entered carrying a tray of coffee and nibbles. “I thought you two might need something to eat and drink while you visit.”

I stood and took the tray from her, catching a wink as she handed it over. Nodding, I replied, “Thank you, Mrs. Hudson, thank you for your kindness.”

Placing the tray on the little table, I doled out the coffee and sat back, sipping the brew and sending more questions Holmes’s way. “I’m intrigued by your trip to Sri Lanka, but also of the one to Odessa.”

“Ah, yes, Sri Lanka was a simple matter of brothers coming to a shared tragedy due to their own ineptitude. My journey to Odessa was both intriguing and parlous, although the denouement was unexpected.”

“Do tell,” I said, sitting back and pulling out my little notebook.

Holmes smiled that wry smile and nodded. "Yes, you can take notes on this one. Though I would ask that you not publish the details for some time yet. As the story unveils, you'll understand why."

"Very intriguing, Holmes, very."

"The tale begins in late January two years past, you may remember the deep snow that lay about, surely."

"Yes. Quite extraordinary, but it eased up in February."

"True. Well at the time, I was quite unoccupied. It seems the extreme cold, mixed with snow, slows down even the most notorious of villains. Except, it seems, across the channel."

"Odessa?"

Nodding, he answered, "Yes, we'll get there. But first, around the 26th, I received a telegram from Mycroft. A simple message to meet him at the Diogenes Club, Stranger's Room. There was no real surprise at the location. Mycroft is not one for any excursions outside of his regular haunts at the best of times. In the middle of a cold winter, I was surprised that he'd even set foot at the club. It was obvious though that he wanted to talk. Pulling on my warmest clothing, I set off into the street and managed to flag down a lone hansom. I found Mycroft quite comfortable in the warmth of the Stranger's Room, alone as well. It turns out he had requested it of some other guests, who were only there because the rest of the club was quite well attended."

"What did you discuss?"

"Patience, Watson, as you should know, a good story is in the telling." Holmes drained his coffee and replenished it, before continuing. "Even though he looked relaxed, and had been provided with brandy and cigars, to elevate his comfort, I could tell from his eyes and manner that he was slightly agitated."

"How so?"

"A twitch of the fingers holding his glass, the disturbed line of smoke rising from the cigar in his other hand. Small signs, but there all the same. As I greeted him and sat, he placed his glass down, picked up a small folio, and glanced at it once before dropping it on the table before me. From the external markings, I could tell it was official Government business, but rather than snatch it up, I simply poured myself a brandy and sat back."

***

"Sherlock," Mycroft began, "Firstly thank you for attending on this vile sort of a day." He shook his head slightly, and picked up his glass, draining it in one long swig, before replenishing. "There are times, I'm afraid, that I come to my wits end with the business I am in."

"And what business is that?" I asked, smiling to myself. "Mycroft tends to be very cagey about what he actually does for Her Majesty's Government. I'm always hoping for a snippet of information but was once again disappointed."

"Never you mind. To be perfectly honest, if you undertake my request then you may gain a little more knowledge on that aspect, than I've ever provided you in the past."

"What is it you wish of me?"

Mycroft studied me for a moment, as if summing up whether to go through with his request, or simply take back the folder and be done with it. He sighed once, then began. "One of the main tasks of any Government is to safeguard our sovereignty, and with it, the borders of our country. We do this through the employment of a Defence force, and also through more covert means. That is, the gathering of information and intelligence, from and about our possible enemies."

"And even our friends, I have heard."

"Yes. True." He took a long drag on his cigar and blew a line of smoke away from us. The tang of its smell told me it was a La Intimidad from Cuba, not one of the standard Partagas on offer at the club. Mycroft must have brought them with him. Sensing my interest, he pulled a small carry case from his pocket and held it towards me. A single cigar remained in the case. Realising that the sole residual cigar was possibly needed to console my brother during the rest of the afternoon, I simply held up my hand and said no. Instead, I pulled out my cigarette case and lit one of my own in response.

Replacing the case, Mycroft continued with his story. "I can't remember, but have you been to Ukraine?"

I shook my head.

"Pity."

"Why?"

"Some knowledge of the area would prove very useful. Regardless, as I was saying, our government, from time to time, feels the need to seek information about our potential enemies."

"Russia?" I said, putting together several facts.

"Yes. Russia."

"Why Ukraine?"

"The security prevalent in Mother Russia is much more entrenched into the souls of the populace, than in its neighbour. The people are very dedicated to their Tsar. Even though we have perceived several groups that are fomenting unrest, the average Russian has as much love for Nicholas as our citizens have for the Queen."

I nodded wondering where this was all going.

"For many years, we have placed members of our bureaucracy in positions within the borders of Greater Russia, to observe and report back regarding the feelings of the populace."

"Sort of embedded agents, or some such?"

"Yes. They aren't there to assist with any instability, only to witness and scrutinise."

"Has one gone missing? Or perhaps dead?"

"Very astute, but yes, precisely that. One of our agents, for want of a better word, has indeed gone missing."

"Where in Ukraine?"

"Odessa. A thriving port city on the Black Sea. From our observations, the place simply yearns for Western freedoms, but is held back under the yoke of Imperial Russia."

"What can I do, then? I'm not a spy."

"No, and that is precisely why I need your services." He reached into his coat, once more, and withdrew a thick paper envelope, which he tossed onto the folder. "I have been asked by my superiors, yes, I do have superiors, to investigate the disappearance of one of our operatives using the name Nikolai Trepoff."

Intrigued, I picked up the envelope and peered inside. It contained a sizeable pile of pound notes and other currencies from Eastern Europe

"A substantial fee for your services, and more to cover any expenses." I didn't wish to appear so gauche as to pull the wad of bills out and count them, but even looking at the thickness and the top denomination, I deemed there to be around five hundred pounds. It struck me that this Trepoff fellow held something of very high import to Her Majesty's government.

"It's not just this Trepoff's location you are after, is it?"

A frown crossed Mycroft's face for a moment before it eased, and he replied. "No. Trepoff is simply the conduit for information. He hasn't been in contact for a good two months now. The trail is probably very cold, and we can't be seen sending in agents, left, right and centre, to investigate, most of them are well embedded in their own little stories, which would be fractured if the local authorities connected them to Trepoff. That's why we need someone like you."

"Or you," I suggested. "Your deductive reasoning and intelligence are equal if not far superior to mine. You've proved that on multiple occasions."

Mycroft chuckled. "Yes, but I'm far from what you would consider a field agent. You've kept yourself at the peak of your physical condition, while I, shall we say, have rather enjoyed life."

"Quite, so. I can only assume that you wish to establish if this Trepoff fellow has been disappeared by the authorities, and whether he had any vital information in his possession."

"Exactly. Though, I have expressed to those that have requested your services, that this could all be a fool's errand. The trail is long and cold, and we haven't picked up any sniff of repercussions from the Russians. I half expect that Trepoff has simply grown bored of his life, found himself a local wife, and gone native. If you track him down, he'll possibly be living in a small yurt on a cattle farm in the depths of Ukraine."

At that, I had to let out a small chuckle. "Does that happen a lot?"

"You'd be surprised. Send a red-blooded man into the wilds of some far-flung exotic country for a year or two, and they develop a taste for the environment and culture. The local females become enamoured by his strange accent, or his physical differences when compared to the local chappies, and anything can happen. Most men in the world are not like you and I, Sherlock. Their sense of duty and diligence in their work is merely a façade that can easily be broken by the slightest hint of the simple life of hearth and home."

"You sound like that is something you've long thought about," I said, half in jest, drawing a slight sigh from my brother.

"I feel that is far beyond me. I have signed up for a life of duty to Her Majesty, and I cannot fathom anything else."

At that point, I moved the envelope of money aside and picked up the folder. Opening it, I found it thick with handwritten pages. A quick scan revealed that most of them were transcripts of reports from Trepoff. The earliest was from two years previously.

Closing the folder, I leaned back and sipped at my brandy. "I'm intrigued. Though, I'll admit that I'm no spy."

"That's for the best. Your task is simple. Travel to Odessa and look into Trepoff's disappearance. That file contains much about Trepoff's cover. His real name was Archie Brand, born and bred in east London, though he did have parents from Eastern Europe, Hungary, I think. You'll be Alexandr Trepoff, his brother. There are identity papers in there, but I suggest you derive a story for yourself. Find some other place of birth, one that you're familiar with. Much easier to keep to the facts if you have prior knowledge."

***

"As Mycroft relaxed back into his seat and went silent, I took his attitude to mean no more information would be forthcoming. I wasted little time on trivialities, promptly finished my cigarette and brandy, and bade my leave, taking the file and envelope with me. Back here in Baker Street, I read through the folio. There was little detail about what Trepoff was investigating or being asked to keep an eye on, except for a line which stated, *Ensure to view the docks and harbour area for military activity*."

"Military activity?" I asked.

"Yes, the Russian navy regularly sends ships through the Bosporus Strait and into the Mediterranean. This avenue is controlled by Turkey, but there is a long-standing convention that applies between the Black Sea countries and Turkey over its use. Odessa, being one of the largest cities on the Black Sea, is a perfect spot for military activity, especially from the Russian forces controlling the city."

"So, what was your plan?"

"I quickly arranged transport to Dover, and onwards to France. If I could catch the Orient Express in Paris, I could make it to Bucharest. From there I planned to embed myself for some days and gain some familiarity with the area and provide details for my cover story. I was to become Alexandr Trepoff, a simple clerical worker from Bucharest in Romania. Nikolai and I had been separated in our childhood, but I had found some records relating to him and wished to reconnect. Our father had recently died, and there was a bequeath for both of us, but I needed Nikolai to witness the documents. It took me a few days to get there but it was worth the trip."

"Simple, but ingenious. If there was money involved, then it would shift suspicion away regarding any espionage."

"My thoughts as well. To ensure to enhance the authenticity, I found a small solicitor's office, and convinced them, with the addition of a small amount of money, to draft a will and other papers."

"But you don't speak Romanian, do you?"

"I didn't. As I said, I had several days to learn. My knowledge was still rather rudimentary but serviceable. I didn't think I'd need an extensive vocabulary for the first part of my journey. My Russian is functional, so I also brushed up a bit on that, and hoped it would see me through in Odessa itself."

"Very good."

"Indeed. From Bucharest, I travelled by slower train to Varna on the shores of the Black Sea. From there I was able to procure passage on a steamer North to Odessa. A journey that took another three days."

"A very mixed journey, and long."

"Admittedly, yes. But, straying from my cabin on the steamer, I was able to practice my Russian with some of the other passengers. Some were from Odessa, others only passing through."

"What did you converse about?"

"I wanted to understand the temperament of the locals in the town. From a couple of older Ukrainians, I caught a sullen undertone of repressed belligerence towards the Russians. The Ministry of Education in Moscow had recently begun to remove the teaching of the Ukrainian language. Only Russian was being taught. One of my acquaintances let loose a string of obscenities at one point against that, before being quietened by the other."

"Hmmm. Perhaps something that this Trepoff fellow may have been keeping an eye on."

"Perhaps. By the afternoon of that third day, we docked in Odessa. I spent an hour familiarising myself with the area and created an escape plan in case it was needed. Finding a modest hostel, I booked a room for several nights, then made my way back to a stable I had seen earlier. There I bought myself a horse."

"Bought? A horse?"

"Yes. The sum that Mycroft gave me was quite substantial. My emergency plan was for a quick exit from the city. A horse would provide that transport. I hoped that if I didn't require it, I could sell it back to its original owner. It didn't worry me even if I had to give it away. So, I paid for several days stabling for the nag, and then proceeded to a nearby market where I procured some food and then headed back to my hostel room until nightfall."

Holmes stopped and refilled his coffee cup. I was happy at that moment as it gave me time to add some more details to my notes. As he sat back and sipped, I took the opportunity to refill my cup. This story was getting intriguing, and it had only just begun.

"Now, that first night was interesting. I had no compunction to play the tourist, and simply ate, and bathed to remove the dust and smell from my body, before donning a costume I had prepared for just that purpose. I chose a style of clothing mostly worn by members of the merchant craft that plied the waters of the Black Sea, providing me with an immediate alibi or excuse if cornered and questioned. My outfit was also of the darkest blue, rather than black, I wished to blend into the shadows and avoid any attention. I set off through my second-floor window and kept to the rooftops. The town was mostly one and two-storey buildings, but packed very closely together, making traversal much easier. When I had to cross an avenue or street, I climbed down to the road level and skulked across in whatever shadows I could find. Unlike London, there was very limited lighting, which made my journey much easier."

"I finally found myself on Pastera Street. Trepoff's rooms were located on the second floor of a small building near the centre. As I skulked along the dim boulevard, I heard the noise of voices coming from a brightly lit building across the way. I found out later that it was the Odessa Music and Drama Theatre. I had arrived on the scene, just as the performance was letting out. Quickly pulling the scarf that I had wrapped around my face and head away, I strode quietly and confidently, mingling with the audience as they left the building, and found the entrance I required. The denizens of that port city are not as concerned with burglary as ours, and I found the main doors unlocked."

"Nikolai's front door was another matter. It was not only unlocked but the entire locking mechanism was broken off. I found it lying on the floor in some detritus beside the external wall. As you can imagine, my internal alarm systems became alert for anything else untoward."

"Why didn't you just leave and return in the daylight?"

"At that point, I was intrigued and needed to see the inside of Nikolai's apartment. Even in the dim light afforded by the dull gas lamps in the hallway, I was able to examine the door. The lock had been broken away by several whacks with a large sharp object, probably an axe. From what I could see, I suspect the assailant was not trying to be subtle. A crack in the door, at about knee height, indicated that he had attacked the lock until it was damaged enough to fall off, followed by a swift kick or two to finish the job."

"Surely that would have aroused others in the building?"

"Ah, that I can assure you did happen, and I'll get to that later. I pushed the door lightly, and it swung inwards, with only the slightest squeal from the old hinges. They were rusted, rather than damaged. With luck, I found a shelf just inside which held a small candle and matches. I had brought my own just in case, but that made it much easier to investigate. Stepping inside, I quickly lit the candle and shed light on the area."

Holmes stopped for a moment and took a long drink from his coffee. It seemed he was steeling himself for the next part of the tale.

"Now, Watson, you and I have seen some horrors in our time, have we not?" I nodded in agreement as several incidents flashed past my eyes. "What greeted me in that place, was possibly one of the worst sights I had seen."

"What was it?"

"Blood. The place was covered in it. It had dried to a dark brown stain, but even in that dim light, I could tell it was blood. From puddles to pools, to splashes and trails. From where I stood, I simply pieced together what I could see. Whoever was inside, when the assailant burst in, tried in desperation to race out of the only available exit. The lone window. It yawned wide open, filling the room with the frigid intensity of the deep winter outside, and snatching away any scent from the carnal display before me. It has surprised me, in hindsight, how I couldn't smell the blood, but on reflection, the chill breeze that entered probably accounted for that."

"If it was as cold as you say, then the blood was possibly frozen as well."

"Yes, markedly so."

"Sorry, I broke your train of thought, you were piecing together the crime."

"Yes, thank you. As I said, I stood on the threshold and viewed the area as best I could. The largest pooling or splashing occurred at the window. Assumedly, the assailant caught the victim as he probably tried to escape out the window. Later examination proved me right. There were deep wounds in the windowsill, where several blows had missed the victim but landed in the wood. Even now I can't be sure how many rained down on the poor unfortunate, but it must have been at least a couple of dozen, such was the extent of the crimson tide."

"That sounds like a crime of passion, more than an execution."

"My thoughts exactly, Watson, my thoughts exactly. Scanning the immediate area, confirmed that as well. I found three sets of boot prints, all of which were stamped as if inked by the victim's lifeblood, and all of which led from the room. That told me that three men entered, possibly at different times. The assailant's boots led from the very depths of the blood. Several tracks showed where he stepped during the ordeal, and where he dallied over his handiwork. His trail led away in a series of staggered steps, as if in a slunk posture, almost as if he was overcome with grief after the adrenaline had dispersed. The second and third sets were more straightforward as if the owners had simply moved into the room to pick up something, then leave."

"How could you tell that?"

"Because one set was reversed at the exit. It looked like two people walked side by side, about six feet apart, and then one turned and exited backwards. I found traces of bloodied footprints in the hallway that confirmed my suspicions. Their footprints were quite pronounced, which would be indicative of them having carried something heavy, say a body."

"The victim?"

"I can only assume. There was no evidence of the body in my line of sight and given there were no immediate signs that it was located elsewhere, it can only have been moved out through the front door or pushed out of the window. I decided to check on the second location once I left the apartment complex."

"Did you work out whether it was this Trepoff fellow?"

"Not at first. Until I had more evidence it was all simple supposition. My first task was to establish that Trepoff was the most likely occupant of the apartment at the time, my second was to uncover any information that he had documented during his observations of Odessa. With an eye on the first, which would require the discovery of identity documents, or unearthing a witness or two, something I would attempt in the morning, and a keen sense of the second, I moved into the apartment, carefully avoiding the splatters and pools of blood. It was then, in that dim candlelight, that I realised whoever appropriated the victim's body, had also returned to investigate the apartment."

"How so?"

"There was more evidence of footprints, mostly partial, but some led through the more far-flung blood spatters and tracked the crimson marks further through the rooms. It was also, at that point, that I noticed several drawers in the nearby bureau were partially opened, or dislodged from their track, as if hurriedly opened and closed with some force. Looking through some of them revealed nothing of import remaining, but it did give me cause to believe that the second set of visitors had a far different motive than the first."

"Police?"

Holmes nodded. "Or worse."

"Worse? What do you mean worse?"

"The Russians employ a covert squad that belongs to the Department for Protecting Public Security. Colloquially they are known as the Okrana. Ostensibly, they are a police force interested in espionage or terrorist activities in and outside of Russia. Though, I have heard they can be employed for more ruthless activities."

"My word. Would they have been responsible for this apparent murder?"

"That occurred to me, but I dismissed it at the time, as the evident ferocity of the attack would only be used if they were trying to send a loud message. That didn't seem to be what had happened, because they would most likely leave the body behind as a form of punctuation."

"Hmmm." I was starting to become happier that I hadn't been involved in Holmes's little trip to Ukraine. "What did you do next?"

"The signs that I could discern indicated that the second visitors moved from the main room into the adjoining rooms. Stepping carefully and as close to the perimeter wall as possible, I moved into the small adjacent bedroom. It only took a momentary glance around the area to see that it had been visited with less care than the main room."

"How so?"

"The sheets had been ripped from the bed. The stained mattress was slashed open; its innards were torn out. The drawers in the little bedside had been pulled completely out, their meagre contents strewn across the floor. The small robe lay open, the clothing snatched from the hooks, before joining the detritus on the floor. Any boxes, or bags, had suffered a similar fate. Someone was in a desperate need to find whatever Nikolai had secreted away in that apartment."

"Do you think they found it, whatever it was?"

"At that point I was unsure. All I could conjecture was that Trepoff had been tasked with observing and documenting the Odessa port. If he had taken notes, then there would need to be a notebook, or papers, or perhaps a diary, of some kind. I took up the search, mostly to convince myself that whatever evidence existed had been found or didn't actually exist."

"He could have simply held the facts in his memory before communicating them."

"True. After a thorough search, I decided to leave. It was growing late, and I didn't think I could garner any more information in the dim light. The scene was far too sullied for that. Leaving, I made my way downstairs, stopping and noting the name on the last door. The name Tsyganov, was written on a small card by the door. Underneath I deciphered that he was the building superintendent. I would make my way to see him first thing in the morning. A quick trip to the side alley proved slightly fruitless. In the darkness, I could neither see any evidence of bloodstains nor marks from where a body would have landed. I mapped the route back to my hostel via the alleyway so that I could conveniently retrace my steps and investigate in the light."

"What were your thoughts at that stage?" I asked. The evidence so far presented left me quite puzzled, and I hoped that Holmes could help me add some context to the tale at the point in time of his story.

"To be honest, Watson, without any contradictory evidence, I simply saw a case of murder or at least heavy violence against the person posing as Nikolai Trepoff. Whether that violence came from the authorities, a robbery attempt or some other intervention was unclear. What was apparent was that someone was intent on finding an item or items amongst Trepoff's possessions. Whether they had or not was another matter. And even with my exertions over the last few days, I slept rather fitfully that night, cogitating on all that I'd seen."

Holmes picked up his cup and noticing it was empty, reached for the pot. When that too was bereft, he simply huffed, placed it down and pulled out his cigarette case. As he withdrew one and lit it, I quickly read through my notes, hiding my eagerness for more of this story. When I raised my eyes towards him once more, I caught him looking at me, with that little smile. He had been waiting until I was ready before continuing.

"That next morning, I ate a light breakfast in the small room on the ground floor, set aside for such, before donning clothes more suited to blend in with the local population and set off for Trepoff's apartment building, once more. It was retracing my steps through that side alley, that my intrigue was quite piqued. As I had noticed from my cursory examination the night before, there was no blood to be seen, and any indents in the dull dirt and mud had been extinguished by recent rains. But," he held up a finger, snatching my attention, "I found the weapon."

My eyes grew wide at that fact, and I simply stared at him in fascination, almost forgetting to take notes.

"Lying in a small patch of weeds growing against the wall of the neighbouring building was a small hatchet. The blade, though sharp, was pitted with small dents and nicks as if it had been used on the toughest materials. The head and handle were covered in sparse spatters of dried blood, though there was an indication from some streaks that most had washed away. Instead of taking the object with me, I found some scraps of material and wrapped it, secreting it behind some cast aside boxes, ready to be retrieved if required."

"It could have just been a coincidence."

"My thoughts exactly, that was why I wanted it available at a later date. My next destination was this Tsyganov fellow, the superintendent. Within a moment of my knocking, I heard him banging around and yelling coarse insults towards me. It was obvious he didn't relish his lot in life. As the door opened, I was greeted with the large frame of a man in his fifties, dressed in little more than a dirty undershirt and pyjama pants. He looked me up and down and a sneer came to his lips."

"What you want?" he said.

"In my broken Russian, I told him I was Nikolai's brother from Bucharest." His face dropped in fear, and I thought he was about to shoo me away, instead, he simply pointed to the stairs, and I caught the words “first floor, number eight,” before the door slammed shut.”

“Surely he knew of the state of the place?” I asked.

“From his expression, I could only imagine he knew something. Regardless, I took his reaction as permission to enter the apartment unfettered, and that was exactly what I did. As expected, nothing had changed, but I was able to see more of the carnage. The attack appeared even more unhinged than I had previously deduced. The hatchet had found its mark on several occasions, but on many more, it had left dents and cuts in the furniture, walls and window seal. I felt a little sorry for Trepoff. Nobody deserved to leave this world through such a violent act, even one undertaking covert work for his government.”

“But you couldn’t be sure that was the reason for the attack.”

“True. I still didn’t know it was Trepoff either. For all I could construe from the evidence, Trepoff may have been the perpetrator, and it may have been in defence. Brushing aside such confused thoughts, I revisited my search from the early morning and was a little disappointed to unearth only cursory items. Some paper, several pencils, and one blank notebook, but nothing that contained Trepoff’s observations. I did however find something that the previous seekers had missed.”

“What?”

"A small hidey-hole in the bathroom. It was tucked down beneath the bath. Two of the ceramic tiles had been loosened and a small hollow had been formed beneath. The contents surprised me, though upon examination I realised it proved Trepoff had been there.”

“What was it?”

“The first was a Webley Mark IV revolver. Standard issue for the English Army. It had either been left by a previous foreign office employee, or by Trepoff himself. His file mentioned that he spent several years in the Army, perhaps it was brought along in much the same way that you or I bring our own revolvers. It was fully loaded, but there were no other bullets, so I decided to take the pistol with me. If Trepoff was gone, he wouldn’t be needing it, if not then hopefully I could have it returned to him. The second item was a buff-coloured envelope. It was filled with bank notes, it was a mix of notes and denominations. Mycroft's envelope held a similar mixture. From the amounts in the envelope, it would appear that Trepoff was given enough currency to see out the best part of a year. It was obvious that this hidey-hole had remained hidden. Even the most diligent policeman would not leave a gun and a wad of money, like that, lying in wait for the owner to return."

"Was the cavity not big enough for a diary or notebook?"

"Yes, it was. But again, I can only suppose about its use and contents. Trepoff may have only used it for the gun and the money. I pocketed the revolver and envelope and as I pondered my next move, a knock came from the open main entrance. Stepping through to the bedroom to investigate, I found an old man standing at the entrance, his watery eyes fell on me as I moved towards him. He appeared to be in a slightly agitated mood and beckoned towards me."

"Gospodin," he said, his head turning to look over his shoulder, "Okrana."

"I realised he was warning me of the approaching secret police."

"The superintendent?"

"I can only assume he had called them. As I reached the exit, I heard voices from the ground floor and heavy boots heading up the stairs. The old man stood in the doorway across the corridor. Fearing detection, I started towards him. As I moved, I spied a cup sitting on a small table. I picked it up and threw it towards the open window, it broke against the glass pane, shattering the window and sending shards into the street outside. I quickly fled and rushed inside the old man's apartment. He threw the door shut and stood with his finger to his lips. My new comrade and I stayed still, listening to the approaching footsteps and voices."

"Okno," a rough voice shouted, before other shouts of "snaruzhi."

"The booted feet retreated. My rudimentary Russian translated the words *window* and *outside*. My ruse had worked. The Okrana had a ghost to chase. I began to speak to my host, but he put a finger to my lips. The heavy footsteps returned. From the sound, I determined a lone figure stepped into the apartment and rummaged around for what seemed like hours before another pair stomped up the stairs and fired off a stream of Russian to the first person. Finally, both men retreated downstairs, and all fell quiet once more."

"Good Lord Holmes, what would you have done?"

"Pleaded my case. I was simply looking for my brother. I had the fake documents. If worse came to worse, I had the revolver."

"What happened then?"

"After another few minutes, the old man let out a long sigh of relief. I pointed towards the apartment and spoke Trepoff's name. The old man nodded, then ran a finger across his neck. That told me almost everything I needed to know about Trepoff's fate. I then said *Okrana*? To my surprise, he shook his head. I asked who, to which he replied, *Dmitry*. When I asked who Dmitry was, he gave a simple two-word answer, *Rosanna's father*, before pushing past me and moving to a nearby rolltop desk. He bent over and wrote on a small piece of paper before returning and handing it to me. It was an address. I recognised the street; it was only two away from where we stood. The name Rosanna Kravchenko was written above it."

"What did you make of it all, Holmes?"

"After the old man ushered me out of his apartment, shutting the door, and from the noises behind locking it several times, all I had was the name and address."

"Was that your next destination?"

"Yes. I made a short stop at the superintendent's apartment. The look on his face when he answered the door, told me everything I needed to know about the visit from the Okrana. As there was nothing more to find in Trepoff's apartment, I knew I wouldn't be returning, so merely nodded towards the man before turning and leaving. I assumed that he would send word to the police again as soon as he was able, so hurried off towards Sadova Street, the address given to me by the old man."

Holmes took a drag on his cigarette and blew out a long line of smoke before proceeding.

***

It was Rosanna that opened the door, a puzzled look tinged with fear on her face. She was young and quite attractive, but her eyes were haunted by some tragedy. I simply said Nikolai's name and any hint of courage left her. Shuffling her distraught and weeping figure inside, I scanned the street, fearful of any witness by police or nosey neighbours. Luckily, the area was deserted, so I took the poor woman into a small reception room and bade her sit down. I found an open bottle of vodka on a nearby shelf and poured her a small measure. Offering her the glass, she downed it in one gulp. The calming effects were almost immediate. She wiped the tears from her eyes, before holding the glass up towards me. The second helping went down slower and enabled her to address me.

"Who are you?" she asked.

"Alexandr Trepoff, Nikolai's brother from Bucharest."

"He never mentioned you."

"We have not spoken in many years. Our father has died, and I am here to settle some legal issues over the will."

"He didn't mention his father either."

"Let us say that Nikolai and our father did not see eye to eye." I broached my next question carefully, but fully expected the reaction. "Can you tell me where Nikolai is?"

As the tears flowed, I brought another glass of vodka and waited for the sobbing to subside. It proved to me that she knew of Nikolai's fate, or at least the rumours of his fate.

"Is he dead?" A drop of the head, a slight nod and more crying. "Was it the Okrana?"

At that, she looked up. Shaking her head, a confused look crossed her face. "No. Why would the Okrana care?"

"Who was it? Do you know?"

"Me papa. He came home and the neighbours told him about Nikolai. He…he…went crazy. He burst in here yelling and screaming at me, then he snatched up the hatchet we use to cut wood and looked at me with such rage in his eyes. I ran into my room and locked the door. I was so afraid. I've never seen him like that."

"Do you know why?"

"No. I heard him come home. There were noises of rage and sobbing. I stayed hidden until all went quiet, and then I crept out and found him asleep in that chair. He was covered in blood, and there were two empty bottles on the floor. I almost screamed when he spoke in his sleep. Nasty words, about foreigners, about me. I was so worried about Nikolai. I left and raced to his house, but all I found was blood, but no Nikolai."

"Did you go inside?"

Shaking her head, she said, "No. I stood in the doorway. I listened, but it was quiet. I didn't want to see him like that."

"You believe your father killed him?"

More tears ran down her face. "Yes. He told me the next day. He said I was never to love a stranger, only a Ukrainian. As he left to go back to his fishing boat, he turned and said if he caught me with a stranger then my fate would be worse than that of my former lover's. He slammed the door, and I haven't seen him since."

***

"What did you tell her, Holmes? No one should have to live under such threats, even from a parent."

Holmes shrugged. "I can only agree with you Watson, but this was a foreign country, with their own traditions. Who was I, an Englishman, masquerading as a Romanian, to advise the young woman? I simply told her to go to the authorities and report her father for murder. At that, she simply shook her head and said they would be worse. It was at that point, that I brought out Trepoff's money and handed it to her. I said that if she felt she was in danger, then she could use the money to leave Odessa and set herself up somewhere safe. Her face showed confusion until she saw the money, and then her eyes simply grew wide as she considered everything I had said."

"Do you know what she did?"

"No. I was near the end of my quest. I only had one more question for her, and that was whether Nikolai had given her anything that he wished to keep safe. Rosanna immediately leapt from her seat and disappeared into a room at the rear of the apartment. She returned; her demeanour thoughtful. She considered the small item in her hands. I believed she wanted to keep it, as the only memory she had of Nikolai, but finally, she held it out towards me."

"It was a small diary. She said that Nikolai left it there and would return when Rosanna's father was away and fill it with words. She mentioned that she couldn't read any of the strange writings. The words were not of her language."

The Okrana had a ghost to chase.

"I took the book and flipped through it. It was indeed a diary, full of notes, diagrams, times and dates. From my quick reading, it appeared to track the movements of ships berthing in Odessa. Trepoff had catalogued the cargo loaded and unloaded. Signs of any troops disembarking. It was everything that Mycroft had hoped for."

"Good Lord, Holmes, what did you do next?"

"What more was there for me to do? I thanked the young woman and wished her luck with whatever choices she decided to make, then I fled into the streets. Once back at the hostel, I had the uncomfortable feeling of many pairs of eyes staring at me. Several of the guests sat around the reception area, they feigned interest in their papers or books, but when I shot a glance in their direction, there was a distinct rustle of items and faces disappearing behind them. Even the manager had a strange demeanour about him. Back in my room, I quickly packed. I believe I had overstayed my welcome and may have attracted the wrong kind of attention. It was the shouts and whistles from the street that spurred me into real action."

"What was it?"

"The Okrana. Like the superintendent at Trepoff's apartment block, one of the other guests must have informed them. Rather than leave through the ground floor or my window, I tracked my way down the second-floor corridor and exited via a window at the end of the hall. I had examined it the day before for just such a contingency. It overlooked the neighbouring roof and allowed me easy access. Within a matter of minutes of scaling across the rooftops, I dropped down to the cobbles outside of the stables where my horse was stalled. The stablemaster helped me harness my horse, and gave me a wink, pointing to a nearby corner that ran behind the stables. He told me to head that way for a mile, before turning back and heading out on the other street that led out of Odessa. He was obviously not one of the cowed citizens under the oppressive yoke of the secret police. I thanked him and spurred my horse onwards."

"As I fled past the buildings, I caught sight of agitated people and dark-clad men, whom I could only assume were the Okrana. Whistles and shouts accompanied the heavy footfalls of boot-clad feet. Within a few minutes, all went silent except the clopping of my horse's hooves on the cobbled streets, and soon we had left Odessa behind."

"That must have been a relief."

"Yes, it was, Watson. Though I would have liked to have learnt more about Trepoff's murder, and the interest that the Okrana had in him. I could only assume that it was they who stole away with his body. Possibly, in the hopes of examining him further, or finding some evidence on his person, or to hold onto it in the hope of unearthing more of our agents."

"But he wasn't killed because he was a spy."

"No. Although it was obvious that Trepoff was of interest to the Russian secret police, his demise came down to a simple case of maddened xenophobia. A father, desperate to keep his daughter under his control, scared of any stranger wishing her away."

"Do you think she took your advice?"

"I can't say. When I handed the journal over to Mycroft, I asked him to send word to Odessa to have the welfare of the girl investigated, but he simply laughed off my suggestion, and implied that I'd gone a little soft and been overly influenced by you."

"And what is the problem with that?"

Holmes smiled. "I must admit that I have missed that influence and am happy you came here today. I hope my little tale has whetted your fervour for more adventures to document."

Looking down at my copious notes, I smiled and replied, "Yes. I think this will keep me quite busy for a while. A strange little case, and one I'm actually happy I wasn't involved in."

The little mantle clock struck twelve. Holmes glanced towards it and smiled before standing and retrieving a bottle of brandy with two glasses. As he poured, he said, "I may have only spent two days acting as a sailor, but I believe that the sun is over the yard arm, so it must be time for one of these."

Sitting, we clinked glasses and enjoyed a middle-of-the-day refreshment.

www.ingramcontent.com/pod-product-compliance
Lightning Source LLC
Chambersburg PA
CBHW030807310726
48980CB00006B/412/J
* 9 7 8 1 8 0 4 2 4 5 8 2 8 *